DOLLED UP TO DIE

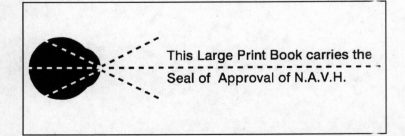

This Large Print Book carries the
Seal of Approval of N.A.V.H.

THE CATE KINKAID FILES

DOLLED UP TO DIE

LORENA MCCOURTNEY

THORNDIKE PRESS
A part of Gale, Cengage Learning

GALE
CENGAGE Learning·

Detroit • New York • San Francisco • New Haven, Conn • Waterville, Maine • London

GALE
CENGAGE Learning®

LIBRARY OF CONGRESS CATALOGING-IN-PUBLICATION DATA

McCourtney, Lorena.
    Dolled up to die / by Lorena McCourtney. — Large print edition.
        pages ; cm. — (The Cate Kinkaid files ; book 2) (Thorndike Press large print Christian mystery)
    ISBN 978-1-4104-6175-9 (hardcover) — ISBN 1-4104-6175-0 (hardcover)
    1. Women private investigators—Fiction. 2. Large type books. I. Title.
PS3563.C3449D65 2013b
813'.54—dc23   2013030040

Published in 2013 by arrangement with Revell Books, a division of Baker Publishing Group.

Printed in Mexico
1 2 3 4 5 6 7 17 16 15 14 13

With thanks to Rosemary Rhodes for her helpful information about the life-size dolls she creates, and to Sherrie Vig for introducing me to the dolls.

1

Case closed!

Until she'd become an assistant private investigator, Cate Kinkaid had never realized how satisfying those words were. Gleefully, she threw her hands up and clapped. She added the time and date to the report and hit the print button.

Okay, the case didn't rank up there with capture of a most-wanted serial killer or an episode of *CSI* on TV, but she had successfully cleared Ridley Jackson of his wife's suspicion that he was cheating on her. Ridley had decided to learn to play the saxophone, knew his wife would disapprove, and had been practicing with friends in a barn out in the country. Having heard the sounds emanating from Ridley's sax, Cate suspected a barn might be the appropriate setting for his musical talent. But her job was just to uncover the facts, not to critique them.

She changed to jeans worn thin at the knees and a faded sweatshirt for an evening with Mitch on a cleanup job for the Helping Hands project sponsored by the church. She and Mitch Berenski had been dating more or less regularly since they met on her very first case. She was headed for the door when the office phone rang. She jumped back to answer it. Mitch? No, an unfamiliar name and number on the caller ID.

"Belmont Investigations. Assistant Investigator Cate Kinkaid speak—"

"Lucinda, Marianne, and Toby have been shot!" a breathless voice interrupted. "All of them! Shot! And —"

"Wait, wait! If there's been a shooting, call 911 immediately! They'll send the police and an ambulance."

"I did call the police. I guess they're coming, but they don't seem in any big hurry to get here."

Three shootings, and officers weren't responding with screaming sirens and screeching tires? That didn't sound like the capable and effective Eugene, Oregon, police force Cate had dealt with. She glanced at the caller ID screen again. J. Kieferson. Something about the name seemed familiar, but she couldn't place it. "Mrs. Kieferson, are you all right?"

"Of course I'm not all right," the woman snapped. "I told you, Lucinda, Marianne, and Toby have been shot! Marianne's head is gone."

A head gone, shot away? "Are you alone? Could the shooter still be nearby?"

"I don't know! I just got home a few minutes ago and found this *massacre*."

"Mrs. Kieferson, you should —" Cate started to tell the woman to lock the doors and stay inside until the police arrived, but if the killer could still be in the house, that was hardly good advice. "Can you get to your car?"

"I guess. Maybe."

"Then go to the car and drive away from there. Contact the police again and tell them where you are. I'd like to help, but violent crime situations are outside our area of investigation."

Uncle Joe had emphasized that when he hired her. Belmont Investigations handled routine matters only. Background checks, serving subpoenas, insurance investigations. Although Cate's very first case had unexpectedly rocketed right into murder.

"You need the police," Cate repeated.

"You won't come, then?"

The woman wasn't sounding too rational, but her reproachful tone jabbed Cate's conscience button. Which immediately shouted, *You can't just ignore this woman and three people shot!* Although barging into a triple homicide scene was a situation Mitch would probably classify as right up there with skydiving with an umbrella. He'd accepted her becoming a full-time private investigator, but he wasn't exactly a cheerleader. He always seemed to think she needed a protector or rescuer, maybe a full-time bodyguard.

"How did you happen to call me?" Cate asked.

"You were highly recommended." Before Cate could ask "Recommended by whom?" Mrs. Kieferson rushed on. "Please, come! I'm at 17453 Randolph Road."

That was some distance outside Eugene. County sheriff's department territory rather than the city police. Cate hadn't dealt with them before.

"I've got to go now," the woman said. "I hear —"

"Wait —"

The phone clicked and went silent. Cate immediately tried to call the number on the caller ID back, but, after five rings, an answering machine clicked on. Leaving a message seemed pointless, and she punched in Mitch's cell phone number. Tonight he could do his protective, knight-in-shining-armor thing. Except that what she got was voice mail.

All the blessings of technology.

She tapped her fingers on the desk. She could wait for Mitch to call back so he could accompany her. But who knew when that might be? She could call Uncle Joe on his cell phone and ask for instructions. He was leaving much of the day-to-day business at Belmont Investigations up to her now, but this was definitely out-of-the-ordinary business. But she hated to interrupt his and Rebecca's anniversary celebration at some classy restaurant.

Octavia jumped up on the desk, her white tail twitching. She tilted her head at Cate, then batted the knob on the top drawer of the desk.

"You want me to look in there?" Cate asked. "Oh no. You may be the richest cat in Oregon. You may soon be queen of your very own Kitty Kastle, and you may accidentally have been helpful before. *Accidentally helpful,*" Cate emphasized. "But I don't think now is the time to take advice from you."

Octavia was an indiscriminate batter anyway. Pens, keys, stray coins, bare toes. Although Cate did have to open the

11

drawer . . .

"Only because the county map is in there," she informed the cat as she yanked the knob. "But you really should get up to date, you know. Everyone uses GPS now."

Except her. She hadn't been able to afford it for her car yet, and Uncle Joe stubbornly believed GPS might send you on a wild ride to nowhere.

She grabbed the map, then spotted something else in the drawer and hesitated.

Uncle Joe's gun and holster, long unused but freshly cleaned and oiled. In a triple homicide situation, having a gun for backup might be a good idea. Was the gun, not a map, what Octavia had in mind?

She slammed the drawer shut. Sometimes it seemed as if her deaf cat knew unlikely things, but Cate was not about to rank them above coincidence.

She couldn't take the gun anyway. Uncle Joe had done the paperwork to make her assistant PI status official, but the state's instructions about guns had been specific.

"Remember, oh brilliant furry one? I can't carry a gun until I'm a fully licensed private investigator." And that wouldn't be for some months yet. Surely deputies from the sheriff's department, well supplied with guns, would arrive before she got to the house on

Randolph Road anyway.

"So you're not so clever after all," Cate told the cat.

Octavia departed the office with tail held high, probably headed for Cate's bedroom. Or maybe Uncle Joe and Rebecca's room, since Octavia seemed of the opinion her presence was desirable everywhere in the house. A definite don't-say-I-didn't-warn-you message stiffened her upright tail.

Cate took a moment to locate Randolph Road on the map, grabbed a jacket, and headed out to her old Honda. She'd call Mitch again from along the way.

Clouds blotted the stars and warned that fall rains were coming soon. Leaves littered the yard and street, and a gusty wind swirled piles at the curb. She took the freeway to avoid slow city traffic, then headed west through wooded hills. By the time she made several turns and reached graveled Randolph Road, the first drops of rain splattered the windshield.

She pulled over and tried Mitch's number again. Again that frustrating voice mail. She left another message and pulled back onto the road. There were no prominent house signs posted out here, just numbers on the rural mailboxes.

And there it was in her headlights: 17453.

She braked. A bullet hole punctuated the 4. Dread at what she was about to encounter kept Cate's foot on the brake. Blood. Death. A killer still lurking? Mrs. Kieferson might even be dead by now.

A dilapidated house stood on the right, the weedy driveway banked with overgrown blackberry bushes. It was obviously unoccupied, so Mrs. Kieferson's place must be the rambling farmhouse behind a chain-link fence on the other side of the road. Two trees canopied the yard, their bare branches reaching skeletal fingers toward the sky. Shrubbery lined the fence. *Concealing* shrubbery, she noted with a certain uneasiness. A dark outline of some other building rose beyond the house.

No ring of police cars. No flashing lights. No ambulance. Strange.

A vehicle was coming up behind her on the road, and she reluctantly turned into the down-sloped driveway to get out of the way. The pickup swept on by, leaving a flash of red taillights and a feeling of emptiness in its wake. Not another house light visible in any direction.

Apprehension tightened her throat again. Yes, the woman had sounded desperate, and Cate wanted to help her. But this was no Ridley-and-saxophone kind of case. There were three dead bodies in there. Or more by now.

She'd just decided she'd call 911 herself when the phone in her hand jingled. She looked at the screen. Mitch!

"Hey, what's going on?" he asked. "Where are you?"

"I had a phone call from a woman. I'm at her place now."

"A phone call about what?" Mitch sounded instantly wary. "Where is 'her place'?"

Cate told him. Lucinda, Marianne, and Toby, shot. Randolph Road.

He groaned. "Cate, get out of there. Now. Let the sheriff's department handle it."

"But the woman said she'd called them, and they aren't here! I can't just drive away. Maybe something's happened to her, and she needs help."

"Do you see anyone?"

"No. There's only one car parked up by the house. It's an older white van." Cate let her car roll farther down the driveway and peered closer. Oregon license plate, with a bumper sticker that read Vote 2008. Did killers drive old vans with out-of-date bumper stickers? "I think it probably be-longs to the woman who called me."

"Just stay in your car, and I'll be there in

a few minutes."

"It took me at least twenty minutes to get here. I think I should go to the house. I'm worried about Mrs. Kieferson."

Silence, as if he were deciding if it would do any good to argue with her. Finally he said, "Stay on the phone, then. Keep talking to me."

Cate kept the phone to her ear, grabbed her purse, and slid out of the car. The gun she wasn't allowed to carry would feel pretty good about now. She knew a little about guns. Her dad had taught her to shoot one back home. She kept a wary eye on the shrubbery as she picked her way around the white van, raindrops sprinkling lightly around her.

"The path to the gate in the front yard fence doesn't look as if it's used much, so I'm going to the back door."

"Keep talking. And be careful."

"I'm heading up to the door now. I still don't see —"

An unearthly sound blasted the night. Cate jumped, then stopped short, her legs too paralyzed even to run back to the car. It came again. A discordant bellow, a guttural roar, a monster in the night. And close, so close —

16

"Cate, what was that?" Mitch yelled in her ear.

A light came on over the back door. A shadowy face appeared in the window beside it. The door opened a few inches, and the face peered around it.

"Who are you?" the woman called.

"Cate Kinkaid. Belmont Investigations. You called me?"

"Oh, I'm so glad you're here!" The door opened wider. The monster noise blasted again, and a matronly shaped silhouette stepped outside and yelled, "Maude, will you shut up!"

The light illuminated movement behind a rail fence, and now Cate saw the source of the noise. Not a fiend or monster.

A donkey. A white donkey. With floppy white ears. She'd been frozen to the spot by the braying of a donkey.

The woman motioned Cate to the door. "Don't mind Maude. She's just like a watchdog, lets me know the minute anyone comes around." She peered at Cate. "Haven't you ever heard a donkey before?"

Yes, growing up in rural southern Oregon, Cate had heard a donkey or two. But they'd never sounded as if they came with monster DNA. "It's been a long time."

"She's really very sweet. She loves apples,"

17

the woman said. "Thanks for coming."

"You are Mrs. Kieferson?" Cate asked. She could see the woman better now. Middle-aged, short gray hair with a permed curl, stout figure in dark slacks, sturdy shoes.

"Yes, Jo-Jo Kieferson. You're a lot younger than I expected." She sounded disapproving. "And a lot more redheaded."

Cate couldn't think of any suitable response to that. At twenty-nine, she didn't think of herself as terribly young, although by Jo-Jo's standards she probably was. And she was definitely redheaded.

She followed Jo-Jo Kieferson through a back porch/laundry room and stepped into a homey kitchen with sunny yellow walls decorated with cute-kitten calendars and wall plaques. Ivy trailed from baskets above the cabinets. A huge teddy-bear-shaped cookie jar sat on the counter. An inviting kitchen scent of vanilla and cinnamon suggested the cookie jar was often full.

It did not look like the proper setting for a triple-homicide crime spree. And Jo-Jo Kieferson was either in shock now, or she'd calmed considerably since that panicky phone call.

"Cate?" Mitch's voice came distantly from the cell phone that had slid to Cate's chest.

18

She yanked the phone up to her ear. "Everything's okay. I'm inside the house now. I haven't seen the, um, crime scene yet."

"Keep talking to me."

Jo-Jo frowned at Cate as if she considered the phone conversation rude.

"I have to keep in touch with my associate," Cate explained to her. *Associate* wasn't quite the right word for Mitch Berenski, but overprotective boyfriend sounded somewhat less professional.

"They're in here." Jo-Jo headed toward the adjoining room.

Heart thudding with apprehension, Cate followed.

2

Cate reported her progress to Mitch. "We're in the dining room now . . . nice, old-fashioned table with claw feet . . . framed painting of Mt. Hood on the wall . . . now going into the living room. Everything's still okay."

Jo-Jo stopped in the archway to the living room. "That's Marianne." She flung a finger toward the figure in a child-sized rocking chair next to the brick fireplace. "As I told you, her head is gone."

Yes, it was.

"Lucinda's over there."

Brown-haired Lucinda, in a girlish pink dress, sat behind an old-fashioned school desk. She was faceless, the front of her head blown away.

"And Toby, with the gunshot hole in his chest."

Toby sat in a window seat, a fishing pole dangling a line into a miniature pond of blue plastic at his feet.

"Cate, I heard that!" Mitch said. "It sounds like a-a slaughter!"

"Well, yes, it is kind of a slaughter," Cate said to Mitch. Marianne's head gone. Lucinda's face shattered. Toby with the hole in his chest. "But they're *dolls.*"

"Dolls?" Mitch repeated.

"They look almost like real children. But they're dolls, big, life-sized dolls." Dead dolls.

The hole in Toby's chest leaked white pellets, not blood, and the remaining section of Lucinda's head was hollow. The pieces of head on the floor were ceramic shards, not bone. No ugly scent of death thickened the air.

Yet it was a macabre scene because the figures appeared so truly childlike. Except for the leaking hole in his chest, Toby looked like a mischievous seven-year-old, sprinkle of freckles on his nose, blond hair tousled. The fact that he was still smiling only seemed to make the scene more macabre. Plus there was Lucinda's eyeball looking up from the floor.

"Did you tell 911 that the, um, victims were dolls?" Cate asked Jo-Jo.

"The woman was going to send an ambulance, so I explained why that wouldn't be necessary. I suppose that's why the police aren't in any hurry to get here." Jo-Jo sounded resentful about this discriminatory attitude toward non-human victims. "Perhaps I should have mentioned it to you too."

Yes, that would have been helpful. Cate made a mental note for future PI reference: *Always inquire if victims actually have human DNA.*

But the police should be here. Even if there weren't actually dead human bodies, someone had been flinging real bullets around.

"Do you know anyone who would want to injure —" Cate broke off and corrected that statement. Dolls, even ones that looked as lifelike as these, didn't suffer injuries. "Anyone who would want to damage your dolls?"

"I think it was me the shooter was after. And since I wasn't home, he just went after Marianne and Lucinda and Toby." Jo-Jo's voice went scratchy. "Destroying something he knew I loved."

"He?"

"My former husband. Eddie the Ex." Jo-Jo said the name as if she'd like to do something personally destructive to him.

"Eddie the Ex might want you dead?"

"Isn't a dead ex-wife usually preferable to

a live one? Although shooting dolls, that might be more of a woman thing, don't you think? Maybe that new wife he left me for did it. If she could steal my husband, I sure wouldn't put it past her to shoot my dolls."

Noises coming from her cell phone reminded Cate that Mitch was still in the loop.

"Cate, I'm coming," he said in her ear. "This is a weird situation. You don't know what else a wacko who'd shoot dolls might do. What's the address?"

"I can handle it," Cate said. "Just go ahead with the cleanup job for Mr. Harriman."

"We can do Harriman another day. I'll call him. What's the address?"

Cate finally supplied it, though she decided this was something she had to get straight with Mitch. Yes, she had called him to come to her rescue a couple of times. She'd had in mind having him come with her tonight. But having an overprotective male trailing along behind was not an image that suggested competent PI. She dropped the phone in her pocket.

Mitch was right about one thing, however. Shooting dolls qualified as weird. Maybe even a psycho thing? "What about the bullet hole in the mailbox?"

Jo-Jo's wave dismissed that bullet hole as irrelevant. "That's always been there. The stop sign down the road has seven of them. I think it's a country thing."

"Where did you get the dolls?"

Jo-Jo looked as indignant as if Cate had just asked if she bought her children at Wal-mart. "I made them, of course. That's what I do. Create dolls, usually in the image of real children. They're very dear to me. And to the people I make them for."

"Did you make Marianne and Lucinda and Toby for clients?"

"No. I keep them here in natural settings as displays of my work." She reached over and smoothed the skirt on the headless doll. "I used a photo of my mother from her third grade class to create Marianne. And Toby is a boyfriend from my own second grade photo."

Jo-Jo wasn't acting as upset as if these were her real children, but a tear dribbled down her cheek. She brushed it away. Something clicked in Cate's head.

"Do you know a woman named Krystal Lorister?" Cate had met the woman with a lifelike doll when she was investigating that other murder case. Seeing that doll in Krystal's reading room with a book in hand, Cate had first thought it was a grand-daughter. "I don't remember the doll's name."

Jo-Jo beamed. "Camille! Yes, of course I remember Krystal and Camille. Actually, she's the reason I called you. Krystal, I mean, not Camille."

"You talked to Krystal tonight and she told you to call me?" Cate asked doubtfully.

"No, no, not tonight. She told me once that if I ever needed help, you'd be the person to contact. That you were really clever at investigating things. So I wrote your name down."

"Krystal thought you might need help?"

"Eddie the Ex keeps trying to weasel out of his alimony. He has the most expensive restaurant in town, making money hand over fist, but he always acts as if he doesn't have two jars of caviar to rub together."

"So now you want me to investigate your ex-husband or find out who shot your dolls?"

"The dolls for right now. But I think they're connected."

Uncle Joe hadn't been happy when Cate got involved in that other murder situation. Belmont Investigations didn't do cops-and-robbers or violent stuff.

But this wasn't murder, she argued with herself, and no killer was involved. And business had been slow. The economic crunch affected even private investigators.

"Belmont Investigations is a business, of course. We charge an hourly rate."

"That's okay." Jo-Jo smiled slyly. "I'll think of some way to make Eddie pay for it."

"Did anyone know you were going to be away from home this evening?" Cate asked.

"I was talking to my friend Donna earlier. I might have told her. I don't remember."

Cate asked for Donna's full name, address, and phone number. She wrote the information in a notebook she always carried in her purse now. "Do you have a list of people who've bought dolls from you?"

"I keep a scrapbook of all my dolls and the people who've adopted them."

"Is there anyone among them who might be angry with you?"

"I don't think so. My customers have always been very nice people." Jo-Jo's eyebrows crunched in a frown. "I don't think not-nice people tend to be interested in dolls."

Probably true. Cate couldn't recall ever seeing a photo of a killer clutching his dolly. "You make the dolls right here?"

"I turned the master bedroom into a workshop. I create everything from the original molds for the head and arms and legs right down to making the clothing myself. I always put my initials on the fabric

26

part of the body, kind of my personal signature." Jo-Jo lifted headless Marianne's skirt and showed Cate the little JJ embroidered on the midsection of the doll. "I've been thinking maybe I should add a belly button, but I haven't decided if it should be an innie or an outie. What do you think?"

Cate figured they had more important matters to think about than innie/outie belly buttons. But still . . . "An innie, I think. Is this a full-time business with you? Or a hobby?"

"It used to be a hobby, before Eddie the Ex had his midlife crisis. Now it's a business. Do you have a little girl or boy? I could give you a nice discount."

Sometimes Cate had fleeting visions of herself and Mitch and a family. She wanted a little girl or boy someday. Both, actually. But she wasn't sure if her relationship with Mitch was headed that direction. "Thanks. I'll keep that in mind. Why do you live so far out of town? Wouldn't it be better to have a location more accessible for clients?"

"That was a glitch in the divorce settlement. Eddie wanted our big house in town. My lawyer said okay, but if Eddie got the big house, he had to buy me another house. Unfortunately the lawyer didn't specify where, and good ol' Eddie stuck me out here in the boondocks. I imagine he and Kim got a big laugh out of that. Kim's his new wife." She paused to glance back toward the kitchen. "Although it's a nice, cozy place, and I like it a lot better than the Ice Cube in town."

"Doesn't it make you uneasy living out here alone?"

"Not really. But I've been thinking maybe I'd move down to California or Arizona."

"You have family there?"

"No. I raised Eddie's two kids, but his son lives back east and his daughter Karen killed herself a few years ago. Karen and Eddie had been estranged for a long time, so that made it even worse for him." Jo-Jo paused and swallowed. She brushed a knuckle across her right eye, then swiped the wet knuckle on her leg. "Karen and I were close when she was little, and I'd kept hoping . . ."

Jo-Jo obviously felt very bad about her dolls, but Cate could see that this other loss went much deeper.

"But Eddie and his son are estranged too, and he never tried to fix that, even after Karen died. He can be stubborn as a mule. Although comparing Eddie and a mule is really unfair to the mule."

"Have you checked the premises to make

sure the shooter isn't still here?"

Jo-Jo glanced uneasily toward the dark hallway leading off the living room. "I didn't want to do it alone. But I don't think anyone's here or they'd have jumped out and shot me by now, don't you think?"

Cate's glance followed Jo-Jo's. Her nerves shrieked an internal alarm siren when she spotted something standing there in the depths of the dim hallway. She touched Jo-Jo's arm and pointed silently at the shadowy outline.

"That? That's my dust mop. I didn't want to get out the vacuum, so I was using the dust mop there in the hallway. I suppose girls your age don't even know what a dust mop is." Jo-Jo's eyebrows pinched together in disapproval of the shortcomings of Cate's generation.

Okay, Cate could see now that the shadowy figure was stick-handle thin. Maybe her nerves were a bit overwrought even if the victims here were only dolls. She certainly did know what a dust mop was, although it had always seemed to her an inefficient way of managing dirt.

"On the phone, you said you heard something. And then you didn't answer when I tried to call back."

"It was a noise, a kind of thud from down

the hallway. I started to go see what it was, but then I got scared and hid over there behind the sofa. The phone's in the kitchen, and it stopped ringing before I got back to it."

Now Cate also heard a noise from down the hallway. Thud. *Thud.* She and Jo-Jo both stiffened as if they'd turned into dolls themselves.

"You have a gun, don't you?" Jo-Jo whispered.

"No."

"I thought private investigators always had a gun. They do on TV."

Cate chose not to explain that she had not yet reached gun-toting status. "Don't you have a gun, living way out in the country like this?" she counter-whispered.

"I bought one when I first moved here. But I accidentally shot the hot-water heater, and after the flood I figured I'd better get rid of it. But we can find something in the kitchen to use as a weapon."

Cate saw herself armed with a potato peeler while searching for a guy brandishing a gun with bullets. "I think we should go out to the car and wait for the police or my associate to arrive."

Then another noise came from down the hall, not a thud this time. A much more familiar sound. Jo-Jo smiled delightedly at the yowl.

"It's just Effie! She must have gotten shut in my workroom. She likes to sleep on an old beanbag chair in there."

Jo-Jo flicked on a hall light and headed confidently down the hallway. Cate followed. Jo-Jo barely got the door partway open when a calico cat even bigger and plumper than Octavia squeezed out and thudded down the uncarpeted hallway.

"Well, what in the world got into her?" Jo-Jo took off after the cat.

Cate turned to follow, then stopped short. No sound came from the room. No thud or thump, not even a rustle or squeak. No drifting scent of male aftershave or feminine perfume. No movement in the skinny oblong of light cast on the bare hardwood floor by the hall light.

But that PI instinct that sometimes surprised Cate suddenly kicked in.

She knew with horrifying certainty that the room was not empty.

3

Cate looked up and down the hallway, frantically searching for something to use as a weapon. Rules or not, maybe she shouldn't have ignored Octavia's advice about the gun in the drawer. But all she saw was the dust mop leaning against the wall behind her. Challenge a gun-toting shooter to a duel with a dust mop? No way.

Retreat.

She moved one foot behind the other, lifting each foot so not even a brush of sole against floor made a sound. Paused. Listened again, ears straining for anything from a breath to a heartbeat in the room. Still nothing except her own hammering heartbeat.

What was his plan? Jump out and start blasting? Or slyly wait for his next victim . . . a live victim . . . to come to him? If so, he was in for a long wait. Because she wasn't coming.

Another silent lift and plant of foot, hand on the wall to steady her balance. Back in the kitchen, Jo-Jo chattered to the cat. One more step and she could turn and run, grab Jo-Jo, and head for the car.

Her arm touched something. It moved . . . She turned, frantically aware that her shoe squeaked on the bare floor as she did so. The dust mop. She grabbed for it. Missed. The dust mop clattered to the floor. Cate went down with it. Her knees hit the floor. Her head banged the wall. Her cell phone fell out of her pocket and skittered down the hallway.

Cate struggled to get up, but the ceiling spun in dizzy circles.

"What in the world?" Jo-Jo clomped down the hall in her sturdy shoes. "What happened? Are you okay?"

Cate heard something else. A car in the driveway, Maude braying to warn of an intruder. She groaned. In a minute, Mitch would burst in, find her sprawled on the floor, and be more than ever convinced she didn't belong in the PI business. Cate scrambled to her feet. She put a *ssshh* finger to her lips to warn Jo-Jo not to say anything more.

"Where's the light switch in the room?" she whispered.

"Right where light switches usually are. Just inside the door." Jo-Jo gave Cate an impatient look and started to step around her. "I'll get it."

Cate flung an arm out to stop her. She picked up the dust mop and turned it so she held it by the mop end. Body hugging the wall so she wouldn't make an easy target of herself in the doorway, she thrust out the handle and pushed the door open wider. No response.

Which meant — what? A patient killer? A tricky ambush?

Even more carefully, she slid a hand through the doorway. A click, and the light came on. Still no response. Jo-Jo apparently caught some of Cate's apprehension because she made no move toward the open door.

How did they do it on those crime shows? Burst through a doorway and instantly step to the side. Of course they were usually wearing protective gear and were armed with something more lethal than a dust mop. A knock sounded at the back door.

"I'll get it," Jo-Jo said and sprinted down the hallway.

Mitch was here. At least she wasn't ignominiously sprawled on the floor. Then, when she heard voices, Cate realized the person at the door wasn't Mitch after all. The deputies had arrived. She heard Jo-Jo bringing them down the hallway.

One officer stopped short when he spotted Cate. "This is the person who shot the dolls?"

"No, no, that's my private investigator."

Cate couldn't think what else to do. She gave them a fingertip wave. *Cate Kinkaid, Belmont Investigations. Have dust mop, will investigate. Dusting optional.*

"We think the shooter may be hiding in that room," Jo-Jo added in a whisper.

Both officers unholstered their guns. Back against the wall, gun raised, one called, "Okay, whoever's in there, come out with your hands up."

No response. The officer repeated the order. Silence, except for Effie padding down the hall and sidling between an officer's spread feet. She plopped down at the door and started washing a hind leg. The two officers exchanged glances, then one stepped forward and burst through the door. The second officer followed. Effie indignantly skedaddled down the hallway again.

No gunshots. No sound at all. Cate stepped up to the doorway and peered inside.

Her PI instinct had been right. The room was not empty. The body lay sprawled on the floor. Male. Dark gray suit. Burgundy tie. Iron-gray beard. Gun fallen to the floor by his hand. Bullet hole in his forehead. Cate's stomach went queasy.

Jo-Jo looked over Cate's shoulder, gave a little gasp, then pushed her aside. "Eddie!" she cried as she ran to him.

One of the officers tried to stop her, but he apparently didn't expect speed or agility from such a grandmotherly-looking woman, and she adroitly ducked under his arm. Her foot hit the gun and she grabbed it, looked at it in horror, and dropped it. She slumped to her knees by the body.

"Oh, Eddie, you didn't have to do this!" Jo-Jo moaned. "I'd have forgiven you for shooting Marianne and Lucinda and Toby."

A surprised officer grabbed and pulled her away. "You'll have to stay back, ma'am. We have to investigate this. You know this person?"

The officer braced Jo-Jo with an arm around her shoulders. She buried her face in her hands. Cate's first moment of surprise slipped into sympathy. However Jo-Jo might bad-mouth Eddie the Ex, apparently she still had feelings for him.

"He's Eddie Kieferson, my ex-husband. I

don't know why he shot my dolls, but he didn't have to kill himself over doing it."

Cate was doubtful about Jo-Jo's conclusion that some overwhelming guilt had prompted Eddie to shoot himself, but she didn't know enough to come up with any different explanation. She couldn't tell what the officers might be thinking. One got on a cell phone and the other herded Cate and a protesting Jo-Jo out to the dining room.

A raucous bray from Maude announced that someone else had arrived, and a moment later Mitch and the officer almost collided at the door. The officer made Mitch produce identification and then planted him in the dining room with Cate and Jo-Jo. Raindrops glistened in his brown hair and darkened the shoulders of his denim jacket.

"You okay?" were Mitch's first words to Cate. His blue eyes searched her face and he touched her cheek as if he'd like to expand that to a fierce hug, but he settled for a squeeze of hand on her shoulder.

Cate assured him she was okay, though that wasn't totally correct. Queasiness still roiled her stomach, and she doubted she could walk a straight line, but she managed introductions — Jo-Jo Kieferson, Mitch Berenski — and gave him a hurried update on Eddie the Ex and what had happened here.

She left out the minor detail of the dust mop.

The sheriff's deputies may have been slow to respond to a doll shooting, but the response to an ex-husband's death was immediate and abundant. More vehicles arrived, officers in uniform and other people in plainclothes. Maude brayed until she began to sound more like a squeaky cartoon character than a monster.

Cate now suspected that when Jo-Jo called 911, they'd thought the doll shooting was vandalism. There'd been a lot of it recently. Doll shootings would undoubtedly have garnered a response soon, but they weren't crisis enough to bring the instant reaction that murder would.

Although this wasn't murder either. Eddie had apparently shot the dolls and then himself. Although . . . did suicides often shoot themselves in the center of the forehead? *Note to self: research methods of suicide.*

Newly arrived deputies separated Cate, Jo-Jo, and Mitch for interviews. The questions Cate was asked seemed routine. Name, address, occupation. She explained why she was here and offered her identification card from Belmont Investigations. That didn't appear to make her and the deputy instant crime-solving buddies. Mitch's interview lasted less than five minutes.

"They told me they might have more questions for me later on, but I could leave for now," he told Cate. Without asking for her opinion, he added, "But I'm not leaving."

Right now, Cate didn't argue with that protective stance. She might not want to admit it, but his male presence was reassuring.

During the time that Jo-Jo's questioning went on and on, a deputy with both digital and video cameras spent considerable time in the room where Eddie's body still lay, then photographed the dolls and living room from all angles. Someone dug bullets out of the walls behind the dolls. Each bullet went in a separate plastic bag. Another person put the dolls in big plastic bags and carried them away.

When the officer finally returned Jo-Jo to the dining room, she grabbed the back of a chair for support and dropped onto the padded seat as if her knees were wobbly.

"They wanted to know all about Eddie and what kind of relationship we had and how long we'd been divorced and was he depressed or had he talked about killing himself. As if I'd know!"

"You weren't in touch with him?"

"I never heard from him except when he objected to some bill he had to pay. Then the officer wanted to know who he was married to now and where they lived. How long I'd lived here and did I have any visitors today. Where I'd gone and when and for how long, what I was doing and who I was with. How Eddie got in the house."

"How did he get in?"

"Probably looked in the dirt in that flowerpot on the back steps. That's where I've always kept a house key, wherever we lived. I wanted to call a funeral home, but they said his body wouldn't be released for a while."

"I think someone from the medical examiner's office has to look at it."

"They said there'd have to be an autopsy. An *autopsy.*" Jo-Jo's daze flared into anger. She jumped out of the chair, hands on hips. "Why do they have to do that to him? He has a bullet hole in his head! He shot himself. What more do they need to know? And they said they might have more questions to ask me later."

"You don't have to answer their questions if you don't want to. You can tell them you want your lawyer present. And then let your lawyer advise you about saying anything."

"Why didn't you tell me that before?" Jo-Jo skewered Cate with a vexed look, as if Cate had neglected a duty, but a moment later she sagged back into the chair. "Never mind. It doesn't matter. Why would I want a lawyer? I didn't do anything. Eddie shot himself," she repeated.

Yes, that was what it looked like. The gun was right there by Eddie's hand, and the deputy's questions about Eddie's state of mind suggested suicide. But the deputy's other questions sounded as if they might have other suspicions. As if they were checking to see if Jo-Jo could account for her whereabouts at Eddie's time of death.

Reluctantly Jo-Jo added, "I suppose I should call Kim and tell her."

"I think the officers will take care of that. Kim is Eddie's new wife," Cate added by way of explanation to Mitch.

"Will you stay with me after they leave?" Jo-Jo asked Cate suddenly. "I don't want to be alone here."

Cate had the feeling that wasn't how this evening was going to play out. She glanced at Mitch again. She knew what he was thinking. *No, no, no. Do not stay here.*

Cate started to say that Jo-Jo could come to the house and stay with her for the night, but Rebecca had recently moved the bed out of the guest room and started using the room for sewing and crafts. With Cate and Octavia moving out soon, their room would then become the guest room.

So instead Cate said to Jo-Jo, "I'll be glad to stay with you." She ignored Mitch's scowl.

As it turned out, staying or leaving wasn't either her or Jo-Jo's decision. A deputy informed them that the house would be sealed off during their investigation. He said he'd accompany Jo-Jo to her bedroom so she could pick up a few items, but he couldn't say when she'd be allowed to return.

"But I don't understand," Jo-Jo said. Her earlier flare of anger had fizzled into bewilderment, and the lines in her face drooped with both emotional and physical weariness. "Maude needs feeding. And Effie too. I can't leave them here alone."

"Maybe you could take the cat with you? I'll see that the burro is fed. And maybe your friends here could take you somewhere?" The deputy gave Cate a questioning glance and in an aside said, "I don't think she should drive tonight."

"I'll be glad to do that."

"But where would I go?" Jo-Jo lifted her hands and looked around, as if the deputy had doomed her to join the homeless under a bridge somewhere.

"What about your friend Donna?" Cate suggested.

"Donna's the biggest gossip in Lane County."

Cate ignored that objection. "I'll call her while you get your things together." She punched the number into her cell phone while the deputy escorted Jo-Jo down the hallway.

When a woman's voice answered, Cate identified herself and, without going into details, said there was an emergency and asked if Jo-Jo could spend the night there.

"Of course she can!" the woman said. "Is she okay?"

"She's fine. A little . . . rattled. She can explain it to you. We'll see you in a few minutes, okay?"

"I'll have tea ready."

After Cate put the phone away, Mitch said, "You can take her in your car, and I'll follow."

"There's no need for that. I'll call you later."

"I'll follow you," Mitch repeated.

"Bossy," Cate muttered.

"Cautious," Mitch corrected. "Because maybe there's a killer out there. And who knows what he may have in mind."

Cate mentally rolled her eyes. Mitch worrying again. Seeing danger lurking behind every bush, bedpost, and burro. Although Mitch did have an annoying habit of being right . . .

4

Cate had found a cat carrier on the back porch and had an uncooperative Effie stuffed into it by the time Jo-Jo returned with an overnight case.

"Thank you for checking every single item I put in there," Jo-Jo said to the deputy, sarcasm sharp as Effie's claws. "I wouldn't want to make off with something that would send your department into a dither."

"We don't go into dithers, ma'am," the officer said politely.

Jo-Jo glared at the deputy, but after he jotted down Donna's address and phone number, she let Mitch take her elbow and steer her to the door. Cate carried the cat carrier with a protesting Effie inside. Once outside, where the rain had settled into a steady drizzle, Jo-Jo jerked away from Mitch.

"I am not going to Donna's and listening to her talk, talk, talk. And I can drive myself," she declared. She tried to grab her overnight case out of Mitch's hand. "I'll just get a motel room. Eddie can pay —" Jo-Jo stopped short, as if it only then hit her that Eddie would never again be coerced into paying for anything. The fight went out of her, and her shoulders sagged.

Maude was silent now. Apparently her job description covered only the announcement of incoming visitors, not exiting ones. But there were other discordant noises. Chatter of radio in an empty police car. Patter of raindrops on car metal. Voices in the house. Effie's jungle-cat screeches.

Cate waited several moments and then said gently, "I'll take you to your friend's place."

Jo-Jo didn't resist when Mitch led her to Cate's car and put the overnight case in the backseat. Cate set the cat carrier beside it. The headlights of Mitch's big SUV followed Cate's Honda onto the gravel road. In the rearview mirror, Cate saw a uniformed figure come out and start stringing yellow tape across the driveway. Jo-Jo remained silent, except for minimal answers to Cate's questions about locating the address, as they drove into town. The earlier daze seemed to have fully enveloped her now. Effie's yowls dropped to occasional plaintive meows.

Donna had apparently been watching for them from the window of her white cottage. The porch light went on, and she opened the door. Cate helped guide an unsteady Jo-Jo to the door. Mitch carried the overnight case and cat carrier, then whispered that he'd wait for her and went back to the SUV.

The woman who met them at the door was about Jo-Jo's age, but her figure was trim in black capri pants, and her blonde hair cut in a stylish angled bob. The first thing she said was, "I didn't know the cat would be coming too." She sounded dismayed.

"Under the circumstances, it seemed necessary."

Then the woman gasped when she saw Jo-Jo. "For goodness' sakes, what happened?"

Jo-Jo's face looked years older than when Cate had arrived at the house. Her hair plastered her head like a permed helmet, her blouse hung out of her slacks, and her shoulders sagged.

Jo-Jo didn't offer any explanation herself, so Cate said, "Jo-Jo has had something of a shock. Her ex-husband is dead and —"

"Eddie the Ex is dead? Well, after all his shenanigans, I'd say good —"

Cate was almost certain Donna had started to say, "Good riddance!" But she managed to morph it into, "Goodness me, what happened? Did he have a heart attack?"

"Actually," Cate said, since Jo-Jo still wasn't speaking, "he was shot at Jo-Jo's house."

"Shot!"

"The sheriff's deputies are at the house, so that's why we had to bring Effie along."

Jo-Jo finally said something. "I think I'm going to be sick." She clutched her stomach, and ominous noises gurgled in her throat. Her eyes lurched into washing machine circles.

Donna grabbed her arm and helped her down a hallway to a bathroom. Retching noises followed, apparently Jo-Jo's delayed reaction to the events of the evening. Cate stood there, uncertain what she could do to help, or if she should just quietly slip away. She finally perched on the edge of the padded bench in the entryway, cat carrier and overnight case at her feet. Effie was either scared or prudent enough to remain silent now.

A few minutes later Donna came for the case, said she was putting Jo-Jo to bed, and asked if Cate could stay a little longer. She motioned toward the living room. Cate used her cell phone to call Mitch out in the SUV to tell him not to wait for her.

"I don't need to leave for a while yet," he said.

A mild statement that Cate knew really meant that whether it was five minutes or five hours until she came out, he'd be waiting. Stubborn man.

Yet the reassuring thought hit her that if someone had followed them from the house, implausible as that seemed, this person wasn't going to get past Mitch.

Eventually Donna did return to where Cate was sitting on a white sofa in the living room, her feet on the ice-blue carpet. Neither sofa nor carpet looked as if cat paws or hair had ever crossed their immaculate surfaces.

"I don't know if I should have done it, but I gave her half of one of my sleeping pills. So what's going on? Jo-Jo wasn't making any sense. By the way, I'm Donna Echelon. Jo-Jo and I are old friends." She offered a hand, nails nicely manicured in a silvery pink that matched her lipstick.

Cate shook the hand. "Cate Kinkaid." She didn't elaborate on an identification.

"Would you like tea? I made a pot of chamomile when you called."

A calming cup of chamomile held a certain appeal right now, but Cate shook her head. "Thanks, no. A friend is waiting for me outside."

Donna dropped to the edge of a chair upholstered in blue velvet. "I can't believe it. Eddie shot. Well, yes, maybe I can believe it," she amended. "I'll bet that new wife did it, didn't she? By now, he was probably cheating on her too."

"Actually, it looked as if he killed himself. He was shot in the forehead, and the gun was on the floor beside his body. He'd shot some of Jo-Jo's dolls before shooting himself in her workroom."

"Really? How . . . bizarre."

"Out of character for Eddie?"

Donna frowned, as if answering that question took some thought. "Once I'd have said way out of character. Shooting the dolls seems to have a certain symbolism to it, and Eddie never had that much imagination. But after he dumped Jo-Jo for that blonde bimbo . . ." She shook her head, her own blonde bob catching highlights from the lamp. "Now that I think about it, maybe I *can* see him shooting the dolls."

"He'd changed?"

"He was certainly different from what he was back when he and Jo-Jo had their burger drive-ins. Before he went all high and mighty with the glass house and fancy restaurant and blonde-babe wife."

"Jo-Jo thinks he went to her house to kill her, and just turned on the dolls when she wasn't home," Cate said. "Though I don't know why he'd kill himself afterward."

"That does seem strange. He waltzed around the restaurant chatting up customers and handing out favors as if he were some potentate reigning over his private kingdom."

"You've been there?"

Donna touched her throat as if she'd been caught in an indiscretion. "Some friends visiting from Portland wanted to go there. I'd rather Jo-Jo didn't know." Her lift of eyebrows asked for Cate's discretion.

Cate nodded. "Jo-Jo seemed to have mixed feelings about him."

"She always talked like he was pond scum, but once she told me she thought someday he'd realize he'd made a big mistake, and they'd get back together."

"If I can do anything to help —" Cate dropped a business card on the coffee table.

Donna picked it up. "You're a private investigator?" She said the words as if they equaled nuclear bomb expert. "You're investigating Eddie's death?"

"No. Jo-Jo had called me earlier, when she found the dolls. Then, while I was at the house, the deputies from the sheriff's department arrived and found Eddie's body."

Cate expected more questions about Eddie's death, but instead Donna tilted her head and studied Cate. "Why in the world would someone like you become a private investigator?"

Someone like you. What did that mean? Cate was uncomfortably aware that the rain had frizzed her usually flyaway red hair, that one knee now poked through a ragged hole in the worn jeans, and that sometimes she looked more teenagerish than twenty-nine. But Donna, with what sounded like a touch of envy, added, "It must be very exciting."

"Mostly not. Our work is usually routine. Actually, I'm still an assistant PI," Cate admitted. "It will be a few months before I get my own license."

"Really, I'm curious. I'm a librarian. Very unexciting. How does one become a PI in a town like Eugene?"

Cate wasn't about to go into what a scrambled-egg mess her life had been. Out of work for almost a year, job prospects as dim as a star in some faraway galaxy. Male relationships like a bad chick-lit novel. Living in a room in Uncle Joe and Rebecca's house. And then along came God's surprise plans for bringing good out of bad. A PI job in Uncle Joe's Belmont Investigations. Mitch. A deaf cat. A house of her own. Well, Octavia's and hers. It was an odd story, tangled up with her one murder case and acquisition of the cat.

"I guess you could say God opened the door, and I kind of stumbled through it. It wasn't anything I planned."

"I'm not very religious, but I remember that saying about God working in mysterious ways. Maybe it's true." Donna sounded wistful, as if her own life could use some mysterious intervention.

"But God always knows what he's doing, even if we don't."

A noise from down the hall made Donna jump to her feet. "I'd better go see if she needs something."

"I'll let myself out. I'm glad Jo-Jo has you to look after her." She stood up. "I'm not sure when they'll let her back in the house. Perhaps you could contact the sheriff's department in the morning and find out."

"I'll do that. Thanks for bringing her here."

Cate stepped out into another downpour. Mitch met her halfway to her car even though rain hammered the sidewalk so hard

53

that raindrops bounced. This time he did wrap his arms around her and shelter her with his body. "You okay?"

Cate had come out of the house thinking all she wanted was to go home and drop into bed, but now she realized she didn't want to be home alone with a vision of Eddie the Ex with a bullet hole in his forehead.

"I could use a coffee or something. Maybe the Espresso Junction over on Sixth Avenue?"

"Sounds good," Mitch said.

Ten minutes later they walked into the warm fragrance of the espresso shop together. Cate stopped short just inside the door. She started a quick U-turn to go out again. Too late.

"Hey, you guys!" Robyn stood up and waved. "Come on over and join us."

Cate glanced up at Mitch. He squeezed her hand. She knew he wasn't overly fond of the fiancée of his business partner in Computer Solutions Dudes, but he, like Cate, was trying hard to like her. Robyn Doherty *was* likable in many ways. Outgoing and friendly, bubbly and energetic, very successful at managing a flower shop her aunt owned. She was also relentlessly money-minded and status conscious, and right now Cate thought if she heard one more word about the minuscule details of the wedding, she'd put her hands over her ears and make a noise a whole lot like Maude's loudest bray.

"I need an opinion on an ankle bracelet," Robyn said when they reached the booth.

Cate swallowed hard to keep a bray from erupting.

"And you probably know what kind of opinion Lance has," Robyn added with an exaggerated roll of eyes at her fiancé. "He doesn't care if I even wear shoes, let alone an ankle bracelet."

"She's right," Lance McPherson agreed cheerfully. "The more I see of this wedding stuff, the more I think we should run off to Reno and do it up quick. With or without shoes."

Cate slid into the booth across from the couple, and Mitch followed. The waitress came, and Cate ordered a caramel latte and Mitch a plain coffee. Robyn had pictures of a dozen different ankle bracelets spread across the table. Robyn did much of her shopping on the internet. Her bead-encrusted, strapless wedding gown had come from San Francisco, the tiara and veil from Houston.

"I think this one would go best with my

shoes," Robyn said, tapping a string of sparkles that might or might not be tiny diamonds. "But I don't want something that will compete with my shoes, do I? So maybe I should go for something simpler, like this." Her finger moved to the photo of a silver chain with a tiny heart pendant.

Robyn rearranged the prints, like a general plotting strategy from reconnaissance photos. "What do you think?" she asked Cate.

What Cate thought was, *Between that $2,500 wedding dress and those $500 shoes, who's going to notice an ankle bracelet?* Since that didn't seem like a diplomatic response, she said, "Um."

Robyn swept the scattered pictures into a pile. "I'll think about it later. But we do need to decide about the sauce for the chicken." She looked at Lance. "I'm leaning toward —"

Lance groaned. "Any sauce is fine with me."

"I have to tell the chef at Mr. K's within the next few days what we want."

"Or you might wind up with naked chicken?" The snarky remark was out of character for Mitch, but he turned it into a gentle tease with a grin. He and Lance butted fists over the table, and even Robyn smiled.

"I know. With you two, ketchup would be a fine sauce. Over hot dogs. And we can have Oreos instead of a wedding cake. Afterward, instead of dancing, we'll all tromp out to the vineyard and stomp grapes in our bare feet."

"Hey, that sounds like fun," Mitch said, and Cate almost wished the facetious scenario were possible. It sounded more interesting than the actual plans. But now she latched onto something Robyn had said a moment earlier.

"Mr. K's is doing the dinner for the reception?" That was the restaurant where Uncle Joe and Rebecca were celebrating their anniversary tonight, so expensive that they'd joked about eating beans for the coming week. Mitch had mentioned taking Cate there sometime, but they hadn't done it yet.

"Mr. K's does all the food for Lodge Hill weddings. The same man, Ed Kieferson, owns both places. I'm sure I've mentioned that before." Robyn gave Cate an annoyed glance, as if Cate not remembering this bit of information was right up there with forgetting the date of the wedding. "The reputation of the food was one reason we chose Lodge Hill. Though it's also such a romantic setting out there in the vineyard. Aunt Carly knows Mr. K too, of course."

"A wise choice, I'm sure," Cate murmured. A moment later, as the name familiarity that had evaded her earlier suddenly clicked into place, she wondered if this would turn out to be such a wise choice after all.

Jo-Jo had said that Eddie the Ex owned that "most expensive restaurant in town." Which would be Mr. K's. And the K of Mr. K's would be Kieferson. Who also owned Lodge Hill, which Robyn certainly had mentioned before. Which was why the Kieferson name had sounded vaguely familiar to Cate.

Cate started to say something to Robyn about Ed Kieferson's demise, but the arrival of her latte, plus an elbow nudge from Mitch, gave her time to reconsider. Robyn was a little high-strung about the wedding . . . make that explosive as a stick of dynamite with a lit fuse . . . and who knew what hysterics this information might bring on?

Instead Cate asked, "There really is a vineyard at Lodge Hill?"

"Oh yes. Rows and rows of grapevines. Although Mr. Kieferson doesn't run the vineyard himself. The manager is this hottie who lives in a little cottage behind the main building." Robyn glanced surreptitiously at

Lance to see if her description of the vineyard manager had any effect on him.

It didn't. Not even when she added, "I think he used to be into motorcycle racing."

Motorcycle racing and raising grapes sounded like an unlikely combination to Cate, but all Lance did was say enthusiastically, "Maybe he's found a new way to stomp grapes, with a motorcycle. I'd like to see that."

Robyn refused to get into any lighthearted banter now. In cool tones, she said, "The grapes are trucked somewhere else for making wine now, although Mr. Kieferson plans to build his own winery later on."

Not going to happen. But instead of pointing that out, Cate said, "Have you ever met Mr. Kieferson?"

"Oh yes. He's been at Lodge Hill a couple of times when I was talking to LeAnne, the manager there. Such a distinguished-looking gentleman. And so elegant."

"Elegant?" Lance snorted. "He's a hand kisser. Can you imagine that? That's why she was so impressed with him. Because he kissed her hand."

"I thought it was sweet. Very old-fashioned and chivalrous."

Lance grabbed her hand and covered it to the elbow with noisy kisses. "How's that for old-fashioned and chivalrous?"

Robyn momentarily looked as if she might toss her latte in his face, but then she laughed. Cate mentally shook her head. She could never figure out if these two were going to have the happiest marriage ever or be in divorce court a month after the wedding.

"How about Mrs. Kieferson?" Cate asked. "Have you met her?"

"She and her mother own some kind of New Age shop, gifts and little one-of-a-kind things. Funky-fashionable, Aunt Carly called it. She knows Mrs. Kieferson's mother too, but I've never met either of them." Robyn's face brightened. "Hey, maybe I could find an ankle bracelet there."

Cate was disappointed. She'd have liked to have an outside perspective on the new wife, something other than Jo-Jo and Donna's not exactly unprejudiced descriptions.

"How's the new house coming along?" Lance asked Cate in what she suspected was an effort to get off the subject of the wedding. "Last time I was by there, it looked almost finished."

"I wish someone was giving me a house," Robyn muttered. "I mean, how often does *that* happen?"

Not often, Cate agreed silently. Something

in which God definitely had a hand.

"Your great-aunt is paying for half our wedding, which is a pretty generous gift," Lance pointed out. This was not something Cate had known before. Either the fact that the aunt was paying much of the wedding costs, or that she was actually a great-aunt. "You don't even like cats, so you probably wouldn't appreciate a ceiling-high scratching pole in the living room."

Robyn wrinkled her nose. "Does it really have that?" she asked Cate.

Mitch answered the question. "The pole doesn't actually go all the way to the ceiling, just up to the walkway that runs through a couple of rooms. Cats like high places."

"Mitch calls it the Kitty Kastle," Cate added.

"Didn't you have anything to say about the house?" Robyn asked. "I mean, who wants a house that's just peculiar even if it is free?"

"It isn't peculiar," Cate said, her tone a little more frosty than she intended. "It's a great two-story, three-bedroom, two-bath house. I picked out the bathroom fixtures and the granite countertops and paint colors myself."

Although it did have a few cat-friendly differences from most new houses. Mr. Ledbetter, the lawyer who was handling construction of the house as part of the estate of the woman who had originally owned Octavia, had diligently researched the internet for helpful ideas.

"Cate will pick out all the furniture herself," Mitch said.

"You mean furniture is part of the deal too?" Robyn asked.

"You can't expect a cat like Octavia to live in an unfurnished house." Mitch managed to sound shocked at the prospect.

"What happens if the cat dies or something?" Robyn asked. "Do you have to give the house back?"

"No. But I'd do everything I could to give her a long and happy life even if a house weren't involved," Cate said firmly. "Octavia is a unique cat, with a personality all her own."

"Well, it's one unusual deal," Robyn declared.

Cate had to agree. Octavia's owner, long before she was murdered, had specified in her will that whoever got the cat also got her house, and she had left the decision about the cat's ownership to her lawyer/executor. Cate hadn't actually saved Octavia's life, but she had kept her from being dumped at the animal shelter, and so Lawyer Ledbetter had decided Cate should be the cat's new owner. Then, after the house burned down, he had also decided a new house should be built to fulfill the provisions of the will. A house suitable for a deaf cat with a trust fund. And furnished, of course, because the original house Octavia should have inherited had been furnished.

Robyn suddenly lost interest in Kitty Kastles and whipped out a notebook. "I almost forgot. I have to change the shade of blue for the ribbons on the wrist corsages for the older women." She slashed through something written in the notebook. "I've been planning on cerulean, but now I realize that just won't work."

"Yes, cerulean would be a disaster," Cate murmured, and then she gave herself a mental whack for the snide comment. She tossed out a word she'd heard somewhere. "What about periwinkle?"

"Periwinkle?" Robyn looked up from the notebook, eyes squinted in thought, and Cate thought, *Oh no, I've just made the faux pas of the wedding world.* But then Robyn smiled and slammed a palm down on the notebook. "Yes! That's it. Periwinkle! What a marvelous idea, Cate. Thank you!"

She appraised Cate with what appeared to

be new respect, as if the periwinkle suggestion had elevated Cate from frump to fashionista. Although what Cate was thinking was that she'd better use her investigative skills and find out what color periwinkle actually was.

5

Uncle Joe and Rebecca were already home when Cate got back to the house. She asked about their dinner at Mr. K's, and they were enthusiastic about the prime rib, and the amaretto cheesecake for dessert.

"I was hoping Mr. K would come around and offer us a free dessert," Rebecca said. "I've heard he does that occasionally. But we never even saw him."

"That's because he's . . . dead," Cate said.

That received a double response. A shocked "Dead!" from both of them. Then, from Rebecca, "Was it on the news?"

Cate told them about Jo-Jo's call, the decimated dolls, and Eddie the Ex dead on the floor with the gun beside him, an apparent suicide.

"Did it look to you as if he'd killed himself?" Joe asked.

"I guess, although shooting the dolls first seems peculiar. And Jo-Jo's house seems like an odd place to kill himself."

"You said there wasn't another vehicle there at the house, so that makes you wonder how he got there, doesn't it?"

"I'm curious," Cate admitted.

"Curiosity can be a valuable asset for an investigator," Joe said. In a sterner tone, he added, "It can also get you in trouble. Big trouble. As we've discussed before, Belmont Investigations doesn't do murders."

Cate determinedly stuffed her curiosity in a mental corner and repeated the line to herself. Belmont Investigations doesn't do murders.

"I was there for several hours, but I'd rather not bill Jo-Jo for the time, if that's okay with you. All I really did was take her to a friend's house for the night, and I think she's short on money."

Uncle Joe nodded. "Write up a report for the files."

Joe was a stickler for keeping a written record of everything Belmont Investigations did. Cate intended to wait until morning to do the report, but she found she couldn't sleep and wound up padding barefoot into the office just after 2:00 a.m. Writing the short report again raised doubts in her mind, but she stuck to the facts and didn't include her questions. Her current case was

66

to deliver a subpoena the following day.

She printed out the report and tucked it in a folder to file later. Then, strictly because she couldn't sleep, of course, not because she was *involved,* she found a book in Joe's criminal research library and read up on suicides. One item she gleaned: gun suicides weren't unusual, but a bullet to the forehead was definitely out of the ordinary. Most gun suicides were done with the weapon stuck in the mouth or aimed into the temple.

Interesting.

Cate spent most of the next day looking for the woman on whom she was supposed to serve the subpoena, finally locating her hiding under a blanket in the backseat of her car. The woman was not complimentary about Cate's talent or persistence in tracking her down. She fired off a barrage of language hot enough to toast Cate's ears, then smashed the remains of a chili dog in her face. The woman had to get close to Cate to do that, however, and Cate triumphantly stuffed the papers down the front of the woman's baggy sweatpants. Subpoena served! And case closed.

This time, when she got home, she found Uncle Joe sprawled on the sofa, leg stretched out on a pillow. The hip he'd broken several months ago still gave him occasional problems and limited his activities. Now he grimaced with a twinge of pain as he shifted on the sofa and lowered the copy of the Eugene newspaper he was reading.

"Your dead man is featured," he said. He handed the front section of the newspaper to Cate.

Cate was headed for the shower to get rid of a chili-dog scent powerful enough to interest the neighbor's German shepherd when she got out of the car, but she stopped to look at the newspaper. The article about Eddie the Ex wasn't the top story, but it was on the front page, with a photo and a headline that read "Death of Prominent Businessman Investigated."

The article was short, as if the law enforcement people had been close-mouthed with information. Ed Kieferson had been found dead in the home of his former wife, Josephine Joanna Kieferson, in a rural area south of town. He'd been shot, but the article didn't go into specifics, didn't call it suicide, and didn't mention the dolls. It gave background information about Kieferson's business interests and named his survivors as wife Kim, living here in Eugene, and a son living back east. Cate was relieved to see her own name was not mentioned.

She studied the photo. A bullet hole in the forehead tended to alter anyone's appearance, of course, but in this apparently older photo he didn't have the beard, and his face was on the chubby side. Not what she'd call, as Robyn had, distinguished looking. Maybe his midlife crisis had included a face-lift? Or maybe he'd grown the beard to mask the saggy jowls visible in this photo?

"I think I'll cut this out and stick it in the file with my report," Cate said.

Cate talked to Mitch later, telling him about her day and hearing about his, and then went into the office to write up her brief report on serving the subpoena. She was surprised when the office phone rang after 10:00. Joe and Rebecca had already gone to bed.

"Belmont Investigations, Assistant Investigator Cate Kinkaid speaking."

"Cate, this is Donna Echelon. Jo-Jo Kieferson's friend?"

"Yes, of course. How's she doing?"

"Not great. An officer was here this morning and asked her all kinds of questions." Donna's voice was almost a whisper.

"But she'd already been questioned out at the house."

"I know," Donna said in a tone that put

69

ominous significance on the double questioning.

"She can't go back to the house yet?"

"The officer said they weren't finished there."

Cate scrunched the phone closer to her ear. "I'm sorry, but I can barely hear you."

"I don't know if Jo-Jo would want me to call you. I waited until after she went to bed, but she may not be asleep yet." A pause, as if Donna were listening for something from the bedroom, then another whisper. "I know you said you weren't investigating Eddie's death, but I think you should be."

"Why is that?"

"I stayed home from work today because I was concerned about Jo-Jo being here alone. She still seems so dazed. I probably shouldn't have listened in when the deputy questioned her, but I kind of . . . did."

"What kind of questions were they?"

"Oh, mostly about where she was, and who she'd talked to. It certainly sounds to me as if they suspect Jo-Jo killed him, though I don't think she realizes that yet. She's just too upset to think clearly about anything."

"Why would they be suspicious of Jo-Jo?"

"Oh, you know. There are . . . peculiarities."

Cate had to agree with that, although she wasn't about to offer her own list of peculiarities. One thing she hadn't thought about before occurred to her now. It had seemed accidental when Jo-Jo picked up the gun beside Eddie's body, then dropped it in apparent horror, but could the police be thinking that might not have been accidental? That she was cleverly making a legitimate reason for her prints to be on the gun to conceal the fact that they were already there?

"Are you suspicious of her?" Cate asked bluntly.

"No! Of course not. Jo-Jo's my friend. I've known her for years. She's a wonderful woman."

Cate thought that statement came with more hasty indignation than actual conviction, and she had the feeling that Donna did have suspicions about her old friend. Still, Belmont Investigations did not do murder.

"It sounds as if the sheriff's office is simply doing a thorough investigation," Cate said. "Actually, law enforcement officers usually treat any death that isn't natural as a possible crime." That information had come from Cate's middle-of-the-night reading. "It doesn't necessarily mean they're suspicious of Jo-Jo."

"They sounded suspicious of Jo-Jo to me." Donna sounded accusing, as if she thought Cate was shirking her duty.

"A private investigator can't just barge in and start investigating the way law enforcement officers do," Cate pointed out. "It's their job to investigate any unnatural death, but a PI doesn't have that right. It would probably be a good idea for Jo-Jo to talk to a lawyer."

"Okay. I'll tell her."

Cate started to hang up, but curiosity got the better of her. "By the way, I understand Eddie's new wife has a store or shop of some kind. Do you know anything about it?"

"The Mystic Mirage," Donna said promptly. "Lots of incense and crystals and candles. Tarot cards. Astrology stuff. Jewelry and some clothing, with a big emphasis on natural fabrics and dyes." Donna spoke in a disparaging tone, but then, as if she made the admission reluctantly, she added, "Although some of it is rather attractive, especially the antique jewelry and the leather sandals. In a, um . . ."

Cate filled in with Robyn's word. "Funky-fashionable way?"

"Yes, funky. But I found her selection of

books really disturbing. Everything from New Agey spiritual stuff to books about Atlantis and out-of-body experiences. UFO books, even some on witchcraft and the occult. Creepy."

"You've been there?"

Moment of silence, as if Donna realized she'd again revealed too much. "These friends from Portland —"

Cate let her off the hook, although she suspected nosiness rather than insistent friends may have motivated Donna's visit to the shop. "I understand."

"And I'll tell you something else. Jo-Jo says the reason Eddie left her was that Kim put a spell on him."

"A spell? Like voodoo or witchcraft?"

"I don't believe in far-out stuff like that, of course," Donna declared. "I think poor Jo-Jo is just desperate to explain to herself how Eddie could up and dump her like he did. But if thinking the woman put a spell on him makes it easier for Jo-Jo, well, okay with me." Donna might have concerns about Jo-Jo's involvement in Eddie the Ex's death, but her loyalty to her friend stood firm as a concrete wall.

"Did you meet Kim when you were in the store?"

"Yes, although I didn't let on that I was a

friend of Jo-Jo's. The mother was there too, and if you ask me, she's the really strange one."

"Did you talk to her?"

"Oh yes. She was pushing her book about her taking people into their 'past lives' through hypnotic regression. She has a 'Doctor' in front of her name and calls herself a metaphysical psychologist, whatever that means. She managed to get herself on a bunch of big TV talk shows, as she made certain I knew."

"Have you read the book?"

"No way! And I don't intend to," Donna declared, and Cate suspected Donna was relieved that it wasn't another indiscretion she had to admit to. "But if anybody put a spell on ol' scumbag Eddie to snag him for Kim, I'd bet it was her, the Queen of Weird."

"But Eddie was already married."

"He probably looked like a great catch, with his fancy restaurant and wedding business and all. Being married is no obstacle to some people," Donna said meaningfully.

"Well, tell Jo-Jo I'm thinking about her and praying for her, okay?"

"But you won't actually help her?"

Cate mentally protested that statement. Prayer *was* help. The most powerful kind of help. But Cate knew what Donna meant. "Maybe I'll drop by and see her."

Cate followed through on her comment about praying for Jo-Jo before she went to bed. The next morning, with her curiosity slithering out of that corner where she'd stuffed it, she spent time on the internet. The internet opened up for Mitch like a jet soaring through blue sky. Cate more often encountered murky clouds and engine trouble, although she had no trouble finding a website for Lodge Hill.

Photos showed a massive log and stone structure with rows of grapevines stretching off in the distance. Weddings could be held outdoors in the "garden chapel," or indoors in what had once been a ballroom. The room could accommodate the largest gatherings or be closed off with screens for "more intimate ceremonies," as the site put it. Plans were to turn the currently unused portion of the building into rooms and suites, although at present a list of "fine accommodations" elsewhere was available for out-of-town guests.

In a history section, the text said the log building had once been a private home belonging to a wealthy mining baron. His widow had started the vineyard after his death, apparently trying to upgrade his image from that of a man who cheated and stole his way to wealth into a genteel grower of fine grapes. The website treated the details in a lighthearted way that made the man who was basically an old shyster into a lovable semi-hero. It said there were even rumors his ghost still roamed the grounds.

The website included a photo of owners Ed Kieferson and wife Kim. In this photo a bearded Eddie the Ex did look quite distinguished. Cate doubted Kim had needed the help of a spell to snag him. Definitely trophy-wife material. Younger than Cate, lush blonde hair, high-wattage smile, beauty-queen figure. The spiel about the couple called them true romantics, dedicated to making weddings "memories to fulfill all your dreams," with the syrupy hope that the ensuing marriages would be as happy as their own. No mention of Eddie dumping Jo-Jo for this current wife, of course.

A Google search turned up a few other sites with information about Ed and Mr. K's restaurant, but Cate suspected computer-expert Mitch could have found much more. She did come up with an address for the Kiefersons' home in the elite Riverwalk Loop area, but the home phone was apparently an unlisted number.

Cate shut the computer down at lunchtime. She remembered to stick the newspaper photo of Ed Kieferson in the file with the notes she had written. Which was when she discovered an odd fact. She had not, as she always did, written "case closed" at the end of the report.

After a moment's thought, she didn't add it now.

6

After a quick lunch with Mitch, Cate spent almost three hours at the courthouse checking on properties for a client whose soon-to-be-ex-husband was trying to hide his assets in a tangle of corporate ownerships. Afterward she drove around by Riverwalk Loop to look at the Kieferson house. She couldn't claim she did it only because she was conveniently in the area, because she wasn't. It was a considerable distance from the courthouse.

It was an area of big trees, and lush landscaping surrounded each house. The Kieferson house stood back from the street, behind a wrought-iron fence and a tall hedge of evergreens. Maples glowed with fall foliage of russet and gold. A modernistic steel sculpture stood in the yard, the gleaming metal swooping in graceful loops and swirls on a marble base. Cate assumed it was supposed to represent something, but she had no idea what. Probably something she was too un-artistic to identify, she decided with a certain guilt. She was the girl who in sixth grade art class did a watercolor of a sunset that someone rudely titled "Barf Soup."

At first, looking through the trees, she thought the house simply had an overabundance of windows. But when she drove on to the spiked iron gate, where the hedge ended, the slanting rays of the afternoon sun turned the glass to blazing sheets of gold. She slowed the Honda to a complete stop, startled. Except for a supporting metal framework, the house was all glass. Glass from ground to roof, corner to corner. Stacked cubes of it, fantastic and surreal, like something drifted to earth out of the future. A red convertible stood in the circular driveway.

A man in a passing Mercedes eyed Cate suspiciously, and she reluctantly moved on. She started to head for home, then changed her mind. Curiosity had brought her this far. Why stop now? A quick search with her cell phone brought up an address.

A sign hanging from a metal crescent moon identified the Mystic Mirage. It was located on the main floor of an old brick building.

The second and third floors looked unused. The window held a creative display of candles, hanging over them copper and bronze plaques and bells with embossed figures of the sun, moon, and stars. A bell tinkled when Cate opened the door. The tiny interior had a pleasantly exotic scent of some incense she couldn't identify, and soft flute music added an otherworldly ambiance. A beaded curtain covered an entrance to a back room. Painted astrological signs dotted the concrete floor. A collection of huge swords, and an enormous brass shield, all vaguely Oriental looking, hung on the back wall.

A woman stood behind the counter. Not Kim Kieferson, Cate saw in disappointment. Although Kim's absence wasn't surprising. Her husband had been dead only a few days, so it was understandable that she wasn't working in the store so soon. Probably she was at home in the glass house with the red convertible outside. Mourning.

Unless she was the killer.

But this woman bore a definite resemblance to the Kim of the website photo. The mother, the Queen of Weird, the one who claimed she could take you on a tour through past lives? Although she didn't look weird. Neither did her silvery laugh sound as if she were in mourning for her son-in-law. She looked slim and polished and sophisticated, blonde hair pulled back into a sleek chignon that would be too severe on many women, but on her the style emphasized aristocratic cheekbones and dark eyes smoky with expertly applied makeup. She wore slim black pants and a cream tunic, and at least a half dozen colorful bracelets circled each arm. An oversized crystal hung on a silver chain around her neck.

She gave Cate a smile and nod to acknowledge her presence, then went on showing the other customer dangly earrings by holding them against her own ears. Cate hoped the stout customer didn't think the earrings would look the same on her as they did showcased against Kim's mother's slender and graceful neck.

Cate strolled the few feet of floor space. There was a display of tarot cards and Ouija boards. A headless mannequin wore a sheepskin vest over a gauzy dress, a rope belt, and cork-wedge sandals, an unlikely combination that managed to look both funky and fashionable. Shelves of books lined a rear wall. Stacked out front was a pile of hardcovers, with a handwritten sign that said Autographed Copies. The book Kim's mother had written? Cate edged closer to get a better look at title and author, but something else grabbed the corner of her eye, and she stopped short.

It was a doll, the size of a seven- or eight-year-old girl. Big blue eyes in a pixie face, with an expression that was both sweetly girlish and a bit mischievous. A ribbon in her ponytail of golden hair matched her ruffled pink dress. A strand of crystals hung around her neck, and she sat in a child-sized rocking chair with one hand resting on a bronze dragon.

Cate stared at the doll in astonishment. It had to be one of Jo-Jo's creations. But here, in the new wife's shop? No, surely not. There must be other doll makers whose work was similar to Jo-Jo's. Maybe someone was even doing rip-offs of her work. Cate remembered Jo-Jo saying she always marked the soft bodies of her dolls with an embroidered JJ.

Cate leaned closer to the doll. She glanced back to make sure the woman behind the counter was still busy with the customer. She lifted the ruffled skirt and was just peering under it as the customer said something in parting and the bell over the door tinkled. Cate heard no other sound, but she felt an ominous presence loom behind her. Her hand froze.

"The doll is not anatomically correct, if that's what you're looking for," a frigid voice said.

Cate looked up to find the woman glaring at her from only a couple of feet away. A red tide of embarrassment flooded Cate's face. The woman thought she was checking *anatomy.* Cate yanked her hand out from under the doll's skirt.

"But I wasn't —" she sputtered, mortified at what the woman was thinking. "I mean —"

Okay, if she wasn't checking anatomy, what was she doing? Did she want to tell this woman she was snooping into Eddie's death, looking now to see if the doll had been made by the ex-wife of her daughter's dead husband? Tell her, as far as Cate was concerned, both she and her daughter were high-priority suspects in his murder?

Because, even if Belmont Investigations didn't do murders, snooping into Eddie's death was really what Cate was doing here. Same as she'd been doing when she checked out the house on Riverwalk Loop. She smoothed the disarranged ruffles and gave the dress a nervous pat.

"She's, uh, really exquisite."

The woman pointedly straightened the do-not-touch sign that Cate hadn't even noticed until then.

"Oh, uh, sorry. Is she for, uh, sale?" Although all Cate could really think was, what kind of person snooped under a doll's clothing to check out anatomy? Pervert? Lech? Whatever, that was obviously what this woman thought Cate was.

"No, she is not for sale," the woman snapped, although Cate got the impression the doll was perhaps not for sale only to her. Because she wasn't qualified to own something so exquisite.

Cate didn't wait to continue the embarrassing conversation. She just turned and thundered for the door. Head down, she thunked head-on into the chest of a man just entering.

He grabbed her by the arms. "What's going on?"

In her distracted state, all that registered was that he was dark-haired, big, and muscular, with a grip that felt like iron bands on her arms.

"N-nothing." She broke away from his hands, almost had another collision with the high handlebars of a motorcycle parked at the curb, and dashed across the street to her car without looking back. Tires screeched as a driver braked to avoid hitting her, then blasted his horn at her.

Finally, in her car, she put her head against the wheel and groaned. She'd just earned what every budding PI needed in her resume. An official pervert designation.

And she still didn't know if the doll had Jo-Jo's identifying initials sewn on the body.

Uncle Joe was again reading the newspaper when Cate got back to the house. Her face still felt warm, embarrassment like a hot cloud enveloping her. Why hadn't she simply made polite conversation and asked where the doll had come from rather than peering under the skirt? Even if she felt a definite antagonism toward husband-stealing Kim, she still didn't like having the woman's mother think she was some groping-hands pervert.

"Heads may roll," Uncle Joe remarked. For a moment Cate felt as if "Pervert" must be branded on her forehead, and it was her head soon to roll. But then he handed her the newspaper he'd been reading. "Take a look."

Ed Kieferson had made the front page again. It was not a release of official information but was instead information the reporter had acquired from "an anonymous source close to the investigation."

The article said that Ed Kieferson's death

was now being investigated as a homicide. Shots fired within the house had come from the gun beside his body, but the fatal shot into his forehead had been fired from a different gun. The handgun beside Kieferson's body was registered to him, and he had recently acquired a permit to carry a concealed weapon. The gun from which the fatal shot had been fired had not yet been located. Authorities were still trying to determine why he was at the ex-wife's house and how he had gotten there. His Jaguar had been found in the parking lot at Mr. K's restaurant. The police had not yet made an arrest, but they were investigating "persons of interest" in the case. A photo of Jo-Jo's house accompanied the article.

Cate figured that heads would indeed roll if the department figured out who had supplied this unauthorized information.

The article in no way targeted Jo-Jo as a suspect, and yet that possibility ran through it like an ominous undercurrent.

"I know things look bad for Jo-Jo, but I just can't believe she killed Eddie. She seemed really broken up when she saw his body. And with him dead, she won't get any more alimony." That seemed a little lame as proof of innocence, but all Cate could come up with to bolster Jo-Jo's innocence was,

"She has a cat and a pet donkey."

"Very admirable, I'm sure. Although the value of their testimony in court may be questionable," Joe observed.

True.

"Look, just because she called you doesn't mean she's innocent," Uncle Joe warned. "I've had clients tell me stories imaginative enough to top the bestseller lists."

Cate had heard a few imaginative stories even in her short time as an assistant PI.

"Try this on for size," he said. "Jo-Jo is a woman scorned, and everyone knows how that can turn even a sweet woman into a flaming maniac. She's out for vengeance. She lures Eddie to accompany her to the house in her car —"

"It's an old white van," Cate scoffed. "Eddie wouldn't be caught dead in it."

"Well, he wasn't, was he?" Uncle Joe pointed out. "Now, once they're inside the house, he gets suspicious and pulls his own gun. But she shoots him in the head, leaves the body lying, returns later, and, with you and the deputies present, is horrified to 'discover' the body."

Cate considered his scenario. "There are some holes in that," she said.

"True," he agreed. "What did she use as bait to get him to accompany her to the house? Why was he in her workroom? Why did he shoot the dolls? How about he didn't shoot the dolls? She did it herself, after he was dead, as part of that amateur suicide scene she tried to set up. And it was a really amateur mistake for her not to realize ballistics tests would show that two guns were involved."

"It could have happened an entirely different way," Cate suggested as she slowly formulated a different scenario.

"I'm listening."

"Eddie came to kill Jo-Jo, but she shot him in self-defense. Then she got scared and ran."

"Possible. But where's the vehicle he came in?"

"Or the new wife Kim, who knows Eddie is a wife-cheater because he cheated *with* her, has now discovered he's cheating *on* her. Maybe he's even going to leave her for the other woman. She chooses Jo-Jo's house as the place to kill him because she figures the ex-wife will be blamed for the murder. She drives him to Jo-Jo's house on some pretext, kills him, and then drives away in the Jaguar and parks it at the restaurant." She paused. "Although I guess that has a few holes in it too, doesn't it?"

Uncle Joe nodded. "But it's not bad. Not

bad at all."

"I just don't think Jo-Jo did it. PI instinct?" Cate asked hopefully.

"Instinct and intuition, like curiosity, can be a great help to an investigator," Uncle Joe agreed. "Sometimes it's all you have to go on. It can also get you into trouble. Like the time I had this great intuition that a teenager I was looking for was hiding out in a barn in back of an abandoned farmhouse. What my intuition didn't tell me was that there was a rotted-out old septic tank by the house."

"Septic tank meaning . . . sewage?"

"If I didn't know that before, I did after I crashed into it," Uncle Joe agreed. "But the kid helped pull me out."

So Joe's intuition had, in a roundabout way, worked. Or maybe it was God working in his mysterious ways again. "So would it be okay if I go talk to Jo-Jo again, maybe do a little investigating into her ex-husband's death?" Cate asked. "I'd really like to help her if I can."

"You want to put Belmont Investigations back into the murder business."

"Well . . . um . . . yeah."

Joe scowled but then gave her a wry grin. "It's what I'd have done back in my hotshot days." He paused. "Thank you for checking with me first. But be observant. And careful."

The warnings were not afterthoughts.

Cate was supposed to meet Mitch at 6:30 at the Hong Kong Restaurant for a Chinese dinner, but he called to say he was working late on a computer systems installation job for a business down in Cottage Grove and could they make it 8:00?

"Great! That'll be fine," Cate said.

"How come you're so happy about it?" Mitch grumbled. "Here I thought you'd be sitting around counting the minutes until you could see me again."

"Oh, I am! Counting seconds, even. A thousand and one, a thousand and two, a thousand and —"

"I believe that's known, in technical terms, as hogwash," he muttered.

"I'll tell you about it when I see you."

"You're planning to do something I won't approve of, aren't you?"

"Bye now."

7

The house lights were on in Donna's house, and she answered Cate's tap on the doorbell.

"Cate! I didn't know you were coming —"

"I thought I'd stop by and see how Jo-Jo's doing."

Donna led Cate to the living room where Jo-Jo sat in the blue velvet chair. She still had a dazed, not-quite-present look. For a moment, Cate wasn't even sure Jo-Jo would know who she was, but the woman blinked, as if coming back from somewhere, and reached for Cate's hand.

With an unexpected spark of life she said, "I knew you wouldn't let me down!"

"We read the piece in the newspaper about Eddie," Donna said. She motioned Cate to a seat on the white sofa.

"And I finally got it through my head what's going on. Eddie didn't commit suicide. He was murdered right there in my house, and they think I did it." Jo-Jo touched her chest, as if she couldn't believe it. "*Me.* They think I shot Eddie."

"What makes you say that?"

"What the newspaper says. The questions they asked me. Realizing that if I were them, I'd probably be suspicious of me too. Discarded wife, bitter about being dumped, getting revenge." She held up her hand and cocked one finger like a gun. "Bang."

"They may think it, but they apparently don't have strong evidence yet, or you'd be under arrest," Cate said. "Have you talked to a lawyer?"

"Right now, I'd rather have you," Jo-Jo said.

A nice vote of confidence. Jo-Jo might have less confidence if she'd seen Cate's undignified exit from the Mystic Mirage.

"I can't pay all your fee right away, but I will pay you eventually," Jo-Jo said. "You can check my credit rating."

Cate doubted Jo-Jo knew how expensive private investigation could be, but all she said was, "We'll work out something. Actually, I did some preliminary investigation earlier today. I drove by the house in town —"

"Eddie's Ice Cube?" Jo-Jo's voice was stronger now, her eyes focused and alert.

Her tone turned scornful. "A million-six. Can you imagine paying that for a house? I told Eddie he was out of his mind, but he just had to have the place."

"I also went over to the Mystic Mirage," Cate said.

Jo-Jo blinked, as if that information dismayed her. For a moment Cate felt like a traitor, fraternizing with the enemy, but finally Donna said, "That was a very good idea, checking it out. Was Kim there?"

"No. An older woman was behind the counter. I'm assuming it was her mother."

"The famed Dr. Celeste Chandler." The disdain Donna put into "Doctor" made it more of a slur than an honor.

"I've never been in the Mystic Mirage. Although I've been curious," Jo-Jo admitted.

Donna prudently remained silent on that point.

"I saw something that surprised me," Cate said. "It was a doll that looked like one of yours."

Jo-Jo straightened in the chair. Her eyes flashed sparks. "Celeste put Kimmy in there?"

"She's one of yours?"

"Of course she's one of mine. She's how Kim met Eddie. The nerve of Celeste! Putting Kimmy in that creepy place."

"I think I need to know more about this."

Jo-Jo said that Kim's mother had admired the doll Jo-Jo had made for their mutual friend Krystal Lorister. "This was back when I was living in the Ice Cube, of course, with a workroom I'd set up in the garage. Celeste contacted me. She said she wanted to commission me to make a doll for her that looked like her daughter as a little girl, and I did."

"It was a gift for the daughter?"

"No. She said she was writing a children's book, about a doll that turns into a real little girl with mystical powers. She wanted the doll to put on the cover, I think."

"So why did she put the doll in the store?" Cate asked. "She and Kim surely aren't into giving you free promotion and advertising."

"I never heard anything about her publishing a children's book." Donna gave an unladylike snort. "Maybe she wanted to upgrade the creepy atmosphere of the Mystic Mirage."

"So what did the doll have to do with Kim and your husband getting together?" Cate asked Jo-Jo.

"Celeste came to pick up Kimmy when I had her done, and Kim came with her. Eddie happened to be home at the time. He had about as much interest in my dolls as he had in flying figs, but all of a sudden he's following them to my workshop and blathering on and on about how creative and artistic the dolls are. Then he invites both of them to the restaurant for a complimentary dinner. I should have been suspicious right then, but it just never occurred to me that he'd . . ." Jo-Jo paused to swallow, and then in a self-righteous tone added, "Of course, once she put a spell on him, he really couldn't help himself."

Donna leaned forward. "Did you say anything to the police about a spell?" She sounded anxious, and Cate could understand why. Talk about spells with the authorities might make Jo-Jo look a little strange herself. Like someone who'd blast away at evil spirits, Eddie included.

"No. I didn't think to mention it." Jo-Jo's eyes brightened. She glanced at the phone. "Maybe I should do that."

"No, don't," Cate said quickly. "Did either of the deputies, when you were questioned at the house or here, ask if you owned a gun?"

Jo-Jo nodded. "Among a zillion other things they asked."

"What did you say?"

"I said no, of course. I don't own a gun."

"You didn't tell them you used to own a gun?"

"They didn't ask that."

A certain innocent logic in that response. Or, an argumentative voice inside Cate's head suggested, perhaps the clever dodge of someone not so innocent?

"You said you got rid of the gun you had. What did you do with it? Just in case the question ever comes up."

Jo-Jo's brow wrinkled. "Well, let's see . . . Why? Does it matter?"

"If the authorities find out you once owned a gun, they may be interested in knowing where it is now. You're sure you don't have it? Because if the authorities search your house and property and find it . . ." Cate left the consequences hanging.

"They aren't going to find a gun in my house," Jo-Jo said. "I was going to sell it. But then I thought, what if it got into the hands of a criminal and he used it to do something terrible? So I took it to that bicycle bridge over the river, the bridge near the mall, and threw it into the deepest part of the current." She looked at Cate with a mixture of anxiety and defiance. "Maybe I shouldn't have done that?"

Cate wasn't certain what you were supposed to do with a gun you wanted to get rid of, but she was fairly certain tossing it in the river wasn't the preferred method of disposal. She also wasn't convinced that was what Jo-Jo had done with the gun. She waved away the question for now. "In this situation there may be a bigger problem."

"I don't understand."

"If the law enforcement people can't find the gun that fired the bullet that killed Eddie, and if they find out you did own a gun, they may suspect you shot him with it. And then threw it in the river."

"But I didn't do that. I threw the gun in the river months ago. And I didn't kill Eddie."

"What time did you leave the house the day Eddie was killed?"

"I don't know, 2:00 or 2:30, I guess. Maybe 3:00. I didn't get home until a few minutes before I called you. And I didn't see or talk to anyone I knew. The deputies kept asking that. In about fourteen different ways."

Cate tried to conceal her frustration. As an alibi, this was about as solid as a mist of lavender-scented room spray. "So where did you go? What did you do? Did you buy anything? Use a credit card? Eat anywhere?"

"Well, let's see. I have a Visa card, but I can't remember the last time I used it. I've never believed in buying things on credit."

Admirable, but not particularly helpful at this point.

"I went to Walmart and looked at some rubber boots, because it gets sloppy out in Maude's pen in the winter. But I decided maybe I could pick up a cheaper pair at Goodwill sometime. Then I went to the mall and looked at some fabrics for an outfit for the doll I'm working on. His name's Jerome, and he'll be a gift from this woman to her granddaughter. Kind of the brother she doesn't have. But I haven't decided how to dress him yet. It's a real problem. I hate those crotch-at-the-knees pants that boys wear now."

No receipts to prove Jo-Jo had even left the house. And Jo-Jo was worrying about dressing her doll. Cate tried to jerk her back to the real problem. "If you didn't buy anything, why did you go to town to begin with?"

"Sometimes I just like to get away from the house. It gets lonely, you know? I did get a hamburger at Biff's Beefy Burgers just before I came home. That's what they changed the name of the drive-ins to after we sold them. But they're going really skimpy on the tomato now. We never did that."

"Did you get a receipt?"

"I don't know. If I did, I threw it in the trash with the other stuff."

"Did you know the person who waited on you?"

"No. They change help all the time."

No young person at the burger place was likely to remember one inconspicuous, older-woman customer. So far, there was no proof at all that Jo-Jo had even left the house that afternoon. But wasn't that, in a backwards kind of way, proof that she had? Because if she was trying to be deceptive, wouldn't she have made a deliberate effort to collect receipts and specific conversations to verify she hadn't been home when Eddie was killed?

Donna suddenly straightened in her chair. "Jo-Jo, sweetie, I think you're remembering wrong. Wasn't it last week you went shopping for boots and fabric? And this week you came to the library and spent the whole afternoon looking at those Arizona magazines?"

Jo-Jo's brow wrinkled. "I don't think so. I —"

"But I'm sure you did."

Jo-Jo started to shake her head, but then a crafty half-smile slid across her face. "You know, you're right. How could I have forgotten?" She turned to face Cate. "I was with Donna in the library all that afternoon. I'm thinking about moving to Arizona, you know."

"But you didn't 'remember' that when you talked to the deputies?"

"I can still tell them." Jo-Jo jumped up with surprising agility. "In fact, I can go to the phone right now and Donna can confirm —"

Cate gave her a light push back into the chair. She turned to Donna.

"Donna, I know you're a wonderful friend, a very loyal friend, and you want to help Jo-Jo. But making up an alibi for her is not the way to do it. We'll just have to work with the facts, whatever they are."

The two women looked at each other. Neither said anything, but a kind of resigned sigh passed between them.

"So who do you think might have killed Eddie?" Cate asked. She let her gaze flicker between the two women. "How do you think Eddie got out there to the house since there was no vehicle?"

"Kim," Jo-Jo said.

"Kim's mother," Donna said. "Kim has the boobs and beauty, and she's not a totally dumb blonde, but Celeste's the brains of the pair. And definitely the CEO. Kim does what her mother says."

"Why would Eddie have come to your house?" Cate asked Jo-Jo.

Jo-Jo wound her fingers together. "I think he realized he'd made a mistake and wanted to talk about our getting back together again."

A possibility that didn't jibe with Jo-Jo's original declaration that Eddie the Ex had come to the house to kill her. "But neither Kim or her mother would have driven him out there to do that, would they?"

Jo-Jo and Donna looked at each other, obviously without an answer to what seemed to Cate an elementary question. Finally Jo-Jo said reluctantly, "Eddie's lawyer has been talking to my lawyer about getting my alimony reduced. I suppose he could have come out to talk about that."

"So Celeste convinced him to let her take him out there in her car," Donna said. "She saw it as a great chance to kill him at Jo-Jo's place, where it would look as if Jo-Jo had done it."

"So why would Celeste want to kill him?" Cate asked.

She expected Jo-Jo to continue with what Cate suspected was a wild fantasy that Eddie was coming back to her, but instead Jo-Jo said, "Greed. As Eddie's wife, Kim inherits the restaurant, the Lodge Hill wedding business, the vineyard, the house, everything. Celeste wanted to get rid of Eddie before he divorced Kim and she wound up with nothing."

A sudden new thought seemed to electrify Donna. "Maybe that's how the two of them planned it from the very beginning. Marry him, murder him, inherit his assets. Maybe they took out a big insurance policy on him!"

A mother-daughter murder conspiracy. Sounded like juicy tabloid stuff. Yet Eddie had that gun, and a permit to carry it, which might suggest a different possibility.

"What about business enemies?" Cate asked.

"Back when we had the burger business, I knew all about everything that was going on, every penny that came in or went out, everyone we did business with. Eddie ran the food part, and I took care of the business end." Jo-Jo sounded wistful. "Later, after we sold the burger business, I managed the wedding business for a while. I liked doing that. But then Eddie said I was working too hard and we should get someone else to do that. What he really wanted, of course, was someone younger to dress up the place." Jo-Jo gave an audible sniff that turned into a gulp and then a sob.

Cate put a hand on her shoulder and squeezed. "I'm sorry. I didn't mean to upset you."

Jo-Jo reached up and grabbed Cate's hand. Cate thought the woman was going to plead for her help, but what she said was, "The sheriff's people took Lucinda and Toby and Marianne. Will I ever get them back?"

Not if they convict you for murder.

"Sweetie, there are more important things to worry about," Donna said.

Right.

Mitch was already at the Hong Kong when Cate arrived. He waved to her from a booth. A candle in a Chinese bowl flickered when Cate slid into the bench seat across from him. Her spirits rose, and some of the weariness dropped away. Mitch did that to her. Sometimes she thought she was falling in love with him. Sometimes that seemed like a great idea. Sometimes it didn't.

"A thousand, seven hundred sixty thousand and one. A thousand, seven hundred sixty thousand and two." Cate touched her chest as if she were breathless. "A thousand —"

"What are you doing?" Mitch asked.

"Counting seconds, of course. Until we could be together again." She smiled at him. "And now we are."

"That's very charming. I'm flattered." Mitch dipped his head in acknowledgment. He also frowned. "But what have you been up to that you're trying so hard to distract me with all this butter-him-up sweet talk?"

"It's graduated from hogwash to sweet talk?"

Mitch's scowl reluctantly turned to a grin, and he shoved a menu toward her.

"Belmont Investigations is looking into the death of Eddie Kieferson," Cate said.

"Belmont Investigations meaning Cate Kinkaid?"

"Well, um, yes."

"Have you told your Uncle Joe?"

"Oh yes." Cate was relieved she could say that. "We discussed it, and I went over to talk to Jo-Jo and her friend Donna."

"Something tells me this death is no longer a suicide."

Cate told him about the newspaper article, which Mitch hadn't yet seen. The waitress came, and they ordered the #3 family dinner for two, wonton soup, barbecued pork, butterflied shrimp, chicken chow mein, shrimp fried rice, and tea.

After the waitress left, Mitch said, "So

you're officially investigating a murder. Cate, do you think you should be doing this, even if it's okay with Joe? Last time you investigated a murder you almost got your-self killed. Twice in one day, as I recall."

"Well, that was an unusually bad day. It's not likely to happen again."

"Tell that to the killers," Mitch muttered.

"The sheriff's department is apparently quite suspicious of Jo-Jo. She needs help."

The waitress brought their tea, and Mitch filled the tiny bowls. "And how do you plan to go about helping her?"

Cate told him she'd started the investigation by looking at the glass house and going to the Mystic Mirage. Which meant she also had to tell him about her undignified exit and the reason for it. She appreciated that he did not snicker, although he did make a couple of peculiar snorts and coughs.

"I'd like to know more about both Kim and her mother. But there's no way I can go in there again." Gloomily Cate added, "Celeste would probably meet me at the door swinging one of those swords hanging on the back wall."

"Maybe I could talk to her."

"You?"

"Why not? It's a public store. I might be looking for a gift for my girlfriend. Something unusual." Mitch tilted his head. "I turn on my magnetic charm and personality, and she tells me everything."

Cate doubted Celeste Chandler would be confessing to murder no matter how much magnetism Mitch turned on, but he might be able to pull something helpful out of her.

"You'd do that?" she asked. "Even though you'd rather I weren't involved in this?"

He reached across the table and cupped her chin in his hand. "Sweet Cate, for you I'd climb the highest mountain, swim the widest river —"

"If the hogwash gets any deeper in here, I'm going to have to start swimming myself." She studied him. "Maybe what you're doing is pulling the knight-in-shining-armor act again. Saving me from my own incompetence as a PI."

"Cate, I do not think you're incompetent as a PI. It's true that I'd rather you came to work with me at Computer Solutions Dudes. But I know you're going to jump into this even if it looks as risky and dangerous as doing a Tarzan swing on a spiderweb. So, on the old theory of 'if you can't beat 'em, join 'em,' I'd like to help."

The waitress started filling their table with steaming dishes, and Cate waited until she was gone again. "Actually, I think it's a pretty good idea."

Mitch's eyebrows lifted in surprise, but all he said was, "Anything in particular you want me to find out?"

As they ate, Cate loaded him up with the information she already had about both Kim and Celeste. "Anything you can add to that would help. Any particular time you can do this?"

"How about tomorrow afternoon? Later, we'll get together in the evening at my place, and I can tell you what I find out." He waved a hand over the table laden with food. "I think we'll have plenty of leftovers for dinner."

8

Cate spent most of the next morning at the courthouse again working on the tangled property ownerships. After lunch she took time out to look up the Kieferson house on Riverwalk Loop in the records of the assessor's office. In spite of numerous amenities, including a temperature-controlled wine room and an indoor pool, the property was not now valued at nearly the $1.6 million Jo-Jo had said she and Eddie paid for it. Property values had gone down everywhere.

When Cate arrived at Mitch's condo that evening, he had the leftovers from their Chinese dinner already in the microwave, ready to heat. The gas fireplace in the living room flickered with cozy warmth, and the open drapes framed a view of city lights from this hillside location.

"Okay, tell me about today," Cate said as Mitch punched the microwave buttons. "What happened at the Mystic Mirage?"

"First we eat, then business."

"This feels like Christmas at my grand-parents' house when I was a kid," Cate grumbled. "First everyone eats breakfast together. Then the dishes have to be done. No dishwasher in their old farmhouse, of course. Only when dishes are all washed and dried and put away does Grandpa hand out the presents."

"Good system." Mitch nodded approv-ingly. "When I'm a grandpa, I think that's exactly how I'll do it."

Mitch would make a great grandpa, Cate decided. She felt an odd little twinge inside. Who would be the grandma?

After their leftovers dinner, which was almost as good as the first time around, Cate expected Mitch would admit he hadn't been able to get anything out of Celeste. Instead he led her to his home office in the other room. With a flourish, he pulled a gold and black pen from his shirt pocket. It looked like an ordinary pen until he used a USB connection to plug it into the com-puter. When she heard a recognizable tinkle, Cate realized what the pen was and what he'd done.

"You recorded your conversation with Ce-leste!"

"I figured that would be better than just

telling you about it. Remember back when I got you that pen that's actually a video camera? I got this at the same time, an audio recorder."

"Why?"

"I guess I'm a sucker for electronic gadgets," he admitted. "Did you know there's a cell phone you can wear on your wrist, with a voice-activated control? Wouldn't that be handy for a PI if he — or she — had one when escaping down the side of a building or cliff, hanging on by his or her fingertips, and needed to make an important call to the CIA or Interpol?"

"Interpol and the CIA aren't exactly on my speed dial, and I don't anticipate hanging by my fingertips from anywhere in the near future. Do you?"

"You never know."

"Sometimes I think you're really a PI at heart."

Mitch grinned and turned up the volume. "Hi. Hey, what an interesting place you have here," he said on the recording, and Celeste's voice responded warmly, "Welcome to the Mystic Mirage."

"She sounds much more friendly to you than she did to me," Cate said. "Is this legal?" she added doubtfully.

Mitch stopped the recorded conversation.

"I did some checking first. It's kind of a gray area, but this state is what's called a one-party-consent state. Which means, so long as it isn't a conversation where privacy could reasonably be expected, then only one person in a conversation has to be aware that it's being recorded."

Mitch turned the recording on again. His voice coming through the computer's speaker system sounded enthusiastic about the jewelry in the glass counter.

"We have some lovely new astrological design earrings that just came in. I can get them out for you."

"Let me look around first. Oh, that little girl was here before me — hey, she isn't a little girl, it's a big doll!"

"Yes, isn't she real looking? Her name is Kimmy."

"She looks like something my girlfriend would really like. I suppose she's very expensive?"

"She's from my personal collection of treasures, and I haven't been planning to sell her. I just thought she seemed so lonely at my apartment, so I brought her here. But wait, I'm getting a real vibe here —"

"She put her hands on her temples and closed her eyes," Mitch whispered to Cate.

"Yes, I can feel it," Celeste said. "A real

111

cosmic connection between Kimmy and your girlfriend. What's her name?"

"Corinne."

"Corinne?" Cate whispered in surprise.

"Yeah. Your middle name."

"How'd you know that?"

"The internet knows all. But I didn't think she should know the name you actually use," he whispered.

"Okay. Thanks."

". . . a really powerful connection between Kimmy and Corinne," Celeste continued.

They'd missed a little, whispering between themselves. Cate wasn't sure why they were whispering. It just seemed appropriate, as if they were eavesdropping on a live conversation.

"More like a common destiny joining them," Celeste said. "Something beyond our limited understanding on this plane."

"She'd make a great used car salesman," Cate said. " 'You and this '94 Buick have a common destiny. You're meant to be together.' "

"I'll have to consider that, then," Mitch's voice said to Celeste from the recording. "My girlfriend also likes to read, and I see you have a great collection of books here."

There were some rustles and bumps on the recording, and Mitch whispered to Cate that Celeste had come around the counter and held out a copy of her book to him. Although the biggest bump had come, he admitted, when he accidentally hit the stack of books with his toe and knocked it over.

Cate could imagine what Celeste would have said to her in that situation, but what she almost playfully said to Mitch was, "Men. You're all alike. You all have that proverbial bull-in-a-china-shop trait."

Mitch apologized to Celeste, then said, "This book looks interesting."

"It is." Celeste gave the silvery peal of laughter Cate remembered from when she was in the shop. "Not that I'm biased in my opinion just because I wrote it."

"You're Celeste Chandler?" Mitch had managed to sound awed. "*Dr.* Chandler, I see here on the cover."

"You can call me Celeste."

Cate could hear a smile and something else in Celeste's voice and statement. Something flirty. "I can't believe this woman," she muttered.

"And your name is?" Celeste added.

"I didn't know quite what to do then," Mitch whispered to Cate. "I really didn't want to give her my name, but I didn't feel comfortable lying about it."

"Mitchell," he'd finally said to Celeste,

without giving his last name.

"Mitchell? I didn't realize Mitch was short for Mitchell." How many other details were there that she didn't know about Mitch?

"Although I must admit doing the book wasn't actually writing," Celeste went on. "I simply recorded what people told me about their past lives and added information that connected their hidden memories with actual history."

"How do you meet these people?"

"I'm a metaphysical psychologist. The people in the book are men and women who came to me with problems in this life, and I helped them understand how their past lives affect their present existence. How about you? Would you like to find out about your past lives?"

"Well, I'll, uh, have to think about it. What kind of past could I have had?"

"Well, you're a big guy. Well built and muscular. An air of self-confidence. Definitely no couch potato."

"She was feeling my biceps when she said that," Mitch whispered to Cate.

"I see intelligence in your eyes. Determination. Leadership. Courage. I'd say that in previous lives you were undoubtedly a warrior, probably a leader of warriors. And women were strongly attracted to you.

Many women."

"She's coming on to you!" Cate whispered indignantly. "What do they call older women who go after younger men? Cougars. She's a cougar, and she's after you!"

"I don't know about that, but she made me uncomfortable," Mitch admitted. "An older couple came in the store then, and I turned the recorder off."

Good thing other customers arrived. Who knows what Celeste might have done next? But all Cate said was, "That's the end of it?"

"No, there's more. I skimmed through her book while they were there. Weird stuff. One man 'remembered' he was President Lincoln in a previous life. He said an unknown 'fact' about his previous existence as Lincoln was that his beard was really itchy."

Mitch turned the recording back on, and Cate heard the tinkle of the bell over the door as the customers departed. Then Mitch's voice saying to Celeste, "This is your place?"

"It was mine originally. Then my daughter's first marriage ended, and she came here to stay with me. So we're partners now. But she just lost her present husband and is in seclusion for a time."

"I'm sorry to hear about your daughter's

husband."

"It's an unpleasant situation. He was shot — murdered, actually. You may have heard or read about it. It's been on TV news and in the newspaper."

"Hey, I think I did. He owned a popular local restaurant?"

"Yes, Mr. K's. It's a tragic situation for Kim. Her first marriage was such a mistake, and now, just when she'd found happiness with Ed, this happens. They've been so blissful together. He was a remarkable man."

"And the police have no idea who killed him?"

"It happened at his ex-wife's home. She's caused them all kinds of grief. A very greedy and vindictive woman, always after money. Ed told Kim he was going out to the house to try to reason with her, but there's no reasoning with that woman. The next thing anyone knows, he's lying dead on her floor."

"You mean the ex-wife may have killed him?"

"That's rather obvious, although it's apparently going to take diagrams or a video for the police to figure that out." A hesitation and a little cough before Celeste continued. "I'm sorry. I get a little emotional about this. I'm afraid my feelings for the first Mrs. Kieferson are more than a little hostile. I guess I'm something of a mother bear protecting her cub where Kim is concerned."

"But why would the ex-wife want to kill him?"

"Is a half million in life insurance reason enough?"

"Jo-Jo gets his life insurance?" Cate's startled question popped out aloud. She slapped a hand over her mouth, as if Celeste might hear. Did the authorities know about the life insurance? Probably. No wonder they were zeroing in on Jo-Jo.

"I'm sure the authorities will uncover the truth before long," Mitch said to the woman. "Well, I'll give my birthday gift for Corinne more thought. Thanks for your suggestions."

"What about a reading on your past lives? It can be very enlightening."

"How do you do it?"

"A light hypnosis. Occasionally something to help a person relax."

"You do the readings right here?" Mitch asked.

"No. I find the familiar setting of a person's home much more conducive to the level of relaxation necessary for full regression."

"Now she's trying to grab an invitation to

your condo," Cate said in what she intended as a whisper but which came out more of an indignant yelp.

"And you really believe everyone has lived lives before this one?" Mitch asked Celeste.

"Of course. In ancient times, in an earlier life, I was an artist, painting on the walls of a cave in France. Later, I was a princess, daughter of an Egyptian pharaoh, poisoned by a half-sister rival. I was a peasant girl in the Middle Ages, pulled out of poverty by a powerful lord to become his wife. But I was unfaithful to him, so in my next life I suffered greatly. We pay for our wrongdoings in one life by what we are and what happens to us in our next life."

"No heaven or hell?"

"We keep coming back in new lives until we're worthy of heaven."

"We're never worthy of heaven," Mitch said with a forcefulness that surprised Cate. "Jesus's death on the cross is our only route to heaven."

"I believe it's dangerous to be so closed minded that we see only one viewpoint when there are many viable viewpoints." Celeste's voice coming out of the computer's speakers had now cooled considerably. "Knowledge about past lives explains why what may appear to be injustice in this life really isn't. We're paying off a debt from a previous life, so we can eventually reach the heavenly existence and not have to come back again."

"But Jesus himself says, 'I am the way and the truth and the life. No one comes to the Father except through —' "

Cate waited for more, but the conversation ended abruptly at that point. "You stopped right there?" she asked.

"Oh, I kept going, but I was so intent on what I was saying that I must have accidentally reached up and slid the clip on the pen, which is the on/off control." Mitch sounded exasperated with himself.

"I think you did great."

Actually, Cate was astonished by all the recording revealed. About Jo-Jo getting a half million in insurance, of course. What was a little alimony compared to that kind of payoff? She was just as surprised with what the recording revealed about Mitch. They'd been attending church together regularly, always on Sunday, sometimes also the midweek Bible study. He actively served with the church's Helping Hands project, as he'd been doing since before she'd met him. And yet he'd always seemed to have some reservations holding him back from full belief and commitment, a kind of quiet foot-dragging. But he hadn't seemed to have any doubts as he talked to Celeste.

As if reading Cate's thoughts, he said, "Sometimes having to state your beliefs to someone else helps clarify them in your own mind."

"And yours are clarified?"

He smiled. "Very clear now."

Cate wanted to clap, but she doubted Mitch would feel comfortable with applause. "So what happened then? Did Celeste get as snarky with you as she did with me?"

"She said she'd still like to do a past-lives reading on me, and then I'd know the truth that those lives existed."

"So are you going to do it?"

"Are you kidding? Let that woman hypnotize me? No way. She might program me to quack like a duck every time the phone rang. But I did ask her if she thought Ed Kieferson getting murdered in this life was payback for something he'd done in a previous life."

"What did she say?"

"She said that Ed had plenty to account for in this life."

"That almost sounds as if she thought he got what he deserved."

Had Celeste decided on murder as pay-

120

back for something Eddie had done in this life? She might be a cougar with Mitch, but she was definitely a protective mama bear when it came to Kim.

A good PI, Uncle Joe had once mentioned to Cate, could sometimes pull information out of people that they never intended to give. And sometimes didn't even realize they were giving. She thought Mitch had done that here.

"Well, even if Jo-Jo gets the insurance, Kim has the big house and a convertible, along with Mr. K's and a vineyard, to comfort her," Cate noted.

Mitch disconnected the pen recorder. "Maybe I'll check into that," he said thoughtfully.

9

Mitch, after reminding Cate they were rescheduled to do Mr. Harriman's cleanup job Saturday afternoon, was already settling down in front of his computer when Cate left the condo. Back home, her cell phone rang just as she walked into the house. Uncle Joe and Rebecca were watching TV in the living room, and she stepped into the office to take the call.

"Cate, hi, this is Robyn. I'm sorry to bother you so late, but there's a problem."

Now what? No doubt a world crisis, from Robyn's point of view. Which probably meant — what? She needed help with the color of her toenail polish for the wedding? Someone to fasten her ankle bracelet? A color other than periwinkle for the wrist corsage ribbons? Which reminded Cate she still had no idea what color periwinkle really was. She gave a resigned mental sigh. "Anything I can do to help?"

"Yes! Thank you so much for offering. As you know, I have six bridesmaids plus my maid of honor for the ceremony."

Well, no. Cate hadn't actually paid much attention to the bridesmaid count.

"My maid of honor, McKenzie, is coming from Denver. Kathi and Rachel live in San Francisco. Susi is flying in from Chicago, and Tiana and Tara are coming up from San Diego."

Cate relaxed. This was something she actually could help with. "I'll be glad to pick up any of them at the airport. Just tell me when."

"No, it isn't that. The problem is the other bridesmaid, Shauna. She's a college friend from Spokane, and she just told me she can't make it to the wedding! Her husband is being transferred to Denver, and that's exactly when they'll be moving." Robyn sounded caught between anguish at this breakdown in her ceremony and annoyance that this friend was actually putting her husband's transfer ahead of Robyn's wedding.

"Well, um, that's too bad."

"So right away I thought of you! You and Shauna are about the same size, and her bridesmaid dress will fit you perfectly!"

Cate felt dismay wash over her like a slosh

of sour milk. She didn't mind the small suspicion that she was chosen primarily because she'd fit the dress, but, be a bridesmaid? Oh no. At one ceremony she'd tripped coming down the aisle and fallen into the lap of an elderly man in a nearby pew. At another, the bride had chosen slim-skirted, goldy-brown gowns for her bridesmaids, and they'd looked like a quartet of overdone corndogs.

"You want me to be a bridesmaid?" Cate asked with the small hope she was mistaken about what Robyn was asking.

"Yes! You'll look gorgeous. So many bridesmaids' dresses are almost hideous, you know? You have to wonder, what was the bride *thinking*? I had to wear this ghastly pink thing one time, and I looked like an escapee from a cotton candy machine. But these are awesome. A lovely, soft celadon. You'll have lots of use for it afterwards."

"Well, um, that's nice," Cate said as she frantically searched for some acceptable door of escape. She had to make an unexpected trip to Siberia? She felt the coming onslaught of a disease heretofore unknown to medical science?

"Cate, I know it's a lot to ask, since we're rather recent friends, but I'd really appreciate it. I-I feel as if the wedding is falling apart."

Cate heard a note of panic in Robyn's voice. Okay, this was really, really important to her. Cate gave a mental sigh. Would it hurt her to help out here?

"Yes, I can do it," Cate said. Then, realizing that sounded more sacrificial than eager, she tried to put more enthusiasm into her voice. "I'll be really happy to do it!"

"Thank you so much! Shauna is sending the dress by Fed Ex, so I'll call you as soon as it gets here and you can try it on."

"I'm looking forward to it."

At least as much as she looked forward to flu shots, foot fungus, and a parking ticket.

But an unexpected thought occurred to her after the conversation ended. As a bridesmaid, and presumably a helpful friend of the bride, she could legitimately go to Lodge Hill and look around. And at the same time she could see what other non-wedding information she could pick up about Kim, Celeste, and the late Mr. K.

There was a frustrating delay before she could go out to Lodge Hill, however. On Saturday morning, when she planned to go, Jo-Jo called. She was still staying at Donna's house in town. The sheriff's department had notified her that she could return to the house on Randolph Road, but they still had her old van, so she was without transportation.

"Why are they holding the van?" Cate asked.

"They didn't say, but Donna says it's because they're looking for DNA or fingerprints or something that would prove Eddie had been in it. Maybe dandruff, for all I know. Eddie was always shedding it. Anyway, if they find something, I guess that would prove to them I took him out to the house and killed him."

"Was he ever in the van?"

"Not since he went all highfalutin and got that Jaguar he tooled around in."

So, hopefully, no remnants of Eddie the Ex would show up in the van. Cate briefly wondered what trophy-wife Kim thought about a husband who shed dandruff. Perhaps a flutter of hundred-dollar bills successfully covered even a snowstorm of dandruff?

"So what I'm wondering," Jo-Jo went on, "is if you could take me out to the house? Donna has some event going on at the library today, and I'm worried about Maude."

Cate glanced at her watch. It would mean

postponing her visit to Lodge Hill, but she could run out to the house with Jo-Jo and still get back in time for the cleanup at Mr. Harriman's with Mitch at 1:00. She didn't want the donkey going hungry. "I can pick you up in about twenty minutes."

"Oh, Cate, thank you! You can add this to my bill, of course. Like I said, it may take awhile, but I will get you paid."

Right. A half million in insurance would cover a lot of investigative work.

At the house, Maude announced their presence with a raucous bray, although Cate thought she detected a certain welcoming enthusiasm in this bellow. Jo-Jo climbed on a fence rail, and Maude rubbed her head affectionately against her.

Animals didn't base their affection on what a person had or hadn't done in the human world, Cate knew. Yet seeing the obvious affection this animal gave Jo-Jo somehow reinforced Cate's belief — or was it more like a hope? — that Jo-Jo couldn't be a killer.

Cate hadn't yet had a chance to ask about the insurance. Jo-Jo had chattered nonstop throughout the entire drive, covering everything from a *Dancing with the Stars* rerun, to the comfortable, new-style mattress on the bed at Donna's house, and a wonderful chicken casserole Donna had fixed for supper last night.

"Eddie would have loved that casserole," Jo-Jo had added, sounding, as she sometimes did, wistful.

Cate followed Jo-Jo inside the barn to Maude's stall, where the manger was indeed empty. Jo-Jo filled it with hay and grain and then got out a brush that looked more like something from a cosmetics counter than a donkey store. Maude stretched out her neck as if she were in donkey heaven while Jo-Jo brushed her, and Cate asked how she'd acquired the donkey.

"A farm over on Kittler Road was foreclosed on, and there were a bunch of animals that had been abandoned. Nobody wanted Maude, and she was so skinny and discouraged looking. I just felt so sorry for her."

Cate smiled. Maude was not so skinny now. And Jo-Jo had not killed Eddie the Ex. Maybe that was a non sequitur, but she was sticking to it.

After Maude was properly tended to, Jo-Jo headed directly back to the car.

"Don't you want to go inside and look around or pick up clothes or something?"

"Not yet." Jo-Jo's throat moved in a big

swallow as she turned to stare back at the house. "Eddie's funeral is Tuesday afternoon, did you know? It was in the newspaper obituaries. I suppose it would be inappropriate for me to go. I'd have to take a taxi anyway. I wonder what they cost?"

"I could take you, if you'd like."

Jo-Jo hesitated for a moment, then nodded. "Thank you. I'd appreciate that." She eyed the door to the house. "I suppose I should go inside and look for something to wear to the funeral."

"You could just go buy something."

"I'd like to look nice. For Eddie. But clothes are so expensive these days."

Finally, an opening. "But you have money coming from Eddie's insurance, don't you?"

"Eddie's insurance?" Jo-Jo sounded puzzled. Then her eyes widened and her mouth rounded into a surprised O. She repeated the words in a different tone. "Eddie's insurance."

"I understand there's a half-million dollars of it."

Jo-Jo didn't ask how Cate knew that. She just kept shaking her head as if stunned. "Eddie's insurance," she repeated once more. "I hadn't thought about it."

Either Jo-Jo actually hadn't thought about it, or she was practicing for a late-blooming career as an actress.

"But you must have known. And that you, not Kim, would get the money."

"It was one of those things the lawyer put into our divorce settlement. That Eddie had to keep me as the beneficiary on his policy. But it seemed like such a way-off-in-the-future thing, and I just never thought about it. I wonder how long it will take to collect the money?" Jo-Jo didn't sound wistful or nostalgic now. Just eager.

"I have no idea. You should talk to the lawyer."

"I will. But I can afford a dress, can't I? I can afford to pay you. I can afford to take a taxi — or buy a car!"

Cate doubted the police would ever believe Jo-Jo had forgotten about a half-million dollars' worth of insurance. Cate was inclined to believe it anyway. Jo-Jo really had been mourning Eddie, not counting a windfall of cash from his insurance.

Celeste had apparently been quick enough to find out who was the beneficiary of Eddie's insurance after his death. If she'd killed Eddie thinking Kim would get the money, this turn of events must be an unpleasant surprise for her.

That afternoon Cate and Mitch went over

to work on the Helping Hands cleanup job at Mr. Harriman's place. Along the way, skillfully weaving through busy traffic, Mitch told her what he'd so far learned on the internet.

"Ed Kieferson was over his head in debt and in so much financial trouble that he was going down like the *Titanic.* The house is almost into foreclosure. The wedding business and vineyard are headed that way. Mr K's restaurant has been losing money like a tide going out."

"But how could that be? It's the most expensive restaurant in town. The most prestigious place to take guests or celebrate."

"Poor management, it looks like. Maybe Jo-Jo Kieferson was the brains in the money department, and, without her, ol' Eddie pretty much ran things into the ground. I'm guessing here, but I doubt Kim knew anything about the financial problems. She's been spending a boatload of money on the house. I did, by the way, pick up the name of a former employee at the Mystic Mirage, if that interests you."

"Yes!"

Cate's surfing on the internet usually wandered along cyberspace rabbit trails that fell into black holes, or sites she backed out of with horrified haste, or computer freeze-ups. But Mitch could extract amazing nuggets of information.

"So Kim is the big loser here," she mused thoughtfully. "Jo-Jo gets Eddie's life insurance and Kim loses everything to foreclosure."

"Not necessarily. There may be mortgage insurance on the property loans. Which would mean, with his death, they'd be paid off."

So even if Mama Bear had been mistaken about Kim getting a big insurance payoff, she might still be a well-fixed widow. Still plenty of motive for Celeste to murder Ed, if she was looking out for her daughter's financial interests.

Kim could have murdered Ed herself, but Cate's PI intuition was on Celeste, the brains and CEO of the pair, as Donna had said. Did the authorities know all these details of the financial picture? she wondered as they pulled into Mr. Harriman's driveway, which was lined with a clutter of broken flowerpots, a cracked sink, and two old birdcages.

Mr. Harriman was a sweet older man. He seemed vaguely baffled by the accumulation of *stuff* in his home and yard. "Things never piled up like this when Emma was alive," he said. Cate and Mitch spent all afternoon on the cleanup, hauling loads to the landfill, the recycling center, and Goodwill. Hard, dirty work, but satisfying. It also prompted Cate to go home and fill two boxes with stuff to get rid of.

After church on Sunday, Cate talked Mitch into driving to Lodge Hill, which was several miles out of town, but a locked metal gate barred the driveway. Had the wedding business and vineyard already succumbed to financial difficulties? But the gate stood open when Cate drove out there by herself on Monday afternoon.

The building, an impressive, oversized home in its heyday, loomed as large and imposing as it had looked in the website photo. The old logs, weathered to a silvery elegance, held an aura of dignity, family history, and old wealth, a wordless assurance that any marriage entered into here would surely age and endure as gracefully as these solid old logs. A hedged enclosure with double wooden doors extended out from one end of the building, and evergreens in huge urns lined the covered walkway that stretched the length of the building. A paved trail led across the expansive lawn and down to a boat dock on the McKenzie River.

There was room for several boats to dock, but only a small rowboat was tied there now.

A single car and a motorcycle stood in the huge parking area. Cate rolled her Honda into the wide space between them. A gold-flecked black helmet sat on the motorcycle seat. The hedge, she noted as she walked toward the main entrance, could use trimming. Perhaps maintenance had been skimped on because of those financial problems?

A sign on the main door, which apparently was not used except for weddings, directed visitors to the office farther down the covered walkway. A guy came out of the office door just before she reached it. Cate wasn't paying any attention to him until he spoke to her.

"Another one. Taken," he said, his tone mournful. He placed a hand over his heart and looked at her with soulful brown eyes.

"Wh-what?" Cate asked, bewildered.

"Good-looking women never come here unless they're getting married to some guy that isn't me." His grin was roguish, his dark eyes flirty, and he was definitely good-looking himself. "Story of my life."

Then he stepped on by her and headed for the motorcycle. Cate stared after him. A big guy, dark-haired, lean and long-legged in jeans, muscular in his denim Levi jacket. He gave her a grin and wave as he threw a leg over the motorcycle, as if he knew she'd turn to watch him.

Inside, no one was at the counter, but it was a room designed to make clients feel comfortable. White leather sofas faced each other across a myrtle-wood coffee table piled with brochures, and a coffeemaker stood on a table in a corner. A sign identified a door on the far side as a private conference room.

A woman who'd apparently been bending down to do something under the counter stood up. "Hi. May I help you?" She was blonde, fortyish, plump but stylish in a burgundy suit.

"Hi. I'm scheduled to be a bridesmaid in a wedding here, and I was wondering about, oh, the facilities and everything?"

"I'd be glad to give you a tour." The woman smiled and held a hand over the counter. "I'm LeAnne Morrison, manager here at Lodge Hill."

Cate shook the extended hand. "Cate Kinkaid. It's Robyn Doherty and Lance McPherson's wedding."

"Oh yes. They have an incredible event planned, don't they? She's an amazing woman, so focused and creative."

Amazing, focused, and creative were perhaps the complimentary terms for a big spender in the wedding world? Cate didn't voice that thought however. She just murmured, "Yes, isn't she?"

LeAnne led the way upstairs, chattering all the way about the facilities, her high heels clicking on the hardwood floors. She took Cate through the dressing rooms and the wedding area, once a ballroom, now called the Chapel Room. It had folding room dividers that could be closed to create an intimate area for a few guests, or left open to accommodate ever larger crowds. LeAnne showed her the one room Mr. Kieferson had completed as a display in his plan to turn the closed-off area into luxury rooms and suites. Before going back downstairs, Cate interrupted to ask a question.

"A guy left the office just before I came in. I was wondering who he is?" Suddenly aware that might sound as if she were some desperate bridesmaid hungry to snap up any stray man, she added, "I thought he looked familiar, but I can't quite place him."

Which was true, she realized. There was something vaguely familiar about the big, dark-haired guy.

"Rolf Wildrider." LeAnne wrinkled her nose as if the name put a bad taste in her mouth. "The vineyard manager. He lives in a cottage out back. Thinks he's God's gift to women, if you know what I mean." She softened the snarky comment with a laugh.

A "gift" Rolf Wildrider probably used with considerable success, Cate suspected. Was that his real name? Somehow it had an invented sound about it. He wouldn't earn any points for a sophisticated approach, but a certain bold charm and rugged good looks perhaps made up for that.

"Another reason I'm here," Cate went on, "is that we understand the owner, Mr. Kieferson, passed away a few days ago. We're wondering if that will mean any changes or complications with the scheduled weddings."

"Oh no, I'm certain everything will transition quite smoothly." LeAnne paused. "Of course, there are always a few complications when there's a death." Another hesitation. "But I'm sure everything will be straightened out soon. Within a few days at most. Not that there are any problems; it's just . . . well, everyone is very upset by Mr. K's death."

What had begun as a reassuring statement had progressed into something closer to an admission of rising panic. LeAnne blinked as if she might be squeezing back tears.

"There doesn't seem to be much going on in the vineyard," Cate suggested. "Are there any problems there?"

"I don't pay much attention to what goes on out in the vineyard. We operate independently."

"Has Rolf Wildrider been working at the vineyard long?"

"Just a few months. I never could understand why Mr. K even hired Rolf. Except that he —"

Cate thought the woman was going to say something more derogative about the vineyard manager, but then she broke off and gave a kind of strangled sob. "I still have a hard time believing he's . . . gone. He was such a generous man. So sweet and softhearted and compassionate and caring."

For a moment Cate spotted definite signs of a crush on her boss, but LeAnne's voice hardened when she added, "At least he was until . . ."

Cate waited, hoping the "until" was going somewhere, but LeAnne briskly started down the stairs. "Mr. K was planning a complete kitchen staff here eventually, but right now everything but drinks come from the restaurant. The chef at Mr. K's is fantastic, and so the reception dinners here are fantastic too."

"You've worked here at Lodge Hill for a long time?"

"I was a hostess at the restaurant, and Mr. K was generous enough to give me a try as manager here. It's worked out great. This was just a big old building going to ruin until he bought and restored it. He had such far-reaching, creative imagination." By now they'd reached the bottom of the stairs. "Mrs. Kieferson — Jo-Jo, not Kim, the current Mrs. Kieferson — was managing the wedding business here at Lodge Hill then, and she was a wonderful help to me."

LeAnne's words about Ed Kieferson were approving, but Cate heard a past tense in them that wasn't necessarily connected with his death.

"Did Mr. Kieferson exhibit some, oh, recent changes?" Cate asked cautiously. "Something that might have a connection with his death?"

"His dumping Jo-Jo and latching on to the blonde bimbo was certainly a change!" LeAnne clapped a hand over her mouth and looked around as if she hoped some mouth other than her own had spoken those words. She cleared her throat and tapped her chest. "You must excuse me. I'm just so upset that I hardly know what I'm saying."

Yes, LeAnne definitely had some ambivalent feelings about her recently deceased boss.

"Will you be staying on?" Cate asked.

LeAnne jerked, as if the question startled her. Because she was thinking about leaving, and she was surprised someone might suspect that? Or was she thinking a mother-daughter conspiracy between Kim and Celeste might have her on a to-be-fired list?

"I assume I'll be staying," LeAnne finally said. "I love dealing with excited brides and helping them make memories for a lifetime."

They finished the tour by going through the kitchen, for which there was a separate entrance, and then the downstairs Reception Room.

Back in the office, LeAnne handed her a brochure. "Maybe you'll want to use our services yourself sometime soon." Before Cate could say there was no wedding in her foreseeable future, LeAnne jumped into an enthusiastic spiel. "You can, like Robyn, handle everything yourself, although we have marvelous packages in all price ranges. Personal attention and service are our specialty here at Lodge Hill. I'm personally present at every wedding."

Cate assumed you had to provide the bridegroom yourself, although maybe briskly capable LeAnne could do that too.

140

But what she said was, "Mr. Kieferson's death . . . It's just so puzzling, don't you think? Who would want to kill such a wonderful man?"

"Yes, very puzzling."

No information there. "Did the police talk to you?"

"Oh yes. They asked about everything from the last time I'd seen Mr. K to financial records and what I knew about Rolf Wildrider."

"Did they talk to him too?"

"I would assume so, though I don't really know. He was in here today only because he wanted to know about Mr. K's services."

Cate wanted to know more about Rolf, but the earlier words "financial records" jumped out at her. She repeated them. "Financial records?"

"I couldn't help the authorities there, of course. I turn everything over to the accountant who handles all Mr. K's business affairs." LeAnne dismissed finances with a wave of hand. "I just hope they don't pin Mr. K's murder on Jo-Jo. She's such a sweet woman. But it was odd, his death happening there at her house."

A thought about LeAnne's quick detour from the subject of finances occurred to Cate. Could LeAnne have a lucrative side business as an embezzler? If Mr. K had found out, maybe she'd had to get rid of him before her crime was exposed? Or maybe the accountant was embezzling money and he had to get rid of Mr. K to avoid exposure?

Uncle Joe always said you had to be suspicious of everyone, but it was confusing when ever-more suspects seemed to be popping out of the woodwork here.

Cate jumped back to an earlier trail LeAnne had opened up about Ed Kieferson dumping Jo-Jo for his current wife. She lowered her voice to a confidential level. "I understand the divorce was a rather messy situation."

"Yes, very messy. Actually, I thought Mr. K might eventually come to his senses and go back to Jo-Jo." A frown line cut between LeAnne's nicely groomed brows. "Not that I'd have gone back to him if I were her."

Was it possible Eddie *had* "come to his senses" and wanted out of the marriage so he could go back to Jo-Jo? And Celeste wasn't about to let that happen?

10

Cate was backing her car around the car parked next to her Honda, thinking about all LeAnne had said, when an unexpected connection popped into her head.

Rolf Wildrider, vineyard manager. Big. Muscular. Dark-haired. A bike rider.

Another big, dark-haired, muscular guy, the one coming into the Mystic Mirage as she barged out. With a motorcycle sitting at the curb.

She hadn't seen him clearly that day. She'd been too flustered, too distracted and embarrassed. But there was a definite resemblance.

Had Rolf recognized her today from that previous meeting? Although he'd been flirty, she hadn't noted any sign of recognition. She had the impression, there on the walkway, that he figured he was, as LeAnne had put it, "God's gift to women," and it was his duty to bestow a passing gift on her.

But Rolf Wildrider may not have been in a flirty frame of mind that day at the Mystic Mirage. Why was he there? Hoping to see Kim and offer the beautiful widow some solicitous comfort?

Although his presence there could have been totally innocent. Kim was actually his employer now. Or maybe he knew, with Ed Kieferson dead, that Celeste would really be the person in control and he'd gone to see her, checking on his job security?

On impulse, Cate took the narrow gravel road that circled around back of the Lodge Hill building. The steep-roofed cottage was only a hundred yards or so from the main building, although a line of evergreens probably obscured view of it from inside the lodge itself. A motorcycle was parked out front. She didn't know much about motorcycles, but, as she got closer, it didn't take any expertise to see that the bike had those same high handlebars she'd almost run into outside the Mystic Mirage. Two more motorcycles stood in a carport attached to the house. They were partially dismantled, and bike parts littered the dirt floor, as if this might be a spare-time repair project for Rolf.

She would, she decided, ask Mitch to put his computer skills to work on Rolf Wildrider.

■ ■ ■ ■

Cate picked Jo-Jo up twenty minutes before the scheduled start of Eddie's service. Ever practical, even if she was coming into a half million dollars, Jo-Jo had bought a black suit suitable for the occasion but not so funeral-ish that it wouldn't be appropriate for other occasions.

"You look beautiful," Cate told her honestly. Jo-Jo had also had her hair done, and the frisky gray curls gave her face a youthful uplift. "Eddie would be proud of you."

Jo-Jo blinked and touched her eyes with the corner of a tissue. She gave Cate directions to the funeral home, where services for Donna's husband had also been held only a year ago.

A considerable crowd filled the flower-laden room. The coffin up front was closed, and brilliant red, spiky-looking flowers that Cate couldn't identify covered it from end to end.

"I wonder why they chose those strange flowers?" Jo-Jo whispered. "Eddie liked roses. Yellow ones especially."

Cate and Jo-Jo slipped into a pew near the rear of the room. Cate didn't see either Kim or Celeste, but Jo-Jo nodded toward a curtained-off area and whispered that was where she and Donna had sat for Donna's husband's funeral. If Eddie's grown son was present, he was also behind the curtain, because Jo-Jo couldn't spot him. Cate wondered if she should be including him on her list of suspects. No sign of Rolf Wildrider.

Cate hadn't really expected to pick up any useful information at the funeral, which was fortunate, because she didn't see or hear anything helpful. But, for Jo-Jo's sake, she was glad she'd come.

After taking Jo-Jo home, Cate decided she'd take advantage of the time for some PI work she'd been thinking might be helpful.

Jo-Jo's rural house was in a dip between two hills, and no other houses were visible from it. Cate drove on by and, from the top of the next hill, spotted a single-wide trailer and several houses. The trailer was closest to Jo-Jo's place. Cate pulled into the driveway.

A hound that looked big enough to drag her away and bury her like an old bone bounded out to meet her. Cate, half-in, half-out of the car, started to jump all the way back in, but then she noted the dog's tail was wagging enthusiastically. She tentatively put out a hand, and the dog licked it.

"Okay, you want to take me to your leader?"

The dog bounded back toward the trailer. Cate heard unidentifiable thunks and clunks coming from around behind it, and she was suddenly aware how vulnerably alone she was out here. Mitch would think this was a terrible idea . . .

Then a yell came from the far side of the trailer. "Yo! I'm around here."

Cate cautiously circled the end of the trailer. A middle-aged man with gray hair and a droopy mustache stood thigh-deep in a ditch with a shovel in his hand. A pile of fresh dirt lined the far side of the ditch. Cate's first macabre thought was that he was digging a grave.

"Septic line's got a break in it." He swiped a grimy sleeve across his sweaty forehead. "Gotta dig it up and replace it. If you're sellin' something, I ain't buyin'."

Cate was relieved that she was wrong about the purpose of his digging. "I'm not selling anything. Actually, I'm looking for information about a neighbor."

"You from the sheriff's department too?"

"Someone from the sheriff's department has been here?"

"Oh yeah. Asking all kinds of questions

about that guy got killed over there." He jerked the shovel handle toward Jo-Jo's place. "But I don't know nothin'. I work nights at the mill and sleep days. Except today I have to dig up this fool septic line."

"Did you happen to hear the donkey bray that day?"

"Deputies wanted to know that too. It could of brayed. I dunno. I was probably asleep if it did, and I wouldn't of noticed if I was awake."

The questions the deputies asked about Maude meant they knew the donkey's braying wasn't random noise-making, that it announced someone was entering the property. So this wasn't a fact she knew and they didn't, something she could whip out as a clever clue to prove Jo-Jo's innocence. It was a mildly deflating realization.

"So you never drove by the place that day, never saw an unfamiliar vehicle there?"

"Nope."

"How about a motorcycle?"

"Might of heard one once. I don't know that it was over there, though. Guy over on Dickens Road has a couple of 'em."

"Oh. Well, thanks anyway, then."

The hound gave her hand another friendly slurp as she headed back to the car. A maybe motorcycle. Not exactly a "gotcha" clue, but possibly a tie-in with Rolf Wild-rider and the guy she'd bumped into at the Mystic Mirage. Who she was almost certain now were one and the same.

The four other people Cate contacted on Randolph Road were equally unhelpful. A sheriff's department investigator had already talked to all of them. No one had seen or heard anything unusual that day, and one woman drew herself up and said frostily, as if Cate had accused her of Peeping Tom activities, "I don't snoop into what the neighbors are doing or who their visitors are."

Uncle Joe had once warned Cate that she might have to interview ten people to get one snippet of information. Today, both here and at the funeral, she'd encountered a fair percentage of that snippet-less number. But surely, sooner or later, if she persisted, she'd run into someone who knew something.

That evening Cate looked up a phone number and called the woman whose name Mitch had given her as a former employee of the Mystic Mirage. Lola Makston was friendly and seemed willing to talk. She said she didn't really know Mr. Kieferson, but he'd come into the Mystic Mirage several times, and she was shocked by the news-paper account of his death.

"Did you ever notice any tension between Mr. Kieferson and his wife?"

"Between him and Kim? No." She paused and then amended that. "Well, maybe. I got the impression he really doted on her, but sometimes she seemed impatient with him. He was a lot older, you know."

"Did he get along okay with Celeste?"

"Well, you know men and mother-in-laws." Cate heard a shrug in the woman's voice, as if she spoke from experience. "Maybe it's especially hard when your mother-in-law is younger than you."

"Did anything in particular happen?"

"He came in once to take Kim to lunch, but she'd gone shopping somewhere and only Celeste was there. He and Celeste got in an argument about something, but I don't know what." Her laugh held a tinge of self-consciousness. "Ol' nosy me, I wanted to listen in. But it was my lunch hour, and I couldn't think of any reason to hang around without it being really obvious that I was listening in. He was gone by the time I got back."

"Did you like the job?"

"It was okay, though I didn't like having to act like I really believed all that tarot cards and past lives and astrology stuff. Kim wasn't so hot and heavy on it herself, but Celeste . . . Actually, Celeste fired me."

"Really? For any particular reason?"

"I didn't know she was listening, of course, but I made the mistake of laughing when I was looking through her book. But c'mon, some guy 'remembering' he'd been Bigfoot in another life? Who wouldn't laugh? But she fired me on the spot."

"Well, thanks. That's interesting information. I appreciate your talking to me." Cate decided to ask one more question before hanging up. "By the way, has anyone from the sheriff's department contacted you?"

"You said you were an investigator, didn't you?" The woman sounded alarmed. "I thought that meant you were police."

"I'm a private investigator working for a client who is concerned about Mr. Kieferson's death." Diplomatically she added, "A client who is also concerned the police may not be doing enough to catch the killer."

"Oh, I guess that's okay then. I'd certainly like to see the killer caught. There is one little thing, though I don't suppose it had anything to do with Mr. Kieferson . . ."

Cate offered quick encouragement. "Any little thing may be helpful."

"One time Celeste got a phone call, and

she was — I don't know quite how to put it
— agitated, I guess you'd say, afterward."

"Scared? Angry?"

"Maybe. I don't know. She dropped a
ceramic wind chime and broke it. She went
to use a ballpoint pen, and it wouldn't work,
and she threw it halfway across the store. I
mean, that struck *me* as agitated."

"Could the caller have been Mr. Kieferson, and he said something to upset her?"

"The call came on the Mystic Mirage line,
and when Mr. Kieferson called Kim, it was
always on her cell phone. But I suppose it
could have been him. Kim was there, and
she asked Celeste about the call later, and
Celeste said it was just some annoying salesman."

"But you didn't believe that?"

"For all I know, it could have been someone from one of her past lives calling up for
a chat." Small, uneasy laugh. "Well, that was
catty, wasn't it? Forget I said that."

"Can you remember anything Celeste said
on the call?"

"I remember her telling whoever it was
that he wasn't welcome there. And if he
started coming around, there could be
unpleasant consequences." She paused to
reflect for a moment. "I've always assumed
it was a man, but it could have been a

woman."

"How long ago was this call?"

"It was a couple days before Celeste fired me, which would make it about three weeks ago."

Which would be before Ed Kieferson was killed. Which might or might not mean anything.

"Thank you. That's very interesting. If you think of anything else, give me a call, okay?" She gave the woman the Belmont Investigations number.

Celeste's caller may have been a persistent salesman, as she claimed. Her end of the conversation could fit with that. But former-employee Lola wasn't convinced, and neither was Cate. Maybe Celeste was talking to a killer.

Maybe a killer she'd hired?

Cate immediately called Mitch to see what he could find out about the phone call to Celeste at the Mystic Mirage, but he laughed.

"Cate, you overestimate my skills."

"I think you're a computer genius." Which wasn't hogwash or sweet talk. He really could make a computer give up an astonishing number of secrets. Maybe sing and dance too.

"That's very flattering, and it's no doubt possible for the police to check phone records. For me it would take some powerful illegal hacking, which I do not do now. Although I have something else that may interest you."

"About?"

"Rolf Wildrider."

The first thing Mitch had found out was that Rolf Wildrider's real name was Robert Johnson. He'd adopted the more colorful name during a successful motorcycle racing career. He'd also gotten into motorcycle stunt competitions, suffered a broken back, and quit that line of work. He'd then gone to college in California and studied viticulture, no hint on what prompted him to go into the study of grape growing. He didn't graduate, which Mitch guessed might be because he ran out of money. He'd made big bucks in his motorcycle career, but he'd lived high and hard enough to run through money as fast as he made it. Mitch hadn't found anything on past marriages or divorces, but Rolf's name had been linked with a fairly well-known model during his racing career.

"So he settled down and became a quiet-living grape grower?"

"Not exactly," Mitch said. "He worked for

a vineyard down in the southern part of the state before coming here, but he got in the middle of some drug deal shoot-out down there. At first it looked as if he was involved in the shooting himself and might be charged with manslaughter, but some witnesses disappeared and that case against him fell apart."

"Witnesses disappeared? Suggesting he had something to do with their disappearance?"

"I don't know. But he was in trouble anyway, because they found out he had a little sideline of growing marijuana along with grapes on the vineyard. He wasn't in jail long, but he's still reporting to a probation officer."

So, caring and generous man that Mr. K was, according to LeAnne, he'd been willing to give Rolf a second chance in spite of his wayward ways? Or maybe those wayward, drug-growing ways were what interested Eddie, and he had in mind adding a sideline to boost vineyard income? And could that have any connection with his murder?

Cate had another case to work on the following day, an investigation assigned to Belmont Investigations by an insurance

155

company. The man they were investigating had applied for disability payments, saying he couldn't work, but the company suspected he was secretly working for under-the-table cash. She had several possible workplaces to check out.

By the end of the day, after slogging around an auto repair shop located in an old barn, two small businesses that did yard-maintenance work, and a woodcutting outfit, Cate had found nothing to indicate the man was doing anything but what he said he did. Which was sitting around a coffee shop nursing a lone cup most of the day, because that was all he could afford.

What she had at the end of the day was a pair of shoes covered with enough oil to excite a drilling company, courtesy of the puddle she'd stepped into at the auto-repair shop. Plus a dent in her car bumper from backing into a stump at the woodcutting site. Where she'd also gotten stuck in the mud and had to pay the unfriendly woodcutters, who hadn't liked her nosy questions, to pull her out with their four-wheel-drive pickup.

She was not in an upbeat frame of mind when Robyn called that evening to tell her the bridesmaid dress had arrived.

"I was thinking you could come over

tonight and try it on," Robyn said.

Cate's first inclination was to make up some wild excuse. Sorry, I have to wash a murderer out of my hair. I have a killer headache. But she squelched that route as unacceptable. Especially with such bad puns. Actually, she decided gloomily, trying on a bridesmaid dress was probably the perfect end to the kind of day she'd had.

"Sure, I'll come over right now."

Cate had never been to the house Robyn shared with her great-aunt Carly, but a Googled map took her right to the beautifully maintained Victorian. Gingerbread decorated the porch, ivy climbed the fireplace chimney, and a ceramic daisy encircled the doorbell. Robyn gave her a big hug at the door and introduced her to Great-aunt Carly.

Carly Simmons was of indeterminate age, white haired but enviably slim and smooth skinned. She was watching a documentary on TV about the poisonous qualities of some jungle plants. Taking notes. Hmm. Cate, operating on that be-suspicious-of-everyone premise, made a mental note of her own in case any plant-based poison cases turned up in the future.

Robyn led Cate upstairs to a bedroom

with a steeply slanted roof and orchid-flowered bedspread and curtains. The dress lay spread on the bed, artfully arranged so it seemed to have an alluring figure of its own.

Celadon. Cate hadn't given much thought to what that color actually was, but now she saw that it was a pale celery. A silvery-grayish, not-too-healthy-looking celery.

She skimmed out of her jeans and sweater, and Robyn helped her step into the dress. She didn't even have to hold her breath or suck in her stomach for Robyn to zip the dress up the back.

Robyn stepped back to look at her. She clapped happily. "Oh, that's awesome. It's a perfect fit! Come look."

She led Cate to a full-length mirror in an alcove at the end of the room.

"I'll go get Aunt Carly," Robyn said. "She has to see this."

Cate studied herself in the mirror. If you wanted to be critical, you might say she looked rather like a stalk of ailing celery, with her red hair a radish on top. But if you didn't want to be so critical . . . the effect wasn't bad. Not bad at all! The dress nipped her waist, the neckline flattered her throat and shoulders, and the color set off her red hair rather nicely.

Of course, the idea Robyn had earlier proposed, that Cate would have lots of use for the dress after the wedding, was high fantasy. She saw no Emmy award banquets or presidential inaugurations in her immediate future. But the gown would upgrade her closet nicely.

Great-aunt Carly made Cate twirl twice, so she could get a 3-D view. She offered enthusiastic oohs and aahs. Then she asked, "What about shoes?"

Cate looked down at her bare toes. Good question.

"Shauna's sandals had to be extra-wide and I knew they wouldn't fit Cate, so I told her to keep them." Missing shoes were no problem for the efficient Robyn, however. "What size do you wear, Cate? I'll order them tomorrow, and they'll be here in plenty of time."

Cate told her size seven, and Robyn made a note of that on a to-do list for the wedding. A list that filled most of two pages and would have made Cate cross out everything and put "elope" on the top line.

Cate thought of something as Robyn started unzipping the dress. "Mrs. Simmons —"

"Oh, do call me Carly," the woman said. "Everyone does."

"Okay. Thanks. I was wondering, I think Robyn told me you knew Ed Kieferson, the owner of Lodge Hill who was killed recently? Murdered, actually."

"Yes. So shocking." Carly touched a veined but elegant hand to her collarbone. "I mean, I know murders happen all the time, even here in Eugene, but I've never personally known anyone who was murdered. Did you know him?"

"His former wife had contacted me about another matter, and I happened to be with her at the house when his body was discovered there."

"Cate is a private investigator," Robyn said.

"Assistant private investigator," Cate corrected conscientiously.

Carly adjusted her glasses and inspected Cate rather differently than she had when she was admiring the dress. "Are you carrying a gun?"

Since Cate was now standing there in nothing but her underthings, she had to wonder where Carly thought she might be carrying it. She grabbed her jeans and slipped into them. She didn't feel like explaining about assistant private investigators and guns, so all she said was, "No, no gun. But I am interested in what you know about Mr. Kieferson."

Carly perched on the edge of the bed. "I knew him only in the way one business-person knows another, not really a personal connection. I did do a big job for him when they had the grand opening for Mr. K's restaurant. He wanted yellow roses every-where. That was before Robyn came," she added, nodding to her grandniece, who was now carefully folding the dress and placing it in a box for Cate to take home. "We still have a standing order for a single rose at each table at the restaurant twice a week, but I don't know if that will continue now that he's gone."

"You didn't have much actual contact with him, then?" Cate asked. She wiggled into her sweater.

"Actually I'm better acquainted with his wife's mother, Celeste, than I was with him."

Even better!

"Well, I did know Celeste," Carly corrected. "We had kind of a falling-out a while back."

"This was a personal falling-out, not a business matter?" Cate asked as she sat down to put her shoes on.

"Yes, although it may have been why they didn't order flowers for the funeral from us.

I met Celeste through a bridge club we both belong to, and then we started going to brunch together occasionally, just the two of us," Carly said. "I enjoyed her. She had lots of inside stories about celebrities she'd met, kind of catty stuff, but fun. She had stories about their past lives too. She kept wanting to do a past lives regression on me. I thought it was all kind of far out, but finally, a couple months ago, I said okay."

"She came here?"

"Yes. She told me to get comfortable in the recliner downstairs. She'd hypnotize me, and then we'd go back in time together."

"And?"

"She couldn't hypnotize me. I just sat there, all bright-eyed and wide awake. So then she said she'd give me something to help me relax. I said no way, I wasn't taking anything. That really annoyed her, and she told me I wasn't cooperating at all. By then I was annoyed with her too, and I told her I was pretty sure neither I nor anyone else had any past lives anyway. That it was all a bunch of hokey drivel."

"I take it she didn't care for that opinion?" Cate said.

"She stomped out, and after that she wouldn't even speak to me at bridge club."

Interesting, but Cate couldn't see that it

aided her investigation. Although refusing to speak to Carly did show a certain vindictiveness in Celeste.

"Did Celeste ever talk about Mr. Kieferson or her daughter's marriage to him?"

Unexpectedly, Carly laughed. "Did she ever. She said the man was a clod. Totally unsophisticated. Uncouth. That he had enough nose hair to make a doormat and terrible dandruff. But those flaws weren't so noticeable, I suppose, when he was waving his money around."

"She said this at the bridge club?"

"Oh no, this was when we were having brunch together, just the two of us. After a couple of mimosas, Celeste could get quite talkative. We laughed a lot. Although one time . . ." Carly's elegantly arched eyebrows drew together.

"Something happened?"

"She hadn't had a mimosa that day, but she was talking about Ed, and she wasn't laughing. I don't know what he'd done, but she said, 'If that jerk does anything to hurt my baby, I'll kill him. I will kill that man.' "

Carly looked up at Cate. She covered her parted lips with her fingertips, as if she'd had second thoughts about sharing that bit of information.

"I think you should tell the police about

163

that," Cate said.

Carly hesitated, as if she were considering a conversation with the police. Then she shook her head and laughed. "Oh, I don't think she meant anything by it. I mean, how many times do people say something like, 'My husband will kill me when he sees that dent I put in the fender.' Or 'I'm gonna kill that kid if he talks back to me one more time.' I've done it. Haven't you?"

"I suppose."

"I mean, I think Celeste is a pretentious quack with all that past-lives stuff," Carly said. "I'm not sure her 'doctor' degree is even authentic. But I think 'kill' was just a figure of speech. I wouldn't want to make unfair accusations. She said some bad things about Kim's ex too."

"Such as?"

"Like there were only two important food groups in his diet, chips and beer. Like he'd rather cheat someone out of a dollar than earn ten honestly. That he was lazy and mean, and Kim never should have married him even if she was pregnant."

"Pregnant?" Cate repeated, surprised. She hadn't heard anything about Eddie the Ex's new wife already having a child.

"She lost the baby when she was a few months along."

"Did Celeste ever mention the ex's name? Or where he is now?"

"Travis something. I don't think I ever heard his last name. I asked her what became of him, and she said he was out of the picture. She sounded kind of, oh, self-satisfied about it, and I've always wondered if she had something to do with getting rid of him."

"He's dead?"

"Oh, I didn't mean that." Carly touched both cheeks in alarm, as if Cate had suggested Celeste had killed him. "I just meant, maybe she encouraged Kim to leave him. Although he could be dead, I suppose. I think he had kind of a wild lifestyle."

So maybe Celeste had experience getting rid of undesirable husbands. And maybe she'd gotten away with murder not just once, but twice?

11

Cate slipped into her jacket and picked up the big box. She couldn't make herself white lie about looking forward to the wedding, but she did manage to say, "I'm sure it's going to be a beautiful wedding."

Robyn reached over and picked up a strand of Cate's red hair. She held it out from Cate's head like some slimy specimen she'd found lurking on a plant at the flower shop. "Your, um, hair," she said.

Cate tilted her head out from under Robyn's hand. "I'll get it cut before the wedding. And use some really strong hair-spray to keep it from flying around."

"A cut would be nice," Robyn said. "But it's the color I'm thinking about."

"The color? What about the color?"

"Well, it's . . . red."

Yes, it was. Cate's hair was red. It had always been red. Barn-paint red. Tomato red. Flaming carrot red.

"The thing is," Robyn said, "my maid of honor and the bridesmaids are dark haired. I thought that would be a nice backdrop to, you know, spotlight my blonde coloring."

Robyn fingered a strand of her own hair that reached below her shoulders in a lush fall of silky radiance. One golden-haired princess of a bride. A herd of dark-haired bridesmaids.

Except one of those bridesmaids wasn't dark haired. Cate was the off-breed red-haired mutt in a lineup of purebred brunettes.

Cate knew she should feel relieved. Here was the perfect opportunity to agree with Robyn; red hair would totally destroy the ceremony. Both she and The Hair must be removed from the scene, or some warp in the universe would destroy the world as they knew it. But at the same time an unexpected indignation erupted.

"You knew my hair was red when you asked me to be a bridesmaid."

"Yes, of course! I just —" Robyn broke off, apparently unable to think of a tactful rescue. "I love your hair. But I'm thinking that maybe, just *temporarily,* you could have it colored for the ceremony? I'll pay for it, of course."

"You want me to dye my hair?"

167

"Everybody colors their hair," Robyn said, emphasizing the more euphemistic word. "I mean, even mine isn't quite this blonde naturally. Didn't you ever want to try a different color?"

Okay, Cate had thought a few times about a change. She'd even tried it once, but the resulting pool-slime green was not a flattering change. ("I've never seen that happen before," the hair colorist had said, looking a little green herself.) Now Cate was out of her comfort zone just being a bridesmaid. To be a bridesmaid with hair dyed to meet Robyn's color scheme was too much.

Carly, apparently sensing rebellion, stepped up. "How about a wig?"

Cate and Robyn repeated the words together. "A wig?"

Robyn jumped on it instantly. "Aunt Carly, that's an awesome idea! I should have thought of that to begin with. Don't you just love it, Cate? You can be a stunning brunette for just that evening, and then you can turn right back into a . . . unique redhead. I'll pay for a wig, of course."

Cate didn't "just love" the idea, but after thinking it over for a few moments, she reluctantly nodded. "I guess I could do a wig."

Robyn tapped her fingertips together in a

gleeful clap. "Great! There's a salon over in the mall with an awesome collection of wigs. I've even thought of getting one myself for, you know, those bad hair days."

Robyn have a bad hair day? Maybe. On the same day pigs flew. In formation over the Pentagon.

"When could we go look for one for you?" Robyn sounded anxious.

"Tomorrow, I guess."

Robyn turned to her aunt. "You don't mind if I take a couple of hours off, do you, Aunt Carly?"

Carly inclined her trim body into an elegant little bow. "Never let it be said that I stood in the way of the perfectly color-schemed wedding." She winked at Cate.

Cate and Robyn arranged to meet at the hair salon the following afternoon. Cate got to the mall early so she could pick up shoes to replace the oil-soaked ones, but Robyn was already looking at wigs when Cate arrived at the salon. She had four possibilities picked out, all dark brown but of varying lengths and styles. A hairdresser sat Cate in a salon chair, pinned her hair up, and fitted the first wig to her head.

Robyn didn't wait for any comment from Cate. She instantly waved a dismissing hand. "Too poufy." The next wig was 'too hairy," whatever that meant. The third, a stick-straight style, made Cate look ready for the morgue.

Then the hairdresser placed the last possibility on Cate's head, and Robyn gave a little gasp. So did the hairdresser.

Cate stared at herself in disbelief. The dark hair was longer than Cate's own hair, with a loosely tousled curl and side-swept bangs unlike anything Cate had ever worn. Her nose went from snub to elegant, and even the shape of her face looked different. In an instant, she had *changed.*

Robyn stepped back. "I can't believe it. You look so . . . not you."

If Cate didn't know the dark-haired woman staring back at her really was her, she'd think the mirror had made a twilight-zone mistake. She looked sultry. Mysterious. A woman who might jet off to the south seas or Paris on a moment's notice. A woman with provocative secrets.

The hairdresser, as if the decision had already been made, asked, "Do you want it in a box, or would you rather wear it today?"

Cate didn't hesitate. Sultry and mysterious was a new and exhilarating experience for her. "I'll wear it."

She walked out of the salon feeling as if

she could do all sorts of new-woman things. Walk into some elite boutique and, without a qualm, try on $500 shoes. Eat caviar without the yuck reaction that it was really just fish eggs. Walk up to Celeste Chandler and say "I know you killed Eddie the Ex, and I'm going to prove it."

Back home, Uncle Joe was in the Belmont Investigations office, on the phone with someone. He put a hand over the phone when Cate entered the room.

"Could you wait in the other room, please? I'll be with you in a minute."

"Uncle Joe, it's me, Cate!"

He peered at her suspiciously, then reared back in the chair. "Cate?"

Rebecca came in the door behind her and said, "I'm sorry. I didn't realize someone was here —"

Cate turned. "Hey, it's me!"

Joe ended his phone call, and both he and Rebecca stared at her. Only Octavia, who wandered in at that moment, seemed unstartled. She pawed Cate's leg in her usual pick-me-up gesture. Cate complied and snuggled the cat against her cheek.

Finally Joe said, "You doing some undercover job I don't know about?"

"No, it's a wig to fit a color scheme at a

friend's wedding."

Uncle Joe still looked skeptical, but Rebecca stated firmly, "It's quite lovely. Are you going to show Mitch?"

Cate hadn't thought about that, but . . . why not?

Cate picked up a pepperoni/mushroom/olive pizza on her way over to Mitch's that evening. She was holding the box in one arm when she rang the doorbell with the other hand at his condo.

"Oh, I didn't know the pizza was being delivered." He reached for his wallet. Then he did that rearing back thing that seemed to go with a hair surprise. "Cate?"

She stepped inside and twirled. "What do you think of the new me?"

"I'm not sure. Give me a minute. What brought this on?"

"Robyn and Lance's wedding. She wants all the bridesmaids to have dark hair."

"I'm glad she didn't have some height requirement that everyone had to be shorter than she is. No telling what she'd have wanted then." He cautiously fingered the dark hair as if he thought it might bite.

"You don't like it?"

"It's not that I don't like it. I'm just kind of used to the old you. The redheaded one.

I mean, you do look nice. It's just so . . . different."

She let him pretend all through the pizza that the change was fine until finally he said, "How permanent is it?"

She went to the bathroom, pulled off the wig, and returned to the kitchen in her normal flyaway redhead state.

He looked at the brown wig dangling from her fingertips. His smile held relief. "Good. I mean, I'll love you even if your hair turns green, but —"

He broke off, and they stared at each other, because this statement was something newer than a change of hair color between them. They were together a lot. They enjoyed each other's company. Cate had tentative thoughts about a long-term future together. She thought Mitch sometimes had those thoughts too. But *love* was a new word between them.

It hung there like a piñata waiting to be whacked.

A strange mixture of confusion and surprise and awkward joy ricocheted through Cate. Had she been waiting for this? She wasn't about to jump to conclusions over a few words that had just popped out, however. Although neither did she want to whack them.

Instead, with purposeful irrelevancy, she said, "Wouldn't Robyn be surprised if all the bridesmaids showed up with green hair?"

"I might surprise you sometime too. My grandfather went bald by the time he was thirty-eight."

I'll love you anyway.

She instantly retracted that mental leap. She wasn't ready for that yet. So this time all she said was, "Bald is beautiful."

The next morning Cate went out to Lodge Hill to talk to LeAnne again. In the distance, she spotted a green tractor and some kind of equipment on a trailer among the rows of grapevines. Several people were working around it. Inside the office, LeAnne was on the phone telling someone that Lodge Hill would be operating as usual, and if the caller wanted a spring wedding it should be scheduled now.

"Wasn't Mr. Kieferson's funeral beautiful?" Cate said after LeAnne's call ended.

"Very well attended," LeAnne agreed.

Was that a polite detour around expressing an opinion of the service? Cate decided to bypass further small talk and slid a business card across the counter.

LeAnne picked it up. "You're a private

investigator?" Accusingly she added, "But you said you were in the McPherson-Doherty wedding."

"I am. I'm also a private investigator."

"Investigating what?" LeAnne asked warily.

"Mr. Kieferson's death. I know you've told the police everything you could, but I'm thinking you were close enough to him to know something important, something no one else might know. Something the sheriff's deputies may not even have thought to ask about."

The flattery had a softening effect on LeAnne. She nodded. But then she stiffened again. "You're working for Kim or Celeste?"

"No. Jo-Jo Kieferson is our client. The police seem suspicious of her."

"That's ridiculous! Jo-Jo is just the sweetest person ever. She wouldn't kill Mr. K even after . . . everything."

"So I'm wondering if you could tell me anything that might help in my investigation for her. Observations, suspicions, guesses, speculations, anything."

"I'd like to help, but . . ." LeAnne lifted her shoulders in a gesture of helplessness.

Cate was undecided whether that meant she didn't know anything, or if the status of her job held her back. Something along the line of "don't bite the hand that feeds you"?

"Mr. Kieferson had a gun, and a permit to carry it. Do you have any idea why he might feel the need for a concealed weapon?" Cate asked.

"Maybe something to do with picking up money at the restaurant? Though I didn't know he carried a gun. I do know Rolf has one. But I doubt he has any permit."

"Why would Rolf carry a gun?"

"Maybe something to do with the people he hires to work in the vineyard? Or maybe Rolf just figures carrying a gun is the macho thing to do."

Cate could think of another reason. If Rolf was into a marijuana-growing sideline, maybe he dealt with people for whom a gun was an essential accessory.

"Do you think Rolf could have killed Mr. Kieferson?"

"I wouldn't rule him out."

"What motive would he have?"

"I had the impression Mr. K wasn't fully satisfied with Rolf's management of the vineyard. I saw him go to Rolf's cottage on several occasions."

Cate could think of at least one motive herself. If Rolf were running an illegal pot-growing operation somewhere out in the vineyard, and Ed Kieferson had been in on it, maybe they'd had a falling-out. Or if Ed *wasn't* in on it, maybe he'd found out and was going to turn Rolf in, and Rolf took a murderous step to prevent that.

"Do you have any other ideas on who could have done it?" Cate asked.

LeAnne took a deep breath and glanced sideways in both directions, as if afraid someone might be lurking and listening. "If I were a betting person, although I'm not, of course, my money would be on Celeste. And the thing is, her conscience, if she has one, wouldn't even bother her. She's so into that ridiculous past-lives stuff that she'd figure Mr. K being dead was only temporary anyway. That he'd be back in some new life before long. Like some cosmic washing-machine cycle, going round and round."

"Why would she kill him?"

"If she found out he was cheating on Kim, she'd whack him. If she thought he was leaving Kim for another woman, she'd double whack him. And she was suspicious of him. She even asked me once if I knew anything about his being involved with another woman."

"*Was* he involved with anyone?"

"He had plenty of opportunity to meet women at the restaurant. But I don't think he was into anything." With a pink bloom rising to her plump cheeks, LeAnne added, with a certain defiance, "He knew I had . . . much admiration for him, and he never tried to take advantage of that. I wouldn't be so sure about what Kim might have going on the side, however." With sudden alarm in her eyes, LeAnne added, "This is all strictly confidential, of course."

"Of course." Cate planted her elbows on the counter, expectantly hoping for more confidentiality, but a young couple with wedding-radiant faces came through the door, and LeAnne, obviously relieved to end the conversation, turned to them as if they were long-lost buddies.

That evening, Cate worked on her report for the insurance company on the man with the disability claim, making an extra copy for the office files. Then she started a list of what she knew about Jo-Jo and the Eddie the Ex case. She used a separate page for each suspect. Celeste. Kim. Rolf Wildrider nee Robert Johnson. Jo-Jo herself. Those were the big suspects. But there was also LeAnne Morrison, a long shot, but with a possibility she was skimming money off Lodge Hill receipts, and Ed Kieferson had found out. Or maybe the accountant had his hand in Kieferson's financial pot. And who was the mysterious person who had called Celeste at the Mystic Mirage and gotten her so "agitated"?

In fact, there could be any number of people who might have killed Ed, Cate realized gloomily. People who weren't even a blip on her radar. Some disgruntled employee at the restaurant. An illegal immigrant worker at the vineyard who thought the top boss might have him deported. Someone who really hated men with dandruff.

The phone rang, and Cate answered automatically. "Belmont Investigations, Assistant Investigator Cate Kinkaid speaking."

"Ms. Kinkaid, I'm interested in possibly hiring you in regard to a situation that has come to my attention. Perhaps we could arrange a personal meeting?" The unfamiliar woman's voice spoke with crisp formality.

"Of course. And you are . . . ?"

"Dr. Celeste Chandler."

Cate choked on her surprise, coughed, cleared her throat, and made some other noises more often associated with barnyard animals than a competent PI. This couldn't be about that day at the Mystic Mirage . . . or could it? Finally she managed to apologize for her coughing spell and croaked, "This is in regard to . . . ?"

"I prefer to speak with you in person. But I can say that it concerns someone I may need to have investigated."

So this hadn't anything to do with Cate's unfortunate inspection of the Kimmy doll's anatomy. Relief whooshed through her.

"You were recommended to me by a friend," Celeste added. "I don't mean to be melodramatic, but I believe it may be a matter of life and death."

"You should go to the police, then."

"I may do that. But I'd like to talk to you first."

"Well, um . . ."

Tempted as she was by the chance to find out why Celeste might want to hire a private investigator, she knew that as soon as the woman recognized her, she'd cut off the conversation like a chainsaw zapping through a marshmallow.

Then inspiration hit Cate. The wig. As different as she looked in it, maybe she *could* carry off a meeting with Celeste.

Mitch and probably Uncle Joe too would point out that this might be the dumbest idea since a local criminal wrote his bank holdup note on the back of an envelope addressed to himself. Celeste Chandler was a possible killer. Unpredictable. Dangerous.

But talking to Celeste might be her best

chance to figure out who killed Eddie the Ex.

Cautiously Cate asked, "When did you have in mind meeting?"

"I have a small New Age store, the Mystic Mirage. We close at 5:30. Could you meet me just after closing time tomorrow, say 5:40? We can talk privately in the back room."

"Yes, I can do that," Cate said.

Celeste gave her an address and an order. "Come alone."

Cate had second thoughts as soon as the call ended. Meet Dr. Celeste Chandler, likely killer, in a back room for an after-hours rendezvous? Alone?

Not a smart idea. Even in a brown wig.

The phone number from which Celeste had called was on the caller ID. Cate could call her back and cancel. Or she could simply not show up.

A better idea crashed into her head. She reached for the phone and clicked a familiar number on her contact list.

12

Mitch eased his SUV to the curb directly in front of the Mystic Mirage. Cate brushed a fingertip across her left eyebrow. The long brown hair had seemed to call for more dramatic makeup, but had she overdone it? The eyebrow felt large as the wing of a jet plane, and her mascaraed eyelashes sticky and clumpy enough to qualify as insect traps. She had an uneasy vision of the eyelashes gluing her eyes shut at some inopportune moment.

At 5:40 this time of year, the cloudy day had already darkened into evening. Rain spotted the windshield as soon as Mitch shut off the wipers, and a flickering streetlight turned shadows into one-dimensional monsters only temporarily trapped in the sidewalk. Wind swayed the Mystic Mirage sign hanging from the crescent moon. A few cars passed by, and in the next block a hand-holding couple emerged from a sandwich shop, but here the street looked like zombie territory. Lights still shone inside the store, but they suddenly dimmed to creepy movie level.

"I still don't like this," Mitch muttered.

Okay, Cate had to admit, she didn't much like it either, and the uneasiness had nothing to do with sticky eyelashes. She couldn't see the Kimmy doll, and the dim light oddly emphasized a wicked gleam of the Oriental swords decorating the back wall. They looked oddly out of kilter now, the display unbalanced.

The situation suddenly seemed decidedly peculiar. Maybe Celeste already knew Cate was investigating Ed Kieferson's murder. Maybe she thought Cate knew more than she did, and this meeting was a clever trap and she'd find herself shanghaied to some snaky, jungly place. Maybe —

Cate determinedly broke off the maybe jitters. She concentrated on putting confidence into her voice when she assured Mitch, "Everything's fine."

"Famous last words."

"We have all the bases covered." She pulled her cell phone out of her pocket to demonstrate. Mitch's cell phone number showed on the screen. "If anything happens or doesn't seem right, I just push the call button. As soon as your phone rings, you rush in and rescue me. Although . . ."

"Although what?"

"Maybe someone else will call just at that time. An old girlfriend. A stray message from outer space. You'll think it's me and burst in like gangbusters just when I'm using my dazzling investigative skills to extract crucial information from Celeste."

Mitch didn't comment on her investigative skills, dazzling or otherwise. "Better safe than sorry."

"You're just full of clichés tonight, aren't you?" Cate grumbled.

"Clichés become clichés because a lot of times they're right."

"How about a 'Don't worry, be happy' cliché?" Cate ended the discussion by leaning over and kissing him lightly on the cheek. "Thanks for coming along as my backup tonight. I really appreciate it." She opened the door.

"Don't forget your briefcase," he said. With what seemed ill-timed curiosity, he added, "What does a PI carry in a briefcase anyway?"

"PI stuff," Cate muttered. She wasn't about to tell him what was actually in the briefcase.

"Don't let her lock the door so I can't get

in," he said as Cate grabbed the briefcase and slid out of the SUV.

Cate's shadowy image in the window as she approached the door showed an unfamiliar, long-haired woman in belted jacket and high-heeled boots. The briefcase bulged with importance. She took a deep breath, blinked her eyes open wide to be sure the lashes weren't stuck together, and pushed the door open.

The bell tinkled as Cate stepped inside. The first thing she saw was the Kimmy doll lying on the floor, the rocking chair overturned. Odd.

A faint scent of an exotic incense still permeated the air, but the flute music was silent now. There was no sound, in fact. No Celeste swishing through the beaded curtain across the opening to the back room. Not even a rustle of papers or scrape of chair to indicate Celeste knew Cate had arrived.

Cate waited a few moments and then called tentatively, "Dr. Chandler?" No answer. She repeated the name more loudly. "Dr. Chandler?"

Again no answer. Except maybe a furtive creak from the back room?

Cue spooky mood music now.

For a moment, Cate's finger almost stabbed that call button, but she determinedly held it back. No creak. Just nerves manufacturing creaky . . . creepy . . . sounds.

She stepped briskly toward the curtain. Light filtered between the strands of wooden and ceramic beads. The strands swayed softly. Had her movement caused that? Maybe. She swallowed. Maybe not . . .

Cate raised her voice so it wouldn't come out shaky. "I may be a few minutes late. I hope that hasn't inconvenienced you?" No answer. Cate lifted her hand to push the hanging strands of the curtain aside, but something made her fingers clutch a handful of beads instead. Celeste had to be there in the back room. She'd dimmed the lights just before Cate arrived. At least someone had dimmed them . . .

Cate swallowed again, but her mouth was so dry the swallow stuck in her throat. "Are you there, Dr. Chandler?"

Silence.

"Are you all right, Dr. Chandler?"

More silence.

Okay, she'd just retreat to the safety of the SUV and call Celeste to announce her arrival. No point in acting like a dumb movie heroine stepping into the monster's den.

Then she spotted movement behind the curtain, as if someone had been bending over and straightened up. And there was something on the floor beneath the beaded curtain . . . Her heart thudded, and her throat went tight and thick, as if one of those wooden beads had suddenly jammed inside it.

A foot.

A foot wedged in a high-heeled sandal. Toes pointed upward. A few inches of shapely ankle and a black pant leg.

And then, stomping down beside the foot, two feet. In heavy black boots.

In spite of all their pre-planning, Cate's finger didn't stab the call button. A more basic instinct took over and a scream welled up from deep inside her, a primal shriek that burst up from her lungs and exploded out through her throat. Even as she knew it was her screaming, the sound seemed distant, alien and unfamiliar, as not-her as the long brown hair on her head.

An arm shot through the curtain. A hand clutched her throat. An eye glared venomously through the beaded curtain. The scream died as the fingers closed around her throat and cut off her air.

Lord, what do I do now? He's choking me. Help!

Panic thundered through her body and brain. Her head felt thick and heavy, clogged . . . her vision darkening even as her lungs burned. Desperately she flung her hands up to ward off the fingers squeezing her from light into darkness.

The briefcase swung upward too. She had no conscious plan to use it as a weapon, but it slammed into something solid behind the curtain, hit hard enough to thunder vibrations up her arm. A grunt of pain and the hand let go.

She dropped the briefcase, staggered, gasped for air, and frantically grabbed the cell phone in her pocket, but the front door was already crashing open behind her. Mitch hadn't waited for the ring of the phone when she screamed. On the other side of the curtain another crash as a door slammed on the far side of the back room.

Mitch yanked the curtain, and half the strands broke and clattered to the floor, wooden and ceramic beads hitting and bouncing. He stumbled over the body on the floor. He looked down. "What — ?"

The roar of a motorcycle blasted from the alley behind the store. Mitch leaped to the door and yanked it open.

Cate's legs wobbled unsteadily beneath her. She looked for someplace to sit, but all she saw was a chair at the desk where Celeste had apparently been working. She'd have to step over the body to get to it. No, she couldn't do that . . . She braced herself against the wall instead. She'd never fainted in her life, but she figured this was how you felt just before a faint. She gasped breath after breath, valuing the air drawn into her lungs as she never had before.

Mitch closed the door and came back to look down at the body sprawled on the floor. His feet crunched on beads.

Plain now why Celeste had not responded to the call of her name. She lay on her back, eyes wide open, their expression shocked even in death. Half the curved blade and the ornate brass handle of a sword protruded from her chest like some macabre ornament.

Cate knelt and pressed her fingertips to Celeste's throat. It seemed the thing to do even as what she wanted to do was run screaming into the rainy night. No movement, no twitch of pulse. Yet the body was still warm, which meant she must have surprised the killer bare moments after he'd thrust the sword into Celeste's chest.

Mitch already had his cell phone in hand, and a moment later he was giving the 911 operator information about location and victim and his own identity.

Cate's glance swung to the polished gleam

of Oriental swords on the back wall of the shop. Also plain now why the display had looked unbalanced. One sword was missing. Because it was now planted deep in Celeste's chest.

Then she glanced around, suddenly aware of what she wasn't seeing. She stepped back to peer around behind her.

Mitch returned the phone to the clip on his belt. "What are you looking for?"

"My briefcase. It's gone! He must have grabbed it."

"Why would he do that?"

"I don't know. Maybe he thought there was something important or valuable in it?"

"Was there?"

"No. Like I said, just . . . PI stuff."

The police must have been cruising nearby, because a squad car, lights flashing, was already screaming to a stop behind Mitch's SUV. Two officers burst through the door, the effect of their entrance marginally diminished when they both did Keystone Kops skids and crashes on rolling beads that had spread like some viral infection.

There was a certain déjà vu about the officers' activities after they collected their balance. Cate had been through this before, on her first murder scene. The officers checking the pulse for themselves, snapping questions, making calls back to the station. More sirens and flashing lights, more officers arriving. A fire truck. An ambulance. One of the officers got the lowly job of corralling the runaway beads.

Passing cars slowed, and onlookers appeared out of nowhere to cluster on the sidewalk. Some even framed their faces with their hands to peer through the windows until an officer herded them back. Cate and Mitch stood out of the way, beside the fallen doll. Cate's cold fingers felt welded together, as if she might never be able to separate them. She looked down and saw she was standing on one of the astrological figures painted on the floor, this one an oversized scorpion. She stepped away from it, her feet feeling crawly.

Even if there was a certain familiarity to this, even if she were a private investigator for fifty years and discovered fifty bodies along the way, Cate knew she would never get used to this. A dead body. Murder.

An officer approached them, and Mitch did the talking first, telling the officer who the victim was and what he knew. That the killer had fled through the rear entrance and escaped on a motorcycle. No, he hadn't seen the man and had only heard, not seen, the bike. Cate gave the facts about who she was, her appointment with Celeste, and her encounter with the man behind the curtain. Details were fading, she realized uneasily, as if her mind desperately wanted to be rid of them.

"You didn't see his face?" the officer asked.

"No. Just an arm and one eye."

"Could you tell how tall he was?"

Cate hadn't thought about the man's size, but this was a good point. "His eye was above mine, so he had to be taller. Over six feet, I'd say."

"How about the color of the eye you could see?"

"I'm not really sure. Dark, I think."

"And the arm?"

"Muscular. Tattooed," she remembered suddenly.

"Can you describe the tattoo?"

"I saw it . . ." Cate hesitated, desperately trying to bring the tattoo into focus. It was there, but it was just beyond her grasp, like a nightmare that left your heart pounding but slid out of full memory when you woke. "Swirls, I think."

She lifted her hand and made wavy motions in the air. "Colored swirls. Maybe a design in them. But I — I'm just not sure."

She squeezed her eyes shut, but if there was a design in the swirls, it stubbornly stayed just out of focus, beyond her reach. All she could really remember was the terrifying strength of the hand squeezing her throat, the feeling that her body might explode with the desperate demand for air.

"Bare hands? Gloves?"

"I —" She squeezed her eyes shut. She should know the answer. But she didn't. She finally shook her head. "I don't know."

"How about a wristwatch?"

"I don't think so . . . but I'm not sure. Just tattoos." Tattoos that she couldn't remember.

"Okay. Anything else?"

"Before he ran out, he must have grabbed the briefcase I dropped, because it's gone."

"Could you describe the briefcase for us, please."

This was pre-murder, and there was no fuzziness in this memory. "Tan leather, fold-over top, with a brass buckle. Hard leather handles."

"Initials or any other identifying marks?"

"No."

"What was in it?"

This time she couldn't get by with a general "PI stuff" answer. Neither could she offer a professional-sounding list of important documents and casework. She listed the actual items, even as a flush of embarrassment rose to ambush the Plum Fatale blush on her face. Notebook and pen. Two Snickers bars. Several of Rebecca's old *Good Housekeeping* magazines. A bag of kitty snacks. And finally, the item she'd most dreaded naming.

"And a, um, old flannel nightgown."

Whatever the officer may have thought about the unlikely contents of the briefcase, he simply listed the items in his notebook without comment and briskly continued the questions. "No identification, money or credit cards?"

"No." Hastily she rushed on to another subject. "I did see that the guy was wearing heavy black motorcycle boots."

The connection she'd been too stunned to make before jumped into her head now. A guy with a motorcycle. Big. Muscular. Like the biker guy she'd seen coming into the Mystic Mirage that day she'd so ignominiously rushed out. Like the God's-gift-to-women manager of the Lodge Hill vineyard. Two guys she'd already melded into one.

Rolf Wildrider.

And he'd seen her. Eye to eye.

13

The police detained them at the Mystic Mirage for another hour, then asked them to come to the police station to sign formal statements the following day.

Cate had debated with herself for a considerable time about giving them Rolf Wildrider's name, her conscience stumbling over a roadblock that could compete with the Great Wall of China. Yes, she was almost certain the hand around her throat had been attached to Rolf's muscular arm and lean body. But she wasn't cross-my-heart positive. Maybe Rolf and the killer just shared some general physical characteristics. What would it do to his future if he really was, after mistakes in his past, now trying to be a good-citizen grape grower, and she entangled him in an unfair accusation of murder?

She didn't even know if he had a tattooed arm. He'd been wearing long-sleeved denim that day she saw him at Lodge Hill, and she had no memory at all of arms on that guy coming into the Mystic Mirage that day.

But neither did she want a killer running around loose, endangering other people because she'd made some unwise judgment about fairness. How fair would it be if he killed someone else?

Including the fact that someone might be her.

Okay, she'd give them Rolf's name. Just as soon as she knew for certain he had a tattooed arm.

Cate's car was parked at Mitch's condo, and they went back there. Mitch didn't have much to say, and Cate knew he was upset by all this. Upset by murder. Upset that the guy got away. Upset that she was involved.

Even though the SUV was warm, Cate's teeth gave a skeletal chatter every few seconds. She kept seeing the bronze gleam of that sword and Celeste's open eyes. The killer's one eye venomously targeted on her. Rolf's eye?

Maybe.

Maybe not.

Now she'd never know who Celeste was considering investigating. Whoever it was, Celeste had obviously been right about meeting with Cate on a "matter of life and death."

Inside the condo, Cate slung her leg over a tall stool at the counter between kitchen and dining area, stiff fingers clutching her jacket tight around her. Vaguely she realized she'd lost the belt somewhere. Mitch made instant coffee, apparently figuring she needed caffeine *now* to jolt her out of this daze, and set two cups on the counter.

"You okay?" he asked.

Oh, sure, she was fine. She'd stumbled across a dead body, the killer had tried to choke her, and he'd seen her up close enough to count her freckles. Just another day in the life of your average assistant PI. But she didn't want to get into that because Mitch would no doubt use it to tell her she should find another line of work.

He also didn't know she thought the guy behind the curtain was Rolf Wildrider. There'd been no time or privacy to discuss that at the Mystic Mirage.

With some hesitation, Cate told him her suspicions now. "Maybe I should have given them Rolf's name."

"Why didn't you?"

"I keep thinking, since you said Rolf was still on probation, that it would be unfair to make trouble for him just because of similarities in size and muscles. And motorcycle. But I still think it was him."

"Maybe you have a subconscious suspicion about any guy with a motorcycle," Mitch suggested.

Cate started to indignantly deny that, but maybe it was true. One had tried to kill her not all that long ago in her other murder case. There'd been trouble with a motorcycle gang when she was a kid back in southern Oregon. Tonight's killer had escaped on a motorcycle. Incidents, she had to admit, that probably tended to warp her viewpoint.

Unexpectedly, after a thoughtful tilt of head, Mitch added, "Actually, I'm thinking about getting a motorcycle myself. It wouldn't use nearly as much gas as the SUV. Will you ride on it with me?"

"I don't think I'm a biker-babe type. Do you even know how to ride a motorcycle?"

"I had a little Honda 250 back in college. It was cheap to run around on."

Cate had no idea what the 250 referred to. Number of parts the bike would break into when crashed? Number of girls it was guaranteed to attract? She waved away the motorcycle discussion.

Mitch went along with turning the conversation away from motorcycles. "I noticed

Celeste had only one shoe on. I wonder if that means she lost the other shoe trying to escape from him?" he asked.

This was something else Cate hadn't noticed. Or maybe she had, but it was trapped back there in her subconscious, like details of the tattoo on the arm.

"I was almost certain Celeste killed Eddie the Ex, but I was wrong, wasn't I? Because now the killer got her too." Cate felt a lump in her pocket and realized she'd somehow come away with a wooden bead. She pulled it out and worried her thumb across the glossy surface.

"What would motivate someone to kill both of them?" Mitch asked.

"I don't know. But doesn't it seem logical that there's a connection?" Something clicked in her head. The dolls! "I don't know about a motive, but Eddie the Ex's killer shot the dolls at Jo-Jo's house. Celeste's killer knocked the doll in the store to the floor. Doesn't doll hostility suggest a connection?"

"Eddie may have shot the dolls at Jo-Jo's himself," Mitch pointed out. "And at the Mystic Mirage, the killer may have accidentally bumped into the doll when he went for a sword on the wall. He didn't take time to chop off its head or smash it."

"I think the doll thing shows they're connected," Cate repeated.

"Are you going to suggest this connection to the police when we go in tomorrow?" Mitch asked.

"Yes, I believe I will."

Mitch slid onto a stool beside her at the counter. "Maybe Celeste did kill Kieferson. Maybe someone objected and decided she deserved the same fate. *Two* killers."

Great. Now they were multiplying like fleas.

"There are other possibilities," Mitch added. "Maybe Celeste's killer was someone just passing by. He decides to go in and grab the goodies, and he winds up killing Celeste just because she's there. Wouldn't a guy planning murder have brought his own weapon?"

"His bike was around back. It looks to me as if he had something planned," Cate pointed out.

Mitch nodded. He shifted on the stool and toyed with his coffee cup. "Look, this is off the subject, and maybe none of my business. But kitty nibbles and a nightgown in your PI briefcase . . . I can't help it. I'm curious."

That had to come up, didn't it?

"It wasn't really a PI briefcase," Cate

admitted. "It was left over from a job I had when I actually did have business papers to carry around. I stuck a lot of stuff in it tonight, just anything I could grab, so Celeste would see a bulging briefcase and think I was a busy private investigator with lots of important cases." She rubbed the large bead hard enough to make her thumb sting. "Okay, I know. Dumb. Foolish pride. Say what you're thinking. Pride goeth before a fall. Whatever."

"Did the nightgown have a name tag in it?"

"Of course not!"

"No problem, then."

"No? I have a problem with it. I feel all . . . creepy and crawly knowing this guy has my *nightgown.*" Even if it was an old one she hadn't worn in a long time and had been intending to throw away. "What I should have done was load the briefcase with bricks. Then maybe I could have taken him out right there."

Mitch made an odd little choking noise. Cate looked at him suspiciously. He clamped his mouth shut, but another guffaw burst through.

"I know it's no time to be laughing," he admitted. "This is serious. But, can you picture this guy when he opens the briefcase? He's thinking bundles of cash or antique jewelry. And what does he find? Kitty nibbles and a flannel nightgown."

Cate didn't want to, but she started laughing too. Until finally she realized she was laughing because otherwise she might start sobbing with tension and shock and fear. Maybe a few tears even leaked out, because Mitch put an arm around her slumped shoulders and brushed a finger across her cheek.

"Sorry. Misplaced sense of humor."

Cate blinked back the tears. "I keep thinking how he was looking right at me. Looking at the color of my eyes. The shape of my nose. The number of my freckles."

"I can't even see your freckles."

The unexpected comment jerked Cate upright on the stool. Hey, that was right! She'd slathered on enough foundation and blush in her makeup mania to frost a double-layer cake. And if Mitch couldn't see her freckles, neither could Rolf Wildrider or whoever was behind that curtain! With different hair, even Uncle Joe and Rebecca had hardly recognized her, and the makeup added another layer of camouflage.

"Whoever was behind the curtain saw me, but he didn't really *see* me," Cate said. A weight of dread fell away. She yanked off the wig, not caring that it left her hair twisted into a flattened tomato atop her head.

"What do you mean?"

Cate held the brown wig out at arm's length. It hung there like some strange creature not yet identified in scientific channels. A hairy new species. She grabbed Mitch's hand and kissed the back of it, her lips leaving a fiery red brand.

He momentarily looked at her as if she, too, were some strange new creature. Then he nodded. "Oh, I get it. Right. You looked too different tonight for the killer to recognize or identify you."

"Exactly."

Now she could find out if Rolf's arms were tattooed without worrying he'd recognize her. She spun the wig around her finger and sailed it toward the sofa. Bull's-eye!

"I don't think I like that gleam in your eye," Mitch muttered.

Cate went home carrying the wig in a plastic bag. When she opened the front door, Uncle Joe was stretched out in his recliner, leg resting on a pillow, and Rebecca was sitting in her chair, reading a *Good Housekeeping*, with Octavia squeezed in beside her.

Cate didn't really want to tell Uncle Joe

that she was now involved in yet another murder, but she couldn't avoid it, of course. In fact, Rebecca looked at her and instantly asked, "What happened?"

Cate set the bagged wig on the floor under the end table and dropped onto the sofa.

She was at the part about the killer rushing out the back door of the Mystic Mirage when she noticed Octavia jump out of the rocking chair. Cate was concentrating on telling Joe about that tattoo she couldn't quite picture and wasn't really paying any attention to where the cat went.

Until she was tying the two murders together for Uncle Joe, and she became aware of peculiar sounds coming from under the end table. She leaned over to look.

"Octavia!" she gasped. "What are you —"

Octavia already had the bag ripped open. Her claws were caught in the long brown hair of the wig. Several strands decorated her head and ears. Cate snatched at the wig, but Octavia raced off, wig flopping around her paws and over her back. She leaped on the sofa, then tore around Uncle Joe's recliner and behind Rebecca's rocker, wig flying. Cate jumped up and dashed after her, but Octavia was in one of her Super-Cat episodes. She dusted the coffee table with the long brown hair. Cate crashed into the table trying to catch up with her. The white and brown streak whipped through the open door of the office and skidded across the glass top of the desk. Cate was too late to catch her.

The wig finally came off when it caught on a leg of the dining room table. Cate picked it up and looked at the tangled strands in dismay.

Hairy confetti.

Octavia jumped up on the kitchen windowsill and washed a paw, complacently announcing in deaf cat terms, *My work here is done.*

"This is coming out of your cat food allowance," Cate warned.

Octavia did a big-deal flick of her tail.

Cate stuffed what was left of the wig in a fresh plastic bag and went back to the living room to finish telling Uncle Joe about the evening. She took the bag with her, clutching it in both hands just in case Octavia was contemplating a second attack.

When Cate finished, Joe's only comment was, "I'm glad you took Mitch along with you." Although he did add, with a glance at the tangled mass in the plastic bag, "I don't believe I've ever seen a cat in a wig before."

It was not, Cate thought with regret, something easily forgotten.

■ ■ ■ ■

Next day, before Cate and Mitch were scheduled to meet at the police station, she was still trying to decide how to approach Rolf Wildrider. Marching up to him and suggesting that it was National Muscle Appreciation Day, and she'd really like to see his right arm — hey, wait, it was a *left* hand that had tried to choke her. He was a leftie!

But being too open about inspecting either of Rolf's arms for incriminating tattoos was hardly a workable idea. Hey, but there was another way to do it. She didn't necessarily have to inspect Rolf's arm in person. She looked up the Lodge Hill number and punched it in.

"Lodge Hill Weddings. LeAnne Morrison speaking."

"LeAnne, this is Cate Kinkaid —"

"Oh, Cate, have you heard? Celeste was killed last night. Murdered right there at the Mystic Mirage! It was on the news as I was coming to the office."

The words almost slipped out. *Yes, I know. I found her body.* She prudently reined them in. Better no one knew that. An unpleasant possibility hit her. Would the identity of the person finding Celeste's body make it into

206

the news reports? If it did, all the killer had to do was turn on the TV to identify who could identify *him.*

"Have you talked to Kim?" Cate asked.

"No. I called the home phone, but calls there are going to voice mail, and I don't have her personal cell phone number. I'm not sure I should book any more weddings. I have no idea what will happen to Lodge Hill."

"Kim owns everything now, not Celeste."

"Well, yes. But Kim, isn't, you know . . ."

"A take-charge person?"

"I've sometimes thought she must call Celeste every morning to ask if she should put her left or right shoe on first." A peculiar sound, as if LeAnne instantly regretted the snide comment and had clapped her hand over her mouth. "Actually, poor Kim. First her husband. Now her mother. It almost looks as if someone really has it in for her."

The idea that both murders had been vengeance against Kim hadn't occurred to Cate. Was the killer punishing her for something she'd done by going after the people she loved?

Could the motive for both murders be in some past or present relationship of Kim's? Maybe a relationship with Rolf?

"Did you call for some particular reason?"

LeAnne asked.

"Well, um, this probably sounds odd, but do you know if Rolf's arms have tattoos?"

"What a strange question!"

Cate didn't intend to reveal why she was asking. She didn't want LeAnne, or anyone else, knowing she knew the killer had tattoos because she'd seen them at the murder.

She'd have to look at those arms herself. Another lightbulb idea. She leaped to it without explaining her question about Rolf's arms.

"Actually, the reason I called, I'm wondering if Rolf ever gives tours of the vineyard? I know someone who's interested."

"Why would anyone want a tour? There isn't a winery, just all those rows and rows of grapevines. But they could call him, I suppose. I can give you the number at the manager's cottage. I don't have Rolf's personal cell phone number. He guards it as if it were some international secret."

Available only to clients of a pot-growing sideline?

"That'd be great. Thanks."

Cate scribbled the number on a scratch pad when LeAnne gave it and thanked her again. Another thought. "Do you think Celeste's death will affect my friend Robyn Doherty's wedding?"

"Good question. Under the circumstances, I'm thinking perhaps I should start looking for another job myself."

Cate didn't immediately try to contact Rolf. She wasn't about to go after an arm inspection solo. Mitch? No. He was big and male and could be intimidating. Rolf would be on guard around Mitch. So who?

Of course!

She looked up another phone number. She recognized the voice that answered. "Calypso Florists. May I help you?"

"Hi, Robyn, it's me, Cate."

"Oh, Cate, hi. Are you wearing the wig? I think you'll feel more comfortable with it the more you wear it."

Robyn apparently hadn't yet heard about Celeste's death, or she'd surely be bouncing off the walls. Cate wasn't going to tell her. The death wouldn't necessarily affect Robyn's wedding anyway.

Hold that thought.

"I haven't been wearing the wig, but I'm sure it will be fine." Although Robyn's question reminded her the wig needed some serious damage control after the attack of the furry tornado. "The reason I'm calling, you know that beautiful vineyard out there at Lodge Hill? I was thinking we could ask the manager for a tour. Wouldn't photos of the vineyard make a lovely addition to your wedding album?"

Robyn didn't enthusiastically jump on the idea, and Cate rushed on, using her own enthusiasm to extol the virtues and beauty of the vineyard.

"Cate, I'm sure it's lovely," Robyn interrupted with polite impatience. "But, honestly, I haven't any interest in seeing a bunch of grapevines or taking photos of them."

"I'd really like to see the vineyard, but I don't want to go alone." Cate let a hint of reproach seep into her voice.

"Get Mitch to go with you."

"You know men. They never want to go shopping or anything." An irrelevant comment, since shopping and grapevines were about as connected as weddings and mud wrestling. Fortunately, Robyn didn't seem to notice that.

"That's true," she agreed. "But . . ."

Cate didn't come right out and say, "Look, when you were desperate I agreed to be your bridesmaid, and I'm wearing this wig for you. You owe me." But she wasn't above giving a strong hint in that direction, and Robyn finally agreed. Cate said she'd get the tour set up and call her.

Next a call to Rolf. Cate let the phone at the cottage ring ten times. No answer, and not even an answering machine picked up. She tried twice more before heading out to meet Mitch at the police station at 2:00.

There, Cate offered the officer the additional information that she thought her attacker was left-handed. She also pointed out a similarity between the doll being knocked to the floor at the Mystic Mirage and the dolls being shot at Ed Kieferson's murder scene. The officer thanked her, but she could almost see his mental roll of eyes. *Just what we need. Another crackpot with a nutty conspiracy theory.*

There was another brief article about Celeste's murder in the Eugene newspaper that day, including what looked like a publicity photo of a smiling Celeste holding a copy of her book. It did not mention a connection between her death and Ed Kieferson's murder, and, to Cate's relief, the person who found Celeste's body was not identified.

Cate spent the next couple of days trying to serve another subpoena. Like Elvis sightings, lots of people knew someone who'd seen the guy she was looking for, but no one could pinpoint where he was now. She drove all the way up to Corvallis on a tip he might be there.

She didn't find him there, but along the way she started noticing high-handled motorcycles. She'd thought they might be a rarity that would link Rolf and the guy coming out of the Mystic Mirage that day, but she lost track of how many she saw on the freeway. She also spotted a middle-aged couple outside Walmart loading groceries into the saddlebags of a high-handled bike. And a high-handled bike ridden by a dark-suited guy with a briefcase strapped on behind was ahead of her in the drive-up window at the bank. Not a rarity after all.

She finally nailed the guy on whom she needed to serve the subpoena at a girl-friend's apartment. She also saw two high-handled motorcycles in the parking lot there. When she got home, on a whim she Googled "high-handled motorcycles" and learned they had a name: ape hangers.

Ape hangers. She giggled all evening about that one.

She gave calling Rolf one more try a couple evenings later and was so surprised when someone actually answered that she stuttered a moment before she got out what she wanted to say.

"I'm, uh, calling about a, um, tour of the vineyard. My friend is getting married there at Lodge Hill, and we thought some vine-yard photos would be nice. Would that be possible?"

"I've showed people around a few times, but the situation here at the vineyard is . . . unsettled."

Unsettled. A nice euphemism for disruption caused by two murders connected with owners of the vineyard? Perhaps murders he'd committed?

"We wouldn't take much of your time." Just long enough to check out your arms.

"I guess I could do it." Nothing flirty about Rolf today. Perhaps not surprising, if he had murders on his mind. And, figuratively at least, blood on his hands.

"Tomorrow morning?" Cate suggested.

"Sure, if you don't mind bad weather and mud."

They settled on 10:30 as a time, and he said he'd meet her at the cottage out behind Lodge Hill. Cate immediately called Robyn. She agreed, with all the enthusiasm of an appointment to see a display of belly-button lint, to meet Cate there.

Cate drove through the gate at Lodge Hill and parked at the manager's cottage at 10:28. The motorcycle was there, complete with ape hangers, but no Rolf came out to meet her. At 10:33, still no Rolf, and no Robyn zipping up in her Subaru. At 10:37, Cate was still alone. Did Rolf expect her to knock?

The day was cloudy and cool, and the wind, as sometimes happened in these inland valleys, carried a hint of raw coastal scent. The cell phone rang in her purse, and she whipped it out. Robyn's number on the screen.

"Cate, hi. Look, I'm not going to be able to do the vineyard thing."

"You promised!"

"I know. But I was cutting some flower stems, and the knife slipped and cut my hand. I'm at the emergency room at the hospital."

Cate's first indignant thought was, *You chopped yourself in the hand just to get out of this vineyard tour with me?* Then she guiltily discarded that petty reasoning. Even Robyn wouldn't go that far. "I'm so sorry. Is it going to be okay?"

"I need stitches, and it really hurts, but I won't lose fingers or anything. But now I'm hearing Lodge Hill may close and we'll have to move the wedding somewhere else. Everything is just turning into a-a disaster."

"I'm sure everything will be all right," Cate soothed, although she decided she'd do a full commiseration with Robyn later. Right now she'd just zip on out of here. Rolf wasn't here anyway. Or, if he did show up, she didn't want to be alone with him. Maybe he'd see past the red hair and freckles to long brown hair and jet-wing eyebrows.

"I'll see if I can find out anything about the wedding situation and Lodge Hill," Cate said. "Thanks for calling. Get that hand stitched up, and I'll check with you later."

Cate dropped the phone back in her purse, and a moment later a big green trac- tor rumbled around the far side of the cot- tage.

14

RolfWildrider, of course. Bundled in jacket, gloves, and a stocking cap that covered him like a Batman costume. He could have tattoos from his ears to his toenails, and she wouldn't be able to see them. He could also be carrying a whole arsenal of guns under that bulky jacket. Maybe a sword or two.

Reluctantly Cate opened the car door. Time to say adios, adieu, so long, Mr. God's-Gift-to-Women.

"Hi," he called when she slid out and stood behind the protective barrier of door. He swung down from the open cab of the tractor, leaving the engine running. "Sorry I'm late. I'm working with the crew putting up some new trellising. You're here to see the vineyard?"

"You're busy, so I won't bother you today," Cate called back. "I can come back some other time."

"No better time than right now. I don't

have to be with the crew every minute. Didn't you say there'd be two of you?"

"My friend couldn't make it after all."

He walked up and half-circled the car, so the door wasn't protectively between them. "You know, you look familiar."

Because he'd seen her through the beaded strands of a curtain at the Mystic Mirage? Clamped his hand around her throat? Panic made Cate wish she had a curtain of steel to draw between them right now. Sometimes it was flattering to be remembered. This was not one of those times.

"I don't think so," Cate said. "I'm sure we've never met."

"Hey, yeah, I remember." His eyes lit up. Dark eyes, she noted. Interested, not venomous. "You were going into the wedding office the other day. Who could forget that red hair?" His grin suggested that surely she'd remember him too. He stuck out a hand. "I'm Rolf Wildrider, vineyard manager."

She stepped slowly out from behind the car door and automatically started to shake the hand he held out to her. A squeamish thought stopped the movement, like a gunslinger in middraw. Was this a hand that had pawed around in her briefcase, run fingers through her nightgown? More importantly, was this a hand that had thrust a sword into Celeste's chest? And tried to choke her? If it was him she'd clobbered with the briefcase, the blow hadn't done any noticeable damage. Or was that a hint of bruise on the side of his neck?

Reluctantly she shook the still-gloved hand. "Cate Kinkaid."

She always carried business cards in her pocket, but she wasn't about to give him one that identified her as a private investigator. Right now, she needed to reinforce the idea that the brief meeting outside LeAnne's office was the only time they'd ever met. Maybe it actually *was* the only time. Looking at him now, Cate wasn't any more certain if his was or wasn't the eye behind the curtain.

"We did meet outside LeAnne's office, didn't we? I was going in to talk to her about my friend's wedding. I'm a bridesmaid."

"Not a bride after all? Maybe there's hope for me yet."

Maybe she should have given his name to the police. If nothing else, he deserved indictment for bad pickup lines.

"Okay, then, let's get on with the tour," he said. "Since there's just you, we can go on the tractor."

Cate glanced over at the rumbling green machine. "There isn't enough room for two people."

"Sure there is." Another grin. "It may be a tight squeeze, but we can make it work."

Cate started to say no thanks. A tight squeeze with Rolf was not on her agenda for the day. But he stripped off a glove, and she caught a flash of something dark above his wrist. Tractor grease? Vineyard dirt? Or maybe a tattoo? If she could just see a little farther up his arm . . .

They wouldn't be totally alone. In broad daylight, with a crew working nearby, she surely wasn't going to find herself buried under a grapevine. "I'll get my camera so I can take some photos for Robyn."

She'd brought the camera along mostly as a prop, but now she reached back into the car and grabbed it. Rolf boosted her into the open cab of the tractor, using a little more familiarity than Cate thought necessary.

The open cab was an even tighter squeeze than Cate had anticipated. There was no space for an extra person to stand, so Rolf gave her half the metal seat and squeezed into the other half himself. Cate squirmed to get as far away from him as possible and found herself precariously perched on the metal rim of the seat.

They bumped over the rough ground out to the first row of grapes, with Cate thinking she was going to have the shape of the hard edge of a tractor seat permanently embedded in her anatomy.

Actually, as both LeAnne and Robyn had pointed out, there wasn't much to see in the vineyard. Rolf kept up a running stream of information, however. The vineyard grew chardonnay and pinot noir grapes, and he pointed out which was which. He spoke knowledgeably about how the rainfall, sunshine, humidity, and temperatures of this area were conducive to grape growing. He wanted to get a new type of trellising system started, something called the Geneva Double Curtain, which would improve the exposure of the grapes to sunlight. He mentioned concerns about a grape mite called phylloxera that could devastate a vineyard, and the problems they also had with scavenging birds.

He sounded informed, even enthusiastic. He never mentioned either Ed Kieferson or Celeste, or any uncertainties about future operation of the vineyard. Cate was curious about the possibility of a marijuana-growing sideline, but if there were such an area, it wasn't included in the tour. She took some photos, but she spent most of her time trying to balance on the edge of the seat and get a look at Rolf's arm. Once, rounding the end of a row of grapes, she surreptitiously tried to slide his jacket sleeve up a few inches, but a sudden jolt landed her hand on his thigh instead.

Appalled, Cate yanked her hand back, but Rolf's smirky grin told her he knew she'd really done it on purpose.

In the area where the crew was working on a new support trellis to replace a section that had collapsed, Rolf jumped down to inspect their work. In the distance Cate spotted a barn and several sheds. She asked Rolf about them, and he said they were left over from a time when the vineyard had also been used as a dairy, and they were just used for storage now.

Back at the cottage, Cate didn't wait for a helping hand to get down from the tractor. She jumped by herself, an exit not rivaling Octavia's land-on-her-feet grace, but at least she wasn't cozied up beside Rolf any longer.

"Thanks for the tour," she called up to him. The wind was getting colder. She shoved her hands in her pockets and turned toward her car.

He jumped down beside her. "Maybe you can bring your friend some other time. The one who's getting married at Lodge Hill."

The conditions weren't ideal, but here was an unexpected opening to ask Rolf a few questions without giving away her own involvement. She hunched her shoulders and moved over to where the big tractor offered some shelter from the wind.

"Actually, Robyn was telling me she'd heard Lodge Hill might close. A death in the family, I think. She's wondering if her wedding will be affected. Do you know anything about that?"

"Two deaths, actually. The owner first, and then his wife's mother just a few days ago. It's going to be rough for Kim . . . Mrs. Kieferson."

Cate noted the correction from Kim to the less personal Mrs. Kieferson. It gave her a mental *hmm.* "Does she have other family?"

"I don't think so."

"The wedding business and vineyard, along with the restaurant too, will be a lot for her to keep going alone. Do you think she can manage?"

"She's going to need all the help she can get, that's for sure."

Cate heard concern and even a hint of protectiveness in Rolf's comment and tone of voice. Maybe even a suggestion of intimacy beyond an employer-employee relationship?

"Have you known the Kiefersons long?"

"I knew Mrs. Kieferson way back when. They lived just down the street from us in Tigard a long time ago."

"Kim was an old girlfriend?" Cate purposely put a playful tease into the question. She didn't want him to know she was really digging for information.

"Not a girlfriend." Rolf sounded unexpectedly serious. "Kim is younger. She was just a skinny little mousy-haired kid in grade school then. With a mother everyone thought was uppity and weird. She had Kim taking private lessons in everything from gymnastics to ballet, even drove her into Portland for some special modeling classes."

Early lessons in how to be a trophy wife?

"I'd left Tigard by the time Kim finished high school, but I heard one time when I went back that right after graduation she married that Travis Beauchamp jerk. They'd moved to Portland or somewhere by then."

Cate made a mental note of the name. Travis Beauchamp. "You knew him too?"

"He was bad news even in high school. In trouble for everything from bullying to swiping pills from a neighbor's medicine cabinet. But I guess Kim saw something in him.

Although sometimes I wondered if she married him just to get out from under her mother's thumb."

"The relationship between Kim and her mother was, um, strained?" Cate asked.

"I guess they've been on better terms since the breakup with Travis."

Cate noted that Rolf didn't mention Kim and Celeste being in business together. Maybe he wanted to stay far away from the subject of the Mystic Mirage?

"What became of the ex-husband?"

"He just walked out, I guess. Although Kim told me once . . . this is strictly confidential, of course." His heavy eyebrows lifted sharply. "Just between friends."

Cate prudently didn't argue the "friends" designation. "Of course."

"She was afraid the guy might show up and try to mess up her marriage to Kieferson."

Someone had obviously "messed up" the marriage. Ed Kieferson was dead. "Why would he do that?"

"I don't know. Just a bad dude, from what I remember of him."

"Did knowing Kim help you get this job at the vineyard?"

Rolf looked surprised at the blunt question. His shoulders snapped back. "No way.

I got this job on my own merits. I have a degree in viticulture. Kim and I were both surprised when we ran into each other here. I didn't even recognize her right off, with her hair blonde now. How come you're so curious about all this anyway?" he suddenly demanded.

Cate noticed that he'd upgraded his education in grape-growing to a college-degree level, but she didn't point that out. "Oh, you know how nosy and curious women are," she said. "In fact, you really know women, don't you?" She added a playful smile to emphasize the blatant flattery about his male expertise. Anything to diffuse his curiosity.

Apparently it worked because his own smile was also playful when he said, "I like to think I do."

"Well, thanks for the tour and information about grapes and all. It was very interesting." Cate headed toward the car.

Rolf caught up with her in a long stride. "Hey, wait, I wanted to ask you something."

Cate started to make an elaborate pretense of looking at her watch to suggest she was in a big hurry, but a better idea jumped into her head. "Do you know what time it is?"

She waited expectantly for a last-minute unveiling of the arm when he pushed up the sleeve of his jacket to look at a watch.

Except he didn't. He pulled a broken-banded watch out of his pocket and held it up. "Snagged it on a grapevine." He turned the watch to see the face. "It's only 11:45."

"Looks like you're a leftie." And maybe he'd snagged the watch somewhere other than on a grapevine? Like on a sword at the Mystic Mirage?

Another grin. "Oh, I'm ambidextrous. Very good with both hands."

There was a double entendre in that, Cate was certain, but she wasn't about to pause and examine it for details. "It's later than I thought. So —"

"Look, I have to go back out with the crew now, so I can't make lunch, but how about dinner tonight?"

"Oh, thanks, no."

"C'mon, you know you're interested. You give me a song-and-dance about two of you coming, and then you show up alone?" Another of his frequent lady-killer grins. "Not that I'm objecting, you understand. It's been a fun morning. You can share a tractor seat with me anytime." He patted his thigh to remind her of her touch there.

Cate was reasonably certain Rolf had no clue she was checking him out as a murder suspect. He thought she had an amorous interest in his body. Time to get out before he came up with some suggestion more outrageous than dinner. Or figured out the truth about her interest.

"Thanks for the invitation, but I'm, oh, you know, involved."

He overdid a crestfallen look. "Oh. Well, okay then. I should have guessed. But if you're ever uninvolved, or just want a little fun on the side . . ." Meaningful smile. "I'm a sucker for redheads."

She took one hand out of her pocket to give him a little fingertip wave of good-bye, then scurried to the car and slid inside.

It wasn't until she'd started the engine that she realized he'd picked up something from the ground where she'd been standing.

A Belmont Investigations business card. She'd accidentally pulled one out of her pocket when she waved at him.

He looked up from reading the card, and their eyes met. He wasn't giving her any God's-gift-to-women grin now. Instead his hard gaze asked, *Just what was she investigating?*

Outside the gate Cate kept telling herself there was no reason Rolf would connect a private investigator's card with a brown-haired woman at the Mystic Mirage. Unfortunately, there was also no reason for her to go to the police with new information about Rolf. She still didn't know if he had a tattooed arm. Now what? Bad-investigation days were even worse than bad-hair days.

Although she wasn't too sure of that when she got home and decided she should do something with the snarled wig. She tried combing it. Brushing it. Shaking it. No use. It still looked like something a cat had attacked with all claws unleashed. Which it was, of course. Octavia watched with an interest that suggested she'd like a second chance at the wig.

Cate finally jammed the brown tangle into another plastic bag and headed for the salon where Robyn had purchased it. There, she told the woman she'd like to have the wig repaired and styled. The woman held up the snarled mess and gave Cate an accusing look that put her in some category of felonious wig abusers.

Cate apologized for the condition of the wig and added, "My cat accidentally got hold of it."

The woman gave her a look that put that statement on a level with "my dog ate my homework."

"It doesn't have to look as good as it did

before, just wearable."

"It's beyond repair. And we don't have another wig of this model in stock. We can order another one, but it will probably take from ten days to two weeks to get it."

The wedding was in less than two weeks, so that was cutting it close. Especially when the woman sounded as if she'd really like to blackball Cate from wig ownership for the foreseeable future.

"Okay." Cate paid for the new wig in advance. "Just call me the minute the new one comes in."

15

Back home, Cate called Robyn from the office phone to ask about the injured hand.

"It's okay, I guess. They stitched it up. It's covered with a bandage the size of a watermelon now."

That was rather hard to picture, but Cate murmured sympathies. "I hope it isn't hurting."

"They gave me some pain pills. But I'm not sure it will heal by the wedding. Oh, Cate, I can't march down the aisle with my hand like this. I'll look like a-a walking mummy! I won't even have a finger to put the ring on."

"Maybe the bandage will be off by then. Or at least the bandage will be smaller."

"My ring finger is all swollen. I had to take my engagement ring off and put it on a chain around my neck."

"Surely the swelling will go down by the time of the wedding," Cate soothed.

"By then my whole hand could be infected. You can get this scary red line, you know, going right up your arm toward your heart. And who knows if there will even be a wedding, since no one seems to know what's going to happen with Lodge Hill," Robyn added with an ominous the-world-is-doomed gloom.

Cate decided there was no point adding to Robyn's doom-and-gloom by mentioning the cat-and-wig disaster. She also realized that at the moment Robyn didn't want sunshiny predictions; she wanted to wallow in her gloom. So Cate spent the next several minutes making sympathetic sounds while Robyn rambled through various dire possibilities. Robyn didn't quite get to hand amputation, but close to it.

Finally, apparently realizing herself that none of the grim possibilities were apt to materialize, Robyn gave a self-conscious laugh. "Listen to me. Pretty soon I'll be obsessing about the building collapsing. The dinner being hijacked. Another murder right there at the wedding."

Collapse of the building or hijacking of the dinner bounced off Cate as unlikely, but a murder at the wedding? That hit her like a sneak snowball attack. With a rock inside. With two murders already, maybe a third was all too possible. Wasn't there some old cliché, the kind of saying Mitch might come up with, about trouble coming in threes?

Robyn didn't seem to notice Cate's sudden silence. "Thanks for listening, Cate. You're a real friend. I feel much better now. My hand probably won't have any more than a Band-Aid on it by the time of the wedding. And surely Lodge Hill won't close down."

"Good thinking."

Cate's hand stayed on the phone when she set it down, her mind stalled on a third-murder possibility. No, not possible. The killer was running out of victims, for one thing.

A chilling truth clobbered her with another sneak attack. Killers never run out of victims.

The phone in the office rang under Cate's hand. That's what phones did, ring, but she jumped anyway. She picked it up, and, without preliminaries, Jo-Jo's agitated voice pounced on her.

"You heard about Kim's mother, didn't you? That she's dead? Murdered."

"It's been in the news."

"Cate, would you believe, the police have been here to question *me* about her death?"

"They think you had something to do with it?"

Jo-Jo couldn't have been the killer herself. It was definitely a male arm that had shot out of the curtain and grabbed Cate's throat. But even gray-haired little old ladies had been known to *hire* killers. And Jo-Jo had all that money coming from Eddie the Ex's insurance.

"They didn't come right out and say that, but that must be what they're thinking. Though I can't imagine why they'd think I had anything to do with it."

How about Jo-Jo taking vengeance on Celeste for killing Eddie? Cate had thought Jo-Jo was the sole suspect in Eddie's killing, but maybe the police had an eye on Celeste too. So the possibility of Jo-Jo hiring a tattooed killer to kill the person who'd killed her ex-husband also loomed for them.

"Pretty soon they'll be digging up cold cases from ten years ago and blaming me for those too," Jo-Jo fretted.

"I'm sure they're just checking out anyone who's ever had any connection with Celeste," Cate soothed. "And you do have a roundabout connection."

"Well, yes. And there wasn't any love lost between us, that's for sure. But what happened to her . . . that's really awful. No one deserves that, not even Celeste. But the police shouldn't be wasting time on me."

Cate repeated her earlier statement about confidence in the competence of the local police.

"If they're so competent, how come they haven't caught Eddie's killer yet?" Jo-Jo retorted. Then in a quick change of subject she added, "Oh, I don't think I told you. I bought a car! A nice 2011 Chevy Malibu. Now I can run out to the house every day to visit and feed Maude."

"I'm glad to hear that. You've received Eddie's insurance money, then?" Enough to hire a killer as well as buy a car?

"No. I signed a contract to buy the car, thirty-six months of payments. I hate to be in debt, but I had to do it, for Maude. Without the alimony money coming in, I've also had to use my credit card for some things. I hope the insurance comes through soon. I need it."

Okay, cancel the hired-killer possibility. Hired killers probably didn't accept Visa or MasterCard.

"Actually, if it weren't for Maude, I think I'd just pick up and head for Arizona," Jo-Jo declared. "The lawyer I talked to said the police couldn't keep me from doing that, unless they actually arrest and charge me with something."

Which they might do. But Cate only said, "Let me know if you decide to do that, okay?"

Cate wanted to make another phone call. She didn't have the number, but even unlisted numbers were supposed to be easily available on the internet. She started looking.

Maybe "easily available" was true for some surfers, but not Cate. People her age and younger were supposed to be the generation that came complete with a computer gene installed, but her installation had apparently been short a few cyberspace screws.

After twenty minutes, she decided there was an easier way and his name was Mitch, who had more than enough computer genes. She called his cell phone. He said he'd see what he could find out and call her back. Which he did, although he didn't instantly rattle off the number. She wasn't surprised that a mini-lecture came first.

"I suppose you're going to do something with this number that I won't approve of," he said.

"Maybe I'll use it to run a scam about how I'm in jail in Nigeria, and would Kim please wire money."

He ignored the facetious suggestion. "I think you're planning to call her and get yourself involved in what my grandmother would call 'a heap of trouble.' "

"Yes, that's my plan. The bigger the heap, the better."

Big, put-upon sigh, but he gave her the number. "Let me know if you need backup again."

"Will do." But not if she could help it. At some point, she had to be able to stand alone as a PI.

"By the way, I have something to show you. I'll come by later, okay?"

"Some new electronic gadget?" she asked.

"You'll see."

Cate dialed the number Mitch gave her. An answering machine picked up after four rings. It felt strange, hearing Eddie the Ex speaking while remembering him sprawled on the floor of Jo-Jo's workroom, bullet hole in his forehead. Eerie. A voice from beyond the grave cheerfully telling her to leave a message and he'd get back to her.

In spite of how the unexpected voice rattled her, she managed to leave a reasonably coherent message for Kim. She didn't have high hopes that Kim would respond, but when the phone rang ten minutes later, she jumped for it hopefully.

Not Kim. A male voice.

"Ms. Kinkaid, this is Roger Ledbetter, of Winkler, Ledbetter, and Agrossi, Attorneys-at-Law."

Mr. Ledbetter was the lawyer handling the estate of the woman who had originally owned Octavia, and who was now overseeing construction of the house that was part of the cat's inheritance. He always identified himself with careful formality. Cate had wondered if he did this to reinforce his voice of authority, or if he had some secret insecurity about people not remembering him.

"Yes, Mr. Ledbetter?"

"I'm calling because the contractor says the house will be ready for occupancy as soon as the final inspection by the building department is complete. So it's time for you and Octavia to give the house a final walk-through to make certain everything is satisfactory."

"You think Octavia should check it out?"

"Don't you?" He sounded taken aback by her surprised reaction and uncharacteristically uncertain when he added, "I've never had a cat. I don't know much about them. But I don't want her to be unhappily surprised by any aspect of the house."

Mr. Ledbetter may not know cats, but he took his job as executor of the estate seriously. He'd even had a private investigator check Cate out before granting her ownership of Octavia. She refrained from saying she doubted Octavia would sue if she didn't like the color of the carpet.

"Okay, I can take Octavia over for a look in a day or two."

Mr. Ledbetter's brisk self-assurance returned. "I'll be in court for the next few days, so I need to meet you there today. Will 3:00 be suitable?"

Spend the afternoon on a house tour with a deaf cat and a lawyer? Not an opportunity to which everyone had privilege. "Okay. We'll be there."

She called and left a message on Mitch's voice mail about meeting Mr. Ledbetter at the house, and that she'd see him and whatever he had to show her later.

Octavia objected to being loaded into the pet carrier, objected to the ride, objected to Mr. Ledbetter peering into the cage when Cate carried it into the house. Objections expressed in yowls and snarls that would do justice to a lion protesting a toenail manicure.

Inside the house, Cate, wary of Octavia's

reaction, didn't immediately turn her loose. She did a quick house inspection herself.

The house truly was a cat wonderland, but it was also a great house for Cate. She was going to love living here! A spacious master bedroom. A second bedroom as a guest room. And the third bedroom she could set up as an office for Belmont Investigations business. Refrigerator with ice maker. Sleek granite countertops. Double sinks in the master bath. Hmm. She'd never mentioned that to Mr. Ledbetter, and now all he said was a tactful, "I thought they might be useful at some time."

Finally, when Octavia's yowls had fallen to a lower decibel level, she unhooked the latch on the pet carrier.

To Cate's surprise, Octavia stopped yowling and stepped out of the carrier with queenly poise. She sniffed around for a while and then climbed the carpeted pole that connected to the overhead walkway. She prowled the walkway through the openings cut through the walls, jumped to the window seat, and gleefully attacked a rope in her screened-in playroom. She also eyed the steel-brushed refrigerator expectantly. Octavia liked her cat food from a can, not running around on teensy-tiny mouse feet.

Hands tucked behind him, Mr. Ledbetter

followed the cat's progress through the house. This was the first time he'd actually met Octavia person-to-cat. "Do you think she'd like a TV in her sunroom?"

"Octavia isn't really into TV." There was an aquarium show that sometimes interested her, but Cate figured the cat could watch that on one of the other TVs. Mr. Ledbetter had already told her she could buy as many as she needed, along with whatever other furniture she wanted. All furnished by the estate.

Finally, after Octavia curled up on the window seat, he asked, "Do you think she likes the house?"

"I'd say she definitely gives it a cat thumbs-up."

Surprisingly, now out of the cage, Octavia also seemed to approve of Mr. Ledbetter. She jumped down from the window seat and wound around his legs, rubbed her head on his shoe, and left a few souvenir white hairs on his dark suit. Hands still behind him, he leaned over to take a better look as she batted at his shoestrings.

"She really is deaf?"

"As a stump." Cate eyed Octavia. "But if she were a person, I think she'd have made an excellent private investigator." Maybe even a lawyer.

"Perhaps I'll suggest to Mrs. Ledbetter that we should have a cat," the lawyer said in a thoughtful tone.

After he left, Cate reloaded cat into carrier, and carrier into backseat of car. "You're a cat kiss up," she stated. Octavia, who always knew when she was being talked to even if she couldn't hear, made a comfortable *mrrow* of agreement. "But I have to admit you're an excellent ambassador for cat ownership."

Cate was just slipping into the front seat of the car when a roar stopped her.

Not a kitty roar.

A motorcycle with headlight blazing growled to a stop behind her car. Panic attack. Rolf had figured out she'd seen him behind the curtain at the Mystic Mirage. He'd tracked her here and now —

Hey, wait, the handlebars on this machine weren't ape hanger high like those on Rolf's bike. Nor was this Rolf taking off a rainbow-streaked helmet and shaking out a headful of dark hair.

She got out of the car. "Mitch!"

He stepped back from the bike with gold specks glinting in the depths of deep purple. "What do you think?" He looked at the big machine with pride of ownership.

"I know you said you were thinking about

getting one, but I guess I didn't think you'd actually *do* it."

"I was at the dealer's when you called."

"I wouldn't have expected you to pick *purple.*" Mitch had never struck her as a purple kind of guy. To find purple depths in him was rather disconcerting.

"It isn't exactly purple," Mitch objected. "I think they call it Night Wine."

"It's purple."

The motorcycle had a big windshield, a big trunk, and big saddlebags. The seat was on two levels, so a passenger sat at a slightly higher level behind the driver. Chrome gleamed everywhere.

Beautiful, in a Darth Vader, death-rocket kind of way.

"What's next?" Cate asked. "A wardrobe of black leather? A tattoo?"

"In the bikers' world, those are tatts."

"I'll keep that in mind."

"No tatts. And that's a very —" Mitch broke off and scowled at her. "What's a word that means something like ageist or racist, except it's about stereotyping guys with motorcycles?"

"Bike-ist?"

"Okay. Bike-ist. You're being bike-ist. Very judgmental, to say nothing of snarky, about someone with a motorcycle. Owning and riding a bike is not a character flaw."

No?

"I don't think I'm expert enough to offer you a ride yet. This is a way bigger bike than the one I had back in college."

Cate squelched a snarky comment about how devastated she was not to get a ride this very minute.

"I have to go to the Department of Motor Vehicles now and get a motorcycle endorsement on my driver's license."

The snark rose again. "Are you sure they'll let you do that without tatts and black leather? Maybe a biker babe on the back?"

"Bike-ist."

Okay, maybe she was, she had to admit. Her personal experience with bikers — the one who'd tried to kill her, plus probable killer Rolf Wildrider, and memory of that biker gang that had taken up residence when she was a kid in Gold Hill — had not left warm, fuzzy impressions. And weren't there statistics about how many more deaths there were per motorcycle miles than car miles?

"Maybe I'm worried about you, charging around on this . . . Purple Rocket."

"I worry about *you,* charging around getting into PI trouble."

Was that a stalemate? The jingle of the

cell phone in Cate's pocket interrupted, and, still eying the motorcycle, she answered it without checking the caller ID.

"Hi. This is Kim Kieferson. I'm returning a call someone made a little earlier? An investigator who had an appointment with my mother?"

Kim sounded more little-girl-lost than sophisticated trophy wife. Cate wasn't about to go softhearted, however. This was the woman who had stolen Jo-Jo's husband.

"Yes, I called." Cate explained the appointment with Celeste without revealing any specifics about when or even if it took place. "Dr. Chandler indicated she was thinking about having someone investigated, and I'd like to talk to you about who it might be. It may have a connection with her death."

"Are you with the police?"

"No, I'm a private investigator. No police connection." Cate thought that information might end the conversation right there, but Kim surprised her.

"I don't want to talk to the police anymore. They make me feel . . . awful. Like I'm guilty of something. Like I'm not being truthful."

Cate heard an unspoken cry behind the words. A cry that said that even if Kim didn't want to talk to the police, she wanted to talk to *someone.* Cate was reminded of what Rolf had said about Kim having no family, and what LeAnne had said about her being so dependent on her mother.

"I can come over any time that's convenient for you," Cate said. "Right now, in fact. I just have to take my cat home first."

Cate glanced up at Mitch and put her hand over the phone. "I won't need backup for this."

"You sure?"

"I'm sure."

"Okay. But call if you need me." Mitch slapped the rainbow helmet over his head and fastened the chinstrap. "I know you didn't mean it as a compliment, but I like your Purple Rocket name." He gave the bike a good-boy pat.

Good, dependable Mitch. He might not approve of her PI activities, but he'd be there, backing her up if she needed him. She supposed the least she could do was try not to be so bike-ist.

"At least the motorcycle doesn't have ape hangers," she said.

"Ape hangers?" he repeated, obviously with no idea what she was talking about.

She felt a little smug knowing something about motorcycles that he didn't. "Look it up." She blew him a kiss. "Love the helmet."

"There's a matching one for you in the trunk."

16

Cate dropped Octavia off at the house and drove out to Riverwalk Loop. There was a number pad at the wrought-iron gate to the Ice Cube, but, as Kim had instructed, she spoke into the black box, and Kim opened the gate from the house. Cate parked behind the flashy Mustang convertible and consoled herself by thinking that her old Honda probably got much better gas mileage.

The double front doors of the house were glass, but a shade was pulled over them, and Cate couldn't see Kim until she opened the door. She had a Marilyn Monroe aura about her, beautiful and voluptuous, but also vulnerable and a little fragile in a pink sweat suit and old brown socks that looked as if they might have been Ed's. Her toe stuck out of a hole in the left sock. But it was a nicely manicured toe.

"Were you at the vet with your cat?" Kim clutched the door as if she needed it for support. "You said you had to take it home."

"I was showing her the new house where we'll be living before long."

"That's nice," Kim said, as if showing a house to a cat was something everyone did. Her gaze roamed the high ceiling of the room, as if she were wondering how a cat might view it.

Cate's gaze followed. The ceiling was solid, not glass. No looking up at the undersides of feet overhead. Good thinking. The statistics on the house at the tax assessor's office had said there was an indoor pool and a temperature-controlled wine room. She'd kind of like to have a tour.

Kim lifted her arms. "I've always loved this house. But now, with Ed gone, it's . . . different." Her arms wrapped around her midsection. "I'm always cold." Could eyes shiver? Her blue eyes seemed to.

Kim led the way into a living room so large that it was divided into several sections by furniture arrangements, each with its own color-coordinated scheme. Three TVs, one enormous, two only semi-enormous. Light streamed through the upper third of the glass window-walls, but shades that rolled up from the bottom gave the room a peculiar underwater feeling. Yet, if the shades were down, sitting here where every passerby on the street could see inside would be very fishbowl-ish.

When she was rich, Cate decided, she wouldn't have a glass house. Although she might go for a Mustang convertible.

Kim motioned Cate to a white leather sofa in the purple-and-white geographical region. She sat down herself, then jumped up as if instructions on being a good hostess had just kicked in. "Would you like something to drink? There's Pepsi or 7UP or wine. Pinot noir and chardonnay, I think. That's the kind of grapes the vineyard grows. Or Snapple or V8 juice? But no coffee. I never could figure out that stupid coffee machine!" She slammed a purple pillow into the sofa, as if pillow or coffeemaker were to blame for all her troubles. "Ed always made our coffee. I haven't had any since he's been . . . gone."

Instructions for operating a coffee machine didn't come with the Trophy Wife Instruction Kit?

Cate gave herself a mental kick. Kim was trying to be nice. She looked as if she'd been crying, although that hadn't turned her face all red and blotchy, the way it did Cate's. Only a hint of blue shadows around her eyes darkened her peachy skin.

"Nothing for me, thanks," Cate said.

Although she had some doubts about Celeste Chandler's character, the woman *was* Kim's mother, and Cate offered her sympathies. "I'm so sorry about your mother. I know what a difficult time this must be for you. I think losing a mother is one of the worst events of our lives. Especially when she was still so young."

Kim blinked and nodded. Her voice was scratchy when she said, "Thank you."

Trying to look professional, Cate got out her notebook and placed it on her lap. She couldn't think quite how to get started, but, unexpectedly, Kim made the first move.

"You said you had an appointment with my mother?"

"Yes, that's right. Had your mother mentioned it to you?"

Kim shook her head. "She hadn't said anything, but I've been thinking ever since you called, and I may know what the appointment was about."

"Oh?"

"I think she was considering having my ex-husband investigated."

Cate had been expecting Kim to say her mother wanted Rolf Wildrider investigated in relation to Ed's death, and now she felt as if some new and ominous figure had peered out of the shadows.

"Why would she do that?"

"It's kind of a long story?" Kim made a question of the statement, as if she were doubtful about taking up Cate's time.

"I have plenty of time," Cate assured her.

"Okay. Well, Travis, that was my husband, just walked out on me. Not a word where he was going, and I never heard from him again after he left."

"Did anyone else have contact with him?"

"I asked a friend once, and he said he didn't know anything. But most of Travis's friends would rather lie than tell the truth any day. Travis used to talk about going down to South America. He said he wanted to live where there weren't so many rules and regulations. So I thought maybe he'd done that. Although sometimes I did think he might be dead. He lived kind of a . . . reckless life."

Cate had a sudden intuition. "Was he into motorcycles?"

"Oh yeah. He never could hold a job for long, but he was good at buying and selling and trading bikes. I got fired from the only job I ever had because Travis came in and accused the guy I worked for of groping me. Which he never had. But Travis punched him and smashed the windows of his car with a tire iron."

"Did you try to locate him after he left?"

"No. Marrying Travis was the biggest mistake of my life. Mom practically begged me not to marry him, even if I was pregnant. And she was right, of course. He had a terrible temper. He put a fist through our apartment wall one time and threw a frying pan through a window. He shot up a bunch of beer bottles right in our backyard. The cops came, and they told him to get rid of the gun or else. He did, but he got another one right away, of course."

Rolf had been right. Travis was a bad dude. A follow-up thought was, *It takes one to know one.* Maybe the question here was, who was the baddest dude?

"Mom said I was lucky I lost the baby too, because that meant I could get on with my life. But I never really felt that way." Kim touched her abdomen as if regret for the emptiness still lingered. "Then, after Travis took off, I moved here to live with Mom and met Ed. The lawyer had to do the divorce some special way, since I didn't even know where Travis was."

Kim may have had a rough life with Travis, and losing her mother was also hard on her, but Cate wasn't about to offer instant sympathy. "But Ed was married. You knew that, didn't you?"

"It bothered me, but Mom knew some people who knew Ed, and she told me they said his wife was naggy and mean and money hungry, and they were about to split up anyway."

An actual account of what the people had said, or a little tweaking by Celeste? Although, even if Kim believed what Celeste told her, that didn't make involvement with a married man morally defensible.

"What kind of marriage did you and Ed have?"

"We were fine. Very happy." Then faint lines cut between Kim's eyebrows, as if an unexpected streak of honesty made her reconsider that instant response. "Of course he was busy and had a lot on his mind. The restaurant and vineyard and everything. And we, um . . . well, he was a lot older. He didn't like dancing and I didn't like golf. I didn't like watching boxing or football on TV, and he didn't like figure skating. I love Mexican food, but it bothered his stomach."

Had Ed Kieferson also discovered there were flaws in trophy wife acquisition?

Kim wiggled the toe sticking out of the brown sock. "Sometimes I even wondered . . ."

"Wondered?"

"If maybe he wished he'd stayed married

253

to Jo-Jo." The wrinkle across her forehead deepened, but she determinedly straightened her back. "But mostly we were happy. Very happy."

That's my story, and I'm stickin' to it.

"Were there money problems?" Cate asked.

"He never said I shouldn't spend so much on the house or yard or clothes or anything." Kim's vague wave took in the expensive furnishings and probably that strange sculpture outside. "But from what the lawyers and accountant are telling me now, yes. Big money problems. I think Ed was just too considerate to tell me."

Or afraid she'd burn rubber taking off in the Mustang if she knew the money supply was fizzling out?

"What will you do now?"

"I don't know. Mom said we could keep things going after Ed's death. I always thought the wedding business out at Lodge Hill was interesting. When I was a teenager, I used to dream about a huge, beautiful wedding. I was always cutting out pictures of wedding gowns and articles about what food to serve at the reception, who stood where in a receiving line, all that kind of stuff. I had lots of weddings for my Barbie and Ken."

Kim leaned her head back and closed her eyes, as if she longed to go back to those days. She didn't say it, but somehow Cate doubted Kim's wedding to bad-dude Travis had lived up to those fantasies.

"Did you and Ed get married at Lodge Hill?" she asked.

"No, we flew down to Vegas. I thought maybe, after awhile, he'd let me take over running the wedding business. I gave him a few hints. But I never wanted to be involved with the restaurant or vineyard. No way. And now . . ." She lifted her shoulders as if she had no idea what to do with them.

Cate started to say that Rolf was there to run the vineyard, but, under the circumstances, Rolf might not be running anything for long.

"What about the Mystic Mirage?"

"Mom handpicked everything for the store. She knew all about tarot cards and incense and astrology stuff. But some of it makes me feel . . ." Kim wiggled on the sofa as if she'd like to squirm out from under the weight of the Mystic Mirage. "Uncomfortable, I guess. Once a woman came in and said we were flirting with demons with the witchcraft books." Kim gave a nervous tinkle of laughter, as if she were embarrassed to be giving that kind of thinking any credibility.

"Did you ever do that regression thing into past lives with your mother?"

"She wouldn't do it with me. I never knew why."

Maybe because Celeste knew it was all a big, fat phony?

Back to the husband before Ed. Kim hadn't really answered Cate's question about why Celeste may have been thinking about investigating Travis. Cate repeated the question.

"I think Travis called the store one time. I was there. Mom said the caller was an annoying salesman, but I just had this, I don't know, *feeling* it was him. I never let her know, but I called a friend back in Tigard to ask if he'd been around there. My friend said yes, and that he'd been asking about me." As something of an afterthought, she added, "And Mom."

"So the friend told him where you were?"

"No. She was suspicious even though he said he needed to find me because my name was on the title of some old pickup he owned. But someone else could have told him."

"Do you think Travis could have killed your mother?" Cate asked bluntly.

She thought the abrupt question might

shock Kim, but Kim clasped her hands together and almost primly said, "The thought has occurred to me."

"Why would he do it?"

Kim's fingers worried a half inch of purple thread hanging from a seam on the pillow. "Mom and Travis never got along. As I said, she didn't want me to marry him. And she was so right. He never actually hit me, but I-I kept thinking he was going to. He broke some guy's elbow when they got in a fight. I know he made money buying and selling bikes, but sometimes it seemed as if he must be getting more somewhere else."

"Doing something illegal?"

"Probably."

"Was he into drugs?"

"I never knew him to use anything, but maybe that was just because I was dumb and naïve. He laughed about some guy he knew who made meth right in his kitchen. I always wondered if Travis helped sell the stuff."

"Did your mother know about his possible connection with drugs?"

"I don't know. Maybe."

They sat in silence for several moments, Kim's expression pensive.

"Could you tell me more about your mother?"

"She had a psychology practice where she saw clients at an office in Portland three times a week. She wrote her book, and it turned out to be really successful. Then she closed her office in Portland, moved down here, and opened the Mystic Mirage."

"Why did she close her office?"

"She said she got tired of driving into Portland all the time." Kim paused to think for a moment. "Once she said something about some clients being really unpleasant."

"Did she have a medical degree?"

"No. But she'd earned a doctorate degree from a special metaphysical college in the Midwest." A little defensively she added, "She had a right to put 'Doctor' in front of her name."

"Why didn't she open the Mystic Mirage in Tigard?"

"She said Eugene was bigger and more sophisticated. That there were more intellectual-type people here because of the university. She wanted me to leave Travis and come here with her right then, but Travis warned me no way was he letting me go. He always acted as if he . . . owned me." She swallowed. "Sometimes I had the feeling he'd rather see me dead than free from him."

Kim wasn't dead, but Ed and Celeste

were. Now that those obstacles were out of the way, did Travis have in mind reclaiming Kim? Or was she targeted as a third victim on his hit list?

"But he walked out on you anyway, even after he said he'd never let you go."

Kim smiled in a way that added a grim maturity to her face. "Travis never let logic clutter up his thinking."

Kim twisted the purple thread around her finger, tightening it like a noose until it cut into the skin. In some peculiar way, that reminded Cate of the hand tightening around her throat. She swallowed.

"Sometimes I wondered if Mom gave him money to leave me," Kim added.

"Would she do that?"

"She might have figured paying him off was the best way to get rid of him. And she had money from her book."

"So why would he have gotten in touch with her now?"

"I don't know that he did get in touch with her," Kim said, with another hint of defensiveness. "I mean, I thought it was him on the phone that time. But my feelings about people . . ." She shrugged and made a *phfft* sound about the accuracy of her own feelings. "Mom had real insights into people. Like how right she was about Travis, and how she could see into people's past lives too."

Kim apparently didn't doubt that there were past lives, or that her mother had the ability to delve into them.

"Even if he contacted your mother, why would he kill her?"

"Maybe he blamed her for breaking up our marriage. Maybe the money ran out, and she wouldn't give him any more. Maybe he turned even badder while he was gone."

Travis was a gun-packing kind of guy. Ed had been killed with a gun. A gun that, so far as Cate knew, had never been found. Which brought up a possibility, of course.

"Could Travis have killed your husband too?"

Kim made a choking sound as if her breath had caught in her throat. Cate realized this was a shocking but not totally new thought to Kim when she said, "Maybe."

"Why?" Although it wasn't a question Cate really needed to ask. The ex-husband viewed Kim as a possession. He had a violent temper. If he figured Ed Kieferson had taken something that belonged to him, he might well have gone into murder mode. "Have you told the police about him?"

"I didn't when Ed was killed. It never even

occurred to me then. But, since I thought he called Mom that time, I did tell them about him after . . . what happened to her."

"What did the authorities say?"

She yanked the purple thread, ripping the whole seam on the pillow. "Oh, you know the police. They don't tell you anything. They just ask questions."

"Do you have any other thoughts about who might have killed your husband? Business enemies, maybe?"

"I've wondered, since I found out about all the money problems Ed was having, if maybe he'd borrowed money from, I don't know, who is it that lends money and then kills you if you don't pay it back? The Mafia?"

Cate had never heard of a Eugene branch of the Mafia, but, who knew? That opened up a whole new arsenal of faceless suspects.

"Is it possible Ed was involved with drugs in some way?"

Cate expected instant denial, but what she got was Kim shifting uncomfortably on the sofa. "After he was killed, and I found out about all the money difficulties, I've wondered about . . . some things."

"Such as?"

"If maybe they were growing something other than grapes out there at the vineyard.

Maybe using those old buildings, barns or sheds or whatever they are. Pot growers sometimes grow stuff indoors, you know, using lights. Travis knew some people who grew marijuana in their basement that way."

"Ed wouldn't have been out there planting and watering pot plants himself. He'd have had to have someone in on it. Who?"

Kim gave a minuscule shrug, and Cate offered a name herself. "Rolf?"

"Rolf got in trouble on some pot-growing thing before Ed hired him."

"Rolf told you this? Or Ed?"

"I knew Rolf a long time ago, back when I was a kid. So we've talked a few times." She jumped up. "But if you're thinking there was something going on between Rolf and me, you're wrong! And I don't really think Ed was into any drug thing either." She slumped back to the sofa, her moment of fiery denial fizzling. "I mean, if he were, he wouldn't have had all those money troubles, would he?"

Probably true. Or maybe there were some guys who could lose money even growing or dealing drugs.

"Rolf also told me he was on probation, and I don't think he'd do anything to risk getting sent back. He said when he was locked up he felt as if he couldn't even breathe. As if the jail cell didn't have enough air to go around. But Ed was really mad at him about something. I think he was about to fire Rolf."

"But you don't know what the problem was?"

"They were pretty close when Ed first hired Rolf. Ed spent a lot of time out at the vineyard. He said they were planning to redo the whole vineyard and plant a different kind of grape. So I guess Ed just didn't like how Rolf was running the vineyard."

Rolf wasn't eliminated from Cate's suspicions, but he'd dropped down on her list. And she had one more question, maybe the most important question of all. "What does Travis look like?"

"Oh, tall. About six-two. Dark brown hair, brown eyes. He used to weigh about 210, but I don't know what he might be now."

The words could describe a lot of men, but one vision in particular jumped into Cate's mind.

A big, dark-haired, biker guy stalking into the Mystic Mirage as Cate barreled out.

"Does he have tattoos?"

"Oh yeah." Kim unexpectedly shuddered. "A big one of a dragon on his back that he got before we were married. And vines twined around hearts and skulls on his arms. I hated them all."

Another vision. A tattooed arm reaching for Cate's throat. Were there hearts and skulls on it? There was *something* in those swirls she'd seen. If she could just see the arm clearly . . .

"Do Travis and Rolf Wildrider look a lot alike?"

"Travis and Rolf?" Kim sounded surprised at the connection. She reflectively glanced up at the blue sky above the shades. "I guess, in a way they do. They're both big and dark-haired. But Rolf is, you know, kind of lean and lanky. Travis went in for a lot of body-building stuff, so he's really muscular. He's good-looking in a boyish kind of way, but Rolf has those smoldery good looks. They aren't guys you'd mistake for each other."

Except Cate was almost certain she had.

17

"Would you excuse me a minute?" Kim said. "I need to put on something warmer. I'm so cold."

Cate had never removed her jacket and now she realized why. It *was* cold in here. Was Kim more aware of expenses these days? Or simply forgetting about such mundane matters as turning up the thermostat? She disappeared around a solid wall at the far end of the room and returned wearing an oversized plaid jacket that looked as if it also may have been Ed's.

"Can you think of anyone other than Travis whom your mother might have planned to discuss with me?" Cate asked after Kim sat down and tucked her feet under her.

"Maybe Ed's ex-wife. Mom said she was greedy enough to do almost anything. She thought all along that the woman had killed Ed." Small, thoughtful pause as if Kim had accepted that assessment earlier but was reconsidering it now that Travis had resurfaced.

"I've met the former wife," Cate said carefully. "From what I saw, the breakup with Ed really devastated her for a while. She's a nice person, actually. Very creative at making those life-sized dolls, like the one she made of you. She certainly didn't strike me as dangerous."

Kim wiggled her toe through the hole in the sock. "Mom could put her own spin on things," she admitted. "But she always had my best interests at heart," she added almost fiercely.

"Have arrangements been made for her services yet?"

"No. I just haven't been able to decide what to do. Her body will go to a funeral home after the autopsy." She broke off as if the word conjured images she couldn't cope with. "Maybe it's already there. I don't know whether she should be buried here, or up in Portland where her parents are, or what."

Kim lifted the pillow and stared at it, as if she might find answers in the purple velvet. "I don't know why she didn't leave instructions." For the first time she sounded on the verge of resentment toward her mother.

"I'm sure you'll make the right decisions."

Kim gave a small, bleak smile. "If I do, it'll be the first time."

It was such a downbeat attitude, but no doubt understandable, given Kim's recent losses of both her husband and the mother on whom she'd been so dependent. Yet Cate suspected neither of them had ever done anything to help her develop the self-esteem or self-confidence she so badly needed now that she was alone. Cate wasn't sure she wanted to do this, wasn't sure she *should* do this, but she took a deep breath and said, "If there's anything I can do to help —"

Kim suddenly sat up straighter on the sofa. "You know, there is something we could do! Mom didn't keep a real day planner, but she wrote appointments and notes on a calendar in her apartment. Maybe she wrote something about an appointment with you and what it was about."

"Have the police been in her apartment?"

"Not that I know of. They're taking the Mystic Mirage apart like they're looking for lost atoms, but they've never said anything about the apartment. If you'd like, we could go over and look at her calendar. I haven't been there since Mom's . . . passing." She stumbled over the euphemism, as if she couldn't say "death" or "murder."

"Good idea," Cate said. "Afterward, we

can stop and get something to eat. You haven't been eating, have you?"

Kim looked around vaguely, as if eating were an unfamiliar concept. "I guess not."

"We can go in my car. I'll drive."

Cate thought Kim might want to change clothes or comb her hair, but she just pulled the plaid jacket tighter around her and headed for the door.

"Maybe you should put on some shoes."

Kim looked down at her feet. She seemed more surprised than embarrassed to see the toe-hole socks. She disappeared again, and this time came back wearing dressy slides that, along with the pink sweatpants and plaid jacket, made a rather odd fashion statement. The fashion police were apparently not on her list of worries now, and Cate liked her rather more for that.

Outside, at the car, Kim stopped suddenly. "Do I need to, um, hire you or something to do this?"

That brought Cate up short too. She already had a client, Jo-Jo. She couldn't take on another client whose interests might conflict with Jo-Jo's. But this case might be connected with Eddie the Ex's murder, which definitely involved Jo-Jo.

"That won't be necessary."

The apartment building where Celeste

had lived wasn't disreputable or ratty looking, but neither was it the upscale complex
Cate had expected. It was simply a single
oblong building, gray-green in color, each
unit with a tiny balcony. The landscaping
was minimal, and the asphalt parking lot
had odd bulges and bumps. Apparently
Celeste's book was no longer bringing in
big money, nor was the Mystic Mirage any
producer of wealth. Had Celeste been looking for something better for her daughter
when she targeted Ed Kieferson and his Ice
Cube house? Maybe thinking some financial
benefit would flow through to her?

Kim pointed to a corner unit on the
second floor. "That's Mom's."

Celeste's apartment stood out from the
others with colorful pots of flowers and a
climbing vine that formed a graceful green
frame around the balcony. A copper plaque
of a sun with fat rays, like those in the
window of the Mystic Mirage, hung in the
center.

There was an elevator, but they took the
stairs. No crime-scene tape barred the door
at 17B. Kim stuck a key in the lock and
opened the door.

Inside . . .

What Octavia had done to the brown-
haired wig, someone had done to the apart-

ment. Kim's mouth dropped open as she stared at the chaos, but nothing came out. Cate stepped around her.

Ripped sofa cushions, overturned floor lamp. A dining room chair flung against a wall, TV screen broken, a vase smashed, wilted chrysanthemums on the carpet. Beyond, in the kitchen, broken dishes and contents of fallen drawers strewed the floor, and the microwave door hung askew. In Celeste's office, papers scattered the desk and floor, and pieces of a broken computer monitor glittered in the carpet. The medicine cabinet in the bathroom had been swept bare, pills scattered everywhere. In the bedroom, the mattress had been pulled from the bed and overturned, clothes yanked from the closet, drawers dumped.

Kim turned slowly in the ravaged bedroom, like a limp doll caught in forces beyond her control.

Cate had heard that the police weren't into tidying things up after they searched a place, but this surely went far beyond police untidiness; this was destruction.

"We need to call the police," Cate said.

Kim didn't say anything. Cate had the impression her mind had simply stalled, as her own had there at the scene of Celeste's murder.

"I wonder how he got in?" Cate said. "The door was locked."

Kim blinked as if Cate's statement made no sense. "He, who?"

"Travis?" Cate suggested.

The name jerked Kim out of that lost space and lifted her into anger. "Travis," she repeated. "He could get in. He knew about picking locks! Some friend showed him. Just for fun, they said."

Had Travis been having "fun" here?

"But why would he do something like this?" Kim wilted back into mental bewilderment and made that slow rotation with her arms outstretched again. "Why would he break in here just to destroy everything?"

Cate made a surveying turn of her own. "I think he was looking for something." With destruction as a bonus. Or fury at not finding what he was looking for?

"Looking for what?" Kim asked.

Cate felt a twinge of impatience. Kim was the one who knew the guy, the one who'd been married to him. If anyone would know what Travis may have been looking for, it should be her.

"Who was the friend in Tigard you called to ask about Travis, the one who said he was looking for you?" Cate asked.

"Melissa Bair. She owns a house now, but

she lived in an apartment next to us, and we got to be pretty good friends."

"I don't suppose you can tell if anything's missing here?" Cate asked.

A useless question given the state of the apartment.

"I don't know what Travis, or anyone else, could steal here. Mom never kept much cash around. She dropped the Mystic Mirage's receipts off at the bank almost every day. She had some diamond earrings and lots of bracelets, but they were mostly those colorful bangle kind."

"A burglar wouldn't necessarily know that was all she had here," Cate pointed out. Celeste was the kind of woman who looked as if she owned expensive jewelry, even if she didn't.

"The only piece of jewelry she really cared about was that big crystal on a silver chain. I don't know that it was worth a lot, but she said it had 'special properties.' But it wouldn't be here, because she always wore it. The . . ." Kim swallowed convulsively. "The police gave it back to me."

A big crystal on a silver chain. Cate hadn't remembered seeing it that night at the Mystic Mirage. Her mind, too frozen by the shock of the murder and being attacked herself, had simply turned off details. But this detail had apparently been buried in her subconscious, because now it leaped into her conscious mind like a photo in 3-D. Celeste's slender throat. A delicate silver chain. A big crystal glittering there on Celeste's blood-stained ivory tunic. Right above the sword in her chest.

"Do you know where she kept her jewelry?"

"In a jewelry box here in the bedroom, I think."

Kim didn't help look for the box. She simply dropped to the edge of the bed and watched Cate probe around in the chaos. Cate came up with an empty, smashed box covered in blue velvet, and Kim nodded to identify it as the jewelry box. Poking further in the jumble on the floor, Cate found a few bracelet bangles, nothing that looked valuable. The burglar had apparently gotten the diamond earrings.

Which meant — what? Just a run-of-the-mill burglar enjoying a destructive fling in the process, especially if the loot hadn't lived up to his expectations?

Cate's PI intuition told her no, and this time she felt confident in the instinct. This was someone with a grudge against Celeste, someone who grabbed the diamond earrings while he was looking for something else. Travis.

Cate called 911. The woman first said, because it wasn't an emergency situation, that it might be a while before an officer could respond. When Cate pointed out that the vandalized apartment belonged to a recent murder victim, the woman said they'd get someone there as soon as possible.

Cate wandered back to the combination living/dining room while they waited. Sliding glass doors opened out onto the little balcony, and Cate could see now that neither the flowers nor climbing vine were real. Kim followed and plopped down on the sofa.

"When did you last talk to your mother?" Cate asked.

"I haven't been in the store since Ed was killed. So . . . I don't know. I guess that morning, probably. She called and wanted to know if I'd heard anything from the attorney about Ed's insurance."

"Had you?"

Kim shook her head. "She said she'd check on it with him for me. We found out after Ed was killed that his ex-wife gets the money from a big insurance policy, but we were hoping Ed had gotten another policy to protect me. But now that I'm learning about all his money problems, I doubt if he did that. I don't know how I'm going to manage without Mom."

No mention of Kim having problems getting along without Ed, Cate noted.

"I can't do it!" Kim hadn't cried before, but tears tumbled down her cheeks now. She brushed at them with a cuff of the plaid jacket in a harsh gesture that somehow seemed more angry and frustrated than grief-stricken. "I can't get along without Mom."

Cate wanted to stomp over to the sofa and shake Kim for such a negative attitude, but again she reminded herself of all Kim had lost. She started shoving kitchen drawers back into cabinets and putting utensils in them.

"Maybe you shouldn't do that," Kim said. "Maybe the police need to see everything the way we found it."

Good point. Cate moved just enough debris so she could sit on the other end of the sofa. Then she jumped up, realizing they hadn't even done what they'd come here for.

"Where's the calendar you said your mother kept her appointments and notes on?"

"In her office."

Surprisingly, the calendar still hung on the wall. The current month had a picture of a quaint-looking seaside village dozing under a Mediterranean sun. Cate flicked the pages. Various of the squares for the days of both past and future months indeed listed appointments and notes. None of them stood out as suspicious. Bridge club. Hair appointment. A book club reading. A couple of women's names and phone numbers that Kim thought had been appointments for past-lives regressions. Cate jotted the names and numbers in her notebook. The square for the day Celeste had met her death was empty.

"We'd made the appointment only the day before, so she probably just didn't bother to write it on here," Cate said.

Only now did something click in Kim's head. "I thought your appointment with Mom was one you didn't get to keep because she'd been killed. But you did keep the appointment, didn't you? You're the person who found Mom's body! Why didn't you tell me?"

"I'm a private investigator. My work is confidential." To ward off further questions, she added, "It isn't something I can talk about."

Kim stared at Cate for a moment, as if

she was thinking about challenging that answer, but finally she changed the subject abruptly.

"I think I'll make some tea. You probably think I don't even know how to make tea, don't you? That married to Ed, all I was supposed to do was sit around and look good. But I cooked and kept house and everything, back when I was married to Travis."

"About Travis," Cate said. "Do you really think he could have killed your mother and done all this because he blamed her for your marriage breaking up?"

"Travis could carry a grudge for a long time." Kim straightened an overturned chair in the dining area. "But I've been thinking while we've been sitting here. Mom was in Tigard not long before Travis disappeared. She was staying in a motel, not with us, because I was afraid if she was at our place Travis might start throwing frying pans or something at her. I thought that was when she might have paid him to get out of my life. But I'm wondering now if she did it some other way."

"Such as?"

"Maybe she knew something incriminating about him. Something bad enough to get him in real trouble. And she told him he'd better just walk away or she'd use it against him."

"Blackmail?"

Kim's delicate brows drew together in a frown, as if she objected to the bluntness of that word. But she finally said, "I guess that's what it would be called, wouldn't it? But she must have had proof, or he'd have ignored her."

Right. Some kind of proof that he'd been searching for here in the apartment. Tearing the place apart in fury. Or frustration? Had he killed Celeste and then come here to the apartment to find that proof, so it wouldn't turn up later to trap him? Or had he come here to search and then gone to the Mystic Mirage and killed her? Had he looked for that proof, whatever it was, there in Celeste's office?

No, he hadn't had time. Because Cate had interrupted. And if Mitch hadn't been there backing her up, she'd have been dead right along with Celeste.

Once more Kim turned slowly to survey the destruction. "I wonder if he found it?"

Good question.

An officer finally called Cate's cell phone. He said no one would be able to come until the following day. They made an appointment to meet him at the apartment at 3:00 the following afternoon.

On the way back to the Ice Cube, Cate tried to get Kim to stop for something to eat, but Kim said she wasn't hungry.

"I've been putting on weight anyway." She prodded a slim thigh with a finger. "Mom said I'd better start taking it off."

Mom, the guiding force behind everything Kim did.

"Don't forget to put your shoes on in the morning," Cate muttered.

They arranged to meet outside the apartment building just before 3:00 the next afternoon. Just an hour before that, Cate thought of something and called Kim.

"I was wondering, do you still have any photos of Travis around?"

"I might." Kim sounded cautious, as if she wasn't sure she wanted to admit to a secret stash of ex-husband photos.

"Could you bring them along? I think the officer might find them useful."

Cate also wanted to see photos of Travis Beauchamp for herself.

Unexpectedly, Kim laughed. "I can do better than that," she said almost gaily. "See you at 3:00."

The hot red Mustang stood in the parking lot when Cate arrived. Kim slid out of the passenger's side. A male figure got out of the driver's side.

Cate momentarily thought it was Rolf. Big, dark-haired, muscular guy. Then she took a second look. Not Rolf. Kim was right. There were definitely similarities, but, up close, you wouldn't mistake the two men for each other.

But here? Now? Cate glanced at Kim in disbelief. Hey, girl, what are you *thinking*?

Kim made blithe introductions. Cate Kinkaid — Travis Beauchamp.

Cate's skin prickled. She saw a malicious eye behind a beaded curtain, a tattooed arm reaching for her. An arm that was close enough to reach out and grab her again.

Cate wanted to get Kim alone and hammer her with questions. What is he doing here with you? Why are you smiling at him?

But that wasn't going to happen because a city police car was already pulling into a space on the opposite side of the parking lot. Reluctantly Cate followed Kim and her ex-husband across the asphalt to meet the officer.

18

Kim gave the officer background information as they went up to the apartment. Cate had expected to have to do the talking, but Kim seemed more in charge today, as if Travis's presence had given her confidence. She had identified him to the officer as a "family friend from out of town." Cate had thought the officer might object to Travis accompanying them to the apartment, but he hadn't said anything. Travis had little to say, but he seemed congenial and polite.

If Kim hadn't already told her about the fist through the wall, the frying pan through the window, his possessiveness, and the possible drug dealing, Cate might have thought Travis really was a helpful family friend. His sleeves were turned back on this pleasant fall day, revealing a couple of red hearts and black skulls within a tangle of varicolored vines.

Was that the arm she'd seen that night at

the Mystic Mirage? Maybe it was. And maybe it wasn't. Cate just wasn't certain. No matter how hard she concentrated, all she could pick up from that terrifying encounter was a vague vision of swirly lines. Although she was positive Travis's arm wasn't one she'd want to see every day over breakfast.

The officer had a portable kit for picking up latent fingerprints. Cate had to explain that hers would be in the apartment because she'd earlier touched a number of items, a fact that earned her a grunt of disapproval from the officer. She kept a hawk eye on Travis as the officer dusted a grayish powder over various surfaces, wondering if he'd be nervous about his own fingerprints showing up, but he seemed unconcerned. Which might only mean that he'd been wearing gloves when he ransacked the apartment and smugly knew the officer wasn't going to find anything that incriminated him.

The officer spent a good hour and a half in the apartment talking to them. He didn't specifically say so, but Cate got the impression he doubted Celeste Chandler's murder and the ransacking of the apartment were connected. He suggested the possibility that the burglar was some lowlife who kept track of reported deaths and used them as his personal reference guide for break-ins. The officer said he intended to talk to other tenants in the building. He also said the police investigation of the Mystic Mirage had been completed, and Kim could go back on the premises now.

After they headed back to their cars, Cate suggested she and Kim go over to the Mystic Mirage and check things out there. It was a lame attempt to get Kim alone to ask her questions, and Travis easily defeated it.

"I could go along and help. But we should go to the funeral home, don't you think?" He touched Kim's elbow lightly. "Get that taken care of?" He sounded concerned about her welfare, solicitous of the strain on her.

"Travis has been helping me decide what would be best for Mom," Kim said. She looked up at him. "Yes, let's do that now. I'll feel better with that worry off my mind. We've decided on cremation," she added to Cate. "No services. We'll sprinkle the ashes out at the vineyard in a private ceremony of our own."

Cate got it now. Got it with a big dose of dismay and apprehension. Kim had been lost without either Celeste or Ed to tell her what to do, and Travis had instantly slithered into that influential job. Right now, he'd managed not only to keep Cate from getting Kim alone, he'd also smoothly cut Cate out completely.

Cate was momentarily inclined to walk off and leave Kim to her gullibility or whatever it was, but a frustrating concern for the vulnerable woman kept her from doing so. She couldn't just leave Kim in the clutches of a killer. Finally she decided there was no way to be subtle about this.

"Kim, could I talk to you for a minute? Alone," she emphasized. Cate thought for a moment that Travis was going to jump in and veto that. His hands balled into fists. She tossed out a diverting statement. "I really need your help with something."

Kim looked up at Travis again. His glance at Cate narrowed, but he apparently decided protest would look suspicious, and stepped back. Or maybe he was already confident enough of his hold on Kim. Cate led Kim over to the far side of some straggly but head-high bushes.

"Kim, what is going on here?" she whispered frantically. "I can't believe this. Yesterday you were convinced Travis may have killed both your mother and Ed, and trashed her apartment too. And today you're taking his advice about cremating her?"

"I thought you needed help on something."

"I do! I need help understanding what you're doing!"

"I can see why you might have reservations about Travis." Kim spoke with an I'm-trying-to-be-patient note in her voice, as if Cate were just too dense to understand. "I did too, when he called me last night from Tigard —"

"How do you know he was calling from Tigard? On a cell phone, he could have been standing here in this parking lot."

"I thought of that," Kim admitted. "But when he got here this morning, he had flowers for me. They were from a florist's shop in Tigard. My favorites, anthurium, from Hawaii."

If Travis had staged a couple of murders, he could certainly stage the production of flowers that looked as if they'd come from a florist's shop in Tigard. And remembering Kim's favorite flowers. A nice touch.

"Anyway, we talked and talked last night when he called, and we've been talking ever since he got here this morning."

"So just like that, you're jumping into a hot new romance with him?"

"Of course not!" Kim's eyes flashed as if that suggestion both shocked and offended her. "I'm still in mourning for my husband. Travis is just trying to help out. He told me how sorry he is about everything. He's changed, Cate, he really has."

Okay, people could change. Cate could grant that. But she wasn't yet ready to jump on Travis's bandwagon. The ex-husband may be saying he'd changed, but the difference between saying it and actually doing it was like the difference between misdemeanor and murder.

"Did he tell you why he left you? Or where he's been? Or why he came back?"

"He left because he just got tired of the responsibility of marriage and wanted out. It was as simple as that. Now he realizes how immature that was, and he's ashamed of himself. He also says he was really stupid. That he was too dumb to realize what he had when he had it."

"And now he wants to jump back into the role of husband?"

"No! I told you. We're not into some instant romance. He's been down in Guatemala. But the buddies he knew who'd gone down there were living like jungle rats while they grew pot. He found out he doesn't want anything to do with that kind of life. He says he got lost out in the jungle one time, lost for ten days out there alone, and it changed him. Straightened out his priorities. He came back to Oregon because he's different now, and his life is going to be different too."

For Kim's sake, Cate hoped that Travis's claim to change was real. But the hope was pockmarked with a dread that if Travis was the killer Cate thought he was, Kim might be risking her life in accepting his claim.

"How long has he been back?"

"He worked down in California for a while after he left Guatemala, so he's only been in Tigard for a couple months."

"Long enough ago for him to make that call to your mother."

"That wasn't him. I asked. He didn't know anything about any phone call. Like I told you, I felt like it was him on the phone with Mom that time, but my feelings about most things are about as reliable as infomercials. It must have been some salesman on the phone that day, just like Mom said. Travis didn't find out until just a couple days ago that I was here in Eugene."

Kim asked. Travis denied. Kim believed.

Which meant she was also believing he couldn't have been involved in either Ed or Celeste's deaths, because he hadn't known where Kim was until a couple of days ago.

Cate wanted to pound Kim the way Kim

had pounded that purple pillow back at the house. *Wake up, girl. Smell the lies!* Frustrated, she asked, "What does he plan to do now?"

Cate was thinking in terms of the next few days, but Travis had already filled Kim with loftier plans.

"He's realized he needs more education," she said. "He's thinking, if he can find a job here, he could start taking classes at the university."

"Classes in what?"

"I don't know." Kim sounded impatient with these picky details. "Maybe architecture or social work, something like that. Something worthwhile."

"That's a rather wide area, from architecture to social work," Cate pointed out.

Kim waved a hand, as if this were irrelevant. "I just know he's already been a big help in deciding what to do about Mom. He says maybe I should go back to school too."

Kill Celeste and then kindly jump in to help decide what to do with the body. Way to go, Travis.

"Kim, don't do this! You can make decisions on your own. You don't have to have someone tell you what to do. Maybe you *should* go back to school. But decide it for yourself. You're not dumb." Naïve about men, maybe, but not dumb.

Look who's talking, Cate had to remind herself. Before good-guy Mitch came along, her past had included a fair number of frogs who hadn't a clue about turning into princes.

"I remember back to a decision I made on my own," Kim said with a certain defiance.

"Marrying Travis."

"A very dumb, very bad decision," Kim said.

"So you think letting him help and advise you now is a good decision?"

Kim managed a smile. "I know. That sounds, um, a little muddleheaded, doesn't it? But we were both so young back then, and we've matured now. He's changed, and I need his help. Neither of us is thinking romance now."

Kim turned, circled the bush, and headed back toward the Mustang and Travis. Kim might not think Travis had romance on his mind. Cate thought otherwise.

The even bigger worry was, what else was on Travis Beauchamp's mind?

On the way home, Cate pulled over to the curb and did a quick search with her cell phone for a number for Melissa Bair in Tigard. She expected voice mail, answering machine, a delay of some kind, but instead a woman answered on the third ring. She sounded harried even in her one-word hello.

"Hi. Is this Melissa Bair?"

Cate had a feeling the woman would prefer to say "maybe" rather than "yes," wary of what the call was about. Instead the woman detoured answering the question by saying, "And this is?"

"Cate Kinkaid. I'm a private investigator here in Eugene. I'm not investigating you or collecting a bill or trying to sell you something," she added quickly. "I'd just like to talk to you. But if this is a busy time, I can call again later."

"With three kids under five, it's always a busy time," Melissa said. Curiosity, however, apparently outweighed the busyness. Or maybe hearing from a private investigator was preferable to a call from a bill collector. "What did you want to talk to me about?"

"A situation has come up concerning Travis Beauchamp. I believe he was a former neighbor, and you knew his wife Kim too?"

"You said you're a private investigator?"

"Well, uh, an assistant private investigator, actually," Cate said. Sometimes she wished honesty about that minor detail wouldn't kick in at inopportune moments.

"Travis has done something that needs investigating, no doubt. What do you need to know?"

"Travis came to you awhile back because he was trying to locate Kim. Could you tell me exactly when he contacted you?"

"Well, let's see. Aaron broke his tooth about three weeks ago, and it was quite a while before that. Maybe when he put the mustache on Tiffany with a marking pen, and I had to — no, I remember now. It was the day Tiffany tried to flush my *Cosmo* magazine down the toilet. Which would make it right about six weeks. I paid the plumber's bill just yesterday."

Motherhood made for a different time line for keeping track of events, Cate realized, but it sounded like an accurate system. Six weeks. That would definitely put Travis's contact with Melissa back before Celeste got that phone call at the Mystic Mirage. Before Ed Kieferson was killed too.

"I was thinking at the time maybe I should call Kim and tell her Travis had been snooping around, looking for her, but I couldn't find a phone listing for her or her mother. I didn't know then that she'd remarried."

"Did you see what kind of vehicle he was driving?"

"Motorcycle."

"With high handlebars?"

"High handlebars? Hey, come to think of it, that's exactly what they were. The kind where your hands are up higher than your shoulders. They look about as comfortable as trying to chin yourself while riding a bike. Tiffany Jean, stop that!" she yelled. A clunk and then a few moments of silence on the phone before Melissa returned. "Sorry about that. Tiff was trying to put our new puppy in the crib with the baby. Where were we? Oh yeah — I knew both Kim and her mother were down there in Eugene, but you can bet your diapers I didn't tell Travis that. He was bad news back when they lived in the apartment next door to us, and I figure he's still bad news."

"Someone else could have told him?"

"Oh, sure. Some of his sleazy buddies are still around, and they probably knew. Is he down there making trouble for Kim? I hope not. When she called me, which was after Travis had been here trying to find out where she was, she said she'd gotten married again."

Even though both Ed's and Celeste's deaths had been big news in Eugene, that importance hadn't carried statewide. At least the information hadn't blipped on

Melissa's radar.

"Both Kim's husband and her mother have recently met their deaths under suspicious circumstances, so Kim is going through a very bad time now."

"Oh no! Poor Kim." With no pause for introspection, Melissa immediately added, "And Travis was involved?"

As if, if there were trouble, and Travis was in the vicinity, it was a foregone conclusion that he was involved.

"No one has been arrested yet."

"You know," Melissa said, "now that I think about it, Travis asked about Celeste first. Then, when I wouldn't tell him anything about her, he gave me that song-and-dance about Kim's name being on the title of some old pickup, and he had to find her. But now that you say something happened to Celeste, his asking about her first strikes me as odd."

Yes. Odd. Of course, Travis may have figured if he found out where Celeste was, that would also lead him to Kim. Maybe he just hadn't wanted to admit an interest in his ex-wife. And then, maybe it was Celeste he really wanted to find.

Why?

"Do you know what Travis has been doing since he got back to Tigard?"

"Actually, I don't think he was here very long. I never saw him again. I figured he'd just slunk back into his dark hole under a rock, or wherever he came from, but maybe he's been down there in Eugene."

Maybe that's exactly where Travis had been. And still was. Pulling Kim into another trap.

Back home, Cate looked in her notebook for the names and phone numbers she'd copied off Celeste's calendar. Uncle Joe and Rebecca weren't home. With Cate handling much of Belmont Investigations's work, they'd taken to helping with renovations on the church or going to yard sales, even an afternoon movie now and then.

An answering machine picked up on the call to the first number, listed on Celeste's calendar as D. Dustinhoff, and a woman's perky voice said, "I can't come to the phone right now. Maybe that means I'm off on a honeymoon in the Caribbean! Maybe I'm hiding in the next room, paranoid about this strange machine that keeps ringing! Maybe I'm having a romantic interlude and don't want to be interrupted! Leave a number, and if you're one of today's lucky chosen few, I'll get back to you. Have a nice day!"

When the machine beeped, Cate, feeling

as if she'd inadvertently stepped into the world of the strange and loony, hung up without leaving a message. Although this did sound like someone who'd gleefully romp around in previous lives.

On the second call, Cate was relieved to hear a nice, everyday, "Hello."

19

Cate identified herself as a private investigator and said she needed to talk to a woman named Susan Linderman.

"About what?"

Now the woman didn't sound quite so nice. The question bristled with hostility, as if Cate had instantly hit a hotline to her nerves.

"Is this Susan Linderman?"

Silence, as if the woman was undecided about admitting anything, although the silence itself told Cate this was the woman she was looking for. She went on as if the woman had agreed that yes, she was Susan Linderman.

"You may have heard about the recent death of a local woman, Dr. Celeste Chandler?"

"Yes, I saw it in the newspaper." She sounded wary, but reluctantly interested.

"I'm involved in a private investigation of

her death, and I understand you had an appointment with her within the last couple of months?"

"Who told you that?"

"In the course of my investigation, I found your name and number in her records."

"How do I know who you are? You could be her killer. I don't have to talk to you!" Mrs. Linderman's blustery voice held an undercurrent of panic.

"Of course you don't have to talk to me," Cate soothed. "But I'd be so grateful if you would. I'd be glad to show you my identification and talk to you in person." Cate half-expected an instant hang-up, but to her surprise Susan Linderman wilted almost instantly.

At the end of a sigh, she said, "I probably should talk to someone." She sounded resigned now, as if it was actually not a surprise someone had surfaced to interrogate her. "I thought about calling the authorities, but then . . ." Her voice drifted off, apparently lost in lack of any good reason she hadn't contacted them.

So what was the reason she should have contacted them? Cate felt a shiver of excitement. Susan Linderman knew something!

"May I come over now?"

"Yes, I guess so." Mrs. Linderman gave an

address, again with that aura of resignation.

Cate Googled the address, and the map took her to an area of modest older homes on the west side of town. She momentarily wondered if Susan Linderman's name had been on Celeste's calendar for some reason other than a regression-into-past-lives session. Somehow she expected a person interested in past lives would occupy a house more esoteric than this ordinary gray, ranch style with a neat chain-link fence surrounding a children's slide and swing set and a flock of pink plastic flamingos.

Past-middle-aged Susan Linderman opened the door before Cate even rang the bell. "I'd, uh, like to see some identification," she said. Her demand tried for belligerence but didn't make it past uncertainty, and Cate suspected a library card would get a nervous nod of okay.

She wore blue slacks with an elastic waistband, pink blouse, old tennies, and an apron. Cate couldn't remember when she'd last seen an apron. The woman apparently noticed Cate's glance at it because she added, "I've been making peanut butter cookies for my grandson. He comes here after school every day."

"I'm sure he appreciates that." Cate offered a Belmont Investigations card and also opened her wallet to a driver's license as identification.

Both could have said Cate Kinkaid, Hired Killer, Discount for Senior Citizens, for all the care Mrs. Linderman took in examining them. She'd obviously just been going through the motions trying to make Cate think she wasn't as nervous about this interview as she was.

"Okay, come on in. We can have some cookies. And tea. Would you like orange-cinnamon delight? Or apple spice?"

Cate had the feeling making tea would help put the woman at ease. "Orange cinnamon would be great."

"Come on in the kitchen then."

Cate followed the woman into a cozy room that reminded her of Jo-Jo Kieferson's country-house kitchen. White cabinets, family photos plastered on the refrigerator, old-fashioned iron skillet on the stove, plastic-topped table. A scent of freshly baked cookies fluttered angel wings over the mundane room and furnishings.

When the tea was ready, Mrs. Linderman started to load a tray to take to the living room, but Cate stopped her. "Let's stay right here in the kitchen. It's so nice and cozy."

Mrs. Linderman took off her apron, and

they sat at the kitchen table. Her tennies shuffled the floor, and she studied her tea as if it held secrets of the universe. Cate nibbled a cookie and remained silent, hoping the woman would feel a necessity to fill the silence with something. It worked.

"This is about my taking that stuff when I went into my past lives, isn't it? Dr. Chandler said it was okay, just a mild relaxant. But . . ." Mrs. Linderman started to pick up her cup, but her shaky hand sloshed tea into the saucer. She jumped up to rip a paper towel off the holder and sop up the spill.

"I'm looking into all aspects of Dr. Chandler's life." Cate carefully kept both her comment and tone neutral, although what she wanted to do was yell, "What stuff?"

"I didn't murder her!"

"I'm sure you didn't," Cate agreed.

Mrs. Linderman sank back into the chair. "I didn't want to take anything. I told her that. But I just couldn't seem to relax enough to get hypnotized, so she said that was the way she'd have to do it. She wanted me to take it with some red wine, but I never drink, not even wine. Duane's father was an alcoholic, so he was dead set against anything alcoholic. So then she said we could use whatever I had on hand, and what I had was root beer, so I went to the fridge and got a can of that. But I still felt uneasy about it."

"This was supposed to relax you to where you could be hypnotized? Or was whatever she was giving you supposed to take the place of hypnosis and put you in the same sort of state?"

"I'm not sure." Mrs. Linderman gave a nervous titter. "Actually, it felt kind of, oh, frivolous, delving into the — I don't know, secrets of the universe? — with a glass of root beer in my hand."

"She didn't say what she was giving you?" Cate asked.

"No. She just said, didn't I ever take a sleeping pill? And I said, well, yes, sometimes I did. I've had trouble sleeping ever since Duane passed away four years ago. She said this was no different than about half a sleeping pill."

"I see," Cate said. She didn't want to let on that she still had no idea what the woman was talking about. She did remember now that Robyn's aunt had said Celeste wanted to give her something, but she'd refused to take it. "Dr. Chandler gave you a pill?"

"No, she mixed something in the root beer."

"Was what she used a powder or liquid?"

"I didn't see. She had this big tote bag. It's funny, I can't remember much, but I remember that bag so clearly. It was a beautiful tapestry material, with golden threads woven in, and leather handles."

"You say you can't remember much. Do you mean you can't remember much about Dr. Chandler, or the past-lives session, or . . . ?"

"It all just seems so . . . far away. Except I remember her lighting this candle that smelled so heavenly. And she drank a glass of red wine herself. The prettiest wine, like a red jewel."

"Where did she get the wine?" Cate asked.

"She must have brought it in that bag. Anyway, I started feeling happy and kind of oh, maybe a little tipsy. Or what I think tipsy is like, because I've never *been* tipsy. Then everything just kind of fades away, and I don't remember anything more until I woke up."

"It put you to sleep?"

"Well, I guess. Kind of. I mean, I woke up. I couldn't remember anything. But I didn't really feel as if I'd been *asleep*. It was more like I'd just lost a stretch of time.

Maybe she hypnotized me after I got relaxed, and that's how you feel after you've been hypnotized."

"So you didn't go into any past lives?"

"Oh, I went into past lives all right!" Mrs. Linderman's face lit up as if an interior bulb had turned on. "I've lived some interesting lives."

"But if you don't remember anything —"

"But I talked up a storm! Dr. Chandler took notes. She said I talked so fast she could hardly keep up with me. All this fascinating information about a life I was living way back in ancient times. I was wearing clothes made of wolf and bear skins, and I carried my baby in a sling made of the special soft skin of some unborn animal. She said I kept stroking the air as if I were actually feeling that soft skin and murmuring to my baby."

Cate made some noncommittal murmurs of her own.

"And then I lived another life when it just rained and rained, and everything started to flood. We decided afterward that that must have been during Noah's time, when he was building the ark!" Mrs. Linderman smiled, as if she was delighted with having been a contemporary of Noah's. "Then I lived in Egypt once, a very hard life, making bricks with straw in them. That sounds like Moses's time, doesn't it?"

"Quite a variety of lives," Cate murmured.

"I also told her about a life when I came across the plains in a covered wagon. I've always been interested in that era." Mrs. Linderman nodded, as if having lived in that era explained why she had an interest in it now.

"You really think Dr. Chandler took you back to these past lives?" Cate said.

"Of course." Mrs. Linderman sounded surprised at the skepticism in Cate's question. "I still have her notes."

"Could I see them?"

"Oh, they're such a treasure I wouldn't dare keep them here. They're in my safe deposit box."

A satisfied customer.

"But I'm still not sure we should be messing around with some things," Mrs. Linderman fretted. "Duane wouldn't approve."

She glanced at a blue vase on a corner shelf — Duane's final resting place? — as if she were afraid he might pop out and wag a disapproving finger.

"He wouldn't approve of the past lives thing, or the relaxant?" Cate asked.

Mrs. Linderman hesitated and finally, like a child who's been caught at something, sighed and said, "Probably both."

"Why did you do it?"

"A friend knows a woman who found out that she'd died rescuing a girl back when the Romans were feeding Christians to the lions. She said it 'opened up new vistas' for her, knowing she'd been a heroine back then." Mrs. Linderman's smile turned self-conscious. "I figured I needed some new vistas in my life. I seem to plod along in the same old rut day after day."

"Do you feel as if new vistas opened for you?"

"Um, well, I guess not," she admitted. She glanced toward the vase again. "Duane would say that it was all phony-baloney. That was a word he used. Phony-baloney. So once in a while I wonder if I was just . . . spouting nonsense."

And maybe she hadn't spouted anything. Maybe Dr. Celeste Chandler had busily scribbled fake notes while her client lay in a silent semi-coma induced by something she'd given her.

"Dr. Chandler charged for these, um, services?" Cate asked.

"Four hundred dollars. That's a lot of money, but what bothers me more is that stuff she put in my root beer."

"You think it may have been something

harmful?"

"I think it was something illegal," Mrs. Linderman said flatly. "And that's why you're here."

This was the crux of her worries when Cate had called, Cate realized. Mrs. Linderman was afraid Cate might be coming with handcuffs and a prison jumpsuit because she'd taken some illegal drug.

"What makes you think it was illegal?"

"I've had pain pills when I hurt my back. I've had tranquilizers and antidepressants when I was so down after Duane died. I have to take a sleeping pill once in a while since then too. But that stuff she gave me . . ." She shook her head. "It was different. It was like it just cancelled out time."

Cate didn't particularly feel like defending Celeste. The woman's excursions into past lives struck her as phonier than the brown wig Octavia had demolished, and Celeste couldn't do prescription drugs if that "Doctor" degree wasn't a real MD degree. But maybe she'd found some way to circumvent that.

"It may have been a legal relaxant you've simply never taken before," Cate said.

"It was something illegal," Mrs. Linderman repeated. "She was murdered, wasn't she? Right when I heard about it, first thing

I thought was that it was a drug dealer or someone like that who did it."

"Do you think she knew it was illegal?"

"Dr. Chandler was a very caring person." Her face brightened. "If she was using something illegal, it was only because she needed it to help people. But if she got mixed up with drug dealers . . . Well, murders and drug wars and drive-by shootings, that's what those drug people do, isn't it? I hope they get whoever killed her."

Cate had to wonder how Celeste had apparently gotten away with this for a considerable time. Perhaps because people expected to be in some altered state with hypnosis, and simply accepted Celeste's explanations.

"I've always expected that someday the authorities would come after me for taking something illegal." Mrs. Linderman was now back to resignation about her future.

Cate patted her hand. "I don't think you have any cause for worry. Even if it was an illegal substance, you didn't know that when you took it."

"What's that old saying? Ignorance of the law is no defense. Or excuse. Something like that." A burden of guilt obviously weighed heavily on Susan Linderman's shoulders. "But I feel better now that I've

307

told you. I'm willing to take my punishment."

"Mrs. Linderman —"

"Susan."

"Susan, you seem to have some familiarity with Noah and Moses in the Old Testament of the Bible?"

"Duane was never one for going to church, but he liked me to read to him after his eyes got bad. Sometimes he wanted to hear something out of the Bible." She tilted her head. "Sometimes he wanted Stephen King or Tom Clancy."

"Try reading in the book of John in the New Testament. And Romans. They'll help you understand what comes after this life. God cares, you know. And you can contact him without having anything in your root beer."

"Maybe I'll do that."

Now Cate had to figure out what to do. Report this to the police herself? She couldn't think Susan Linderman needed punishment for anything she'd taken. Could Celeste's use of an illegal drug have any connection with Ed Kieferson's death?

Should she ask Kim if she knew anything about what her mother used to deal with hard-to-hypnotize clients? Another thought occurred to her. Was the reason Celeste had never done a past-lives regression on Kim because she didn't want to give her own daughter some illegal drug?

20

Back home, Cate wrote up notes about the interview with Susan Linderman to add to her growing file. She called the hair salon, but her replacement wig hadn't come in yet. Only one more week until the wedding next Friday night. Octavia had been staring at her while she made the call.

"You're lucky Robyn didn't want white hair, or I might be wearing yours on my head," Cate said. Octavia ignored her and batted at the phone. Cate pointed out that she wasn't expecting any calls, but the cat kept staring at the phone.

And Octavia was right again. The office phone rang only a moment later, just as the notes were spewing out of the printer.

"Coincidence," Cate mouthed at the cat before she said aloud, "Belmont Investigations. Assistant Investigator Cate Kinkaid speaking."

"My caller ID shows I had a call from this

number. So I'm calling now to find out why Belmont Investigations is interested in me. It's not every day I get a call from a private investigator! In fact, I've never had a call from an investigator. I'm all in a dither! If you could see me, you'd see I'm goose-bumpy all over."

"This is D. Dustinhoff?"

"It is. Destiny Dustinhoff. Although, if you're investigating, you probably already know that the name my parents gave me is Diane. But the name we're given is not necessarily our Destiny — so I changed mine! Dustinhoff really is my last name. Not that it's so great, but it is the original. I took it back after I gave Pinocchio Paul his walking papers."

"Pinocchio Paul?" Cate repeated doubtfully.

"You know. The creepy little wooden guy whose nose grew when he told lies? Given ol' Paul's creative talent for lies, it's a wonder he didn't need a wheelbarrow to carry his nose in."

Cate hid how taken back she was by this barrage of unasked-for information by muttering her all-purpose "um."

"So, why did you call me? Am I on a terrorist list of OOWs?"

Again all Cate could do was repeat her

caller's peculiar words. "OOWs?"

"Outrageous Older Women. Although I really think of myself as a GYT."

Cate didn't want to ask what that meant. She refused to ask. But the next words out of her mouth were a repetition of the letters. "GYT?"

"Gorgeous Young Thing, of course." Destiny Dustinhoff sounded victorious. "You're not the Belmont of Belmont Investigations?"

Cate repeated her identity. "Right now, I'm investigating the death of a local woman, Dr. Chandler, and I found your name —" Cate broke off and tried again. "I mean, I'm investigating another murder, a different murder, and this death seems to be connected with that, and then —"

Cate broke off again. Now she was rattling on like Diane Destiny Dustinhoff herself. Maybe it was an infection, virulently contagious even over the phone, and next she'd be telling the woman how she became an assistant private investigator, how she had this deaf white cat who'd wrecked her wig and knew when the phone was going to ring, and her favorite guy had just rattled her cage by getting a motorcycle. Although it didn't have ape hanger handlebars.

She took a deep breath and tried for brisk

professionalism. "I understand you had a recent meeting with a Dr. Celeste Chandler."

"Yeah, and now she's dead. That's kind of spooky. And I'm dead serious about that. Uh-oh. That didn't come out right. Dead serious, get it?"

Got it. Didn't care for it.

"I understand Dr. Chandler did some kind of sessions that were supposed to bring up memories of lives you've lived before. A past-lives regression, I believe it's called."

"Right. I had great past lives. I was the palace spy for a queen back when an ol' Egyptian pharaoh was building himself a pyramid, and Queenie was afraid he might be going to stuff her in it and take up with the court bimbo. I was a dancer in some other exotic court, a real dynamo with the swirling veils and diamond in the belly button. But once, back in the Wild West days, I was hung."

Cate didn't want to ask, but curiosity overrode the reluctance. "What did you do to get hung?"

"Stole this fantastic horse named Midnight Meteor that could run like the wind! I was a man in that life. We aren't always the same, you know. There were some other lives and deaths too, if you'd like to hear

313

about them?"

"I think these are sufficient to give me an idea of what Dr. Chandler was doing."

One thing Celeste did, Cate could see, was recycle time periods. She researched something such as ancient Egypt, and then everyone just happened to have an old Egyptian past life.

"What did you think of the experience?" Cate asked.

"It was, oh, you know, kind of like going to a fortune-teller, except instead of going forward to what's going to happen, you go backwards."

"You don't take it all too seriously, then?"

"I'm not sure I believe it. But I'm not sure I don't believe it, either. I keep an open mind about all things!"

An open mind could be a good thing. Or a flytrap for any weird idea sailing around the universe.

"Do you remember telling Dr. Chandler about your lives as you were experiencing them, or did she report to you afterward what you'd said?"

"You think the doc was a big quack, don't you?"

"I'm just investigating the death. What I really need to find out is, did Dr. Chandler hypnotize you? Or give you something that put you in a kind of hypnotic state?"

"Is that what this is about? Like maybe she gives you some drug to get you hooked, then she goes for the big bucks by supplying you with it?"

Cate gave Diane Destiny Dustinhoff credit for an active imagination. This particular thought had never occurred to Cate. Could Celeste have been selling more than candles and books and astrological earrings there at the Mystic Mirage?

"Anyway, she didn't give me anything. I can get hypnotized at the drop of a Frito. Zing! At a party one time, this guy was fooling around with hypnosis, and I was the one who got hypnotized when he was trying to do someone else. Then he gave me this posthypnotic suggestion that whenever I heard the words 'What time is it?' I'd start doing a Lady Gaga imitation. I'm pretty good at it too. Though it doesn't always work now." She sounded disappointed.

Talking to Destiny Dustinhoff, Cate decided, was like carrying on a conversation with a chatty tornado. And you never knew which way the wind might blow.

"Could she have slipped something into a drink, and you didn't know it?"

"I didn't eat or drink anything while she was there."

So, Celeste hypnotized if she could, helped things along with a dose of something if she couldn't, or if she was in a hurry.

"Do you know anyone else who went into a past-lives regression with Dr. Chandler?"

"Yeah, my friend Pam did it. You know, come to think of it, Pam said Dr. Chandler gave her a glass of wine to help her relax. And she thought there was something in the wine."

"She could taste something?"

"I don't remember about that. Anyway, whatever it was, Pam blamed us, because we'd, oh, you know, kind of pushed her into going to Dr. Chandler. I was hoping the doc would give her some posthypnotic suggestion to loosen her up a little. Maybe have her get a whole new wardrobe of miniskirts. Or pole dance around a tree in the park."

"Um," Cate muttered.

"But the whole thing really upset Pam. She said it made her feel as if she'd fallen into a black hole. She couldn't remember a thing. She said Dr. Chandler could have made her tell secrets that were none of the doctor's business. Although Pam is so prim and prissy that I figured her deepest secret couldn't be more than hiding her broccoli under a napkin instead of eating it when she was a little girl."

"How long was she in this 'black hole'?"

"She didn't say. But I don't know that it was really as bad as she said. Pam is kind of . . . well, we call her Paranoid Pam, if that tells you anything. She quit taking some vitamins because she thought the company was putting something addictive in them."

Not your most reliable witness, perhaps. Cate asked the question anyway. "Could you tell me how to get in touch with her?"

"She moved to Texas or someplace and we never heard from her again. Maybe that was Dr. Chandler's posthypnotic suggestion."

Or maybe Paranoid Pam just had a brilliant idea about getting far away from her so-called friends.

"Okay. Well, thanks." Cate had one more question, strictly extracurricular curiosity, she had to admit. "What do you do? I mean, do you work somewhere?"

"You've never heard of Destiny Dustinhoff? Well, you and most of Eugene, I'm afraid. Story of my life." Melodramatic sigh. "I'm a deejay! 'Nights with Destiny.' From 11:00 p.m. till 2:00 a.m. on the local AM station. A little talk and a lot of music now, but I'm hoping we can turn it into a call-in talk show. If this podunk station ever gets more than one phone line."

With Destiny's line of chatter, Cate had no difficulty saying sincerely, "I'm sure you'll be very good at that."

"If you ever need a deejay, master of ceremonies, anything like that, just remember, I'm your Destiny. Call me."

Don't hold your breath.

As if Destiny heard the unspoken words, in a more serious voice she added, "Actually, I really am a pretty good deejay. And I have my own sound equipment."

Cate tried to call Mitch, got his voice mail, and left a message asking if he'd like to come for fajitas that evening. The phone rang again as soon as she hung up. Caller ID showed that it was Jo-Jo, so Cate didn't bother to identify herself.

"Hi, Jo-Jo. I've been meaning to call and check in with you."

"Bad news, I'm afraid. First thing, I'm moving back out to the house."

"That isn't so bad, is it?" Cate asked. "I'm sure Maude will be glad to have you back. It's a little far out of town, but it's nice out there in the country."

"Oh, well, that part's okay. That's not the bad news. The bad news is, I heard from the lawyer, who just heard from Eddie's insurance company. There isn't any insurance after all."

"No insurance? You mean Kim gets it instead of you?"

"No. There was supposed to be some way set up so Eddie couldn't let it lapse, but he managed to get around that and hasn't been paying the premiums. So it's gone. I'm sorry Eddie got himself killed, but sometimes I just get so mad at him. I've been telling myself he was there at the house because he wanted to get back with me, but I'm thinking now that's about as likely as Maude taking up crocheting. He was up to no good."

"That is bad news about the insurance," Cate said, although she also was thinking that Jo-Jo's more realistic view of Eddie the Ex was probably good.

"On the bright side, maybe no insurance will convince the police I didn't have anything to do with Eddie's death. I didn't have anything to gain from killing him."

Cate appreciated Jo-Jo's attempt to look on the bright side, although she suspected the police would still be thinking Jo-Jo could have murdered to get insurance money she thought at the time she had coming. Cate saw no point worrying Jo-Jo about that detail, however, and she said, "You lost the alimony payments from him too, so that should be further proof to them."

"Right. But Celeste's apartment was broken into. Did you know that? I suppose they'll be asking me about that too. Like, since I wasn't getting insurance money, maybe I'd just grab something valuable at the apartment."

"I've been doing some investigation into whether there could be a connection between Eddie's and Celeste's deaths."

"That's the other bad news. I have the car to pay for, and those bills I ran up on my credit card. My only income is this little pittance of Social Security, and what I can make with the dolls. So there's no way I can afford a private investigator now, and I'll have to let you go. Not that you haven't been a great investigator!" Jo-Jo added hastily. "I just don't have the money for a private investigator now."

"I'm sorry to hear that."

Sorry because she felt the whole two-deaths-and-a-break-in situation needed investigation. Sorry because now Belmont Investigations wouldn't be getting what should have been a decent PI fee. Sorry because she'd be losing a PI connection to the crimes. As Uncle Joe had pointed out in the past, she couldn't just go digging around in crimes like a redheaded gopher; there had to be a client.

"Unless I could pay you with a doll?" Jo-Jo added hopefully. "Or maybe two?"

Cate had never expected to get rich as a private investigator, but neither had she expected to work for dolls. Even life-sized ones. But then, she'd never expected to want to solve crimes and see justice done like she did now that she was a private investigator.

A century ago doctors sometimes worked for a chicken or eggs, maybe a cow if it was a really big disease. Maybe those times were coming back.

"I could probably use a doll or two," Cate said. They'd look nice in the new house. Unless Octavia chose to dismantle them as she had the brown wig.

"Great! I'd love to do a red-haired girl for you. I've never done a redhead! You come on out to the house, and we'll talk about that, okay?"

"I'll do that."

"I'm thinking I'll try to get a part-time job, so maybe I'll have some money to pay you too."

Given the economy and shortage of jobs, Cate suspected Jo-Jo might not find many doors open to her. But if anyone could do it, Jo-Jo probably could. Kim could take lessons in standing on her own from Jo-Jo.

"So, are you still my private investigator?" Jo-Jo asked.

"Assistant private investigator," Cate reminded her.

"Whatever. Maude and Effie and I are looking forward to seeing you whenever you have time to come out. I'll have some great doll ideas for you. And cookies."

Robyn called and said the sandals to go with the bridesmaid dress had arrived, and Cate went over to pick them up. Mitch came for fajitas that evening. He and Uncle Joe spent most of the time at the table talking motorcycles, and after dinner they put the bike in the garage and examined it under the lights like scientists studying a UFO. Even Octavia, instead of spitting at the unfamiliar machine, crawled over it from front fender to rear taillight, as if it were some fascinating new cat gymnastics apparatus.

"Traitor," Cate muttered at her.

No comment from Octavia. She just curled up on the motorcycle seat and purred.

By the time Mitch was ready to leave, he told Cate regretfully that it was too late to give her a ride tonight.

Be still, my disappointed heart, she muttered inwardly, but aloud she murmured politely, "It is late." Traitor Octavia objected with an outraged yowl when Mitch gently removed her from the motorcycle seat.

"I'll call you tomorrow," he said.

Next morning, Saturday, Cate spent time on the internet using Uncle Joe's special PI databases to look for information about Travis Beauchamp. One part of his story checked out. There was an old pickup registered in his and Kim's names at their old apartment address. There were also a couple of motorcycles registered to Travis.

Cate was trying to decide where to go from there when the office phone rang. She got only half her usual identification out before the female voice interrupted.

"Cate, I'm so glad I caught you!"

"Kim?"

"Something's happened. I don't know what to do!"

Which seemed to be Kim's theme song.

"Isn't Travis there to help you?"

Okay, snarky question. Cate was about to revise it and reluctantly offer her own help when Kim said, "Travis isn't here! They arrested him."

"For killing Celeste?"

Brief moment of silence, as if Kim was appalled that Cate could even suggest that.

323

In a small voice she said, "I shouldn't have called you, should I? You've already made up your mind about Travis."

Yeah. Bad dude.

"What was he arrested for?"

"Something that happened up in Tigard. They had an arrest warrant from there. They put handcuffs on him and took him away! I didn't even get a chance to talk to him."

"Where are you?"

Kim named a motel Cate had never heard of over on the north side of town, not one of the nicer chains. "Travis has been staying here."

"Okay, you should just go on home for now. Stay calm. Call your lawyer. If he can't help you, he'll refer you to someone who can."

"I can't even go home! I don't have a car here. We came on Travis's motorcycle to get his things. He hadn't brought much with him, but we were going to take what he has back to my place."

"Why?" Cate asked bluntly.

"Because the house is huge, and there didn't seem any point in his paying for a motel when I have all that space. It's not what you're thinking! Not something . . . personal between us. Just a matter of convenience."

Yeah. Right. Very convenient for Travis and whatever slimy scheme he had in mind.

"Anyway, that doesn't matter now. What matters is that he's in jail. The officer did say he'd be transferred up to Tigard, but I don't know when."

"The police were there waiting at the motel for him?" Cate asked.

"I don't know how they knew he was here in Eugene, but we saw a police car at the motel office as soon as we rode in. Travis started to make a U-turn and leave, but the police car backed up and blocked the way."

Didn't the fact that Travis had been going to cut and run from the police tell her something?

"Everything's falling apart, Cate! I don't know what to do. LeAnne called this morning. She's quitting at Lodge Hill. She's leaving Wednesday!"

"She isn't giving you any notice?"

"She says they need someone at this place down in California right now, and she isn't going to risk losing out on the job."

Cate wasn't surprised that LeAnne was bailing. Who knew what was going to happen with Lodge Hill now? Although it did seem unfair to Kim that LeAnne was doing it without sufficient notice. Another thought: Robyn. What would LeAnne's departure do to Thursday's rehearsal dinner and Friday's wedding?

"Okay. Calm down. I'll come to the motel and get you."

A minute of silence. Cate thought Kim might be about to melt into a puddle right there in the motel, but unexpectedly she took a deep breath, as if she were making a determined effort to pull herself together.

"I'm sorry. This isn't any of your concern, is it? I can call a taxi to get home. I'll come back in the Mustang. Maybe they'll let me in to get Travis's things. I can bring Rolf with me to drive the motorcycle back to my place. I grabbed the key when they arrested Travis."

"Is his motorcycle the kind with handlebars that stick up really high?"

"What difference does that make?"

"It's part of my investigation. I think they're called ape hangers."

"Yes, the handlebars are that ape hanger style." Kim gave an unexpected giggle. "Travis got mad at me because I found that funny."

The term had struck Cate as funny when she first heard it too, but at the moment she wasn't exactly in a humorous mood.

"Does Travis know I found your mother's

body at the Mystic Mirage?"

"I didn't tell him. Well, not exactly, anyway. But I suppose he could have figured it out from something I said."

Maybe Kim couldn't recognize a blessing in disguise, but Cate could. The authorities might not yet have Travis Beauchamp fingered for Celeste's and Eddie the Ex's deaths, but being in jail got him out of the way at least temporarily. Hopefully long enough so Cate could dig up the evidence to nail him for murder. She felt a little safer already.

"Just wait there. I'll be by in a few minutes, and we'll figure out what to do."

Cate located the motel address with her cell phone. She didn't have to tell Uncle Joe what she was doing. He and Rebecca were making the rounds of yard sales this morning. Rebecca wanted to buy an old treadle sewing machine for the old-fashioned décor she had planned for the bedroom when Cate moved out.

The motel wasn't rock-bottom sleazy, but a sign, with two letters missing, offered weekly and monthly rates. A baby stroller lacking a wheel stood outside one door. The motorcycle was parked at an askew angle among a handful of nondescript vehicles in the parking lot. Kim, looking puppy-lost —

although still a gorgeous puppy — sat with her chin in her hands on the curb nearby. As soon as she spotted Cate's Honda, she ran and jumped in as if it were the last lifeboat off a sinking *Titanic.*

21

Without asking Kim's opinion, Cate headed to the closest Dutch Brothers espresso stand. She ordered two hot lattes, handed one to Kim, and pulled the Honda into a parking spot out on the street.

"Okay, now tell me everything."

"I've already told you," Kim protested.

"Tell me again."

Travis had come to the house for breakfast. Apparently falling into her old, do-what-Travis-says mode, Kim had made pancakes and eggs for him. He said he was worried about her being there alone and asked if there was some out-of-the-way space in the house where he could stay to make sure she was safe.

What came to Cate's mind was that old cliché about letting the fox in the henhouse to guard the chickens. Travis had slithered his way into the driver's seat of the Mustang quickly enough; here he was trying to dig in even deeper. All on the basis of being "worried" about Kim.

"And you have no idea why the police arrested him?"

"Something about a burglary in Tigard."

"A recent burglary, or one from back before Travis went to Guatemala?"

"A recent one."

Cate didn't point out that this hardly looked like the actions of a changed man, but Kim's averted eyes suggested she knew what Cate was thinking.

"A burglary Travis claimed he didn't do?"

"I told you, I didn't get a chance to talk to him!" Kim flared. "But he kept telling the officers they'd made a big mistake, that he didn't have anything to do with any burglary."

Reluctantly Cate said, "I suppose that could be true."

Kim gave a big sigh and poked at the whipped cream on her latte. "I suppose it could. I'd like to believe him." A fierce jab at the whipped cream. "But I guess I don't. I'm also thinking that he wanted to stay at the house because he doesn't have any money, not because he had any big concern about me. Travis is still . . . Travis."

Except that now Travis might also be a killer.

"But I don't feel I can just abandon him. I mean, burglary is, well, *awful,* but I still don't think he killed anyone." She glanced at Cate and added, "Even if you do."

"So, what do you plan to do?"

"Maybe they'll let me in to see him, and I can figure out something then." Kim gave Cate another sideways glance. "Will you come with me?"

Visiting a scumbag ex-husband in jail was well down on Cate's list of Things I've Always Wanted to Do. *Do I have to, Lord?* she wailed silently.

The Lord, as was often the case, let her conscience provide the answer. *You couldn't abandon a deaf cat when she lost her owner. Can you abandon a confused friend when she needs you?*

"Okay, we'll go see Travis," Cate said. "But we're not taking him any hacksaw blades so he can saw his way out."

"Well, that wasn't fair," Kim grumbled as they drove away from the big brick jail, where both county and city inmates were held.

They hadn't been inside long. Making a jail visit had turned out to be more complicated than just showing up and asking to see someone. The inmate had to fill out a form before he could receive visitors, and the form could be submitted only Monday through Friday. Kim wouldn't be getting in to see Travis anytime this weekend. Cate didn't say so, but she was relieved.

They also didn't know any more about when Travis would be transferred to Tigard. Kim couldn't call him, but he would be allowed access to a phone if he wanted to call her. She had also been assured that there wasn't a one-phone-call limit.

Cate took Kim back to the Ice Cube. She offered to stay with her, but Kim, even though her own attitude toward Travis had frosted around the edges, still seemed a bit miffed by Cate's attitude toward him. Cate went on home, and Mitch called right after lunch. He said he'd be over in a few minutes to take her for that first ride on the bike.

"Okay." Cate felt as resigned as Susan Linderman had sounded about being questioned. A dark and inescapable fate. "What do I wear?"

"Jeans and a heavy jacket. I have the helmet for you. Weather report says there may be scattered showers, but nothing to worry about. You're going to love bike riding, once you get a taste of it. Maybe you'll want to get a bike of your own."

Right. Maybe she could also learn to love

turnips, spiders, and things that go bump in the night. But invest in a Purple Rocket of her own? Sure. The same day she tried bungee jumping. Without a bungee.

"Okay," she said. "See you in a few minutes."

Mitch arrived. He helped Cate strap on the helmet with zigzagged rainbows, which had a clear plate across the face. Mitch mounted the big bike gracefully. Cate managed to catch her foot on the backrest as she climbed on, twist her knee, and clunk her helmet on a handlebar. Boings echoed inside her head, and only Mitch's quick grab kept her from splatting on the pavement.

It was not, she thought gloomily, a good omen for her first ever motorcycle ride.

Feet still planted on the pavement, Mitch turned his helmeted head to ask if there was anywhere in particular she'd like to go. Cate suggested Jo-Jo's place. She may as well accomplish something useful on this jaunt.

She quickly learned several things about bike riding. Some were good: she did not have to wrap her arms around Mitch's body to keep from flying off into space. She could brace herself against the sturdy backrest and grab handholds right next to the passenger's seat. She felt reasonably secure, and the seat was surprisingly comfortable. She had a feeling of being more closely attuned to her surroundings, a part of them in a way that riding in a car couldn't offer. They breezed through interesting pockets of warmer air here and there. She smelled the tang of a pine tree as they rode under it. A small boy stared at them with awe, as if they were riding a magic bolt of lightning. Cate waved at him.

"You're enjoying this, aren't you?" Mitch asked over his shoulder. "Be honest now."

"It's better than, oh, falling out a fifth-story window." Actually, quite a bit better, she added grudgingly to herself.

But she found some aspects of motorcycle riding close to terrifying. Never had she felt more insignificant and vulnerable than when an eighteen-wheeler roared by. The huge tires rolling only a few feet from her face made her head spin dizzily. Those tires also shot out road water like wet missiles. She came close to full panic when another truck driver didn't see them and stopped barely inches behind them at a stop sign, the big truck looming over them like a panting monster. And when she looked down and saw the road zipping along bare inches under her feet, it almost seemed to be pulling her down into it.

She was relieved when Mitch eased the bike into Jo-Jo's driveway. Maude instantly announced their presence. Jo-Jo's car wasn't in the driveway, but Cate went to the door. No response to her knock.

"I guess I should have called first," she said when she walked back to Mitch and the bike. "Maybe she hasn't moved back out here yet."

"That's okay. We're in no hurry." Mitch held out a palm. "It's starting to sprinkle anyway. We can wait in the barn, and maybe it'll pass over."

He drove the motorcycle under a shed-type overhang on the barn and got a rag out of a saddlebag to wipe a few sprinkles off the seat and glossy purple finish. Cate wandered over to scratch Maude behind her big white ears.

After twenty minutes, Jo-Jo hadn't arrived, and the rain was falling harder.

"I guess we'd better go," Mitch said. "It doesn't look as if it's letting up."

Not only not letting up, the rain was falling in a downpour now, gleefully repudiating that optimistic weather report.

"This is the sprinkle you mentioned?" Cate asked.

If Mitch heard her, she couldn't hear his response over the hammer of rain on her helmet. A couple miles farther on, with Cate thinking these helmet faceplates really should come with windshield wipers, he pulled into a little country store. Cate followed him inside, mostly to get out of the rain. He bought a carton of big garbage bags. She watched, puzzled, as he pulled one out and used a pocket knife to cut a hole on each side and a larger hole at the top. He handed the black bag to her.

"There. Instant rain gear."

Cate had never been a stickler for fashion, but she had always worn items that could actually qualify as clothing. "You want me to wear a garbage bag?"

He was already busy cutting on the second bag. "Suit yourself. I'm going to."

Cate, looking at the rain outside, felt dampness already seeping through her jacket, and grimly slid her head and arms through the openings. Mitch put his on. When they went outside, he looked big and bulky and masculine. In a window of the store, Cate saw her own reflection. She looked like an overweight witch with a bad sense of fashion. Mitch easily hiked his garbage bag up to swing his leg over the bike. Cate managed not to twist, dislocate, or break anything.

They rode through onslaughts of rainwater

from above, rainwater splashed sideways by passing cars, more rainwater bouncing up from below.

Finally, back at the house, Mitch steadied the bike while Cate dismounted. "You okay?" he asked.

"I'm home safely." She unfastened the helmet and slid it off her squashed hair. "I guess I should be grateful for that."

"I'm sorry. This isn't how I intended your first ride to be. I guess I should have waited when they said it was going to sprinkle. But I was just so eager to take you for a ride." Behind the face plate, Mitch's eyes looked dark and anxious.

Yes, Mitch had undoubtedly had good intentions. But what was that old saying? The road to destruction is paved with good intentions. A very wet road, in this case.

Mitch swiped a finger across her wet eyebrows. Unexpectedly he grinned. "The garbage bag is quite becoming. Black is definitely your color."

Cate wanted to be grumpy. In spite of the garbage bag, cold rainwater dribbled down her back. Her jeans, where they'd stuck out from under the bag, clung to her legs like wet paint. She was cold as a plastic-covered Popsicle. Of all the drawbacks to being a biker babe, this was not one she had anticipated.

Yet, with Mitch grinning at her so hopefully, she couldn't help the beginning of a smile of her own. The bike ride was a new and memorable adventure. No rut in her life with Mitch in it. And it tended to put life's problems in perspective. Who could be too serious about life while wearing a garbage bag?

"Does this make me a full-fledged biker babe?"

"Definitely the queen of the biker babes." He brushed back a strand of wet hair plastered to her face. "I'm hoping you'll give the Purple Rocket and me another chance."

"I'll think about it." She paused, and the smile got a little more genuine. "Yeah, I probably will."

"And won't this make a great story to tell our grandkids someday?"

Our grandkids.

It had a nice ring to it. She wasn't jumping on it with joy, but she did manage to say, "Do you want to come in and warm up for a while?"

"Thanks, no. I'm going to head on home and get the bike put away. I'll meet you at church tomorrow?"

Cate nodded. He lifted the faceplate on

his helmet, leaned over, and gave her a kiss that felt warm and wonderful even with rainwater dribbling down her face.

Yeah, life could be good even in a garbage bag.

Cate showered and wrapped up in a flannel robe. With Uncle Joe and Rebecca out to a potluck dinner with friends, she had leftover fajitas for dinner, propped pillows on the bed, and settled down to read. Octavia snuggled up beside her. Her cell phone sitting on the nightstand rang without any pre-notice from the cat. She saw from the ID that it was Kim's number. She was tempted to ignore it, but an inevitable sense of concern made her sigh and pick up the phone.

"Hi, Kim."

"Cate, I know I probably shouldn't call you. I know you're unhappy with me. I know I'm probably being paranoid or something. But I just have this awful feeling. Like a big rock or something is about to crash down on me."

Not a good feeling in a glass house. "Has something happened since I saw you this morning?"

"No. I've just been sitting around, thinking I should be here if Travis called."

"Um."

"You must think I'm the most helpless person in the world."

"I think you have strengths and capabilities, but you've let your mother and Travis and even Ed convince you you're nothing but a dumb blonde who can't do anything on your own."

Unexpectedly, Kim managed a laugh. "Come on, Cate. Don't be shy. Just tell me straight out what you think."

"Maybe that was a little blunt. But —"

"It's okay. Thanks for being honest. I think I'll, uh, go fix myself some tea now. Probably I'm just all nervous for nothing."

Maybe. Maybe not.

"I'll get dressed and come over."

The house was all lit up when Cate arrived. Apparently Kim's apprehension had overridden worries about paying a big electric bill. Although the house was cold inside, and Kim had been huddled in front of a small heater by the sofa rather than turning up the thermostat on the main heat. She was wearing the old plaid jacket again, plus two pairs of socks now.

"Did you and Rolf go over and get Travis's bike?" Cate asked.

"No. I couldn't get hold of him."

340

Cate started to ask if she'd left a message for Rolf, but the cell phone in the pocket of Kim's baggy jacket played an incongruously upbeat guitar riff. Kim looked at the ID but apparently didn't recognize whatever was there.

She answered the call with a tentative hello. Then, after a moment, she said, "I was wondering if you'd call."

That didn't necessarily identify the caller as Travis, but Kim looked at her and gave a little nod that said it was him. Cate was surprised that they were allowing him to call from the jail so late on a Saturday night. It was past 9:00 already. Kim didn't move away, but Cate, even though she was curious, felt awkward overhearing the private call. She started to move over to the black-and-white seating area. Kim made a downward movement with a hand to stop her, touched a button on the phone, and a moment later Travis's voice came out of the speaker.

". . . big mistake, but I don't know how long it will take these idiots to get it straightened out." He sounded odd, his voice hoarse or whispery.

"How did they make this big 'mistake'?" Kim asked. Cate heard the quotation marks around mistake. She wondered if Travis did.

"Remember my buddy Jesse? He got caught trying to sell some stolen stuff on Craigslist. When they nabbed him, he told them I'd been in on the burglary."

"Why would he do that if you weren't involved?"

"Oh, you know. Sometimes they give you a deal if you rat on someone else. He was already mad because I hadn't brought a ton of pot back from Guatemala. But it's like I already told you, I'm through with that life."

"Jesse always was getting in trouble."

Cate could hear Kim softening toward Travis and his I'm-a-changed-man combined with my-friend-done-me-wrong story.

"I tried to get in to see you, but they wouldn't let me in," Kim said. "Do you know yet when they'll move you up to Tigard?"

"No idea. Look, can you do something for me? I need to get my bike away from the motel. No telling what might happen to it there in the parking lot. And I need my stuff out of the motel too."

"I'll get an employee from the vineyard to move the bike. I grabbed the key. I'll see if I can get your things out of the motel too."

"Great! I knew I could count on you, babe. You're the best! There is one other thing." Travis didn't wait to see if Kim was agreeable to something more. "I don't know when they'll set bail. Probably not until —"

"Could you talk a little louder? We — *I* can barely hear you."

"I can't talk any louder," he said, though the whisper did go up a notch in volume. "I'm on a cell phone, hiding out under a blanket on my bunk. Cell phones are illegal in here, but this guy got one smuggled in. I'm paying him a hundred bucks to use it for fifteen minutes. He wouldn't have trusted me for the money except he was impressed when I told him who you were. He's heard of Mr. K's expensive restaurant."

What Cate heard was that the cellmate was counting on Kim for that hundred bucks, though Kim didn't seem to pick up on that.

"Won't you be in trouble if they catch you with the phone?"

"Big trouble. But I had to talk to you, Kim. I just had to. Everything was going so good for us, and then this. I used up the one phone call they allow by calling Jesse to try to get him to tell the truth about the burglary."

Cate felt a sudden shift in Kim's view of Travis. They already knew the one-phone-call limit wasn't true.

"Anyway, what I need is money to pay the

bail so I can get out of here," Travis said.

"How much will bail be?" Kim asked.

"I don't know. It's only a burglary charge, so probably not more than $25,000."

"Travis, I can't come up with —"

"You don't have to come up with the whole amount. I think they only require 10 percent, something like that."

"It doesn't matter how much it is. I can't come up with *anything.*"

"What do you mean, you can't come up with anything? That old guy you married was loaded. I checked. Million-dollar house. Expensive restaurant, big vineyard, high-class lodge of some kind. Probably a boat-load of stocks and bonds and cash too. Get some of it for me, babe. I need it. *Now.*"

"I know it looks from the outside like we were rich, but I have maybe fifty dollars in my checking account."

"Oh, come on," Travis scoffed. Then, as if he'd had a sudden suspicion, he said, "Is that redhead there with you? She's filling you full of a bunch of baloney about me, isn't she? Don't trust her, babe. She —"

Travis broke off abruptly, and Cate's PI intuition kicked in with the realization that he was only at that moment finally putting details together. That she was the one who had found Celeste's body that night at the

Mystic Mirage. That she was the one he'd tried to choke through the beaded curtain.

"Cate has nothing to do with this," Kim said. "And I'm telling you the truth. I don't have any money."

"Borrow some."

"I can't! I'm already up to my ears in debt!"

"Then hock something. Sell something. I don't care what you do. I can't talk much longer or they're going to bust in and catch me. Just get the money and get me out of here, or —"

Travis stopped, but the word hung there like a bomb about to explode. *Or.*

"Get you out of there, or what, Travis?" Kim said, her voice going unexpectedly calm. "You'll kill me like you did my husband and my mother?"

"I didn't have anything to do with either of their deaths. I told you that!"

"I think you did."

"So now you're threatening me? You're going to sic the cops on me for murder? Do that, and I'll just have to tell them a few things about your precious mother." His voice had risen out of the whispery range, even if that put him in jeopardy.

"What do you mean?"

"I mean, your dear mother was using a

drug on her so-called patients. A very illegal drug."

"I don't believe you," Kim said, but her voice faltered.

"No? Well, I know it for a fact, babe. If she couldn't get her 'patient' hypnotized right away, she slipped 'em some Rohypnol. Or maybe you've heard it by its more common name, the date-rape drug? It put her patients out quite nicely, and they couldn't remember a thing about what went on during that time. Then afterwards Celeste fed them any kind of wild story about their past lives that she wanted to."

"I-I don't believe you. You can't know that."

"Kim, babe, I was the one getting the Rohypnol for her, so I definitely *do* know. And why do you think she dropped her Portland business like a hot potato? She had a couple of those so-called patients threatening to sue over what she'd given them."

Kim's mouth dropped open, but forming words seemed beyond her.

"Anyway, you get me the bail money and a few thousand extra, or all this comes out. Your mother may be dead, but this will make an interesting addition to her obituary, don't you think? 'Well-known local meta-psychologist' or whatever it was she called herself. Or maybe it will be, 'Well-known hypnotist Dr. Celeste Chandler revealed as illegal drug pusher.' "

Cate could hear an ominous ring of truth in Travis's threat. He'd do it, even if the revelation backfired and got him in more trouble. She knew Kim could hear it too.

"Did my mother give you money to get you out of our lives?" Kim demanded.

"She gave me money, all right. A nice bundle. When I told her that if she didn't come up with it, the police would get all the facts about the magic secret to her big success with that so-called past-lives regression rubbish."

"You blackmailed her!"

"It got me out of being married to you, and I had a nice nest egg to finance an escape too."

"Why did you come back?"

If Travis's disdainful attitude about their marriage hurt Kim, she wasn't letting it show.

"Money, of course. I ran out and I need more. Those idiots down in Guatemala couldn't grow pot any better than I could send a rocket to the moon. But Celeste got hard-nosed about it. Said she didn't have anything to give me."

So he killed her when she wouldn't pay

347

off again. And trashed her apartment for whatever he could find. What about Ed Kieferson's murder?

"But then you looked like a pretty good bet, rich widow and all," Travis added.

"So now you're trying to blackmail me," Kim said.

"I'm just telling you the facts, babe. About what's going to happen if you don't get me that bail money, and more, or if you try to pin some murder on me. But you get the money, and everything will be fine. We can start a great new life together, right there in your big glass house." His voice softened persuasively. "We were pretty good together, babe. Things just kind of went wrong. But we can make it really good this time."

Travis could go from telling her how glad he was to get out of their old marriage to how great a new one would be. As Kim had once said about her ex, Travis never let logic clutter up his thinking.

"Maybe I don't care what you tell the world about my mother!"

"You care."

Kim's moment of silence said he was right, but her voice was a little sad when she said, "Then maybe you should have checked on the real level of my wealth before you killed her."

Kim hit the button that ended the call. The cell phone rang again a minute later. Kim didn't answer it, and, without listening to whatever message Travis may have left, she erased it.

22

Cate and Kim sat there in silence, the only sound the faint hum of the small refrigerator in the bar area in a corner of the room.

"Do you believe what Travis said about your mother and giving the drug to her clients?"

"Yeah, I guess I do." Kim still sounded sad. "But it's a good thing Ed never knew, or he'd have been mad enough to kill her himself. Someone gave his daughter that date-rape drug once. What happened while she was knocked out with it left her so disturbed and depressed that she killed herself a couple years later. It was all before I knew him, of course, but he was still really bitter about it. He said anyone who gave a woman that drug ought to be —" Kim shook her head. "Well, Ed could get pretty graphic about that."

Jo-Jo had mentioned the daughter's suicide but not this detail.

"Are you going to get the money for him?" Cate asked.

"I suppose I could hock something. I have some jewelry Ed gave me. And there's lots of stuff around here that's probably hockable." Kim gazed around the room as if sizing up the dollar value of lamps and furniture and knickknacks. "I hocked things now and then back when Travis and I were married."

"Do you think helping him get out is a good idea?"

Kim turned to look at her. "What do you think?"

Cate resisted the urge to jump up and wave her arms and shout "No, no, no, don't help him get out!" Instead she said, "You have to decide this, Kim. It's one of a lot of decisions you're going to have to make for yourself now."

Kim hesitated for a long moment. "No, it isn't a good idea, is it?" Another long moment of thought as she weighed the decision. "And I'm not going to do it."

Cate again resisted an urge, this one to stick two fingers in her mouth and blow a raucous whistle of approval. Instead, she merely nodded and said, "I think that's a good decision."

"But I think hocking or selling something

is definitely a great idea. I need money to pay the bills. Maybe I could even sell enough to get the house out of foreclosure!" Kim jumped up. She grabbed a free-form sculpture from the coffee table, small and squiggly looking but undoubtedly expensive. "I don't need all this stuff!" She sounded unexpectedly amazed about that discovery.

If Travis's threatening call had made Kim see that she *didn't* need all the stuff that surrounded her, then it had accomplished something worthwhile after all. Kim set the sculpture back on the coffee table, then picked up an elaborate vase filled with drooping flowers, gave it an appraising inspection, and decisively set it beside the sculpture.

Cate was about to suggest Kim could add that strange sculpture out in the yard to a list of disposable items, but Kim suddenly dropped back to the sofa. She clasped her arms around her body as if she'd gone cold again.

"But he'll manage to get the bail money somehow, even if I don't give it to him. Travis can be . . . resourceful."

Oh yes. He'd blackmailed his way to a trip to Guatemala. Gotten hold of a cell phone in jail. Definitely resourceful.

Kim's throat moved in a convulsive swallow. "He'll get out."

That realization obviously scared Kim. It scared Cate too. Because what the words told Cate was that this was no time to feel complacent or safe simply because Travis was behind bars. He would get out on bail, so she had a very limited window of time to get evidence against him about murder before he came after one or both of them.

"But I'm not going to worry about that now," Kim declared with determination in her voice. "He surely can't get out on bail for a few days yet. Probably not until they take him up to Tigard. There are small weddings scheduled for both Tuesday and Wednesday evenings at Lodge Hill. LeAnne says she'll handle the Tuesday one, and I'll be there with her to learn all I can so I can do the Wednesday one alone. I don't even know exactly what she does or how the food for receptions is coordinated with the restaurant. Or a lot of other things."

"Thursday is the rehearsal dinner for my friend Robyn's wedding. I don't know anything about weddings, but I'll be there and help any way I can. And then Friday is Robyn's wedding."

"That's a big wedding, isn't it?" Kim's brief burst of confidence sounded on the edge of crumbling.

Yes, that herd of bridesmaids, a wedding gown from San Francisco, and a color-coordinated hair scheme probably qualified as big and complicated. "You can do this, Kim. Remember all those weddings you had for your dolls? All those wedding articles you read? And you wanted Ed to let you manage Lodge Hill, didn't you? Now you can do it."

"But even if I manage that, there are so many other problems! This house and the vineyard and the restaurant. The Mystic Mirage too."

"Take them one at a time. You're not dumb. Or helpless."

"You think so?" The sideways glance Kim gave Cate looked hopeful, but her voice sounded skeptical.

"God gave us all talents or abilities of some kind. Running a wedding business may be one of yours. I'll pray for you."

"Pray?" Kim looked surprised. Her gaze darted around as if she suddenly feared God might be spying on her through a glass wall. "What good will that do?"

"You might be surprised."

Cate offered to stay the night with Kim, but Kim shook her head and smiled wryly.

"With Travis behind bars, I'll be fine."

■ ■ ■ ■

Cate called Kim's cell phone number right after church the next morning, and Kim was indeed fine. She surprised Cate by saying she was at that moment at the Mystic Mirage, putting bargain-basement prices on everything for a going-out-of-business sale. She'd gotten hold of Rolf. He and a friend were coming by the Mystic Mirage that afternoon to pick up the key to the motorcycle, and then he'd ride the bike out to the vineyard for storage.

"I decided I don't want it at the house," Kim said. "I also called the motel and asked them to store Travis's things until he could pick them up. They weren't happy about it, but I don't want his stuff at my place either. Monday evening I'm meeting LeAnne out at Lodge Hill, and we're going over information about how things work there."

"You sound as if you have everything under control," Cate said. "I'm impressed."

"Maybe it was that pep talk you gave me. Or the prayer."

Cate and Mitch went for another ride on the motorcycle that afternoon. Cate still wasn't putting bike riding at the top of her list of favorite activities, but it had edged off of her Things I Never Want to Do list. Even though the day was sunny and unseasonably warm, she prudently took along her garbage bag.

They rode east from Springfield on the highway that followed the McKenzie River and wound back into the mountains. Fall colors blazed on the forested hillsides, and they took side hikes, once to see a covered bridge, another time to stand close to a waterfall. Mitch swung her hand as they walked. They had a late lunch and turned around at a little place called McKenzie Bridge.

"Well?" Mitch said when they coasted to the curb back at the house just before dark.

Cate flexed her hands. She'd kept a lifeline grip on the handholds most of the time. "I had fun. I enjoyed the ride. There's a nice sense of freedom on a bike."

"Good."

"But I'm still not rushing out to buy a motorcycle of my own," she warned.

He leaned over and kissed her. "You'll always have a place on mine."

Midmorning on Monday she drove back to the motel to see what she could find out about Travis. Yesterday's warm fall day had given way to blustery clouds, and rain spattered the windshield as she parked by the office door.

The motel looked the same as it had when Cate and Kim were there on Saturday. Baby stroller by a door and nondescript cars in the parking lot, although today a cleaning cart stood by an open door to a room. She was surprised to see Travis's motorcycle still angled at the curb. Rolf obviously hadn't come for it yet.

Then a red Camaro pulled in right behind her and parked beside the bike. Rolf got out on the passenger's side. He was wearing jeans and a heavy denim jacket and carried a plain black helmet in one hand. A curvy blonde got out of the driver's side of the car. She looked as if she'd just stepped out of an ad that said "Don't you wish your jeans fit you like this?"

Cate didn't want to explain her presence here to Rolf. She scrunched down in the seat. She'd just sneak away before he saw her, and return later.

Fat chance.

Rolf, apparently equipped with invisible antenna that detected redhead vibes from across a parking lot, turned and instantly spotted her. He waved, dropped the helmet on the seat of the motorcycle, and headed toward her as if they were old friends. Reluctantly, reminding herself she should be nice to him because he was helping Kim, she opened the window. She probably owed him nice anyway, since she'd had unwarranted suspicions of him. The blonde shot eye icicles across the parking lot.

Rolf braced his arms on the window frame and leaned down to peer inside. "Hey, I didn't expect to see you here." He gave her a raised eyebrow and smirky grin. "Meeting someone?" He glanced around the parking lot as if looking for likely prospects. "You should tell him you deserve better than this rat hole."

Cate ignored his insinuation that she was here for some midday tryst. "Kim said she'd asked you to pick up the bike and take it out to the vineyard. I'd thought you were doing it yesterday."

"Got busy," he said. "You and Kim BFFs now?"

Best Friends Forever. Cate was surprised Rolf knew the term. She jumped the conversation in a different direction. "A friend is getting married at Lodge Hill Friday night. She was concerned the place might be closing down, but Kim is planning to keep it going." Which wasn't an answer to anything he'd asked, and didn't explain why she was

358

here, but she hoped the small avalanche of irrelevant information would muddle his attention.

"I've been wondering about the vineyard and whether I ought to start job hunting."

"I don't know about that. Did you know Travis was here in town before Kim called you about his bike?"

"This is Travis's bike?" Rolf turned and gave the motorcycle a reappraisal. The blonde looked ready to storm across the parking lot and grab him by the ear, but he didn't seem to notice. "Kim didn't mention that. She just said a friend's bike was here, and asked if I could take it out to the vineyard and store it for a while."

Me and my big mouth.

"So, isn't that interesting," Rolf mused, his gaze still on the bike. The blonde crossed her arms and started tapping a toe. "Kind of makes you wonder, doesn't it? Ol' Travis shows up, and pretty soon both Kim's husband and mother are dead. I guess I'm not surprised Kim decided she needed to hire a private investigator."

"It's not Kim I'm working for." Too late Cate thought she should have phrased that differently, because her words made it all too obvious she was working for someone else, but Rolf just laughed.

"For a while there, when you dropped the Belmont Investigations card that day I gave you the tour of the vineyard, I wondered if you were investigating me."

"Guilty conscience?" Cate smiled to suggest it wasn't a serious question.

"I'll bet you know all about my little brush with the law at the vineyard where I worked before, don't you? Six months incarceration, two years probation. Enough to scare a good ol' farm boy like me straight for life."

He didn't sound worried about what she might know, and Cate didn't let on whether or not she knew anything about his marijuana growing. "So, you want to tell me all the details about that?" she asked as if it were a playful challenge.

"Sure. Over drinks and dinner? Anytime," he shot back. He grinned, and she couldn't tell if he actually thought she might accept the invitation or if he was just making flirty small talk. "But now I'm wondering, where is Travis, that he's not around to take care of his own bike?"

Cate hesitated, but she didn't see any reason not to tell him what had happened. "Travis had a little brush with the law of his own. They arrested him here at the motel a couple days ago."

"Hey, couldn't happen to a more deserving guy, could it? What for?"

"I think it was a burglary charge up in Tigard."

"Is Kim all shook up about it? Or is she thinking Travis maybe did something a lot worse than burglary right here in Eugene?" He gave her a meaningful lift of eyebrows. He, too, had quickly jumped to a suspicion of murder.

"I'm just a private investigator, not a mind reader."

"Too bad. Mind reading could be really helpful for a private investigator, couldn't it? Maybe that's what Kim's mother should have been. She liked digging around in people's minds and lives."

"I only met her once, so I didn't really know her."

He slapped the window frame as if putting a punctuation mark on the conversation. "Well, you tell Kim that if there's anything else I can do to help, just let me know. She's had a rough time. You might tell her Rolf says to watch out for ol' Travis too. He came down here for a reason, and I doubt it was because the lattes are better here. Travis is always looking out for Travis."

Cate wouldn't argue with that. "I'll tell her."

361

"I'll be happy to help you out too, you know. Any way I can. Any time." His grin gave the offer a sly double meaning made even plainer when he winked and added, "And I don't do cheap motels. First class, all the way."

Cate wanted to be angry with him. First he suggested she was meeting someone here at a motel room. Now he was offering . . . something. With a girlfriend standing only fifty feet away. He was an egotistical jerk. But maybe he couldn't help it. Once a lady-killer, always a lady-killer. It came out of him as naturally as hot air escaping a balloon.

"I'll keep that in mind."

"You know, there is something." His tone unexpectedly went serious. "If you are investigating Travis in connection with the deaths . . ." He lifted a questioning eyebrow.

Cate didn't acknowledge any connection with an investigation of Travis, but curiosity made her say cautiously, "And if I were?"

"You might want to make a run up to Tigard and ask some questions."

"Ask questions of whom?"

"Go to a bike shop called Ric's Rough Riders. Travis and his friends always hung out there. Let 'em know you're not expecting anything for free, that you're willing to

362

pay for information. Travis likes to brag about his exploits, and his friends are the kind who'll sell each other out for a dollar-ninety-eight. You might pick up some interesting information."

"I doubt Travis was going around bragging even to his friends about murder."

"But he might have said something about how rich his ex-wife was now. About how he figured on getting her back, and he wasn't going to let her crazy mother or her overage husband stand in his way." He nodded meaningfully. "You don't know just what you might find out."

There was also, Cate remembered, that friend of Travis's named Jesse whom Travis said had connected him with a burglary he hadn't been involved in. Jesse might have some interesting information, if Cate could get it out of him.

"You heard something about Travis up in Tigard?" she asked.

"Me? Nah." Rolf slapped the frame again and backed away from the window. "I haven't been in Tigard for a while now. I'm just a grape grower, minding my own business, workin' hard, staying on the right side of the law."

Cate resisted a glance toward the blonde. Workin' hard. Yeah, right. "Okay. Well, thanks."

He swept the few moments of seriousness away with a jaunty grin. "Don't forget my offer."

Cate pulled out of the motel parking lot. She drove several blocks, parked in the parking lot of a boarded-up restaurant, and waited for fifteen minutes before cautiously returning. Both bike and Camaro were gone. She went into the office and handed the older man at the counter her Belmont Investigations card. He stared at it as if he thought it might catch fire any moment.

"We run a family business here," he stated. "Nothing that needs investigating."

Cate wasn't sure that was true, but she gave him her most winning smile. "It's not you or the motel we're interested in. It's a guest who stayed here for a while. Travis Beauchamp? The man who was recently arrested."

"His wife sent you for his stuff? She wanted us to store it, but we're not in the storage business. People forget something in a room, we hold it three days, then out it goes." He made a *pfft* sound and twitched a bony thumb toward the door.

Cate was surprised. Weren't there laws or regulations about what a place like this was required to do with left-behind belongings? Maybe not. Or, if there were, this guy just twitched his thumb at them. She also noted that Kim had identified herself as Travis's wife, apparently trying to give herself some authority over his belongings. Cate started to say no, she didn't want Travis's belongings, but on second thought she cut off the words. Maybe this was an unexpected opportunity.

"Did he have a gun? Or drugs?"

"A gun or drugs?" The man sounded outraged that she'd think anyone in his establishment might possess such items. "If there was anything like that, I'd of been calling the cops the minute we found it. All he left is some clothes, the usual stuff. Jeans and shirts and underwear. Shaving gear, a few papers in an envelope. Some fancy skin lotion and hair gel stuff. Smells like rotten roses. Can you imagine that? Biker guy like him using skin lotion and hair gel."

Cate would have doubted the guy ever smiled, but the skin lotion and rotten-roses hair gel brought a snicker. He yelled back into the living quarters at someone named Elsie, then motioned Cate to follow him outside. He unlocked a room holding various cleaning and yard supplies and pointed to a couple of boxes on a bottom shelf. The tops of the boxes were folded over, so Cate couldn't see what was inside.

"How long did Mr. Beauchamp stay here?" Cate asked.

"I dunno. I'd have to look it up." His surly tone suggested he'd do that about the same time he offered free lodging for the homeless. "Week or ten days maybe."

Which meant Travis had been here long enough to murder Celeste and search/trash her apartment, but not long enough to kill Ed. Although he could have been in Eugene much longer at some other motel, of course. So what would he have done with the gun that killed Ed? Toss it, probably. But just maybe he'd stuck it in the saddlebags or trunk of the bike.

Although there was still the possibility Celeste herself had killed Ed before Travis arrived in town, and his murdering her had been unrelated to Ed's death. There seemed to be more than enough hostility for two murderers here.

"Did he have any visitors while he was here?"

The man drew his skinny frame up indignantly. "We don't spy on our guests." But, after a brief pause, he added, "I figured him for having women friends. Good-lookin' guy, you know? But I never seen any."

"Did he pay with cash or a credit card?"

The money question apparently reached the motel owner's limit on information sharing. "You got any business asking all these questions?" he demanded. He eyed the boxes as if he might be about to change his mind about them.

"I'm just trying to help the family," Cate said. She hastily scooped a box off the shelf. "And I do thank you very much for the help."

She headed for her car with the box in her arms. "I'll be right back to get the other box," she called over her shoulder.

She wanted to look for the envelope right away, but a quick glance showed her that someone, probably the person named Elsie, was watching from a window. She hurriedly got the second box and slammed the trunk lid shut on both boxes. She went only as far as the parking area of the closed restaurant before stopping again to open the trunk.

Travis Beauchamp apparently wore his clothes until he ran out before he did laundry. Cate gingerly held two plastic bags of dirty clothes at arm's length and examined them from the outside only. His personal gear consisted of throwaway plastic razors, a spray can of shaving foam, a scruffy-looking toothbrush, a flattened tube of Aquafresh toothpaste, a bottle of mouth-wash, and the previously snickered-at skin lotion and hair gel. The motel man had a talent for descriptive scents, however. Rotten roses it was. She fingered through the few items of clean clothing, and finally, right at the bottom of the box was the manila envelope.

Sealed.

She hefted it in her palm. Not heavy or thick. But maybe rich with incriminating secrets? Could she get it open without leaving traces of her snooping?

A moment later she realized she should have just ripped the envelope open instantly. Because now, quicker than a freeze-up on her computer, her conscience had kicked in. Killer though Travis might be, could she rightfully rummage around in his private papers? Regretfully, she dropped the envelope back in the box. As an ex-wife from whom Travis was trying to extort money, maybe Kim was entitled to open it.

What Cate wanted to do right now was rush up to Tigard and start asking questions, but it was time, not conscience, that held her back. Investigating Travis wasn't a paying proposition for Belmont Investigations, and husband-following was. Which is what she and Uncle Joe were scheduled to do for the next two days. But right after that — no, she couldn't go then, either, she realized in further frustration. She'd have to wait until after the wedding.

But she did have time, she decided after a glance at her watch, to stop by the Mystic Mirage and see what Kim thought about opening the envelope.

Kim's red Mustang stood at the curb in front of the Mystic Mirage, and Cate parked behind it. The street wasn't busy on this blustery Monday morning, and the other parking spaces in the block were empty. A sign reading "closed" slanted across the inside of the door. Kim must be inside working on the going-out-of-business sale.

Cate headed for the door, but it resisted her push. Locked. She rattled the handle, tapped, and then pounded on the door. No response.

Odd. Even if Kim was working in the back room, surely she could hear Cate's hammering. Cate felt a shimmer of uneasiness.

She moved over to the window, cupped her hands between her face and the glass, and peered inside. Kim had been re-arranging merchandise, and Cate could see where she'd put tags on items with a red line drawn through the original price and a new price below. The Oriental swords had been removed from the back wall.

Maybe she should go around to the alleyway and pound on that back door. The one through which the killer had escaped that other time.

She wouldn't let her mind latch onto the thought that instantly rammed into her head. The thought that Travis had already gotten out on bail, and he'd been here again, and Kim —

Cate ran to the window on the other side of the door. It gave her a new angle of view. Celeste's books were scattered on the floor, and a Ouija board lay broken among them. Now she also saw the Kimmy doll sprawled on the floor, back of her head smashed in but her face still sweetly smiling.

The big brass shield that had hung on the wall with the Oriental swords lay on the floor now.

Two jeans-clad legs stuck out from beneath it.

23

No, no, no, not Kim too! Shock and pain and a desperate blast of failure roared through Cate. She hadn't known Kim long. They were far from being the BFFs Rolf had suggested. But Kim had seemed on track for making something of her life, and Cate had hoped she could do it.

Even though Cate had known Travis would probably get out all too soon, she'd expected him to be behind bars for a few days yet. But he had gotten out, and he'd done far more than make good on his threat to destroy Kim's mother's reputation. He'd taken deadly aim on Kim herself.

Cate mentally hammered herself harder than she'd pounded the door with her fists. She should have done something to prevent this. Made Kim more aware of the danger. Convinced the police Travis was a killer. *Something.*

Was he still lurking inside, just as he'd

been after he thrust that sword into Celeste's chest?

Cate backed away from the window and frantically dug in her purse for her cell phone. She punched in 911 and told the dispatcher what she could see. Body on the floor. Brass shield half covering it. Door locked. Same address where a murder had taken place not long ago.

The dispatcher told her to return to her car, lock the doors, and stay on the phone. Help was on the way.

Cate followed instructions and stayed on the phone until she heard sirens in the distance. She returned to the window then. She felt a desperate need to *do* something, even if it was only watch over Kim's body sprawled on the floor.

She blinked when she saw the jeans-clad legs again. Was that a toe moving? It couldn't be. But then the shield moved, like some big brass beetle scuttling sideways. It slid aside, and Kim slowly sat up. She put a hand to her head and then looked at her bloody fingers as if they belonged to someone else.

"Kim! Kim! Are you all right?" Cate pounded the glass.

Of course Kim wasn't all right. Blood streaked her face and matted her hair. Cate could see where all the blood was coming from now. A gash slashed across her forehead and into her hair. Kim looked Cate's way as if she heard something but couldn't focus on what it was. She struggled to her knees.

"No, don't get up!" Cate yelled. "Stay there! Help is coming!"

Kim disappeared on the far side of a display table as she struggled to stand, only her white-knuckled hand clutching the table visible. Then she was upright, wobbling as if standing were an unfamiliar experience for her. She squinted in Cate's direction, then moved by grabbing one display table, then another. Cate kept yelling at her not to try to do anything, but Kim determinedly kept coming. She used only one hand. The other hung awkwardly at her side. It was bloody too, and there was a crooked place between shoulder and elbow that shouldn't be there. She reached the door just as a police car squealed to the curb, an ambulance right behind it.

Kim swayed back and forth at the door, but she managed to turn the deadbolt with one hand. Cate stepped aside as a police officer rushed forward. Kim lost her tentative balance when her hand slipped from the knob. She collapsed to the floor as if her brain had lost communication with her legs.

Cate had no chance to say a word to her. The EMTs rushed in, and only moments later they had her on a stretcher headed to the ambulance. Cate ran alongside.

"Kim, who did this to you?" she demanded frantically.

Kim's mouth opened, and her gaze briefly focused on Cate, but she couldn't seem to shape her mouth to form words. Then the EMTs lifted her into the ambulance, and the doors closed behind her. Another police car and officers arrived in a wail of sirens. The officers jumped out.

"Her ex-husband tried to kill her!" Cate yelled to them. "I've got to go with her."

"Hey, you can't leave!" an officer yelled back as Cate headed toward her car. "We have questions —"

"Travis Beauchamp!" Cate grabbed one of her ever-ready Belmont Investigations cards and tossed it in their direction. "He just got out of jail. He tried to kill her!" she repeated.

She jumped in her car and followed the wail of the sirens. They took Kim to the same hospital where Uncle Joe had been taken when he broke his hip in a fall from a ladder some months ago, so Cate had some familiarity with it. She headed for the entrance to the emergency room.

She doubted she'd get to see Kim anytime soon, but she was determined to wait until she could find out how bad Kim's injuries were. An officer showed up a few minutes later. They wouldn't let him in to see Kim either, but Cate gave him what information she had about both Kim and Travis. He didn't tell her anything in return. As Kim had once said, the police don't give you information; they just ask questions.

Okay, Travis Beauchamp, Cate thought to herself after the officer was gone. You just lost your right to privacy.

Back at the car, she slid into the front seat and picked up the manila envelope. A fingernail under the flap, some wiggles with her finger, and it was done. She pulled out the contents.

A title and registration for the motorcycle, Travis's name only. An insurance endorsement. A folded sheet of notebook paper with some dates and abbreviations and other figures on it. A passport and a receipt from the motel where he'd been arrested, plus a receipt with earlier dates from another motel. Cate studied the dates, calculating back to Ed's death. Yes, Travis had been in Eugene then.

She went back to the sheet of notebook

paper and studied it again. There were day and month dates but not years, cryptic abbreviations, and two sets of other numbers. Slowly, because of what she already knew about Travis, an interpretation emerged.

Maybe the police would scoff and say this was no proof of anything, that it could be a record of when Travis made his rare trips to the laundry and how much he spent. A record of gambling wins and losses or a rating system on women he'd dated. But Cate knew what it was. This was Travis's private record of dates and amounts of Rohypnol supplied to Celeste, and the money amounts, written without dollar signs, of what she'd paid him. The abbreviations were still meaningless. Maybe the supplier from whom he'd obtained the drug?

Travis had tried to extort more money out of Celeste, probably with the same threat of disclosure of the drug she was still giving her clients. But she wouldn't, or couldn't, pay him. And now she was dead.

Cate went back to the emergency room and settled down to wait endless hours. They weren't endless, but it was more than three hours before they let her into one of the curtained-off cubicles. Kim's eyes were closed, her upper body slightly raised on the bed. The blood had been cleaned off her face and the gash on her head bandaged. An IV line led to one hand. Her other arm wasn't bandaged, but it seemed to have some protective or supportive enclosure around it.

"Kim?" Cate whispered.

Kim's eyes opened. Her gaze wavered for only a moment before focusing on Cate.

"Kim, who did this to you?" Cate demanded. "Travis?"

"Nobody did it to me," Kim said. She sounded hoarse but mentally aware. And a little annoyed. "Couldn't you see what happened?"

"No. I followed the ambulance. I've been here ever since."

"Sweet Cate." Kim sounded grateful but mildly frustrated, as if Cate were a lovable but not-too-bright pet. "Thanks for getting me here."

"Are you in pain?"

Kim moved her shoulders and winced. "I'm not ready to go dancing."

"What have they done for you?"

"Put stitches in the gash. CAT-scanned my head. X-rayed everything else. Looked at my eyes. Tapped my knees for reflexes. Tested my blood for who knows what." Kim's voice gathered strength as she related what she apparently considered medical overkill. Then she looked down at the motionless arm. "And I managed to really mess up my arm. They're going to do surgery and put a metal pin in it tomorrow." Almost as an afterthought, she added, "And I have a concussion. They're going to do an MRI too."

"You seem to be talking okay, so that's good."

"Talking as well as your average blonde bimbo klutz, I suppose."

"Kim, stop that!"

Kim sighed and then grimaced as if that movement hurt too. "I think your prayers got hung up in call waiting or voice mail. Or maybe God just cuts you off if he doesn't want to listen."

"God listens, but he works on his timetable, not ours. And I didn't pray that he'd make all your problems disappear, just that you'd be able to manage and cope with them."

"Well, thanks. I guess."

"But what do you mean nobody did this to you? I saw you there on the floor, Kim. I thought you were dead under that brass shield! Did he hit you over the head with it? Throw it at you?"

"I wanted to get all those stupid swords down off the wall. I couldn't find a ladder."

Cate had noticed that the swords were gone from the wall, but she failed to see the connection here. "So . . . ?"

"So I piled up some stuff to climb on. A stool from behind the counter. Some of Mom's books on top of it. I could reach the swords with that, but I still couldn't get a grip on the shield. So I added a stack of Ouija boards and some magazines —"

"You were climbing on a pile of books and Ouija boards?"

"It seemed like a good idea at the time," Kim muttered. "I remember reaching for the shield, and slipping and grabbing at it to keep from falling. And then, this big crab was rushing up at me —"

"Crab?"

"You know, one of the astrological signs Mom had painted on the floor. And then, I just can't remember."

Cate leaned against the bed as her brain slowly rearranged facts. No one had tried to kill Kim. She'd created a Leaning Tower of Ouija and fallen. The brass shield had crashed down and slashed her head. She'd smashed into the concrete floor and knocked herself out.

"I guess I should have waited until I could get a ladder," Kim added.

"You think?" Cate said. A fall. Yet she was

reluctant to release Travis from responsibility. "What about Travis?"

"What about him? I called the jail. They're transferring him up to Tigard today."

"I found some papers among his things at the motel. They look like a record of the Rohypnol he sold to your mom."

Unexpectedly, Kim gave a gurgly laugh. "Yeah, that sounds like Travis. It was something that always seemed strange about him. He was such a slob about most things, but he kept records on everything from what kind of mileage we got on the car to how many kilograms of electricity we used every month."

"I think that's kilowatts of electricity."

"Whatever. I threw out boxes of the stuff when I came down here to live with Mom."

Okay, so Travis hadn't tried to kill Kim today, and he kept great records, even of his illicit activities. Which didn't mean he hadn't killed Celeste. Yet at the moment Cate's own accusation of Travis to the police at the Mystic Mirage struck her as wildly melodramatic. As a PI, she needed to establish credibility with the police, not make herself look like a hysterical crackpot shouting impossible accusations. Once they found out Travis was still in jail, that she was wrong about his getting out, which meant he couldn't possibly have had anything to do with Kim's injuries, they'd be skeptical of anything else she had to say. Especially an odd list of dates and figures she claimed was a record of Rohypnol sales.

"But now I've got a big problem," Kim said.

Kim had a lot of problems, but Cate didn't point that out.

"I was supposed to meet with LeAnne at Lodge Hill tonight. And be at weddings Tuesday and Wednesday evenings. But I don't know when I'll even get out of here. There was something about possible bleeding or swelling around the brain. As if my brain wasn't a big enough mess already."

"There's my friend Robyn's rehearsal dinner on Thursday too," Cate added reluctantly. "And her wedding on Friday."

"Yeah, well, my being there isn't going to happen." Kim gave a frustrated flop of feet, then winced at the pain that followed.

"Maybe LeAnne will stay on for a few days, since it's an emergency?"

"She made it plain when she first said she was leaving that she didn't care how inconvenient it was for me, she wasn't doing anything to jeopardize her new job. My stupid fall isn't going to change her mind. She liked Ed's ex-wife, but she's never had any use for me."

True. LeAnne had said as much to Cate.

"What I need to do is hire someone to take over at Lodge Hill temporarily. Because even when I do get out of here, I have the restaurant and house and Mystic Mirage to take care of."

"There is someone," Cate said slowly. "Things have no doubt changed since she was at Lodge Hill, but she knows the general way things operate there. It probably wouldn't take her long to catch up on details with LeAnne."

"Who else would know anything about Lodge Hill?"

"Jo-Jo."

"Jo-Jo?" Kim repeated the name blankly, then recognition kicked in. She repeated the name as if it hurt her teeth. "Jo-Jo, as in Ed's ex-wife?"

"She used to run Lodge Hill. Before Ed had his midlife change of direction." Or whatever it was.

"How could I possibly work with her? I mean, it would feel creepy," Kim said. "She'd never come to work at Lodge Hill anyway. She must hate me."

"She needs a job, even a temporary or part-time one. She isn't getting any insurance money. Ed squirmed out of paying the premiums, and the policy lapsed. She also doesn't get alimony from him anymore."

Not that he'd left Kim in a much better position, with big debts and foreclosures looming. Good ol' Ed. He'd managed to leave not just one but two wives in financial straits. Although Kim did have all those, as she put it, hockable items, which Jo-Jo didn't have.

"Jo-Jo isn't my responsibility!"

"At the moment, you probably need her more than she needs you," Cate pointed out.

The fingers on Kim's one working hand pleated and repleated a fold of the hospital sheet for several long moments.

"I was wrong, wasn't I? I've been thinking about it ever since you first came to talk to me. I never should have gotten involved with Ed when he was married. Wrong, wrong, wrong."

Cate wouldn't argue that. She expected Kim to add something putting blame on her mother's matchmaking, but all she did was say it again, her tone turning softer and a little sad. "Wrong."

A nurse came in to check Kim's IV, and Cate backed away from the bed. "I'd better be going now."

"Will you come back?"

"Yes, but I don't know exactly when. I

have a two-day surveillance job starting tomorrow. Uncle Joe is going to show me how to follow someone without getting caught or spooking the person. He thinks this will be a harder job than the one time I did a small surveillance job on my own."

"That almost sounds like fun. Watching someone when they don't know it. Why does this guy need to be followed?"

"His wife thinks he's cheating on her. She's going out of town and wants to know what he does while she's away."

Kim pleated the sheet again. "Maybe Jo-Jo should have hired a PI."

Cate went back to the Mystic Mirage. The officers were no longer there, but no crime scene tape blocked the door. Kim's Mustang was still parked on the street. Cate peered through the store window again, this time seeing the damaged doll and the fallen shield and books from a different perspective. Not a crime scene. Just a, as Kim had put it, stupid fall. A flying book had probably taken out the doll.

She went to the police station, hoping to find the officers who'd been at the Mystic Mirage, but she wound up telling a different officer about her mistaken accusation that Travis had tried to kill Kim. He wrote it all down, but she had the feeling that by the time she was done, she'd come off sounding like a Nancy Drew wannabe with serious credibility problems.

She didn't mention Travis's other crimes. She'd have better proof when she made the accusation about murder.

24

Cate spent the next two days sharing surveillance with Uncle Joe. Unfortunately, the
wife's suspicions proved correct. This was a
cheating husband.

Cate showered as soon as they got home,
then went to the hospital. She found Kim
in a regular room now. No flowers. Kim's
arm wasn't in a cast yet, apparently because
of the surgery, but it was immobilized. She
said she was doing okay, but she sounded
jittery when she added that she wouldn't be
released until later in the week because they
were still concerned about her concussion.

"I contacted Jo-Jo," Kim added. It
sounded like a decision she'd made reluctantly. "She's taking over managing Lodge
Hill temporarily. LeAnne is already gone."

"Good. I'm proud of you. You're taking
charge."

"She sounded nicer than I expected," Kim
admitted. "But don't expect us to do the

BFF thing. We aren't going to be doing each other's hair and texting twenty times a day."

"You don't have to be friends, but, at the moment, you need each other."

"Yeah, I guess so. Hey, I remembered something. My head was too fuzzy to tell you when you were here before. Although it probably isn't important anyway."

"Remembered what?"

"When I was going through stuff getting ready for the closing sale, I found a little camera in a cardboard box by Mom's desk." Kim looked off into space thoughtfully. "Actually, it almost looked as if it were hidden there. It was down under some strings of Christmas lights we used in the windows last year."

"Did you look at the photos on it?"

"I tried to, but I couldn't figure out how. I'm not too good with figuring out how things work."

Right. Kim was the woman who couldn't figure out the coffeemaker in her own kitchen.

"Maybe it's broken anyway, and that's why she threw it in the box. Photography used to be a hobby of hers, but she hadn't done much of it lately. I put the camera in the Mustang. Is the car still there at the Mystic Mirage?"

"It was the last time I looked. But I don't have any way to get in it."

"I think the keys are in the clothes I was wearing when they brought me in here. They're in a plastic bag over there in the closet."

Cate went by the Mystic Mirage as soon as she left the hospital. A minute later she had in hand the small camera Kim had tossed in the backseat. Cate was no camera expert. She tended to use her cell phone to take an occasional photo, and didn't even own an actual camera. But this one didn't look complicated, no fancy settings. She sat in her own car and expectantly pushed a little button labeled "Power." What would she see? Something that incriminated Travis? This must be what he'd been searching for in Celeste's apartment!

But what Cate saw was a little blank, dead screen.

She pushed more buttons, twisted a dial, clicked an up-and-down thing. Nothing. No lit-up screen. No hum of lens gadget opening. She gave the camera a couple of frustrated shakes.

Which didn't, of course, make it work.

Maybe the camera was broken, and Celeste had just discarded it in the cardboard box. Uncle Joe would probably know how to tell. But he and Rebecca were already on their way to the coast, taking a few days off after the surveillance.

Okay, once again she'd have to call on Mitch for help.

Cate called Robyn at the flower shop first, ordered flowers for Kim's hospital room, and told her about the change in managers at Lodge Hill. She was afraid Robyn might go hyper, but at the moment Robyn was more concerned about her arriving bridesmaids and where she was going to put them.

Cate stopped by the Computer Solutions Dudes office, but Mitch was out on a consulting job. That evening and Thursday morning, Cate was busy ferrying bridesmaids from the airport to the house. All were chattery and vivacious and suitably brunette.

At noon on Thursday, Robyn took the entire tribe of maid of honor and bridesmaids to lunch at Mr. K's. It was a bubbly, giggly gathering as they reminisced about their college days together. Cate felt out of place, but she was more concerned about the restaurant.

Some definite glitches surfaced. The service was erratic, with their orders somehow mixed up with orders from another table. The garlic was so strong on the croutons in Cate's Caesar salad that she had the feeling her breath could out-flame any stray dragons. Kim definitely had management problems here.

Over dessert, Robyn made the announcement, apparently as much a surprise to the other bridesmaids as it was to Cate, that the rehearsal that evening would be a full dress event. Except for herself, of course, since the groom couldn't see the bride in her gown until the actual wedding. There were murmurs of protest that no one ever did it that way.

"It *is* my wedding, and I want to try out everything to be certain it's all going to work," Robyn countered, in her sweetly bullying way. "And Cate, you'll wear your wig, of course."

Cate's wig. Which at the moment consisted of a plastic bag of cat-shredded brown stuff, suitable only as nesting material for some desperate bird. She'd planned to go by the wig shop Friday morning, and if the wig hadn't come in by then, buy whatever was available in stock. Now she tweaked the timing. "Of course," she murmured. "I'm looking forward to it."

After Robyn paid the bill, she went to

check with someone about the buffet for the rehearsal dinner that evening. She came back looking as if she'd stumbled over a horde of giant cockroaches in the kitchen.

Cate pulled her aside as they went out to the parking lot. "Is something wrong?"

"The main chef, the one I'd talked to about both the rehearsal buffet and the reception dinner, has quit and gone to Portland."

So here was another person apparently thinking, like LeAnne, that with only Kim in control, it was time to desert the sinking ship.

"Will that affect the buffet tonight?"

"An assistant chef assured me everything is 'under control.' Wasn't that what someone said just before the *Titanic* went down?"

"It'll all work out fine," Cate soothed.

Not, she hoped, Famous Last Words.

"Yes, it came in this morning." The clerk at the wig boutique smiled brightly and pulled a round box out from under the counter. Cate was relieved that this was not the woman who had earlier seemed inclined to blackball her from wig ownership. "Would you like to try it on?"

"I'm sure it's fine."

"This wig isn't exactly like the other one.

They were out of that model, but the only difference is this one is a little longer. This model would normally cost considerably more, but because they couldn't accommodate you with the model you wanted, the price is exactly the same!"

Yes, the same. Exorbitant. "Thank you. I appreciate that."

She consoled herself with the thought that she might find some undercover PI use for the wig eventually.

Back home, she called and talked briefly to Mitch. He was not happy about having to do the tux thing two nights in a row, but he was on his way to pick up all the tuxes from the rental outfit now. The guys could then all change into them at Lodge Hill. He said if Cate would bring the camera to the rehearsal, he'd take a look at it.

That evening, Cate draped the dress in the backseat of her car and set the boxed wig on the passenger's seat. Octavia had batted hopefully at the box several times, but Cate had kept it securely taped shut to prevent a second wig demolition.

At Lodge Hill, Cate's Honda gave an unexpected cough and rattle when she turned off the engine. She felt a brief panic, but determinedly decided it was something to worry about later. No time for it now. She retrieved the gown from the backseat and carefully folded the skirt over the hanger so it wouldn't drag. Gown in one hand, wig box in the other, she'd just started across the lighted parking lot when a pickup pulled out of the driveway leading back to Rolf's cottage. She didn't think he saw her until the pickup suddenly swerved and stopped beside her.

Rolf rolled down the window. "So, this is the night of the big wedding?"

"No, just the rehearsal dinner. Did you get the motorcycle moved over here okay?"

"Yeah, it's out in my carport. If you ask me, Travis oughta junk it. Engine sounds like a garbage disposal grinding up bones. But I guess that doesn't matter, since he's in jail anyway."

"He'll probably be out on bail soon."

"I hope he stays away from Kim. She has enough troubles without him hanging around."

One point on which they were agreed, although all Cate said was, "It's nice of you to help her out with the motorcycle."

"That's me, ever the nice, helpful guy." He smiled. "Don't forget how cooperative I am. Anytime. And I have this weakness for redheads."

But I don't have a weakness for guys with a God's-gift-to-women complex.

Inside, Cate headed up the stairs to the dressing room, but she detoured when she spotted Jo-Jo and a woman in a Mr. K's uniform setting out hors d'oeuvres in the main Chapel Room.

"It's great of you to be here," Cate said.

"I feel as if I'm fraternizing with the enemy," Jo-Jo grumped. "Imagine. Me, helping Eddie's new wife."

"Widow," Cate pointed out. "And you said you needed a job."

"Ex-wives and current wives shouldn't get along. It's unnatural. Like a fox and chicken being friends." Jo-Jo scowled as she arranged tiny crackers with caviar on a silver platter. "But she isn't weird, like I thought she was." Another pause and scowl. "Actually, I kind of like her."

"Is everything going okay here?"

"The hors d'oeuvres are fine, and I made up a big bowl of punch, but someone from the restaurant called and said they had a problem with the van delivering the food for the buffet and it would be late. Then the minister called. I was just going to find Robyn and tell her he said he'd be late too."

"I'll tell her. You just take care of things here."

394

"Okay. Oh, I wanted to tell you. I've started your redheaded doll. You are still my private investigator, aren't you?"

"I'm kind of sidetracked with the wedding and all, but I'm definitely working on it."

"Good."

Jo-Jo's cell phone rang, and Cate headed for the dressing room. Behind her, the photographer had arrived and was photographing the hors d'oeuvres.

The other bridesmaids, plus the maid of honor, Robyn, and Aunt Carly, were already in the dressing room. Cate noted that a small Band-Aid was all Robyn needed to cover the cut on her hand now. Robyn's cell phone rang while Cate was hanging her celadon gown on a rack with the others just like it. Hanging there together, they had the strange look of oversized clumps of genetically altered celery, a salad experiment gone awry. But, Cate hurriedly reminded herself, her gown had looked great when she put it on.

Robyn pressed her phone to her chest. Her face had that this-can't-be-happening-to-me look.

"That was the wife of the guy I hired as master of ceremonies and deejay for the reception. He was supposed to be here for the rehearsal tonight too." She looked down at the cell phone as if it were some alien machine receiving unwelcome signals from another galaxy. "He has laryngitis."

"What about tomorrow night?" a bridesmaid asked.

"His wife said he's been sick like this before. It usually lasts four or five days." She took a deep breath. "But everything is going to be all right," she said, as if it were a mantra she was repeating regularly. "Surely nothing else can go wrong."

Cate hated to have to tell her that more *had* gone wrong, but she repeated what Jo-Jo had told her about both the minister and the buffet being late.

"Should we get dressed?" a bridesmaid asked.

"Not yet," Robyn said in her tone that suggested the entire wedding was on the brink of extinction. "I need to talk to Lance."

Robyn hurried off, and the bridesmaids milled around, although Cate gave them credit for not being the kind of friends who made catty remarks the minute one of their group left the room. They just talked about how stressful this was for Robyn.

Yes, it was stressful, Cate had to agree. But it would be less so if Robyn would just lighten up about details and be glad she was marrying a great guy.

Then she had a different thought about the voiceless deejay, the late minister, and problems with the buffet.

Perfect timing.

25

Cate slipped out the main entrance and circled the hedged enclosure. She'd wanted the chance to see if the saddlebags on Travis's motorcycle held anything useful, perhaps even the gun, and here was that chance. Rehearsal delayed, so no one would miss her for a few minutes, and Rolf was gone somewhere in his pickup.

A yard light on a tall pole lit up the area around Rolf's cottage, but the light didn't spill into the carport. It was a dark cavern of shadows, and Cate hesitated. But Travis's bike was in there somewhere, and she made herself plunge into the darkness.

Once in the carport, her eyes adjusted, and she could make out dim shapes of the bikes that looked as if some motorcycle-hungry monster had been chomping on them. The place smelled of oil and paint and other unidentifiable scents of repair work. She touched something that made her foot jerk back . . . alive? No, just a tangled electric cord. Then her other foot hit a metal something, and down she went. Face first in the dirt.

She lay there a minute, disoriented by the shadows and her spinning head and the taste of oily dirt in her mouth. She finally squirmed to a sitting position and wiped a hand across her face. Her nose felt as if it had been squashed into a new shape. A little late, she remembered the bullet-sized flashlight on her key ring and groped it out of her pocket. Its tiny beam showed oily spots on the knees of her jeans and what looked like the remains of motorcycle warfare around her. Bike parts everywhere.

She tried to see a silver lining as she struggled to her feet. If the carport floor had been concrete instead of dirt, she and Kim might have had matching concussions.

She balanced herself with a hand on the skeleton of a motorcycle and flicked the beam around the carport. Travis's bike stood near a counter along the back wall. She headed for it, picking her way through the booby trap of bike parts. Maybe future generations would drill for oil here. Rolf seemed to have spilled enough of it.

The first thing she discovered was that she couldn't open the saddlebags. She leaned over to focus the flashlight's tiny beam on the small lock. TV and mystery-novel PIs always seemed to know how to open or circumvent locks, but Cate had no such expertise. It wasn't a formidable-looking lock, but poking at it with a fingernail resulted only in a broken fingernail. But another flick of her flashlight beam revealed tools scattered on the counter behind the bike. She grabbed a screwdriver.

She was trying to ease the screwdriver into the lock when she heard a car engine, and then the carport blazed with light. She looked up into a blinding glare of headlights. She squinted and held up a hand to dim the glare, and through a space between her fingers saw Rolf's pickup stopped just outside the carport. A car, the red Camaro she'd seen at the motel, pulled in beside it. Cate's first frantic thought was *hide*! The next thought was *where*? She didn't look enough like a bike part to just blend in.

She flicked the flashlight off, but a moment later Rolf hit a switch by the door, and overhead fluorescent lights flooded the entire carport.

Her next thought was defensive. Why should she hide? She might not be handling this in the most orthodox manner, but there was nothing actually wrong in her doing this. Hopefully. Although the screwdriver in her hand felt as incriminating as a burglar's leg climbing through an open window.

Cate expected immediate confrontation, but what Rolf said mildly was, "If you're trying to hotwire the bike, I don't think that's the way to do it. But if you want to learn, I can show you how."

Cate straightened from her bent position. "Well, uh, thanks. But I guess not. This is Travis's bike, isn't it?"

The blonde woman was out of the Camaro now, standing at the edge of the carport with a DVD case in one hand and a frown on her face. She wore tight jeans, high-heeled boots, and a black turtleneck decorated with sparkly stuff. "What's going on? Who's she?"

"Cate is a private investigator," Rolf said. He sounded amused. "Apparently she's doing some investigating."

Cate held up the screwdriver and studied it as if baffled. "Which end of this is it you're supposed to use?"

Rolf laughed. "Kim wants to know what's in the saddlebags of her ex-husband's bike?" he asked. Before Cate could mumble an ambiguous reply, he added, "I put the keys in the house. I'll go get them."

Maybe she should have enlisted Rolf's

help to begin with. He seemed cooperative enough.

"I thought we were going to watch *Spider-man,*" the woman complained.

"This won't take long," Rolf said. "You can go on inside and get the DVD set up."

Rolf headed for the door to the house, but the woman looked undecided about following him. Finally she planted her boot-clad feet in the dirt floor of the carport, crossed her arms, and studied Cate suspiciously.

"I'm Melody Ketchison," she said. "You two seem to know each other."

"Hi, Melody. I'm a bridesmaid at a wedding tomorrow night, and the rehearsal dinner is tonight." Cate motioned toward the bright lights of Lodge Hill filtering through the trees as if that explained everything. "There seem to be problems with both the minister and the buffet."

Cate had found that a barrage of irrelevant information was a useful PI technique, and it seemed to work now.

"I've heard it's really nice but awfully expensive to have a wedding there," Melody said.

"I think it's the man you're marrying that matters more than where the ceremony is held or what it costs," Cate said.

"Yeah, that's true." Melody glanced toward the door again as if evaluating Rolf's qualifications in that area. Personally, on a list of Would I Want to Marry This Guy?, Cate's list would have the No Way box checked by Rolf's name. But she didn't say that. The woman turned her suspicions back on Cate. "How do you happen to know Rolf?"

Rolf came out of the house dangling a key ring from a forefinger like a trophy, so Cate didn't have to answer the question. He fitted one of the keys into the lock on the saddlebag. With his left hand, Cate noted.

"You haven't looked in here already?" Cate said.

"I wasn't curious enough before." Rolf smiled as if they were in some conspiracy together. "But if you and Kim are interested, so am I. I'm thinking you both figure Travis was up to his ears in murder, don't you?"

"The guy who owns this bike is a *murderer*?" Melody took a step backward, as if the motorcycle might reach out and grab her.

Rolf turned the key and lifted the lid on the saddlebag. In doing so, the sleeve on his left arm pushed up.

Cate reeled and had to catch the back fender of the bike for balance. Because at that moment, all that had been hiding in her subconscious since that night at the Mystic Mirage popped into Technicolor memory.

A left arm bursting through a beaded curtain. An arm with a multicolored tattoo of swirled lines, and in the center of the lines a malevolent dark eye.

The same dark eye she was seeing right now.

Rolf looked up. "You okay?"

Their eyes met, and she desperately willed hers not to give away any hint of recognition. Or to find any recognition in his.

"I-I'm just a little shaky, I guess. I fell over some piece of a motorcycle and hit my face in the dirt just before you got here." She ran her fingers across her squashed nose. "Didn't your mother ever tell you to put things away?"

"My mother never put *her* things away. Beer bottles and cigarette butts all over the house." Rolf reached over and brushed a finger over Cate's cheek. There was an odd intimacy to the touch that made her shudder. Oil and dirt smudged the finger when he took it away. He wiped the finger on his jeans. She wiped her face with both hands.

"I suppose you're going to sue me now," Rolf said. "Stress, pain and suffering, brain damage, warts, flat feet, et cetera."

Cate tried to match his teasing tone. "Probably more money in that than in being a PI."

"Sorry to have to tell you, but my entire fortune is tied up in bike parts. But maybe we could work out some other deal." Cate heard the suggestion of some risqué double meaning in his banter, but she was relieved. Because it meant Rolf was still being Rolf, confident any woman within range was smitten by his masculine charms. He hadn't caught her shocked moment of recognition, and he still hadn't recognized her.

It didn't escape Melody's attention that something was going on, however. She wrapped a possessive hand around Rolf's arm. "C'mon, let's go watch this DVD. She can look in the saddlebags by herself."

"No, I'm interested too." Rolf impatiently shook off her hand. "Maybe Travis keeps his gun in here. The one he shot Kieferson with."

What Cate wanted to do was get out of there. Run, run, run. Before Rolf somehow did recognize her, and his playful teasing turned deadly.

But she forced herself to watch Rolf pull the contents out of one saddlebag and dump them on the motorcycle seat. No gun. Just more dirty clothes. Plus a couple of

Styrofoam cups, a Sonic hamburger wrapper, and an empty Dr Pepper can. One thing to be said for Travis. Not a litterbug. Travis dutifully packed his trash away in his saddlebags.

The other saddlebag held a scrunched-up leather jacket with a carton of garbage bags on top. Cate almost smiled. She knew what those were for.

She also knew something else now. Travis was a lousy husband, a blackmailer, and probably a burglar. But he wasn't a killer.

Cate's almost-smile turned to a shiver.

The killer was right here beside her.

She studied him furtively as he dug to the bottom of the saddlebag. He dragged out a bottle of cologne, opened and sniffed it.

"Try this. Does Travis really think women go for a smell like this?"

Rolf thrust the open bottle under Cate's nose. Rotten roses.

Cate's nose automatically wrinkled. "Maybe he figured dabbing on cologne was easier than washing his clothes."

She managed the snarky comeback even as the thought that filled her mind was that Rolf might have better taste in cologne than Travis did, but Rolf was the *killer*. She'd abandoned her first suspicions about Rolf in favor of Travis as murderer, but she'd been right the first time. Nerves prickled her body and trickled icy sweat down her ribs. She had to go to the police and tell them she'd remembered the tattoo on the arm that night at the Mystic Mirage. And that she knew who the arm belonged to.

Would they believe her? Or scoff at this miraculous return of memory? She had no explanation to offer for why Rolf had killed Celeste. Or what he was searching for when he trashed her apartment, which he must also have done. Or if he'd killed Ed too.

Cate swallowed. The thoughts in her head suddenly seemed so loud that Rolf surely must hear them. She covered them with a white noise of chatter.

"Well, I'd better be getting back to the rehearsal dinner. Mr. K's restaurant is doing the buffet. They do all Lodge Hill's food, you know. But I think they're having problems there since Mr. Kieferson died. You two enjoy that DVD. *Spiderman,* you said it was, didn't you? I've heard it's good."

"Hey, you could stay and watch it with us," Rolf said. "We'll pop some popcorn to go with the wine."

"She could watch it *with* us?" the woman echoed with appalled indignation.

"Sounds like fun, but I am a bridesmaid. I guess it takes practice, that's what this rehearsal dinner is all about. So we won't make a mistake and all go down like a line of falling dominos during the ceremony."

Cate backed away as she chattered. She wondered about leaving Melody here alone with Rolf. But Melody was a girlfriend, no threat to him, so surely safe enough.

"Thanks for finding the keys," Cate called back from outside the carport. "I'll tell Kim that it was just more of Travis's dirty clothes in the saddlebags. Maybe they'll teach him how to do laundry in jail! See you later," she added with a perky wave as she headed for the driveway.

Behind her, she heard Melody ask suspiciously, "What does she mean by that?"

Good. Rolf would have his hands full placating her. As soon as Cate got back to the lodge, she'd call the police. No, she'd go right to the station after the rehearsal. That way she could do a sketch of the tattoo for them. Once it had been only a shadow out of reach in her mind, but now it felt scorched on her brain.

But no need to panic right now. Rolf hadn't recognized her from that night at the Mystic Mirage, and he hadn't caught her shock when she recognized his arm.

Back at the entrance to Lodge Hill, Cate rushed inside and upstairs to the Chapel

Room. There, bridesmaids in gowns and men in tuxes, along with Aunt Carly and a few other people Cate didn't know, milled around the table set up at the rear of the room with hors d'oeuvres and a crystal bowl of punch. She spotted Mitch, indeed looking like a best man, the best man ever, and nothing to do with the wedding. She wanted to tell him what she'd just found out, but Robyn rushed over and grabbed her.

"Where have you *been*? We're about to start the rehearsal. And what happened to you? Your nose is all red. And your face is filthy!"

Cate covered the offending nose with a hand. "The minister got here?"

"No, we'll have to manage without him. Just go get your gown and wig on." Robyn shoved Cate none too gently toward the dressing room.

Cate washed the smudges of oil and dirt off her face, sloshed more cold water on her nose, and pulled the gown over her head. Robyn had zipped it up easily the one time Cate had tried it on, but now she had to twist into pretzel contortions to do it herself. Thankfully, a glance in the full-length mirror showed that the dress still looked great. She piled her hair on top of her head and anchored it with a few pins.

She yanked the round box open but stopped short when she pulled out the new brown wig.

The clerk at the hair salon had been half right. The wig was longer. But "a little longer" was an understatement. When she got it on her head, the brown hair swung somewhere in the vicinity of her tailbone. She stared at herself in the mirror.

This wig, like the original one, transformed her. But it was not that sultry-smoky-sophisticated glamour transformation. Were there somewhere five horses bereft of brown tails because all those appendages were now hanging from Cate's head?

And no flattering sidesweep of bangs here. These bangs enveloped her forehead like some fungal growth crawling through her eyebrows.

Maybe no one would notice. She shut out the cynical *Yeah, right* that followed the hopeful thought.

She slipped into her high-heeled wedding sandals and thumped out to the Chapel Room.

Little frown lines gathered between Robyn's brows when she saw Cate. "The wig looks . . . different than I remember."

"I feel so glamorous." Cate whirled, and

the long hair swirled around her shoulders. In the other wig, the flying hair would have looked dramatic, even romance-heroine lush. In this wig, it was more like the five horse tails were trying to find a fly to swat.

Robyn opened her mouth as if she were going to say something more, but she had problems other than a horse tail wig at the moment. She turned away and started arranging — and rearranging — bridesmaids and groomsmen. The woman photographer scooted here and there photographing everything until Robyn growled, "Not now!" at her. Cate found herself at the end of the lineup without a groomsman partner.

The bridesmaid ahead of her also lacked a groomsman. "Two of them didn't show," she whispered to Cate.

Robyn, ears apparently tuned to dog-whistle sensitivity level tonight, overheard. "They had car trouble, that's all. *That's all,*" she emphasized, as if trying to convince herself the two hadn't deserted like the proverbial rats from a sinking ship.

But so many car problems — the buffet van, the minister, and now the groomsmen — did seem odd. A virulent car plague going around?

"They'll be here tomorrow night," Robyn said. The determination in her voice had an "or else" lurking at the end of the statement.

It was an odd rehearsal, with Robyn both a participant and director, and no minister, but Robyn staunchly managed it like a general preparing troops for battle. Three times they went through it, Lance and Mitch entering from a side door with an invisible minister, the march down the aisle between the rows of chairs, Aunt Carly giving Robyn away, and the triumphant recessional. Always Robyn found some detail unacceptable.

Until finally even usually amiable bridegroom Lance balked at a fourth rerun, for which Cate was grateful. Her feet were cramping in the sandals with higher heels than she ever wore, her bumped nose felt as if it were turning bulbous on her face, and her nerves screeched as if Octavia had them in her claws. As soon as she could get out of here, she was going to the police with what she knew about Rolf. She'd ask Mitch to go with her and along the way explain to him what she now knew.

After the end of the rehearsal, everyone tromped downstairs to the Reception Room, grumpy moods lifting with the prospect of food. But the long table where the buffet should be was empty as the cupboard in that Old Mother Hubbard nursery rhyme.

Robyn stared at it as if this were the disaster to end all disasters.

Jo-Jo, unexpectedly smiling, rushed out of the kitchen and up to Robyn. She whispered something, and Robyn unexpectedly smiled too. She freshened like a wilted plant just watered.

"Good news, everyone! The food will be on its way shortly. So everyone just relax." She turned to Jo-Jo. "Perhaps you could bring the punch bowl down and refill it so we'll have something to drink while we wait? It is marvelous punch."

"Well . . . uh, certainly."

Cate followed as Jo-Jo headed for the kitchen. "Is something wrong?" she whispered.

"Only that I used every bottle of ginger ale in the kitchen to fill that bowl the first time. There's plenty of fruit juice in the freezer to make punch, but not a drop of ginger ale. The punch is flat as old pond water without it." Jo-Jo glanced back over her shoulder. "And the natives are getting restless. To say nothing of the bride herself."

"Okay, you start mixing fruit juice. I'll go find ginger ale."

Cate followed Jo-Jo to the kitchen, by unspoken agreement their steps calm and unhurried so as not to give any hint of panic. But once in the kitchen, Cate dashed up a narrow back stairs to get her purse and keys from the dressing room. She didn't like running off to the store in her bridesmaid gown, but she hadn't time for the unzipping contortions.

Downstairs, Jo-Jo held the door open for her. "Get some oranges too," she called as Cate took off across the parking lot. "They'll look nice sliced thin on top."

Cate picked up the skirt as she ran so it wouldn't drag on the asphalt. Then she had to stop. Stupid sandals! She hopped from foot to foot as she snatched the sandals off, and then sprinted barefoot to her car. At the door, she thrust the key in the lock, got the door open, tossed purse, sandals, and herself inside, and jammed the key in the ignition.

And listened to the engine grind uselessly. *R-r-r-r, r-r-r-r, r-r-r-r,* hopeless as her computer showing that blue screen of death. Maybe there *was* some virulent car plague going around tonight. She'd have to go get Mitch.

The car door opened just as she reached for the handle. She looked up in relief. Mitch had followed her!

Not Mitch.

Rolf.

26

Cate froze as she looked up at him. Was he seeing her as Cate? Or as the dark-haired woman he'd tried to choke at the Mystic Mirage? And why was he here?

"Oh, Rolf! You startled me."

"You startled *me*." He said it with a peculiar little smile that made Cate's scalp prickle under the wig.

She glanced around him. "Where's your girlfriend?"

"She's a jealous freak. She got it in her head that you and I have this hot romance going and took off like that well-known bat out of you-know-where."

"That's ridiculous!"

"She'll be back." Rolf sounded as if he didn't care one way or the other. Right now, his focus was only on Cate. A focus that made her hands clutch the steering wheel as if it might try to escape. Which is what she wanted to do.

"Great dress," Rolf added. "Though I can't say as much for the wig."

Great. Now she was getting fashion critiques from a killer. Yet it wasn't that flip thought that made her stomach churn and her palms slicken. It was the raw knowledge that this was *real,* that this man standing beside her car had held a sword and rammed it into Celeste's chest. A killer.

Yet she couldn't acknowledge she knew that. If she could just make Rolf think she didn't know anything or that he'd made a mistake —

"Look, I'm sorry, but I'm really in a hurry. We're in the middle of a ginger-ale emergency, and I have to run to a store."

Cate grabbed the handle to yank the door shut, but Rolf obviously recognized that as illogical, because he'd heard that *r-r-r-r* too. The car wasn't going anywhere. He jerked her to her feet, but his body trapped her between the car door and the driver's seat.

"You're trying to lock me out? Now, Cate, that's rude, don't you think?" He kept a steely grip on her shoulder with one hand and lifted a hank of brown hair with the other.

Think! Jab him in the eyes with her car keys? That was supposed to be an effective technique. Right. And whose agile body was going to twist around to the other side of the steering wheel and grab the keys? Not hers.

"Like I said, you startled me when I first saw you there in the carport. I was almost sure then, when all I could see was your face in the little light from your flashlight. So I had to wonder what the woman from the Mystic Mirage was doing in my carport. Then I saw that unmistakable red hair, and I was confused."

He said the word with a hint of reproach, as if his confusion were some fault of hers. He smoothed the brown hair of the wig in a way that made Cate shiver. Almost a caress. Almost a threat.

"I really do have to go after that ginger ale —"

"But then I was positive when I sneaked upstairs and played Peeping Tom watching the rehearsal. And realized it was you all along, the redhead in a brown wig. Though you sure had me fooled before tonight." He tapped her forehead as if chastising her for the deception.

Cate determinedly detoured his statement of recognition even as it sent ripples of panic through her. "The bride insisted on the wig. Maybe you noticed the bridesmaids are all brunettes? Her color scheme, you know, to emphasize how blonde she is." Cate managed an exaggerated roll of eyes. "The others are all natural brunettes, but I had to get this wig to fit in. I know how it looks. Like I stole the tails off a herd of horses! Then a couple of the groomsmen didn't show up, and now the buffet is late, so Robyn wanted more punch while we waited, and I really have to get the ginger ale for the punch. Before Robyn goes into orbit or the wedding party turns into a mob rioting for food and drink."

The barrage of irrelevant chatter didn't work this time.

"Shut up, Cate. I know who you are and what you saw at the Mystic Mirage. And then when you saw the tattoo on my arm tonight . . ." He shook his head. "I could practically smell the panic. Just like now. Not a good scent on you, Cate. Worse than ol' Travis's cologne."

She'd thought he hadn't noticed anything about her reaction there in the carport, but she'd been wrong. Maybe *dead* wrong. Maybe he'd have done something right then, but he couldn't with jealous Melody standing there tapping her booted toe. She tried to keep from swallowing convulsively.

"I-I don't know what you're talking about."

"Have you talked to the police yet?"

Cate started to babble a denial. No, she hadn't talked to the police, hadn't told them anything about him! So everything was fine. Then she realized that was exactly the wrong thing to let him know.

"Yes! I-I called them as soon as I got back from the carport. They'll be here any minute now. They know all about you. Your arm, the tattoo, everything!"

For a hopeful moment, Cate actually thought he bought it. He'd turn and run. Instead he laughed.

"You're a lousy liar, Private Investigator Cate Kinkaid."

She automatically started to correct him. "Assistant —" She broke off as she realized that scrupulous honesty about her PI status wasn't going to win her any brownie points at the moment. And what she should be doing was screeching her head off.

She gave it a try. "Help!" The first word came out a squeak instead of a scream. She lifted her head and got it up to a yell. "Mit —"

Before she could get the name out, he clamped a hand over her mouth and yanked her around with his other hand so her back was to his chest. Over the hand clamped at her mouth, Cate's gaze jerked to the brightly lit windows of the Reception Room. She saw what he was also seeing. Nothing happening there. No one looking out a window. No one rushing out the door to help her.

She tried another yell. Great. Now she sounded like a moose in labor. And earned herself a vicious dig of fingers into her jaw.

Now what? Rolf seemed to be considering that question too, even as his arm crushed her ribs and his hand smashed her mouth.

Was grabbing her some unprepared, impulse decision? Like killing Celeste with a sword snatched off the wall? Maybe that plague her car had caught was a good thing. It kept him from just throwing her in the trunk and taking off. But now he didn't know what to do with her?

She wasn't going to stand here and cooperatively wait while he decided on a suitable course of action. She tensed her leg and kicked backward into his shin.

Barefoot, that had about as much effect as a marshmallow attacking a refrigerator, and all it did was make her heel hum with pain. She tried to bite his hand clamped over her mouth, but she couldn't even get her mouth open.

She was breathing hard, at least as hard as she could breathe with her mouth clamped shut and her lungs compressed under his arm, but he wasn't even puffing. All he did was mutter, "Nice try, Ms. PI."

She tried again, a backward punch with her elbow into his ribs.

But all that blow did was the funny-bone thing that made her elbow feel as if she'd stuck it in an electric socket, and his only reaction was a grunt. He whipped her around until they were facing the river. Moonlight turned the flowing water to liquid silver. Lights glittered on the far side. A scent of smoke drifted from the back side of the vineyard, incongruously bringing a nostalgic memory of bonfires back home when she was a girl. The dock and little rowboat looked picturesque as an artist's moonlit painting.

She hadn't realized it was such a beautiful night until now. Enough to take your breath away. Except hers was already taken away by the harsh grip over her mouth and around her ribs. A killer grip. And she knew he wasn't admiring the view. What was he thinking now?

The stark thought that this might be her last moonlit night here on earth hit her. Because Rolf couldn't let her live with what she knew about him. The only question seemed to be how he intended to do it.

Lord, help me, guide me! Send someone!

421

Tell me what to do!

Where was that van from Mr. K's with the buffet food? Where was some couple coming out for a romantic stroll in the moonlight? And where, when you needed one, was a smoker sneaking out for a puff?

Rolf made up his mind and started walking her across the parking lot. His knees bumped the back side of her legs. She stubbed her bare toe on the asphalt and stumbled, but his grip didn't loosen. She made the only noise she could, a squeak of protest, when they reached the road that led around to his cottage and the sharp gravel bit into her bare feet. He didn't slow down, just yanked her higher so her feet dangled above the gravel.

His grip didn't soften, but once they were around the line of trees that concealed the cottage from Lodge Hill, she felt him relax slightly. She stiffened when they reached his pickup . . . he was going to throw her into it! No, he bypassed the pickup and plunged into the dark carport. He circled the dismembered motorcycles and took her to the counter at the back wall. He had to take his arm from around her ribs so he could use his hand, but he slammed her against the counter and held her immobile with his body.

With his free hand he flicked the switch on a fluorescent bulb that buzzed to light over the counter. He grabbed a roll of duct tape hanging on a nail on the wall.

With killer resourcefulness and one hand still over her mouth, he held the roll to his teeth and loosened a six-inch strip with his other hand, then used his teeth to tear it off the roll. Much more competent with teeth than she was. He slapped the strip of duct tape across her mouth as he pulled his other hand away. With both hands free and his body still pinning her against the counter, he quickly added several more strips of tape across her mouth.

He twisted her palms together, efficiently wrapped duct tape around her wrists, and shoved her toward the door that led inside the house.

Inside, the first thing she saw was a dim vision of a woman in a long, pale dress with dark hair hanging at a peculiar angle. A moment later she realized this refugee from a cheesy horror movie was *her,* reflected in an uncurtained window at the far end of the living room.

Maybe someone would see her?

No. The vineyard started back there.

Other than her own reflection, the small house looked incongruously cozy. Coffeemaker and toaster on the kitchen counter, row of duck magnets on the refrigerator, faint scent of fried bacon and onions in the air. The living room sofa was brown suede with a scattering of orange pillows, bright Navajo throw rug on a hardwood floor, TV with a stack of DVDs beside it. A table held an assortment of cups and trophies, most with a bronze or silver motorcycle and rider on top. An arched doorway opened onto a hallway.

Rolf didn't offer her a guided tour of his motorcycle race trophies. He shoved her through the hallway and into a bedroom. Cate made an instinctive squeak-yelp of terror.

He flicked a light switch. "Don't worry. I've lost my taste for redheads. This is strictly business. Although I must admit you do pack an interesting briefcase."

He bent down and with several more wraps of duct tape fastened her ankles together. Now she knew what the roped and tied calf felt like at a rodeo she'd seen once. Except here there was no quick release coming a minute later.

Rolf yanked the closet door open, studied the interior, and apparently decided against it. Why didn't he just throw her in the pickup and take her somewhere? He'd have to kill her before he dumped her, of course. But surely that wouldn't be a problem for him.

She snapped a curtain over the thoughts. Don't give him ideas he hadn't already thought of!

He looked over at her, still standing where he'd left her, since a bunny-hop attempt at escape hadn't seemed too workable.

"You're a problem, you know that?" he grumbled. "We'd all be better off if you'd just concentrated on Travis."

Keep him talking, her instincts shouted. Yeah, right. And I should do that how, with my mouth taped shut?

"A beautiful body in the river, that's what this needs. Yes, that'll work! Such a gorgeous moonlit night, and you went down to the river. You even took off your shoes to walk in the grass. Perfect!" He studied her as if seeing her traipsing gaily to the river. "You walked out on the dock. A tragic slip. A fall into the water. A heartbreaking accident."

That'll never work, you idiot. I was going for ginger ale. I wouldn't take time for a stroll to the river. And it's too cold for barefoot.

But even if the police quickly figured out that her body in the river was no accident, it would be too late. She'd already be dead.

"So all I have to do is keep you hidden

until I can get you down to the river."

Apparently silence here was working the same way Uncle Joe said it did when someone was being questioned. Most people felt a compelling need to fill a silence, even if it wasn't to the person's best advantage. Not that knowing more in this situation was any advantage for Cate. All it did was start a quiver in her stomach that threatened to send her into a full-body quake.

Rolf knelt down and lifted the blue bedspread as if checking for under-the-bed bogeymen and monsters, but she could see, as he obviously did, that there wasn't enough space to shove her under there. And the only bogeyman was out here.

"Hey, I've got it!"

He left her standing there, obviously confident of her inability to hippity-hop to escape, and a moment later she heard the door to the carport open. The duct tape felt as if it were cutting off circulation to her hands, but she could move her arms and wiggle her fingers.

She hopped over to a four-drawer dresser and studied the items scattered on top. A small pile of change. Four quarters, a dime, and three pennies. A sock with a hole in the heel. Two red-striped hard candies. A box of tissues. A pocket calculator. Could Nancy

Drew or Jessica Fletcher turn any of that into a weapon or way of escape? Cate couldn't.

But hadn't LeAnne said Rolf had both a landline and a cell phone? If she could just get out to that phone, and dial 911 . . . How to dial it momentarily stopped her. But she'd do it with her elbow or her tongue if she had to! She was frantically hippity-hopping out to the living room to find the phone line when he came back from the carport with a stepladder and screwdriver in hand.

He met her at the bedroom door. "Going somewhere?" he inquired. He pushed her aside and she teetered on her taped feet as he answered his own question. "I don't think so."

He set the ladder up in an inside corner of the bedroom, climbed up on it, and used the screwdriver to remove the screws on a small panel overhead. The ceiling was plywood, not sheetrock, the screws hidden in the textured beige paint, and the panel had a layer of pink insulation attached on the attic side. Then, as if Cate were a sack of onions, he threw her over his shoulder and hauled her up into the attic. She heard the dress rip as they went through the opening. In the dim light coming from the bedroom below, all she could see was a steeply slanted roof and a pink sea of more insulation.

He plopped her down somewhere between the panel and the back wall, breathing hard himself now. "That ought to hold you while I keep everyone busy so they won't have time to come looking for you." He leaned over to check her duct tape bonds in the dim light. "Too bad you're going to miss the wedding. But that dress isn't looking too good anyway."

Language wouldn't have been possible, Cate realized, if God hadn't given us movable lips, and hers weren't moving. Not that Rolf's monologue really needed a response.

"None of this would have been necessary, you know, if ol' Kieferson hadn't gone all high and mighty. It wasn't as if his hands were so pure and spotless."

Rolf disappeared back through the opening down to the bedroom, and a minute later the dim light in the attic disappeared as he fastened the panel in place. A brief silence, and then she heard a dull thump when he bumped into something taking the ladder outside, and then a second thump of the door closing.

For a moment she thought about what Rolf had said about Ed Kieferson. Ed's hands weren't pure or spotless, but he'd gone high and mighty. About what?

She'd have to figure that out later.

If there was a later.

27

The attic smelled dry and stale and hostile, not cozy and friendly like the attic back home when Cate was a little girl crawling into her secret place to read on a rainy day. And this attic was also claustrophobic, as if the unseen roof above were relentlessly moving down to crush her.

Determinedly, she pushed it back and reinforced the push with a deep breath.

She wiggled her toes, then her fingers. They were all there and moving. Good. Although at the moment wiggling them seemed an ability about as useful as Octavia doing square root calculations in her head.

Because the bottom line was that even if her fingers and toes could tap out Morse code, she was still stuck here. Tied up and trapped until Rolf came back and took her to the river. She fought down the panic threatening to engulf her.

What do I do, Lord?

She waited hopefully, but no big voice boomed out that help was coming, and all she had to do was sit there and wiggle her extremities until it arrived.

Instead, what came was a voiceless push. *Don't just sit there, do something. Let the Lord help.*

If she could get to the panel that opened down into the bedroom, maybe she could shove it off with her feet. She'd have to fall through the opening, but she'd be out of *here.*

She wrestled her body in that direction, bumping over rafters and flopping into the hollows of insulation between them. Over the second rafter she heard the dress rip again. Definitely no presidential balls for her in this gown. By the third rafter, her skin itched and burned from fiberglass insulation prickling inside her dress and between her toes.

By the fourth rafter, she realized she should have counted rafters when Rolf brought her up here. Because now she had no idea where that escape panel was. She angled her body around so she could thump her feet on the bedroom ceiling below, but nothing gave way on the sections she tried.

She had to stop and rest for a moment. Which was when she heard rustles and

431

squeaks from a corner. Mice? There were *mice* up here, and any minute they'd be running over her as if she were some newly discovered mouse playground. But she also realized the darkness wasn't quite as dense as it should be. There was a lighter oblong at the far end of the attic, on the back side of the house. A window!

She rolled and twisted and scooted toward it. Her tied-together feet tangled in the dress, caught a toe in a tear, and ripped it further. Several times the wig snagged on something, and finally it pulled away from her head.

There's your playground, mice. Go for it.

Finally she was at the window. She twisted her legs sideways so she could peer out. If the glass had ever been cleaned, it wasn't within the last decade, but the sight was glorious anyway. Dark sky dusted with stars, moonlight, rows of grapevines, light from Lodge Hill filtering through the trees!

Yeah, a great view. But she was still trapped here.

With sudden determination, she twisted around, lifted her bare feet, and smashed through the window. Shards of glass peppered her legs, but cold night air flowed into the attic.

For a moment, déjà vu rolled through her.

She'd been here, done this, on her one other murder case, when the killer locked her and a friend in a third-floor closet. She'd gotten away then, but that time her mouth and wrists and ankles hadn't been taped into uselessness. And she was no Houdini able to slither out of all restraints.

Some ideas, Lord?

She lay on her side against a rafter and tried to scrape the duct tape off her face. Had Houdini ever had to cope with duct tape?

But she did have those wiggly fingers. She sat up again and tapped her fingertips together. Rolf was a killer. He'd efficiently used a gun on Ed Kieferson and an Oriental sword on Celeste. But could he have made a mistake when trussing her up? Wasn't it written somewhere in the Bad Guys Book of Rules that you tied a victim's hands in back of her, not in front?

She put her hands to her face. Her palms were mashed together, which meant her fingers weren't in good position for creative walking, but she managed to snag the end of a strip of duct tape. She couldn't get a good grip, but she pulled and felt the strip slowly peel away from the other strips on her face.

Hope surged through her. She got a

finger-lock on another strip and pulled again. This time she was down to skin, and she out-squeaked the mice.

She'd had her legs waxed once, and after the burning, my-skin-is-gone feeling, she'd vowed that even if she got to be hairy as King Kong, she'd never wax again. She hadn't that choice with the duct tape now, because this wasn't about smooth legs, it was about her life. She gritted her teeth and pulled three more times to finish the job. She checked the results with an air-kiss and a jaw wiggle. Yes, everything worked.

She could smell smoke from the old grapevines smoldering on the burn pile at the back of the vineyard. No . . . She sniffed again. This scent was sharper, not so clean and sweet smelling. She stuck her head out the window. A wisp of smoke rose above the line of trees. Someone, tired of waiting for the buffet, had decided on a weenie roast in the fireplace? Or some exotic delicacy Robyn had ordered for the buffet had caught fire?

Apparently no one had missed Cate yet. She didn't hear her name being called into the night. Which was a little insulting, wasn't it? Apparently she could be kidnapped by aliens and zapped off to some strange planet, and no one would even notice. But Rolf had said he was going to keep everyone too busy to look for her . . .

She finally made the connection. Smoke — fire — Rolf!

A frantic bite at the tape holding her wrists told her she wouldn't be able to chew through it. But she managed to snag the end of the tape in her teeth and slowly, oh so slowly, unwound it. She took only a moment to rub her numb wrists and hands before freeing her ankles and feet.

She used a hold on the window frame to lever herself to her feet. She had to hunch over, because the ridgepole above her wasn't high enough to stand upright, but she stomped each foot a couple of times to bring back feeling.

She'd broken out of that locked closet by making an escape line using clothes hanging in the closet, but here there were no convenient racks of cocktail dresses and sweatpants and Hermes scarves to tie together.

But she could rip strips off the dress and make a line to lower herself to the ground!

She'd just made the first tear when she heard the last noise she ever wanted to hear. The door downstairs closing. Rolf was back.

No time to construct an escape rope. She peered out the window again, leaning over to look down this time. A bare wall dropped straight from the window to the ground, no foot- or handholds. Below, old lumber was stacked against the house on the left side, a pile of discarded motorcycle parts on the right. If she didn't hit dead center between them —

Dead center. She shivered. Poor choice of words.

Shouts from Lodge Hill made her look that way again. Flame! But now she could hear something ominously closer. Rolf was working on that ceiling panel. She closed her eyes for a last moment of prayer — *I need your help now, Lord!* — used her fist wrapped in insulation to break out the remaining shards of glass, and climbed backward out of the window. The dress caught on something, and she ripped it free.

Bits of glass clinging to the window bit into her arms and hands as she let herself over the edge. Her toes scrambled for footing, but there was nothing. Finally she was clinging only by her fingers, her bare feet dangling in nothingness.

Where was a nice, boring day as a PI when you needed one?

She remembered Mitch mentioning that voice-activated, wristband cell phone. He'd said it might come in handy if she were ever clinging by her fingertips somewhere. She also remembered her blithe response: she didn't need one. She'd been there, done that, and she didn't anticipate dangling by her fingertips anytime in the near future.

Famous last words. Apparently window-hanging was her PI specialty.

Except a moment later, she wasn't hanging. One hand slipped, then the other, and she was falling. Bumping and thumping. Sliding, scraping, and scratching. Her fingers clutched for handholds that weren't there. Her toes grasped for footholds that didn't exist. But her dress, billowing and tangling like a deflating parachute, snagged on everything, jerking her this way and that. One foot banged into the pile of motorcycle parts, and she heard the crash of metal as her own body crashed into the ground.

The impact rattled her from toes to teeth, and she just lay there, shooting stars criss-crossing her eyes and her ears ringing. But a moment later she realized the stars were inside her head, and she couldn't see. She couldn't see! No sky, no moon or stars. The impact had done something to her eyes —

She flailed frantically, and suddenly her vision came back. No, she hadn't been blinded. She'd just been tangled like a bridesmaid mummy in the dress.

Thank you, Lord.

But what she could see was Rolf leaning out the window and looking down at her. For a moment she thought he might jump right down on top of her, but he disappeared, and she heard him crashing across the rafters.

How fast could he get down here? Faster than a speeding bullet?

She scrambled to her feet, snatched up the gown hanging in tattered ribbons around her, and careened toward the line of trees, unmindful of her bare feet. Rolf had to go around front to get out of the house. She had a head start on him. She'd tried out for track when she was in high school. If she could just beat him through the trees —

A frantic twist of head showed that even with a late start he was no more than thirty or forty feet behind her. And gaining. Oh yeah, she remembered now. She hadn't been fast enough to qualify for the track team.

She tried to scream, but she was running so hard that she had no breath left for yelling. She burst through the trees, and the flames flared into full view, eating like some blazing demon into the back side of the Reception Room. Sirens wailed in the distance.

Cate's frantic gaze took in guys in tuxedos with a hose, Jo-Jo's waving arms directing them where to fasten it. Rolf was so close now she could almost feel his breath.

But if she could just get a few feet closer, he wouldn't dare attack her in full view . . .

She let go of the gown and raised her arms to wave for attention. The tattered gown fluttered and trailed around her. Her feet tangled in a torn strip, and down she went. She screamed as a weight fell on her back. A hand covered her mouth to silence her scream.

But this time she reacted before it could clamp down. *Bite!* She bit, clamping down on a finger. Not a great experience, she realized, but she forced herself to hold on. Rolf shrieked in what she irrelevantly thought was a rather unmanly way.

But Rolf had a new technique too. He whacked her alongside the head with his other hand, and she let go. Before he could grab her again, she scrambled away, digging in with fingers and elbows and toes. She chanced a frantic glance backward, then blinked and sat up.

Strips of bridesmaid gown tangled like celadon tentacles around a male figure rolling on the ground trying to escape them.

Cate struggled to her feet, yelling now,

waving her arms. "Help! Help!"

A tuxedoed figure spotted her. He ran toward her. She pointed to Rolf, still draped in bridesmaid gown remnants but now rising from the ground.

Mitch didn't ask questions. He took one look at Cate's bedraggled condition and leaped on Rolf. They both went down in a tangle of flailing arms and legs, jeans on top one moment, tuxedo the next.

Another tuxedoed figure ran up and stared for a moment, and then Lance leaped into the fray too. Three thrashing and twisting bodies and arms and legs.

A fire truck roared around the far end of Lodge Hill. A police car followed, then another fire truck. The trio on the ground rose like some six-legged monster draped in tangled strips of celadon. Cate stood there in her own knee-length tatters of what was once a bridesmaid's gown.

The tuxedos hadn't fared too well either. One of Mitch's sleeves dangled by threads from his shoulder. Lance's dirt-stained knees showed through rips. Rolf glowered between them, Mitch twisting one arm behind him, Lance doing the same with the other arm.

Jo-Jo and groomsmen ran up. Behind them the fire truck started pumping water on the flames. Robyn and the bridesmaids tore around the end of the hedged enclosure like a flying wedge of celery-colored birds in high heels.

Cate thought Robyn would start wailing about her ruined rehearsal, asking what happened to Cate's gown and wig, but she took one look at fiancé Lance, with dirt on his face and exposed knees, gave a little shriek, and ran to him. He didn't let go of Rolf, but he put his other arm around Robyn.

Two policemen raced up. They stopped short at the sight of the odd tableau of a wedding party with various wardrobe malfunctions. Rolf spoke first.

"Get these idiots off me! They attacked me, and I was trying to get to the fire and help —"

"He wasn't helping! He was chasing me! He tied me up in his attic. My wig is still up there! I had to jump out a window to get away. He killed Celeste and Mr. Kieferson, and he was going to kill me too! Because I saw his arm, and it has a tattoo with an eye in it and that was the arm and tattoo I saw when Celeste was murdered!"

"She's crazy!" Rolf yelled.

"Okay, everyone calm down now," an officer said. "Let's get away from the fire and we'll get to the bottom of this."

"He started the fire too!" Cate yelled.

"She's lying! Let me loose!"

The officer moved over to where Mitch and Lance weren't loosening their holds on Rolf. For a moment Cate thought he was going to order them to release Rolf, but he spotted something at Rolf's feet.

A knife! Rolf had been chasing her with a knife!

The officer reached out and rubbed Rolf's dirt-stained shirt between his fingers. He held his fingers to his nose.

"I was working on a motorcycle. I spilled gas on my shirt," Rolf muttered. After a moment's hesitation, he added belligerently, "I'm not answering any questions. I want a lawyer."

"I think that can be arranged," the officer said.

A man in a dark blue suit came around the hedged enclosure.

"Pastor Dietrichson," Robyn said.

"Someone around front, your aunt I believe, said everyone was around back here." The pastor looked questioningly at Robyn, and she nodded. "I'm sorry I'm late. I take it I missed the rehearsal?"

The minister's gaze took in the bedraggled wedding party, officers, burning hole in the wall, fire trucks, and Rolf with the officer now snapping handcuffs around his wrists. Mitch came over and wrapped an arm around Cate's shoulders. She realized she was shivering now, both from the chilly night and nerves. His warmth and strength felt good.

"Maybe this would be a good time to ask if you'd like to come work for Computer Solutions Dudes?" he whispered.

As good a time as any, Cate realized. At the moment, being a PI in a bedraggled bridesmaid's gown, with a fixation on window escapes, didn't really seem like the right answer to that age-old question, What do I want to be when I grow up?

Hey, but there was something —

"Not today. I just captured a killer!"

"*You* captured a killer?" Mitch yanked his tuxedo sleeve free of its few remaining threads and handed it to her.

"Okay, *we* captured a killer. And Lance too."

"Will there be a wedding?" the minister inquired politely.

Everyone looked at Robyn. Cate mentally tallied up the damages.

Her bridesmaid's gown in tatters, her wig gone. There went the color scheme.

Two tuxedos ruined.

"The van that was supposed to deliver the buffet never showed up," Jo-Jo offered. "Someone called and said the restaurant has just closed down."

The master of ceremonies/deejay had laryngitis.

"I don't think Lodge Hill will be usable," Jo-Jo added. She glanced back at the burning area. The firemen had the blaze knocked down, but a smoking hole yawned in the wall.

"Perhaps the wedding should be postponed," the minister suggested.

Cate expected tears of anguish and despair from Robyn, maybe even a genteel faint on this disastrous occasion. Yes, postponement was the only solution. Robyn's perfect wedding was in ruins.

Instead Robyn wrapped an arm around her fiancé's waist. "Lance could have been killed! This guy had a *knife*. But he's here. I'm here. We love each other. There will be a wedding."

Robyn looked around defiantly, as if she expected objections, but everyone, including Cate, simply looked at her in astonishment. Robyn had finally gotten her priorities right.

"That's an excellent attitude," Jo-Jo said. "I can make punch."

"I know a deejay," Cate offered. Thoughtfully, remembering Destiny Dustinhoff's posthypnotic tendency toward impromptu Lady Gaga imitations, she added, "Just don't ask her what time it is."

28

It was a beautiful wedding.

Cate and the bridemaids spent most of the day on the phone, notifying guests of the new arrangements, and that evening Aunt Carly's house overflowed with people and the flowers originally intended for Lodge Hill.

The minister showed up on time.

Bride Robyn dazzled in her wedding gown. The groom and best man wore spotless blue suits. All the groomsmen showed up, but there wasn't room for all the bridesmaids and groomsmen in the ceremony, so the entire entourage was scrapped. Cate came in her natural flyaway red hair and a blue dress that Mitch especially liked, with Band-Aids on her various cuts and scratches. Other bridesmaids went creative with everything from sequins to a flowered muumuu.

The minister asked if anyone had any

objections to this union, and no one did. He pronounced Lance and Robyn husband and wife, the groom kissed his new bride, and in his enthusiasm stepped on her floor-length veil. The veil ripped. The tiara crashed to the floor.

There was a moment of dead silence among the guests as Robyn stared down at the fallen ornament. Cate expected her to burst into tears. But then the new and improved Robyn picked up both tiara and veil and waved them like trophies overhead, and everyone applauded.

The pizza parlor delivered five different kinds of pizza, plus platters of spicy Buffalo wings. Jo-Jo's punch, with plenty of ginger ale, was a big hit.

Destiny Dustinhoff emceed the introductions at the reception, and deejayed the music with no lapses into Lady Gaga solos.

Robyn threw her bouquet. Cate wasn't trying to catch it, but it smacked her in the head and fell into her hands. The bride and groom dashed out to their car to speed off to their honeymoon on the coast, everyone throwing birdseed.

The car wouldn't start.

Mitch loaned them his SUV.

Later, Cate drove him home to his condo in her car.

"I had my doubts before, but I think they're going to make it," Mitch said in a satisfied way. He glanced over at Cate. "You okay?" They hadn't really had a chance to talk before now.

"A little stiff and sore." She'd fallen, been trussed up like a rodeo calf, jumped out a window, and been tackled by a killer. She had a right to be stiff and sore.

Mitch reached over and touched her cheek. "A few cuts and bruises too."

"Just another day in the life of a private investigator," Cate said.

"That's what I was afraid of."

Then she remembered something. The camera. It was still in the backseat of the car. At the condo, they took it inside, where Mitch quickly figured out that the problem wasn't a highly technical one.

"It needs new batteries."

He supplied the two AA batteries, and then they were looking at a series of photos. Ed Kieferson's Jaguar parked at Jo-Jo's house. Ed digging his fingers into the flowerpot on the back steps for the key. Ed leaning inside the half-open door of the house. A motorcycle and rider, apparently just arrived, behind Ed's car. Cate couldn't tell who was under the helmet.

"I wonder how she was getting these

photos?" Mitch said. "Couldn't they see her?"

"She could have parked behind those big blackberry bushes around the deserted house across the road and come over on foot. That's what I'd have done."

Mitch nodded. "And used a zoom."

The figure from the motorcycle was at the door in the next photo. He'd half turned, helmet off, as if looking around to be sure no one was watching him.

"Rolf," Cate breathed.

Rolf was coming out the door in the next shot. Even in a still photo, he was obviously running. He was holding something close to his body.

A gun.

"So now Rolf takes off on his bike, but Kieferson's car is still there," Mitch mused. "But it was gone when you got there. What happened to it?"

Good question. "So do these photos prove anything?" Cate asked.

"I don't know. But I think the police will be interested."

They were.

During the next month, repairs at Lodge Hill were under way with insurance money. Jo-Jo and Kim had an agreement that Jo-Jo would manage the wedding business until Kim was ready to take over. Jo-Jo had decided not to move to Arizona. She'd found a free companion donkey for Maude, and, now that she had a friend, Maude had abandoned her watchdog brays.

Kim wouldn't be taking over Lodge Hill for some time, however, because she was starting classes in business management at the University of Oregon in the spring. Her arm was healing nicely. The Ice Cube had been foreclosed on, so Kim was now living in the one room Ed had completed at Lodge Hill in his grand plan of making it into an actual lodge. She had come to church with Cate and Mitch a couple of times.

A neighboring grape grower was dealing with the bank to take over purchase of the vineyard.

The chef at Mr. K's had returned, and a group of employees were getting together to buy out and reopen the restaurant as Chef Dior's. Kim included much of the contents of the house in a wildly successful closing-down sale at the Mystic Mirage. Cate bought several items for her new house.

Cate hadn't intended to ask Mitch for help when she chose furniture for the house, but she spotted a great leather sofa in a furniture store window near where they had lunch one day. Once inside, he pointed out a beautiful dining room table, and before long almost the entire house was furnished.

Was it a little scary that they had such similar tastes?

Cate wrote up her final report for the files. Belmont Investigations. Cate Kinkaid, assistant private investigator, Case File 36-M. (She'd tacked on the M to indicate it was a murder case.) The report included both solid facts and some of what Uncle Joe called "informed deductions."

Cate had been called in to identify the wig and an empty briefcase the police found in a search of Rolf's cottage. The officer handling the search turned out to be the same one she'd met when Celeste's apartment was trashed. On a you-didn't-hear-this-from-me basis, he suggested Rolf had been searching for the camera there, that Celeste must have threatened him in some way with what she had on it. Cate also learned that the search of his cottage had turned up the handgun from which the bullet that had killed Ed Kieferson had been fired. Fingerprints had been wiped off the handle of the sword that killed Celeste, but Rolf had missed an incriminating print on the blade. Why had Celeste been considering hiring a private investigator? Cate could only speculate that it had to do with Rolf or Travis.

Things were looking good on the case against Rolf, the officer said. Or bad, from Rolf's viewpoint.

A news report said a police search of the old, unused buildings at the vineyard revealed that they weren't so unused after all. They held a small but sophisticated marijuana-growing operation. Rolf had a couple of illegal immigrants working there, and they, in exchange for indemnity, had much to say about the pot-growing operations. An unexpected find for police was a rather large stash of Rohypnol also in the building.

Beyond this point, Cate had to use those informed deductions to answer various questions about the case in her report.

Why had Ed Kieferson gone to Jo-Jo's house that fateful day? It could have been to win Jo-Jo back, but Cate's own conclusion was that he'd gone to demand a reduction in his alimony payments, and shooting the dolls was a warning to Jo-Jo of what he could do to her if she didn't cooperate. Would he have carried through on the threat? An unanswerable question.

Why had Rolf followed Ed that day? From

what Kim had said about Ed's fierce antagonism toward Rohypnol, it seemed likely that
he'd found out Rolf was supplying Celeste
and maybe selling the stuff elsewhere too.
Rolf knew Ed was going to turn him in and
he'd soon be back in jail. Rolf wasn't going
to let that happen. He'd followed Ed with
the deliberate intent to kill him that day.
Which he'd done.

But Celeste had followed too. It seemed
unlikely the three vehicles had been in
parade formation going out to Jo-Jo's place,
and somehow Celeste had arrived before
Rolf, which was how she'd gotten the
incriminating photos. Cate figured Celeste
really did suspect Ed had something extracurricular going with some woman. She'd
followed him to get proof of that infidelity
and unexpectedly got a different kind of
proof. So why hadn't she turned the photos
over to the police? Maybe she didn't want
to lose her Rohypnol supplier? Maybe she
figured she could use the incriminating
photos for leverage to get her supply free?
Maybe she was just glad Ed was dead so
she didn't have to do it.

Ed's Jaguar. How did it get back to town?
Rolf must have moved it back to the restaurant parking lot. Why? Maybe so it would
throw suspicion on Jo-Jo by making it look

as if Ed had gone to the house with her in the van. Rolf was a tough, resourceful guy. He'd have found a way to get back out there and retrieve his motorcycle.

Who had called Celeste that day at the Mystic Mirage, and who had Cate bumped into that time she fled the store in embarrassment? Travis Beauchamp? Who had now done a plea bargain on the burglary charge and received a short sentence.

Cate would add a copy of the newspaper account of Rolf's trial to the file later.

Case closed.

Now here they were at the big event on a cooperative day in November. The yard had been nicely landscaped, the hillside sloping down to the street terraced and planted with grass and shrubs. In the spring it would bloom with azaleas and lilacs, and Cate herself had added a section of iris bulbs Rebecca had donated from her yard. Cate hadn't gardened since she was a girl back home, but she was looking forward to planting tomatoes and lettuce and onions out back next spring. Mitch had said, "Don't forget carrots," and she'd told him to bring his own carrot seed and give it a try.

The outside of the house, with rock trim and big windows, looked like any ordinary house, but everyone knew about the cat-friendly differences inside. A Kitty Kastle.

A sunny breeze fluttered the wide red ribbon with a bow that crossed the front door. Mr. Ledbetter stood beside it with scissors. Cate stood on the sidewalk, Octavia grumbling from the cat carrier at her feet.

Behind Cate stood Mitch, Uncle Joe with a cane, and Rebecca. Rebecca had asked if a few people from church could come. Lance and Robyn, back from their honeymoon, had asked if they could come. At the last minute, Cate had invited the Whodunit ladies, who'd known Octavia's original owner, to be there. Mrs. Ledbetter had come with her husband. So, it was quite a crowd now gathered for the grand opening. A few curious neighbors had also assembled at the foot of the driveway to watch.

"Are we ready?" Mr. Ledbetter asked.

Cate nodded. Octavia yowled.

"Very well, then. I, Roger Ledbetter, designated by Amelia Robinson as executor of her estate, which duties include providing a proper home for her beloved companion, Octavia, do hereby present this house to Ms. Cate Kinkaid and Octavia, as their mutual residence." Mr. Ledbetter cut the ribbon with a big flourish, unlocked the door, and with another flourish presented the keys to Cate. "I hope you'll both be very happy here."

Cate stepped inside. She stopped short for a moment, startled as always by the life-like appearance of the redheaded doll sitting on a chair in the foyer. Jo-Jo had presented her with this doll a few days ago. Jo-Jo hadn't named the doll, saying she'd leave that up to Cate, and Cate was still mulling possibilities.

Everyone crowded in, filling the living room. Cate made certain the door was closed, and then unlatched the door on the cat carrier.

Octavia, with her usual regal attitude, strolled out. She eyed the crowd, then ignored them, as if such an entourage were her due. She inspected the doll, climbed her cat pole, and sat her plump rump down on the walkway to survey her domain and subjects below.

"What does she think?" Mr. Ledbetter asked.

"If she had thumbs, I'm sure she'd be giving it a thumbs-up."

"Good." He made a little my-work-here-is-done dusting motion with his hands. "If you'll excuse me, I want to go talk to some-one . . ."

His wife, who'd been standing next to

him, watched him go over to Mitch. Then she pulled a photo out of her purse. "This is Ellouise." The photo showed a calico cat with a chewed-on ear, not lovely, but Mrs. Ledbetter beamed with pride. "I never thought Roger would want a cat, but when she showed up at our door, he let her come in. We're both quite taken with her."

Cate glanced up at Octavia and gave her a thumbs-up. Cat ambassadorship successful.

"But I'm rather concerned about Roger's interest in that young man's motorcycle." Mrs. Ledbetter gave a worried glance at her husband and Mitch deep in discussion. "He wouldn't want a motorcycle too . . . would he?"

"There's some kind of magnetic attraction between men and bikes." Cate patted Mrs. Ledbetter's shoulder. "You'll get used to it."

"If he does get one, I'm never getting on it," Mrs. Ledbetter vowed.

Cate just smiled. Famous Last Words.

Mr. Ledbetter had provided snacks and drinks, both people and cat varieties. Various people came by to congratulate Cate on her new home, but finally they were all gone, and it was just her, Mitch, and Octavia.

Cate plopped down on her new leather

sofa. Nice in a cat world, because it wouldn't accumulate cat hair. Mitch had suggested the big, soft pillow for Octavia's use at one end of it. Octavia now came down from her high perch and curled up on the pillow beside Cate. Mitch dropped down beside Cate too.

They made, Cate reflected, a rather nice little family.

"Great place," Mitch said.

"I think so too."

"Now that you're a, um, solid citizen homeowner, and you have a milestone thirtieth birthday coming up soon, I'm thinking maybe you'll want a solid-citizen-type job. Not one where you're being chased by killers, bound up in duct tape, climbing out of windows, et cetera."

"And this solid-citizen-type job would be . . . ?"

"There's a great opening in the office at Computer Solutions Dudes. Good pay, full benefits, congenial boss."

Cate considered the offer. For five seconds. "Thank you, no."

"No?"

"No."

Mitch gave an exaggerated sigh. "I didn't think so." He pulled a small package out of his pocket. "Wristwatch-type cell phone.

Voice activated. So the next time you're hanging out of a window, you can call me, okay?"

"But I'm not going to be —"

He touched her lips with a finger. "Or you can use it when you're trapped in a dungeon, hijacked in a hot-air balloon, or spread-eagled on railroad tracks. Whatever."

"Don't be ridic—" Cate broke the statement in mid-word. Given her propensity for dangerous situations, who knew when she might need Mitch's gift?

"Just remember, I'm always here. Just waiting for your call." He grinned. "Or even if it isn't an emergency, and you just want me, I'm available."

"I'll remember that."

Octavia woke up, strolled across laps as if they were her personal red carpet, and plopped down, head and front paws on Mitch, rear end and tail on Cate.

Cate petted her end of cat. Yes indeed. A nice little family.

ABOUT THE AUTHOR

Lorena McCourtney is a *New York Times* bestselling and award-winning author of dozens of novels, including *Invisible* (which won the Daphne du Maurier Award from Romance Writers of America), *In Plain Sight, On the Run, Stranded,* and *Dying to Read.* She resides in Grants Pass, Oregon.